MW00379321

THE GOOD WITCH OF THE SOUTH

Also by T. C. BARTLETT

SANDHILL PUBLISHERS

Children's Picture Books

It's Music Time
(Independent Publisher Book Awards - Gold Medal Winner)

A Dog Named Zero and The Apple With No Name
(Voted by Kirkus Reviews as one of the Best Picture Books of The Year)

You Can't Tickle Me
Never Was a Grump Grumpier
Eat, Eat, Eat! Cheese, Cheese, Cheese!
The Lost and Lonely Tumbleweed
Birds Fly, A Cat Tries
The String
You Have To Do What I Say
Letting Go

THE CREATIVE COMPANY
& HARCOURT BRACE

Tuba Lessons
(Published in ten different languages)

Author website: tcbartlett.com
Author email: tc@tcbartlett.com

Publisher website: sandhillpublishers.com
Publisher email: sandhillpublishers@gmail.com
Sandhill Publishers, LLC, Nashville, Indiana

Printed in the United States of America
Library of Congress Control Number: 2019904301

ISBN-13 978-1-7339086-2-7
ISBN-10 1-7339086-2-5

To Kim, my North Star
&
To Noelani T.,
for her courage, her strength,
and her beauty when she
dances across the stage

*A*uthor's *N*ote:

*I*t might be of some interest to know in L. Frank Baum's classic 1900 children's novel *The Wonderful Wizard of Oz*, Glinda was the Good Witch of the South, not the North. She was also known as Glinda the Good.

The Good Witch of the North was never named in Baum's books about Oz. But he did give her the moniker Locasta for his musical extravaganza titled, *The Wizard of Oz*. Baum's musical premiered in 1902 at the Chicago Grand Opera House and later moved to the Majestic Theatre on Broadway in 1903, where it ran for 293 performances until 1904, followed by traveling tours.

In the 1939 MGM movie *The Wizard of Oz*, with Judy Garland, the North and South Ozarian Witches were combined for the sake of the film and for no other reason. As well, in Baum's book, the magic slippers are silver and were changed to ruby slippers for the movie to take greater advantage of its technicolor cinematography, which was relatively new in 1939.

THE
GOOD
WITCH
OF THE SOUTH

AN OZARIAN ADVENTURE IN THE LAND OF OZ

T. C. BARTLETT

SANDHILL
PUBLISHERS, LLC
AN AMERICAN PUBLISHING COMPANY

*Take heart to all who
fly over the rainbow—and be warned—all that
you know to be the truth
will be something entirely different
somewhere else . . .*

Prologue

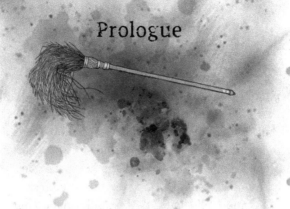

*There is no greater threat to freedom than that which comes
from wickedness.*

        —*Dorothy Gale,* A Call to Arms
           Appeal to The Great Head, Emerald City, 1939

Many unexpected events ensued after the
Wicked Witch of the West was vanquished—a nicer way of saying
liquidated or killed—or, as some said, the crusty old tart was
murdered by the little redheaded, freckled-faced country girl from
Kansas, Dorothy Gale. The thing is, it doesn't matter how you wish to
remember that momentous historical event. That is entirely up to you.
The fact of the matter is, the meltdown of the fiendish western witch
destroyed her iniquitous behavior. And a good thing, indeed, no doubt
about it; just ask the Munchkins and the Winkies. Both of which know
the loss of freedom and being held under the thumb of wickedness.

But stories abound about Dorothy Gale and the demise of
the Wicked Witch and what happened after. They have circulated,
become swollen, and have faded throughout the ages, taking on new
form and luster with each telling, all the way up until now, as I tell you
of what really came to pass during those perilous days that brought
Oz to its knees.

⁊ ♦ ⁌

On that eve when Dorothy snuffed the life out of the evil witch,
the Enchanted Forest was ripe with delicious, red apples ready

for the picking, but only if you asked the trees politely. A terrible storm was creeping in from the east, spitting, sputtering, and wailing with violent intent. Nightmarish, deep purple-and-black early summer thunderclouds mounted, billowed and surged thousands of feet up, choking the troposphere. The temperature dropped, and miles away thunder echoed as gnarled fingers of lightning spat out in all directions from the portentous clouds blocking out the western sky. As the wind picked up, it whipped and batted the lit candles in the lanterns hanging on the walls of the Wicked Witch's castle to a flickering frenzy.

When Dorothy asked if she could have the burnt broomstick the malicious hag had used to try and set the Scarecrow on fire, the head guard, Lucius, asked, "Why? Why would you want a keepsake that carries with it so much evil?"

"To prove to the Great Head that wickedness has been destroyed."

Lucius looked into Dorothy's sparkling earnest sapphire blue eyes, studying her. *Such a brave child*, he thought. Holding the broomstick in both hands while on bended knee, he happily handed the burnt broomstick to the sweet young girl. "Please take this with you, and with our blessings," he said with relief and exhaustion that was evident within his kind, golden-colored eyes and etched across his brow.

He then paused as he stood and looked down upon Dorothy, giving her a gentle, soft smile. "The witch was a dangerous tyrant. We had no way to expel her from our thoughts until you destroyed her evil wickedness. So please take this too." He handed Dorothy the golden cap that gave the one who possessed it three wishes to summon the king of the winged monkeys to do their bidding. "A gift. May it help you find your Kansas."

With a soft and kind voice, he then explained how the witch had stolen the magical cap from Quelala, the first king of the winged monkeys, and selfishly used her wishes to build her army and subjugate and oppress all the good people who lived in Winkie Country. At the thought of the witch's demise, his smile became broader. The light from the lanterns cast an eerie glow on his ice-blue and yellowish-green skin, as he raised his pike above his head, proclaiming, "Hail to

Dorothy! At last, the wicked old witch is dead!"

Then all the guards joined in, their cries echoing throughout the corridors of the castle. "Hoorah! Hoorah! Hail to Dorothy! The wicked old witch is dead!"

The thunderclouds finally broke loose and the first hard drops of rain fell, washing the last remains of the slimy goo left behind from the melted witch out through the drainpipe and down into the Western River two hundred feet below, never to be seen again.

Meanwhile, in the great hall of the castle, the dreariness of the stormy night didn't stop the celebration. Joyous and hardy laughter continued long into the evening as everyone ate and drank, hailing Dorothy, the Scarecrow, the Tin Woodman, and the Cowardly Lion.

E ating so much food and drinking more than they should have— including Dorothy—eventually lulled them all into a deep slumber, except for Lucius.

The Wicked Witch of the West had performed horrible magic on Lucius, transforming him in a significant way from the inside out. The process took weeks, with many dark spells tweaking and twisting every cell in his body. He told me it was like being stung by a thousand wasps. But when the wings started to grow, the pain was . . . well, it was indescribable. (The other gruesome acts of evil I cannot, and will not, tell you.) Suffice it to say, the witch was a horrible creature who cast her black magic for her own corrupt and avaricious needs, without any concern for the good people she persecuted. It changed Lucius, infusing him with something foreign to his nature. He became an entirely different thing, a strange being, half himself, and half something else.

At first, once he recovered from the witch's spells, he felt ashamed, embarrassed, and guilty—because he *liked* having wings. He fell in love with flying and became addicted to the rush of it, the thrill of it. Still, his guilt and embarrassment nagged at him, and he never went anywhere without wearing his captain's coat to hide his wings, to keep his shame to himself.

The Land of Oz had weathered tough times brought on by the evil of the loathsome Witch of the West. Lucius was only one of the thousands of victims she'd experimented on, tortured, or killed. He was glad the wrinkled old crone was dead. But he worried that another storm would brew, one murderous and desperate, if he didn't act quickly and hide the witch's baby daughter—his daughter—in a place of safekeeping. For without his consent, while under the evil witch's spell the Wicked Witch had made him her consort. As a result, they had a baby girl, Elleanora, and Lucius loved her despite her fiendish, monstrous mother and the circumstances of her birth. He had promised himself that she would never know wickedness. He also couldn't take the chance that the Great Head, the Wizard of Oz, would condemn his daughter to death just because she was the spawn of such a perniciously foul and sinister being.

So that very night, when all were asleep (some snoring and moaning from far too much ale), he stole away into the dark, cradling his daughter in his arms, and traveled to the other end of Oz, to Quadling Country. There, good fortune fell upon him and he found love and married Glinda Goodwitch, the Good Witch of the South.

You may be asking yourself, who is this person telling this tale? Pay no attention to the man behind the curtain, as it were; who I am is of no consequence.

I will tell you this: I was there that joyous but stormy night when Dorothy doused the Wicked Witch with water and destroyed the demon-magic that was sweeping through the great land of Oz. And years later, I fought in the last great war in Oz and watched my sisters, my fellow warriors, my friends, fall by my side. I held their heads in my arms as they took their last breaths, and shed all the tears I had for those I loved and lost during that senseless and most egregious of campaigns.

Only a handful are still alive who remember. I am one of those who has not been dropped in a box and planted in the dirt for the worms to gorge upon their flesh, a witness to the story you are about to read. That is all you need to know. It will be up to you to decide if what I tell you is the truth or not.

Sadly though, history has the most obnoxious habit of repeating itself. There will always be wickedness slithering in and out of the dark shadows of this world, waiting for the right moment to show itself. And when it washes across the land, it comes for us all, cloaked in colors that are dark and dangerous.

*T*he Goodwitch castle sits peacefully in the southern portion of Quadling Country. It is a vast realm that embraces a wide variety of geography and climate, and stretches out over four thousand miles from horizon to horizon, covering almost the entire southern portion of the world.

The heart of the country is flat and temperate, much of which is scattered with fertile farmland and small villages. Sightly North of the Goodwitch castle are the great Quadling Peaks, which mark a five-hundred-mile straight line from east to west. Beyond that, further north and past the City of Emeralds is the Impassable Desert that stretches out from the northernmost borders of Gillikin Country. To the south is the Great Sandy Waste, which has remained uncrossed, and to the West is the expansive and mostly unexplored Enchanted Forest.

In recent years, darkness has been growing unchecked in the West and slowly rolling east into Quadling Country, with rumors of a demon fairy putting a spell on the citizens of Winkie Country to build an army.

All who live in the great and wonderful land of Oz are worried, and for good reason . . .

PART ONE

RUMORS
OF
WAR

One

She crouched like a spider clinging to its web, waiting patiently for an unsuspecting insect to fall into her trap. Her left hand grasped the gilded flagpole, while the other gently moved across the cold, smooth slate shingles on the turret roof of her bedroom. The triangular flag above her head—frayed at its tip—whipped and snapped from a robust and single-minded breeze, like a bullwhip nipping the hindquarters of a bull. She shivered. Her stomach churned. Bubbled.

The *rush*. Oh, the rush. The thrill of it. It made her heart race.

It was calling her. A little danger, a little risk. With each thud, she could feel her blood coursing through her veins, making a sound like war drums pounding in her ears. The sound of being *alive* and the need to be steering her own fate—for better or worse. She inhaled deeply, feeling her ribs expand with the brisk, early morning spring air. She smiled. The rush filled her, made her body warmer, and gave her ice-blue, greenish skin a rosy glow. Yes, excruciating as it was, she had to wait. So she waited.

Perched a few hundred feet up on the highest point of her mother's castle while spying on the ant-like creatures swarming below always seemed to snap things into perspective for Samantha; it brought the world into focus. Sounds were more animated, colors more penetrating, exuberant, energetic. Hazy, turbulent thoughts became sharp, concise, and joyful memories, luminous and forceful. She could feel every muscle, every tendon in her body compress, coiling to a tight spring ready to release at just the right moment. It made her feel more like who she was meant to be—more alive, more real, more everything.

འ ◆ ལ

E veryone called her Sam. It was a nickname she adored; it made her feel different. It made her feel strong, secure, and connected somehow. Sam's eyes narrowed, the rush growing and growing, churning, bubbling. And waiting. From this height, the Yellow Brick Road, with its various switchbacks, slithers its way over hills and valleys like a snake rustling through thick brush. She could see miles across Quadling Country. Her eyes scanned anxiously through the dawn's half-light. She could also see the Red Brick Road off to the west, but only bits and pieces of it, peeking out from a break in the carpet of trees or rolling through farmland or when it climbed both sides of a U-shaped valley. The other brick roads, the Green and Blue ones, were hidden from her sight. But all brick roads start and spiral out from the town square of Munchkin City, each taking off in different directions. They traverse the four quadrants of the great land of Oz and end in the very center of the world, where the City of Emeralds, the capital of Oz, spreads out in all its sparkling glory.

She loved this view. The pinkish morning sunlight breaking over the crest of the great Quadling Mountain Range clad in wind-buffed and hard-packed snow. The bright, crisp sky with scattered puffs of white. The deep, long shadows. She loved all of it—she couldn't get enough of it. And each time she found herself taking in this sight she released a soft, contented sigh. Perfect days like this were not uncommon, but as of late they had become harder to find, and it was tempting to believe they were becoming mere illusions. Not this day, however. Today was perfect, despite what was veiled in the background of Sam's thoughts.

She leaned out to look over the slate-shingled roofline. Directly below her was the castle's keep, where the elite castle guards, mostly women, were doing their early morning training with swords, pikes, bows and arrows, and maces. From such a height, it wasn't difficult for Sam to recognize people from the tops of their heads, especially for Saran. She could always pick out Saran, even if all she had to go on was the click of Saran's heels on the flagstone floors or the sound of her light, understated laugh behind closed doors. Saran was Sam's favorite of her mother's personal guards. The one her mother trusted the most. She was the captain, the First Consola, a position that was highly respected and aggressively sought after, a rank only the strongest and most daring ever achieved. And Saran, with her long white hair braided in cornrows and her chiseled features had *brave* written all over her. She was worthy of the position she held: a fearless warrior. Sam's eyesight was keen. She could change the focal length in her eyes and could easily zoom in on her prey. And spying on the First Consola during her morning routine gave Sam a particular thrill to the start of her day. One she anticipated with intense enjoyment.

When the guard next to Saran removed her helmet to dry the sweat on her face with the scarf from around her neck, Sam noticed the guard's unmistakable bright, strawberry blonde hair. It was Lillith, Saran's second. A powerful, tall, strong woman, quiet and kind—a woman of few words. But make no mistake, she'd slice off the head of a snake in a blink if it were venomous and about to strike. She wore a black patch over her left eye. A visible whitish scar ran from the top right side of her forehead. It started an inch above her hairline where hair didn't grow, down through the center of her eyebrow, disappearing behind the eyepatch. The cicatrix continued below the empty eye socket and along her cheek, ending near her ear—a remembrance of a battle hard fought to keep evil at bay and the sacrifice it took.

Next to Lillith was another solider. She was much older than Lillith and Saran. Sam recognized the soldier's weapon and could never forget her well-lined face, always walking around with a grim expression. Her palms were grotesquely seamed with scars, but it was the mace she held in her hands that drew Sam's eye: a round ball of iron that was studded with steel spikes, each sharpened to a pinpoint.

A natural killer, Sam thought. But a mace was merely window dressing unless wielded with the ferocity to make it useful. The soldier's choice of weapon should have chilled her, but instead, Sam was comforted by the presence of this woman, this royal guard, who had clearly lived with violence for so much of her life and had pledged loyalty to her mother's realm. *"Loyalty comes from how a queen rules the land,"* her mother had told Sam many times. *"Not from gold or silver, but with an open and honest hand."*

Lillith was muttering to a different soldier standing several arms' lengths from her right, waiting respectfully for her turn to spar with the First Consola. Suddenly, the soldier and Lillith looked off in the direction of the drawbridge. Then Sam heard someone on a horse— no, three horses. She could not make out their voices, but she did hear the echoed clacking of the horse's hooves on the cobblestones before they emerged from around the corner. The riders wore the uniforms of messengers. The colors they carried and the cut of their saddles said they came from the west, from Winkie Country. One of the men handed Saran a scroll as he spoke to her. They tipped their heads to each other and the horsemen cantered off, their horses placing their feet delicately, as it was dangerous to ride too quickly across the cobbled courtyard.

With urgency in each step, Saran and Lillith disappeared from Sam's view, no doubt to deliver the scroll to her mother, the queen, while the other guards continued their morning routine. Sam didn't have any desire to know what cheerless report had been written on the scroll, no need to understand what was going on. But when three couriers are sent to deliver a message, the news they bring most certainly will not be good. That thought gave her no pleasure.

Right now, all she wanted to do was think about the rush, and yet she found her mind drifting away from the thrill of it. Sam was determined not listen to her worries. She would not allow dark clouds to smother a perfect day, so she searched for something else, something that made her smile, something more pleasing to her, something that pushed her concerns to the back of her mind. She closed her eyes and let the cool morning breeze tiptoe across her face. She'd hardly seen her mother and her stepsister for a week as they wrestled with the messages and the messengers, in hopes they could slow down what they were sure was coming. There were rumblings of dissent from the western country of the Winkies—whispers of a nameless evil, a terrible sorceress, someone who put all who looked upon her under her spell. Another Wicked Witch of the West perhaps, or something much darker and more sinister. The gossip was that someone from the land of the Winkies, either a good fairy or good enough to look it, had carried a bit of demon-magic east across the border into Quadling Country, the country ruled by Sam's mother, Glinda Goodwitch.

It was said that this enchantress, whomever or whatever she might genuinely be, had set herself up as the Queen of the Winkies. And to make matters worse, and possibly dire, the rumors alluded to the fact that this nameless witch had forced taxes on the local farmers and townsfolk to support the raising of an army to overthrow Glinda, with the intention of taking control of the City of Emeralds in order to sit on the Great Head's throne. It was well known that Glinda was the greatest and most powerful of all the witch fairies in the land. If anyone had the desire to rule the land of Oz, had the audacity to even try, their first course of action would be to dispose of the Good Witch of the South. And if they were able to accomplish the unthinkable, the usurper would then merely take a casual walk into the capital to grab the Wizard of Oz by the throat and force him to his knees.

Sam opened her eyes and blinked twice, needing a moment to think and recall something else she had heard. There had been another rumor, a much fainter one, a suggestion that was only whispered behind closed doors: this enchantress had found a way to fly over the rainbow to the land of Kansas and had killed Dorothy Gale and snatched the golden cap out of Dorothy's cold, dead hands to use for herself, to sway the winged monkeys and take control of the

Winkies to build her army. This rumor was far more worrisome, for if true, having the golden cap would make this dark fairy an even more injurious adversary.

Her mother's army was a mixture of women and a few men from every country, providence, and region of Oz—formidable, proud warriors who would defend their queen and the people of Quadling Country at all cost, sacrificing their lives if need be. They believed there was no such thing as a no-win scenario. Only a few soldiers were from Winkie Country, and oddly enough, they had been missing since the rumors began. Every bit of strange happenings, hearsay, and gossip only added weight to the rumors that wickedness was once again seeping out from the west, creeping out of Winkie Country and pushing its evil self into Quadling Country.

There were also whispers that the Cowardly Lion, the King of the Enchanted Forest, was missing. Some said he'd been captured by the unknown villainous witch, held in a cage and deprived of food, just as the Wicked Witch of the West had done. Others were heard saying that he'd been slain and left for crows to pick on. There was even fearful prattle that the Tin Woodman had been turned into a beehive, fulfilling a promise made by the Wicked Witch of the West, and that the enchantress was using the Scarecrow's straw for her mattress and bed pillows. *Rumors*, Sam thought, *are only rumors until proven otherwise.*

But Sam knew her mother never took rumors lightly.

Her mother was ageless, a good fairy witch, both beautiful and young to all those who looked into her scintillating, kind, pure winter-blue eyes, with a pearl of timeless wisdom that was apparent by how she ruled Quadling Country. Her skin was a pale lime green and her hair was a rich, reddish-gold color that fell in flowing ringlets over her shoulders. She was deeply loved and respected by all the people, especially the animals (speaking and nonspeaking alike) and all the other remarkable creatures who lived in the kingdom of Oz. Queen Goodwitch was a great queen, a thoughtful and fair queen who made sure that the poor were fed and the sick doctored, sitting on her throne dispensing justice to those who couldn't seek justice for themselves.

Glinda had decided not to give credence to the rumors, or rather to give them just enough consideration to not discount them completely, so that none of the Quadlings she was the protector of, or the Munchkins who loved her so, would think she shunned the worrisome chatter out of fear. The good witch queen publicly announced that she would make an informal, but royal, visit to Winkie Country to personally speak with Rumpart, the King of the Winkies, in the hope that it would ease any concerns her subjects had, as well as any doubt that seemed to sit lightly in her own mind.

With her would go her First Consola, Saran, the commander of her army; her stepdaughter, Elleanora; a substantial portion of her elite guards; and the same of her court, with all its finery, jewels, and gowns, for a grand show of courtesy. While doing so, she would politely show the army at her back and remind Rumpart of that fact. He was the king for no other reason than his father had been king. But Rumpart's father had been a much better man, a wiser and kinder one, a respected ruler who had been fair and understanding. He was much loved by his subjects and had promised the Tin Woodman—who had given him the crown—that he would never allow slavery to befall the Winkies ever again, as it had when the Wicked Witch of the West ruled Winkie Country. But Taggart Rumpart II had none of his father's qualities. He cared only for his own well-being and personal wealth; he was unpredictable, and easily bribed. If he were indeed under the spell of this so-called devilish siren, it would be a capricious royal visit.

Glinda's plan was both challenging and dangerous, but she wished to prevent a civil war, not provoke one. She would have to choose those to go with her with the utmost care and caution.

"But you're going," Sam said one day to her stepsister, Elleanora, when they were riding together out in the meadow where she could ask her sister without her mother around. "You need me by your side."

Elle grimaced and looked at Sam with a furrowed brow. "I knew you'd feel this way. And so does Mother . . . ," Elle hesitated and continued, "She knows you want to be a mounted soldier in her army.

But now is not the time."

"If not now, then when?" Sam growled under her breath.

"I don't know," Elle replied honestly, shrugging her shoulders and trying to keep the conversation light, even though she knew Sam wouldn't let it go.

"I'm ready," Sam continued, raising her voice. "You know I'm ready!"

"Mother wants you here. You can throw as many tantrums as you like, but you're not going, and that's the end of it!"

"I'm not throwing a tantrum," Sam protested loudly. She dropped her head, rubbed her eyes with the palms of her hands, then lowered and slowed her voice to a softer, gentler tone. "I'm just saying that I know that you know I'm ready." Then she looked at her sister with pleading eyes. "You could talk to Mother. You could convince her."

Elle knew Sam was ready, but she also knew their mother had a reason for everything she did. So Elle ignored Sam and hoped to change the subject by saying, "There's been a new rumor. People have said they've seen dragons."

"Are you sure? Where?" Sam questioned quickly, a look of surprise etched across her brow. "Dragons in Oz? That can't be true."

"It's what I was told. One of the small villages on the southwestern border of Quadling. A village named Blackwood."

৵ ◆ ৶

E lle was beautiful, with her emerald-green skin glistening in the sunlight and her bright-red hair curled and pinned into a glossy, braided, regal tiara. Her naturally glowing ruby-red lips needed no painting. She carried the sweet scent of cinnamon, Sam's favorite spice. Maybe it was her green skin that made her smell so delicious, but Sam thought it was more about the close bond they shared. She could always tell when Elle was close by, and that is why Elle never won at hide-and-seek when they were children—the cinnamon gave her away.

Elle rode her horse, Vail, with her characteristic lightness, agility, and grace. She was a tall and stately young witch, about an inch over six feet, and she outweighed Sam by a third, though only three years older. There was more of their father in her than her wicked witch of a mother. Elle's size conveyed a ripe, billowy, almost intrusive presence, and Sam was not far behind at five feet eight. Even with Elle's overpowering features, she gave off a flavor of total femininity, both compelling and kind. If she wore striped trousers, a vest with a long overcoat, and a stovepipe hat, she'd be worthy of a bronze statue next to the one of the Wizard in the great central forum of Emerald City. And she was becoming a powerful witch too. She'd learned so much about casting spells, and good spells at that, laboring over ancient texts and spell books thought to be lost to dust and decay. She was practicing all the time, teaching Sam; though Sam was more into sword fighting and shooting her bow than she was into casting spells.

Sam thought how gratified their father would be if he knew that Elle was a good witch and would never turn dark, never use demon-magic, never be wicked. She knew deep down that Elle was proud to bear the name Goodwitch, and carried it with dignity. But Sam had it in her mind that she, a queen's daughter, might go; a queen's daughter who was the queen's only child and about to turn sixteen *should* go, even though she hadn't proven herself yet. A queen's birth daughter—of the queen's blood—should have a right to go.

Not to say Elleanora wasn't Glinda's child. Although she was her stepchild, Glinda loved Elle as her own. So much so that after their father vanished, Glinda filed papers for Elle's adoption, signed and sealed by The Great and Powerful Wizard of Oz himself. But as much as Sam desired to be a part of her mother's retinue and stand alongside her mother, it was what Elle had said about the talk of dragons that disturbed her. She didn't know why it bothered her so much. A story she was told, perhaps? A book she'd read once? A dream? Sam didn't know and couldn't remember, but something was nagging at the back of her brain, telling her she needed to find out. Just the thought of seeing a dragon made her shiver. Made her curious. Which her mother said would one day be her undoing—her overactive curiosity and her tendency to jump blindly into the fold, not thinking before she leaped.

But Sam had known they would not let her go. She had known her mother would not dare take her along to confront the rumors of war and find out if dark-mischief and a new, powerful, villainous witch were brewing in the west. Then again, Sam knew she could not help asking—any more, she supposed, than a seed could stop from sprouting. Her mother was always fair, but she was also hard— qualities expected of a queen and of a mother. If Sam completed all of her schoolwork by dinnertime, her reward was to pick a book from the library and stay up reading until her eyes failed her. Or, if by the end of the week she had all her chores finished and had done all her homework without any complaining, she and Elle were allowed to take off on a camping trip for the entire weekend. There had been many nights when Sam had been good and didn't cause any trouble for the guards or Augie, her chambermaid, when she was allowed to stay up until dawn reading a particularly exciting book and allowed to skip her chores. And it is of no great surprise that there had also been times when Sam became tired of the constant schooling and simply refused to do anymore. When that happened, there were no stories, no library, only studies and chores, and the granite disapproval of her chambermaid's face and her mother's stern rebuke. And lately, Sam had done everything asked of her, without protest.

What troubled Sam now was that her mother had been so busy of late and concerned enough about the rumors that Sam knew she would have to wait to confront her and wait again, until the time was right. But mostly, what occupied her thoughts was how to set aside her fear of asking her mother's permission to ride by her side to confront Rumpart, knowing very well that her mother's answer would certainly be a resounding, but kindhearted, *no*.

But the time had been getting close to being almost gone. After dinner, a few days before Elle and her mother were to leave to meet with Rumpart, Sam pulled in a deep breath of courage and asked,

"Mother?" Her voice had opened as thin as paper. It had gone to a higher pitch, as it always did when she was nervous and afraid, seeming not her voice, but a stranger's—shaky, soft, and insecure. *A silly quality for the daughter of the queen to have,* she always scolded herself. As far as Sam was concerned, it was one of the many flaws in her character she was embarrassed about and hoped one day she would overcome. She wanted more than anything to prove to her mother, and her sister, that she was brave and could face trouble straight on with courage and confidence. Elle would always say to her, *"Your courage is too bound up with your fear to be your ally."* But the day her father disappeared was the day that changed everything for Sam. How she felt about herself, how she viewed the world around her and her place in it. The only time when Sam wasn't afraid was when she was flying. Then, everything had order, everything was clear. She wasn't afraid of anything.

Early that evening, when she was walking down the long spiral staircase from her bedroom on her way to dinner, her stomach was doing flip-flops, her fear growing. And now, sitting at the dining table, waiting for the right moment to ask her mother if she could ride with her to Rumpart's castle, her heart was pounding like thunder around her temples, giving her a headachy feeling. She felt the slightest trickle of tiny beads of sweat forming across her forehead, an itchy feeling she was trying her best to ignore. Everyone, including Elle, Saran, Lillith, and the other elite guards, were leaving the long dining hall. Most likely, Sam thought, they were preparing for another weary and worried evening of whispered discussion about the never-before-seen sorceress and the dark smoke moving in from the west.

When she spoke, they paused and all of them turned and looked at Sam and then to Glinda. She wished they were not there, and she wondered if they could see her legs trembling and hear the quaver when she spoke. Her mother was waiting for her to continue with her question. Swallowing, Sam continued. "You ride soon to check on Rumpart?" She could feel Saran's and her sister's eyes burning through her, but she kept her own fixed on her mother.

"Yes, we are going to Winkie Country to meet with Rumpart and quell the rumors concerning him and learn about this enchantress. To find out who, or what, she is." A little of the smile that made Sam feel loved crept into her mother's eyes and Sam's fear eased, but only slightly. "When we go, we will go with my soldiers to show our resolve." The queen's smile widened. "Yes, we go to talk with Rumpart and see what mischief he might be involved in."

Saran added, "We have some hope of maybe catching the mischief before it grows." Everyone was not of a mind to say dark, or magic, or any variation that alluded to another wicked witch or another witch's war. "And if we find that Rumpart is under some unnatural spell, we'll bottle it up and destroy it." Saran's mouth turned up at the corners into a wry smile.

Sam looked at her, and her own mouth found a slight grin. It was so like Saran to treat her as part of the company, as part of the royal court, instead of just the youngest daughter of the queen. Saran would let her go. She knew she would, but it was not Saran's decision.

Sam turned back to her mother. "I wish to go with you, Mother?" Her voice was little more than a quiet squeak. She wished she was in the room alone, without the rest, without her sister, so they would not see her knees beginning to fold up under her like a newborn calf's. "I want to prove myself and stand by your side in battle, like Elle did when she fought alongside you to push the wood trolls back into the Enchanted Forest."

The silence went suddenly tight, and her sister closed her eyes. Then it was broken with Elle's high-pitched laugh. "What should we expect, Mother, when our honored First, your Consola, gives her lessons in swordplay as she did me, and she races around the castle yard unchaperoned riding and practicing with her bow, with never a reprimand or a slap for any misdeed from that cranky, loving, crusty old crow who serves us both as a maid? I blame you, Mother, and I blame our father—and Saran too."

Elle's smile grew bigger, and she laughed again, and so did all the others, including Glinda. And then with a firmer voice, Elle said, "It was your love and encouragement, Mother, that made me a strong woman. Why would we think otherwise for my sister? We should not be surprised at all that her reckoning would come to haunt us, as it has."

Sam felt the blood mounting even more to her face, and she was already flushed with it. Not because of embarrassment, but because of the love for her sister and her sister's undying support. The silence resettled around them and Sam watched her mother. How beautiful she was, how graceful, how commanding, and at times, frightening. "Please, Mother. I am good with my sword."

"She is, my queen," Saran politely broke in. "As rusty and cracked as that old slasher is, your daughter wields it with great skill. A natural skill."

"Samantha . . ." Glinda began, looking directly from Saran to her beautiful young daughter. The gentleness of her mother's voice and the fact that she used *Samantha* and not *Sam* told Sam everything she needed to know. Her face dropped in an instant as the queen continued. "Your time will come, but not now. I need you here—one person of royal blood staying to show the Quadlings they will never be left without hope." Glinda reached out to Sam. She held her tightly and kissed her forehead, saying softly, "Will you do this little thing I ask of you?"

Sam gave her mother a kiss on the cheek in return and put her lips to her mother's ear. "I'll do my best. I promise." When Sam pulled away she bowed and curtsied. But when she walked to the door at the end of the dining hall, her legs were still a little weak, and the pit of her stomach gurgled like it'd been gutted and scooped out with a spoon. But she also had a slight grin grow on her face when a thought hit her with a soft knock. *I wouldn't mind sitting on the throne and being the queen for awhile.* Her lips turned up at one corner, her eyebrows scrunching, as she calculated and then whispered for only her ears to hear, "*Uhmm,* what do you suppose my first queenly proclamation should be?"

That conversation with her mother was still fresh in her mind, and now, days later, as Sam looked out and stood on top of the castle, everything seemed transformed, yet very peaceful. But somehow things were different, slightly off balance. She could sense the morning air was heavier, and the soft morning light was changing rapidly. She heard a whinny, opened her eyes, and turned her head to the sound. Jo, her father's warhorse, now hers (one of the rarest of breeds: a horse of a different color), was grazing in the meadow next to the stoned-sided stables. Looking down on him from the top of her bedroom roof, he reminded her of a miniature dollhouse toy she used to play with when she was a child. She grinned and giggled from the tickle the thought gave her. She could tell he was prancing about with his nervous gait, impatient, turning an angry scarlet because she hadn't been down yet to brush him and give him his morning treat. She would, and soon, and he'd return to his cool, soft cream color. *You can be so dramatic*, she thought with another short giggle.

The rush. Oh, yes—the *rush*. And the waiting.

But the thrill—it was definitely the *thrill*.

S am was a beautiful good fairy witch with thick, auburn hair mixed with golden strands of spider silk braided into cornrows, sprouting out from beneath her crown like long, electrified caterpillars. Her crown was made from a rare santhosian grapevine that had fall and spring leaves growing from it, with grass-like shoots and tree branches extending out. The crown was very much alive, separate from Sam yet attached, connected to her, with an intelligent and more often than not, an aggravating mind of its own. It was vigilant, aware, always on the alert. It guarded her. Protected her. And warned her of trouble.

When she felt extremely high-spirited, snowflakes surrounded her, appearing out of thin air when she was flying and disappearing before touching the ground. Her skin was a mixture of wintery ice-blue and spring green with a soft swathe of darker green covering her golden-colored eyes—the same dazzling, deep rich gold of her father's eyes—and she wore the green mask running across her face like a badge of honor a warrior would wear into battle. There was a sprinkle of freckles that gently danced across her nose and cheeks, and tiptoed softly along the ridges of her pointed ears. And as if someone had dipped a thumb into dark green paint, she had a narrow green band running down from the center of her lips to just under her chin. Some people said her greenish mask and chin stripe were an unfortunate birthmark, the mark of her father, Lucius. But Sam was proud of that fact and wore the birthmarks with great pride.

Almost eight years ago, he disappeared. Unlike Sam, her mother and Elle thought he was dead, and none of them talked about it anymore. She loved her father and missed him terribly. Thoughts of him appeared silently, out of nowhere, like a mysterious dark shadow come to life. Like now. It made her eyes pool, but the rush was more than she could endure, and she let it out in one giant wail, tipping her head back as she wiped her eyes with the back of her hand.

"I LOVE FLYING!" A beefy gust of wind slapped her hard. She grinned, relishing its power, egging it on to give her more. The cool, early morning air filled her lungs, blowing her braids across her shoulders. Sam's heart raced, her body flushed with adrenaline and the sheer joy of abandonment, the taste of freedom, of letting go.

"No more waiting," she whispered to herself. Her eyes narrowed to tiny slits. She released her grip from the flagpole, stood up, looked down at the deadly drop, down to the keep, and noticed that Saran and Lillith had returned to their sparring. She gulped as much air into her lungs as she could, extended her wings, then pressed them tightly against her back as she launched herself out into space. She held out her arms, executing a perfect swan dive out and over the turret roof, and for a moment, everything stood still, tranquil and private. She smiled, counting to herself. *One* . . . flying was the rush. The speed was the rush. The ground one hundred feet away. *Two* . . . the sound of the air *whooshing* past her was the rush. The ground fifty feet away. Now thirty. Moving faster and faster was the rush. Her smile grew wide. Twenty feet . . . fifteen.

"Three!" she screamed out loud, and unfurled her wings as fast as she could. Her powerful pinions were opened to their full length—

fourteen feet across—translucent pearl, gold, and green, shimmering like jewels in the morning light.

When her wings caught the air, Sam was yanked up hard and fast. Saran and Lillith and the other guards all looked up at the last second. They ducked their heads as Sam soared only inches away, pushing the air around them with a *whoosh*, like a fireworks rocket exploding from its roost, leaving a trail of snowflakes behind like pixie dust. She let out a deep-throated howl and surged upward, feeling every pull of her shoulder muscles, the air whistling past her ears, the breeze drying her tears, zooming past the waving flag on top of her bedroom roof, soaring high above the castle.

Instead of a gentle tilting of her wings and gliding in a wide arc, Sam swung around, lurched, tucked, and dived again.

Once more, Sam swept her wings back, turned a sharp angle and plummeted, racing faster and faster to the ground, racing for the rush, back to the keep. She spun until the castle guards thought she was out of control. The guards braced themselves for another flyby and dove to the ground, hugging it with their chests, lying as flat as they could.

Saran opened her eyes, just a slit, in time to see Sam's wings reach out at the last second, fill with air, and swing the princess upward again. Sam had zoomed past with incredible speed, so close that Saran could have reached out and touched her. A blast of wind hit Saran squarely in the face as Sam zoomed past. She got up with a humph, shook snowflakes off her head, brushed the dirt off her tunic, looked back at Sam, and gave a grudgingly approving smile.

Sam giggled, screamed in delight, and circled her bedroom tower twice before softly landing on the balcony. She turned around and looked over the railing and was laughing so hard her ribs stung from each gasping outburst. She raised her arms above her head and waved to Saran and Lillith, blowing each a kiss, first with her left hand and then with her right, and then waving and laughing again.

Two

H er head was alive, wide awake, turned on full blast from her morning flight. Flying was everything to her. It motivated her. She felt the same each time she'd take the deep dive off the castle tower. The exhilaration, the buzz, the thrill, the rush, it was so vividly before her and around her that she could barely hold a thought. Every inch of her skin was tingling, every hair on her arms dancing so that the door of her bedroom was half-open before she heard it. Her grapevine crown nipped her head, warning her. Sam was sprawled out on her bed. She spun around and sat up. It was only Augie, bearing her breakfast tray, and Sam scowled.

Augie glanced up at Sam's sour face and scowled back. "Out flying again before you've had food in your belly, I see."

She'd most likely been chosen as Sam's maid because she was so iron-willed, recalcitrant. *A tough, ornery old bird*, Sam thought sourly. But then she noticed the smell from the steam that rose above the tray and Augie's furrowed brow of fret. Sam's own face softened and her stomach growled.

"You must eat, lassie," Augie said sternly.

"I really hadn't thought about it," Sam replied, and this was true. When the dawn's dim gray light peeked into her bedroom, all she could think about was leaping off the tower again. "It slipped my mind."

"It's always slipping your mind," Augie groused with a huff, placing the tray on the sitting table by the balcony before lifting the cloth napkins off the plates. "All you think about is flying, flying, flying.

Nothing but flying. You need to eat!" She squinted one eye and pointed her finger at Sam. "If it weren't for me, you'd be folly for the dirt, so eat." She looked sharply at her young charge, held a napkin between her fingers, and lifted it to Sam as the worry mark that etched itself on her forehead deepened. Sam crossed her arms, lifted her shoulders mirroring the same sharp look back as the maid continued. "You shouldn't be so stubborn. Now, eat before it gets cold."

Sam got out of bed, her eyes shooting daggers at the old Munchkin. "I'm not stubborn," she muttered stiffly. When she took the napkin, she pinched one corner with her thumb and index finger in defiance. Then she pursed her lips and sat down.

"Headstrong. Pigheaded. Whatever you want to call it," Augie sighed. "I call it stubborn. And a chancer, takin' advantage of your lucky britches, you are. It's not good for you. It will make you old before your time is up."

"Oh, like you," Sam returned in a teasing way.

"Like me," Augie teased back, a smile touching the corners of her concern. "A feeble old bat?"

"I will stop my *stubbornness* if you will worry less."

"I will worry less," Augie replied, "when the strange magic coming out of Winkie Country is put to rest. You need to eat and keep your strength up—we don't know what role we all might have yet to play in this mischief." Seeing worry cover Sam's eyes, Augie then said, with a grin to distract her, "Jo is angry with you 'cause you're late."

"He told you this, of course," Sam said with delight as she put scrambled eggs on a piece of buttered toast and took a healthy bite.

"Aye, he did. He's as scarlet as I've ever seen him," Augie replied as she placed a small satchel on the foot of Sam's bed. "I brought you some apples for his morning treat. I put an extra one in. You'll need it to appease him for sure."

"I'll go soon," Sam said with a gentle smirk. "Jo will have to wait." Her eyes twinkled and her smirk became a grin. "I was *told* by an old bat I must eat." She picked up another piece of toast, sloshed grape jam on it, added some bacon and some eggs, and took another big, healthy bite, smiling as she chewed. "Happy now?" she said, her mouth full of food.

Sam loved her father's horse. He was a symbol of hope to her— an unwavering hope that perhaps, one day, her father would return. And her love for horses was equally matched by Augie's affection for them too, and for the fact that Augie was always roaming the stables and pastures beyond them, rubbing the horses down and giving them a bath any free time she had. It was well-known to everyone in the castle the great care and respect Augie gave to all the animals—the talking ones and the nonspeaking ones.

Sam walked over to the balcony, wiping jam off her chin with her napkin. The sun was much higher now, and the wind had lessened. She leaned over the railing and peered down at the keep. There were more fast-paced comings and goings across the courtyard. She saw more messengers and two young women racing on foot wearing the livery of the queen's army; they had red sashes on their forearms, which meant they were part of the detachment that handled supplies. Preparations for her mother's entourage for the trek west to meet with King Rumpart were moving at a pace faster than Sam had expected. During peaceful times, Sam only saw the everyday goings-on in the castle: guards sparring, castle staff bringing in supplies, or occasional guests riding in to pay their respects to her mother or to ask for a favor.

She heard a loud crash from nearby, and the sound of shattering ceramic hitting the stone floor, and a gasp. "Oh, my—" Sam said as she rushed into her bedroom.

"Whatever you're gonna say," Augie said with a huff, "I've thought of it already."

Silence.

Augie was standing with her head and shoulders bowed, staring at the tray turned upside down on the floor. "It just slipped out of my hands." The dishes were a beautiful, thin, pure white Gillikinese ceramic with a strawberry vine patterned edging, made at the renowned Gillikin pottery manufacturer from the northernmost part of Gillikin Country over three hundred years ago. "Your mother is gonna be so disappointed in me."

They stared at the plates. Sam knew her mother wouldn't be upset because dishes could be replaced. Augie had mended Sam's breakages when she was a baby, though not the fancy plates she ate off of now. Her broken plates and bowls as a child were heavy earthenware and easily repaired. And Sam managed to break more than a few, sometimes just for fun.

A difficult child?

Yes, at times.

What child isn't?

But it was always Augie who came to the rescue to fit the bits together with glue, making it a fun project for the both of them. Sam had been an unusually large and awkward child who seemed able to break things merely by being in the same room with them. She was not a particularly clumsy young woman—she had grown into her large skin and indeed wasn't as awkward as she once had been. But she still had her moments. It was a little comforting to see Augie as the clumsy one for a change.

"Can you fix them?" Augie asked softly. "With your magic?" Sam nodded her head, closed her eyes, took in a gentle breath, concentrated, and slowly moved her hand back and forth over the broken dishes. The shattered pieces started to twitch and wobble, trying their best to wake up. All at once, the fractured shards came to life, shaking just a little at first trying to figure out where they belonged. Then they danced and twirled to music only they could hear, fitting themselves back together as if they'd never been broken.

"Oh, lassie." Augie said in a grateful, hushed tone. "You're getting so good with your magic." She exhaled a sigh of relief, pushing both hands together under her chin as if in prayer. Then, carefully, one by one, they placed the repaired china onto the breakfast tray. "Thank you, milady."

"Elle is a good instructor," Sam replied as she vaulted onto her down-filled bed, bedsheets flying up with a *whoosh* on both sides of her and floating down slowly as the air escaped. She folded her arms around one of her large pillows. "She is the one who is getting good with her magic. Really good."

"She is a natural, like her mother," Augie remarked.

"The wicked one?" Sam teased.

"Of course not, silly." Augie lifted her eyes to Sam, who was still stretched out on her bed, listening, holding the pillow close to her chest with her legs spread out in a relaxed, ungainly way. "I never think of that old bat and her demon-mischief these days. Your mother has shown your sister what it is to be a good witch, not a wicked one. That's why the Quadlings love her so, as do the Munchkins who have accepted her with open arms and adore her as much as they do your mother."

Augie had come to serve Glinda as a child, some two hundred years before Sam was born, for Munchkins and fairy sorceresses, like Augie and Glinda, live very long lives. And despite being over two centuries old, Augie didn't look a day over a hundred and fifty, though one could see that time was indeed slowing her down, changing her. It was putting gray in Augie's once-thick purple hair and giving her a noticeable paunch, a perfect complement to the crinkles lacing her kind orange eyes. It didn't take much imagination to see that Augie had once been beautiful. She was half of Sam's height, which was tall for a Munchkin. She insisted that those who were from the most southern region of Munchkin Country were taller than their northern cousins because the food grew taller in the south and so did their irascibility.

Sam lifted her eyes to Augie, who had walked over to the left side of Sam's bed and sat on the edge of the mattress. She gave the gruff old Munchkin a hug, and Augie gently pushed back enough to look into Sam's eyes with a half-smile and put her palm on Sam's cheek.

"I hate seeing you so young and dealing with such serious adult matters."

Sam let go of her hug, and her eyes turned involuntarily to the dull old sword hanging at the foot of her high-curtained bed. She sighed and stared at the palms of her hands, striped with calluses and scarred with old blisters from sword, shield, and bow practice. "I am more of an adult than you think, my grumpy old caretaker."

"You know that the rumors are just rumors and nothing more."

"Yes," Sam said slowly. "Before I had even heard any of the whispers, Saran, and Lillith, and Elle had been training me harder than they had before—much harder. They've been preparing me, I'm sure of it. I knew it then, and know it even more today. I am the daughter of the queen. A daughter who hasn't proven herself yet." She paused. "Augie," she said before the other had a chance to break in, "tell me the story about my father."

"Story?" said Augie, trying her best to appear unfazed. She was always careful when talking about Sam's father—one of the reasons Sam was so persistent in wanting to know more. And each time Augie told the story it made Sam's eyes pool, the tears soon falling like water endlessly rolling down a stream. They both would end up spilling waterworks until there were no more hugs to give each other for comfort, until their eyes lost their wetness and became sore to the touch. But Augie knew the story had to be told again and again so that the memory of Sam's father would never fade. "Which part?" Augie then asked.

"When he meets Mother."

"Aye, right. When your father first set his dazzling, gold-colored eyes on your mother, he was smitten," Augie began. "It was like all the evil darkness and torture he had endured at the hands of the Wicked Witch of the West turned to ash and fell back into the dirt where they belonged. He told me this one day when he was peeking out the window and watching you practice swordplay with Saran and Elle, with those cute little wooden swords you girls used when you were children."

"The day he disappeared," Sam added.

"Aye, the day your father disappeared. Eight years ago, next week, on your birthday, Princess."

"Did my mother use a potion or a spell so he'd marry her?" Sam asked with a grin and a stubborn squint, ignoring Augie's reference to her birthday.

"I suppose she did, if you believe falling in love is no different than a spell. Your father was a strong, powerful, and loving man. A strapping pure-barry, as we say down south. A right handsome lad. A real looker." She winked at Sam and gave a wily grin. "It's no wonder the queen fell in love with him. He was dedicated to your mother; he helped her in everything that came with ruling a country. He adored you and Elle. And his wings—oh my, they were magnificent," she quietly exclaimed, shaking her head from side to side, and closing her eyes as if she were reliving a private moment with Sam's father.

Augie clasped her hands together with controlled excitement and placed her fingertips on her lips, inhaling deeply and spreading her arms out as far as they could reach. Then she let the air out of her lungs slowly before she said another word. "When your father unfurled his wings and took you flying before your own wings were strong enough, well, he looked like a guardian angel from heaven. He loved you girls so much—" Augie's eyes opened. Her hands fell into her lap as if the memory were more than they could handle.

Sam interrupted. "You tell it like he's gone forever, like he's dead."

"I don't mean to do so."

"He's going to return. One day, he will fly home. I am sure of it." Sam did not want to think about something unpleasant, something that built a wall across the past.

"Yes, one day," Augie said with a forced smile, even though she had her doubts. "Your father will return."

"I like to hear your stories."

Augie laughed, then said in a gentle tone, "I like to tell them."

"Did you see him disappear?" Sam asked, sitting up cross-legged.

"No, but one of your mother's guards saw him flying above the castle, as he often loved to do, like you do now—and then a bright green explosion knocked the guard to the ground and when she looked up, your father had vanished."

"Am I like him? The way folks say?"

"Yes," Augie said. "You have the best of both. Your father and your mother are in you, and that's something to be very proud of. It is why you are so delightfully stubborn."

↬ ◆ ↫

They'd had this conversation many times before, many times in the years since that fateful day when Sam's father had seemingly evaporated into thin air. Over those years, Augie kept telling the same stories, and Sam kept asking again and again for her to tell them, certain that there was a mystery to be solved behind his disappearance.

Augie wanted to believe too, but in her heart, she was much more unsure. Sam's mother and Elle wouldn't discuss her father with Sam anymore, beyond telling her that they missed him, which Sam found reassuring as far as it went. He was alive, though, of that she was sure. And whether the truth behind the mystery was known by anyone or not, she promised herself she would one day find out what happened to him.

"Tell me about my mother," Sam said, putting her hand over Augie's.

Augie considered. "Aye. Your mother. I've known the queen for centuries. I knew your mother when she stood against the subjugation of the talking animals and for their right to speak their mind. I stood alongside your mother with my two swords, one in each hand, in the battle she fought against Mombi, the Wicked Witch of the North, to restore Princess Ozma to the throne." Augie was quiet for a moment. Her eyes seemed to be looking far into the past before she continued, Her voice softened. "Mombi wasn't a natural born witch, but very clever. But not as clever as your mother. Instead of putting the wrinkled old crone on trial and sending her to the gallows, your mother stripped Mombi of all her magic powers so she could never harm anyone again.

"I was also standing next to your mother when your mother first met Dorothy Gale. We stood there in the middle of Munchkin City, gobsmacked, as we watched Dorothy's house fall out of the sky and squash the Wicked Witch of the East like a bug. The house hit the ground with a thunderous crash, breaking the house in half. Then silence. Absolute silence. The next second, every Munchkin in the entire city yelled at the same time, raising their arms in the air."

Augie chuckled. "I'll never forget that old hag's legs stickin' out from under the house, with her black-and-white striped stockings and the ruby slippers she was wearin'. It was the only part of her left after the house practically pushed the evil gorgon to hell where she belonged. I always thought those stockings looked silly on such a wicked old bat. What a sight it was. Aye, a day to remember." Augie paused with a sigh and rubbed the palm of her hand gently along Sam's shoulder. "Your mother is courageous and very powerful, but also very kind, and forgiving, as you know. She is a fierce and courageous warrior in combat. You and your sister are so much like her."

Sam and Elle had read all the books by the famous Gillikin authors about wicked witches. They'd spent many lazy days reading historical novels about Oz, especially the ones written about Sam's mother and her bravery in battle. They had gone on school field trips to the Emerald City and seen the play *Wicked Days*. It was always a little strange watching the story of their mother and Elle's evil mother, with Dorothy and her funny little dog, Toto, unfold before their eyes on a stage with song and dance. But their favorite place to visit was the Natural Historical Museum of Oz, and their favorite display was the famous burnt broomstick given to Dorothy by their father.

"I could stay right here all day and be perfectly happy listening to your stories," Sam said to Augie. "There are times I never want to leave my bedroom." It was her refuge, a place of soft blue and yellow tapestries hiding the cold, stone-gray walls—a shelter of silence, reflection, and meditation. She and Augie had private moments together here, their confidential talks. It was her hidden hideaway, the highest point in the castle. Sam spent most of her time in this room, except when she was buzz-bombing the guards and sparring with her sister and Saran, or riding Jo.

"Jo!" Sam said with a gasp, throwing back the pillow. "He must be really pissed off with me now."

"Watch your language, lassie!" Augie snapped as she stood up from the bed.

"Fine," Sam retorted with a furrowed brow. "He must be really *distraught.* Better?"

"It'll do. Now, be off with you. You've got chores to do."

Sam picked up the satchel with the apples, threw its long strap over her head and shoulder, and was about to run down the stairs when she laughed. "I don't need stairs." She spun around, dashed out onto the balcony, and without missing a beat, leaped over the railing, unfurled her wings, and took flight.

❧ ◆ ❧

S am took a big bite from one of the apples as she flew and couldn't help giggling, thinking of Augie fussing over her and how she enjoyed her fussing. *"Aye, lassie. You need to eat."*

Every morning when Sam flew down to the horse barn to visit Jo, she liked to pretend that the grooms didn't notice her. She tried to be as stealthy as possible, something she was trying to improve upon but had not yet mastered. The head groom, Roman, always made sure no one bothered her private time with Jo. He understood what she had done for Jo to bring him back to life. The poor horse had been a lost soul for the longest time until Sam and Elle started grooming him and riding him every day. Now there was a bond between them, a trust that could not be broken. And what Sam gave to Jo, he gave back to Sam, for she often felt lost without her father, and Jo was the invisible thread that kept that connection tied together.

As she landed on the hard-packed dirt floor in the barn, she instantly could tell that Jo was upset with her. Not because he had turned a deep scarlet, but because he was acting like a spoiled child, a brat, picking up one of his hind hoofs and stomping the ground when she came into his stall. Not only that, but when she approached him, he turned his head away and stomped again, making it clear he'd been wondering what had become of her and why she was so late. And when she gathered up his grooming brushes and walked him outside, he reared up on his hind legs, turned away from her, and trotted over to a patch of blue bunchgrass to munch on the slender stems, ignoring her and turning bright orange.

Jo was her favorite horse in the stable. It was an enormous stable keeping all of the horses for her mother's elite guards. Jo had been her father's horse when she was just a small child. When her father put all the fancy trappings on him Jo looked magnificent in a royal cavalcade, with orange reins, a crownpiece and cheekpieces, an orange skirt attached to the saddle, and a full, sparkling silver breastplate.

Sam slowly walked up to him and gently rubbed his neck. His neck muscles twitched with each stroke. "I have not neglected you," Sam whispered in his ear. "Don't even try to make me think so." She firmly patted him and rubbed his nose with her hand. She could tell that Roman had already brushed him to a high gloss, but she knew Jo liked to be fussed over. He had calmed down, but only a little, and snuffled her all over, partly to make sure she'd brought him his treat, partly to reassure himself that she had in fact finally arrived, and partly to let her know that she was almost forgiven for her lack of punctuality.

He rubbed his nose along Sam's temple, pushed out a breath, and rolled a dark, reproachful eye. It took the extra apple before he truly forgave her and let his angry colors turn to his calm-colored cream, and then Sam fetched the brushes and groomed him while he stretched his neck and made amusing faces of enjoyment.

Sam relaxed as she brushed Jo, something that always happened to her when she was around him. And in doing so, with each brushstroke the thought of the commotion in the keep with the mysterious scroll from the messengers—and the threat of darker days—quickly faded away, like dandelion seeds blown by the wind.

Three

When Sam was only a child, she idolized Jo. He was her father's famous and fierce war stallion. The Quadlings, as well as Sam, were in awe of Jo's grand, courtly manner. Everyone loved how he held his head up high and swished his tail back and forth with an imposing swagger when her father rode him off to battle. Jo was always the first horse in the procession and larger than all the others. Sam thought it so impressive—and frightening at the same time—when he would rear and strike. He'd press his ears flat so that his long, wedge-shaped head looked like a Quadling cobra ready to strike fear into the enemy. But on the day of her father's disappearance, Jo must have been a witness to the event, for at the very moment the legendary green flash streaked across the sky, Jo took off at full gallop across the grazing meadow as if to rescue his master, forgetting about the hacker thorn bushes fencing the perimeter. He tried to force his way through, only to be ensnared by the foot-long thorns. And the more he struggled to escape, the deeper the barbs pierced into his flesh, cutting him severely.

Roman was shaken when he ran up to Jo, who was thrashing about, neighing and stomping the ground, kicking up dirt, flinging his head from side to side, unable to escape the sharp thorns. Roman had seen many animals maimed and crying out in distress over the years, but this was Jo, and the cries he made were harrowing.

There was a deep gash across his right flank and hip, nearly eighteen inches long, as deep as any sword could have slashed, and many smaller cuts as well. When Roman was finally able to cut Jo free and attend to the horrible gash, he found tendons and muscles severed, and his first thought was that he'd have to end it there. But when he looked at the horse's face, with his lips curled back from his teeth and the whites showing around his eyes, Roman thought of Lucius and Sam and Elle and could not—would not—take the life of such a noble animal unless there was absolutely no other choice. And in Roman's heart, he was sure Jo wasn't done yet and that he was going to find a way to bring the proud stallion back to the living so he could carry another brave warrior on his back.

Sam was the first to fly out to the meadow to see about Jo, with Elle only a wingtip behind her. It was a long and slow walk back to the barn, the four of them, Sam and Elle on either side of Jo, and Roman in the lead, but Jo set the pace and was stubborn enough to make it. Roman knew this stubbornness was what the warhorse would need to recover from such serious injuries. Roman decided that if the horse was strong enough to walk back to the barn on three legs, then he was strong enough to recover. He owed him that chance at least.

Jo sidled up the last small hill to the royal stable, limping so badly he could barely inch his way into his stall; with a liberating sigh, he lay slowly down in the straw with a weak groan. "He's a strong one, I'll give him that," said Roman grimly, and then sent for the healers. But when they came, each time they approached Jo in his stall, he surged to his feet and raised up to attack them, turning a fiery red and making it all the more difficult to administer a healing treatment. When the physicians tried to pour a relaxant down Jo's throat, it took all of them and a rope twisted around the horse's jaw to contain him. Even that wasn't enough to control his combative spirit. Jo continued to fight back each and every time a healer came near. But when Sam approached, he didn't put up a fight. He'd relax a bit and lay down from exhaustion. Sam would kneel down and rub his face, from his eyes to his nose, to soothe and give him reassurance. And each time, when he finally calmed down into a quiet, soft and delicate blue, it was only then that the healers could do their work.

It took much time for the wound to heal after the practitioners stitched Jo's leg up. It had healed well on the outside, as far as everyone could tell. But the healers did not believe that the warhorse would ever fully recover. The physicians had told Roman at the time that Jo would always be lame. But Sam and Elle didn't believe it—they refused to.

"He's our father's stallion," Elle said firmly and with pride when Roman told the princesses what the healers felt about Jo's chances and also what he thought was right.

"It's best to let him graze and play for the rest of his days," he told the girls.

"He's more than just a horse," Sam said, her eyes pooling. "He's the fine thread that links us to our father."

The day when Jo was finally strong enough, they turned him out into a pasture of his own, private and away from the other horses, with hope that it would soothe his soul and heal his will. It was the perfect place for Jo to fully recover—if, and only if, he had the intention to do so.

The meadow was covered with delicious, chest-high green grass. There was a cluster of ancient torillian singing maple trees for shade clumped together next to a running brook to drink from and a small pond to soak in, with mud at the edge for rolling. When the breeze washed against the trees, they sang a soft and soothing melody that would lift and calm anyone's spirit, man or beast alike. And Sam and Elle, with Roman's help, built a sturdy, dry shed so Jo could have a place to go when it rained.

This is perfect, Sam thought to herself after building the hut and looking out over the lush green field. *Absolutely perfect*. She truly believed Jo would recover and be the grand war stallion he was born to be. But for a time, even with the beautiful surroundings and the powerful love from Sam and Elle, the horse wouldn't eat all his grain; he would only nibble or knock his bucket of food over with his nose. He wouldn't let anyone groom him, and each time Sam and Elle tried he'd back away, or set his stance, shaking his head as if preparing to charge. Even still, every day Sam and Elle faithfully brought him fresh grain and read books to him.

In the evenings they would walk away, hoping that the next day they'd find Jo greeting them at the gate with an impatient look in his eyes as if to say, *What took you so long?* But Jo only grew thin and began to lose his strength and his desire to live. And for most animals, once their will has been crushed, they will stop eating and let nature do the rest. It was a testament to Sam and Elle's good character that they were not willing to give up.

᠀ ✦ ᠀

As the days gradually edged forward, Jo became weaker and weaker.

"We are not going to let our father's warhorse become food for the dogs," Sam said to Elle one evening, opening a new sack of grain before they left Jo for the night. It had been two months since Roman pulled Jo from the hacker thorns. There was great concern indeed that the horse would not last much longer if he didn't start eating more. He was so weak now that when Sam and Elle approached him, he didn't put up any kind of fuss. The great warhorse didn't back away or try to fight them anymore, and to their surprise, he actually allowed them to groom him.

"He reminds me of a puppy, lost and unloved," Elle said, picking up a grooming brush. "Like he's waiting to be found. And he eats only enough to keep from dropping dead."

"But we *are* loving him," Sam said. "We tell him that every day. We talk to him. We read to him. Every day, we're loving him." Sam poured the last of the fresh grain into Jo's bucket and walked over to him, putting her arms around his neck and nuzzling her cheek against his warm body. The appendages from her crown twirled and mixed with his mane, giving their love as well. "Why is he not getting better,

Elle? Shouldn't he be getting better?"

"I might have an idea."

Sam snapped her head up and quickly replied, "Use your magic, Elle." Sam picked up a grooming brush and carefully started brushing his wounded flank, being ever so mindful of Jo's tender scar. "Use your magic," she repeated.

"No, not that," Elle shot back. "Magic and potions aren't any good when someone has lost their will. It doesn't work like that." Elle held Jo's face with both hands and put her cheek against his, rubbing his jaw. "Mother taught me not to use my magic to force anyone to do something they don't want to do."

"Then what?" Sam questioned.

"He's a stubborn old nag, but I think he's lonely."

"But he has us," Sam said.

"We're not enough," Elle replied. "I think he misses Vail."

"Your horse?" Sam said with a smile. "Maybe you're right. Vail is the only other horse he will tolerate."

E lle had no early memory of when she was born, and no memory of her wicked witch of a mother either. All she had were the stories her father told her and what she read in books. She wasn't even a year old when her father stole her away from the nightmare he endured at the hands of the Wicked Witch of the West. Glinda was the only mother she knew, and the castle they lived in the only home she had any memory of. Elle was so pleased by Sam's birth, so excited that she would have a sister, someone to share secrets with, someone other than herself living in such an enormous castle. It wasn't long after Sam was able to walk and run that the two of them became inseparable.

Elle couldn't wait for Sam to grow old enough to fly. Having a sister as a flying companion was electrifying, and Elle was determined to show Sam all the tricks she had learned. Elle's father taught her everything about flying and her stepmother, Glinda, taught her the finesse of flight. There was no greater pleasure than soaring with her father and stepmother, and having a sister to share that joy made Elle feel as if her family were complete.

Yet, at the same time, she felt a great burden: the responsibility of being the older sibling to guide and protect her little sister. And now, seeing Sam so consumed with worry about Jo, Elle felt like she had to do everything in her power—except using magic—to help Jo find his way back to the light. Not just for Sam's sake, but also for Jo's sake, to save a rare and beautiful creature of Oz.

Sam, however, was by nature the type of child who got into trouble first and thought about it later. Elle, being the bigger, older sibling did her best to help Sam make good choices. Elle would always tell her, *"Everything we do, every day, is make choices, good or bad. We must choose wisely. We must choose well. In the end, we either stand tall on the side of light or fester bent over in darkness."* As far as Elle was concerned, Sam still hadn't quite learned that all-important lesson of not rushing headfirst into the fray—not completely. Sam continued to have moments when thinking first simply would never do. *"You're as stubborn as Father,"* Elle said to Sam over and over.

It wasn't always the perfect friendship as they grew up. And when they fought, it was epic. Elle and Sam made a fearsome pair, facing off when irritated with each other, and they always liked to use the castle garden as their battlefield, glaring eye to eye, ready to brawl like two injured bulls in a bullfight. Elle had come to her full growth and beauty on her sixteenth birthday. And on that morning, Elle had been pampered and primped in preparation for the grand celebration. Her long, full, vibrant, unruly red hair hung past her hips in heavy waves and was skillfully straightened, braided, and held in place by a golden webwork of silk decorated with pearls for that special day. But that morning, Elle's cheeks flushed with rage, staring at Sam until they were as red as her bright ruby lips. And when Elle smiled, the truth of the quarrel was painfully apparent—Sam had crept into Elle's bedroom that night and changed out her toothpaste with coal dye.

Now, when Elle smiled her teeth and lips were as black as pitch. With her emerald-green eyes opened to their fullest, as they were in that moment, one could see steam rising from her body as the sunlight glanced over her.

Elle knew immediately who had done it, and Sam—who would not tell a lie—said, "You should be grateful. I could have shaved your head, you snore so loudly." Her lips curved devilishly as she grinned at Elle, and it brought Sam's high cheekbones into impish prominence.

Elle growled, "I could turn you into a toad, but Mother would be pissed at me and not at you for what you've done, so I won't."

"Watch your mouth," Sam scolded as she wiggled her finger back and forth at Elle, her grin turning into a broad open smile from ear to ear. "Such language is unbecoming of a princess."

As their arguments would escalate, Glinda and Lucius always had Elle carried off in hysterics. Then they would banish Sam to her room with no supper. But confrontations of this nature were few and far between, as there was a bond so strong between the two of them it couldn't be broken. They would protect each other with their lives, a blood pact they had made. This connection, this conviction, became so keen they found they could talk to each other through their minds. It wasn't a full conversation—not entirely—but they could pass a few words at a time back and forth to each other, and it proved handy on many occasions.

Once, during school, in the locker room after gym class, Sam yelled in Elle's head, *The bucket!* But it was too late. Elle didn't turn away quickly enough and a bucket of water balancing on the top edge of the door spilled over and onto Elle, soaking her clothes from top to bottom. A mouthful of water escaped and dribbled down her chin.

Sam got a towel and handed it to Elle, grinding her teeth and saying, "This time, you should use your magic. I am sure it was Shannon and her party of snobby nobodies."

"They don't know," Elle said calmly as she wiped the towel over her face. "They don't know water won't destroy me. They don't understand it's not the color of a person's skin that melts them. It's the wickedness inside them." Elle took her shoes off and let the water trickle out. "Look how wicked they are with their ghost-white, brown, orange, and yellow complexions. I'm proud of my emerald hue. It's the wickedness inside you that turns your heart black, Sam. Never forget that." Elle put her hand on Sam's shoulder and put her shoes back on. "It's the small things we do, the simple acts of kindness that hold back the darkness inside us. I won't let the dark control me, ever."

Sam put her hands on Elle's shoulders and they touched foreheads, something they had always done to show their bond. And Sam's voice inside Elle's head asked, *Promise me?*

And Elle replied, *Promise.*

"Well," Sam said out loud with a deep growl and evil smirk, "I'd like to be a little wicked. How do you turn someone into a sniveling pig?"

Elle shook her head. "Do you have any idea what the headmistress and professors would do to us if we got caught?" Sam pursed her lips, trying to stifle her mirth, but her eyes were positively giddy. "It's not funny!" Elle snapped, holding back a tickle of laughter growing in her throat.

"I'm not saying we leave her a pig forever. Just 'til the end of third period," Sam said, forcing back a smile she knew would hurt her cheeks if it exploded on her face. "Or . . . fourth period."

"We can't." Elle stopped, her eyes squinting in thought. "A pig?"

Sam was trying so hard not to laugh, trying so hard to look serious, concerned, and sincere. Elle couldn't help but grin, and that was a mistake because when she did, a stomach full of laughter escaped from between her lips, and now they were both laughing big, rolling belly laughs.

It was a shared feeling of kinship between the girls, and one that made them understand the trapped and restless feeling Jo was going through. The terrible gash on his flank had healed months ago, and even though he had a bit of a limp, he didn't seem to be in any real pain. The girls believed he needed kinship. They both had visited him every day over the months, but he was no politer to them than he was to Roman, and it hurt them to look at his loneliness.

The day they escorted Vail into the pasture, Jo's first impulse was to charge her. Vail did not move—she just looked at him and shook her head with a snort. Jo raised up on his hind legs and jostled his front legs as if to charge. But Vail shunned him and dropped her head, shaking her mane and swishing her tail and began grazing, paying no attention to Jo's posturing. Jo turned his back to Vail, dropped his head halfway, and stood still. Sam, Elle, and Roman waited for two hours, and the stubborn warhorse didn't move an inch. They took Vail back to her stall, feeling terribly disappointed that afternoon.

"I thought for sure, Elle, your idea was going to work," Roman said to them.

"Me too," Sam agreed.

"I know it's the right thing to do," Elle said with confidence. "We'll try again tomorrow."

"Yes, and we need to go to the library and bring more books with us," Sam said. "These will be long days for sure."

That evening, in the castle library, Sam idly ran her fingers over the spines of the books lined up on the rows and rows of shelves. She pulled down one that had a decorative, tooled binding. She opened it and found the pages were beautifully designed as well. It smelled musty and old, the writing detailed and intriguing, filled with mystery. *Perfect*, she thought.

Elle, meanwhile, found a couple of books about casting protective spells she hadn't read yet. The sisters went back to the pasture the next day, and the next, and the day after that, bringing Vail with them each time. It became a daily routine—good exercise and fresh air for everyone. It was quiet and peaceful in Jo's pasture, and the girls always brought apples and laid them on the ground next to their blanket, where they would read their books about the history of Oz and magic spells, have picnics, and hope that Vail would make some magic of her own to help Jo.

Jo didn't exactly canter up to the girls on the day he finally acknowledged them. He didn't give them an eager whinny of greeting. But he was waiting at the gate entrance, waiting for them to arrive, which he had never done before. An excellent sign. And when Elle and Sam walked in with Vail, Jo followed them to the grove of trees where they always laid out their blankets and set out seven apples all in a row on the ground a few feet away.

Jo stayed back far enough that at first, the girls thought he was going to act like he did on all the other days before. Vail started grazing immediately, before the blankets hit the ground, as she was one horse who'd never overlook the chance for fresh, cool sweetgrass.

"He's acting like he always does," Sam said sourly.

"Be patient," Elle replied. "We have everything to gain if we're patient. Read your book." The girls rolled onto their stomachs and opened their books. Within a couple of minutes, they could hear Jo's hoofbeats. He was moving closer . . . *thunk, clump, pause* . . . And with each pause, he'd snort and blow air, softly stomping the ground with his front hoof and lifting his injured leg slightly off the ground to give it a short rest. The girls held their breath and crunched their shoulders, eyeing each other, tingling with hope. Sam peeked over the pages of her book. "Don't look," Elle whispered, "just wait." *Thunk, clump, pause* . . . *thunk, clump*—stop. Then they heard the delicious crunch of an apple. They smiled at each other and then they heard more crunching and they smiled again.

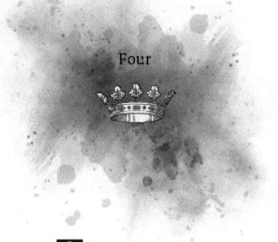

Four

On days when Elle couldn't be with Sam and Jo, Augie stepped in and shared time with Sam and the injured horse. Augie had been keeping a very sharp eye on the situation, for she loved that horse as much as the princesses did. Augie was thrilled when Sam told her the news that Jo had finally eaten the apples; she sighed deeply with relief and began providing them in greater quantity. There had been many a night, after supper, when she found Sam and Elle asleep in the shed with Jo, nestled in the fresh hay. She'd wake them with her heart beating in her mouth, worried Jo would reject her because she had invaded his domain, but he did not revolt. Jo accepted her as he did the girls. Her heart throbbed again when she knew she'd have to wake her charges and send them to their proper beds. She could hear what Sam would say: *"Fuss, fuss, fuss. You're always fussing, Augie."* It took a couple swats on their legs and a pinch or two on their feet to get them to move, but all of them remained excited that Jo had made the choice to live.

⚘ ◆ ⚘

On the eve of Jo's rebirth, when Sam and Elle went to the castle library in search of books to read to Jo, Sam took her time looking, for she indeed loved the library and the knowledge hidden among the multitude of pages. She had a powerful connection to books and couldn't help but let her fingers roll over their spines each and every time she made a visit to the library—every single book, row upon row of books, shelves upon shelves, each one different, each one a mystery. But with one ornate book she found, Sam felt a special connection. It was as if the book were calling out to her, persuading her to pick it up and read it, daring her to open it and turn the pages. It was so utterly different than any other book in the entire library. When she reached up to pull it free from the bookcase, she hesitated for just a moment before her hands grabbed onto the spine. She swallowed hard, taking in a quick breath and letting it out slowly. Her entire body shivered as she held the book in her hands, and her crown stretched out as far as it could to rub the worn and cracked leather binding; the book, too, shivered from the touch. The cover, meticulously hand-tooled, was embossed with the word *Oz* in the center, circled by a dragon. Sam carefully opened the cover and instantly fell in love with the book, its decorative pages, its intoxicating, musty smell, and her eyes grew larger and larger with each turn of a page when she gazed upon the fancy scrollwork.

It told of the history of Quadling Country and the castle they lived in and how it came to be that the first Wizard of Oz sat on the throne to rule the land and built the City of Emeralds. It was filled with all of Ozarian history, stretching back to the dawn of Oz before the Crossing Over, before there was a land to rule. Her mother often said that history was everything and not forgetting about the past was the most important thing, as it was in everyone's nature to make the same mistakes over and over. Her mother would say, *"It is our duty, nay, it is our gravest responsibility that we learn from history, from our past, with the hope of never repeating the same mistakes."* She had looked hard at Sam when she said so, her eyebrows folding down, showing the importance of her words. But this book had never been given to Sam as part of her royal education and she wondered why not, because the book was so interesting, so unusual, and she was sure her mother would want her to know everything there was to know about Oz and its past. It wasn't at all like the books she was forced to study—dry and long-winded, making it impossible to keep her eyelids from drooping and sometimes from closing completely. The facts in her study books seemed written in the most straightforward language, rigid and conventional. Whereas this book that she had found, or as she thought, had found her, looked and felt unlike any she had ever seen before.

At first glance, she had a peculiar sensation, like she wasn't supposed to read it, but she thought for sure her mother wouldn't mind. Education was one of her mother's pet obsessions, so surely it would be okay. The book was ancient, faded with age, and the style of lettering was so strange to her. She had to work very hard to decipher a lot of the words, and some of them had archaic and unfamiliar meanings even when the letters were clear. It was worth it, though, the extra work, because the book told her more about her mother and all of Oz than any other she had read. It was like finding her mother's hidden diary. But the most intriguing of all was the chapter about dragons and how they only appeared when gloomy and foul days smothered the land. What amazed her was that there were only two types of dragons: one a horse-sized, nasty, mean-spirited creature that would fry a child and swallow it whole given a chance, and the other a great beast, a dragon to be truly feared, the one that ruled the others—the alpha dragon. This incredible animal was a huge, scaled, vicious, destructive monster (the size of three barns attached in a row), with a wingspan so enormous it blackened the sun.

The author of the book said dragons could be controlled by an evil sorceress, a dark witch with dark magic, but only a wicked one, not by a good witch fairy. Sam wondered why it had to be a ruthless reprobate who could wield so much power over such a savage and vicious animal. And yet at the same time, it seemed logical to her that one type of evil would give rise to another. The book didn't explain, because the author didn't know. But did it really matter? Not really. The fact was, based on the information from the book, dragons could only be controlled by a wicked witch, and if that happened, everyone in Oz would be in peril. In Sam's day, all the wicked witches had been destroyed—or so it was thought—and the dragons had ceased to exist.

With each paragraph Sam read, the more intrigued she

became. According to the book, the smaller dragons were extremely dangerous—known only to hunt in packs, with no fear. They were cunning, treacherous, and contemptible creatures, with an overpowering, bloodthirsty desire to kill indiscriminately, using their teeth, claws, and fire to decimate their prey. The book took dragons as serious threats. It said that even while no dragon had been seen since all the wicked witches were eliminated, their eggs lay dormant, hidden deep underground in unknown caverns scattered all over the land of Oz, waiting to be born again and used by the next wicked necromancer. And once awakened, they would wreak havoc for all people and animals—no one would be safe—for the knowledge of how to hunt and kill them would have been forgotten.

From the author's point of view, the story of the dragons wasn't a mere legend to be rattled off to children at bedtime to make sure they stayed in bed and didn't sneak out at night. Dragons were real and something to pay heed to without question, not creatures to be turned into a bedtime fairy tale. Sam questioned why anyone would write a book like this were it not the truth, and write it with such care and detail too. The book described in depth how dragons had short, stubby legs on wide, reptilian-like bodies, and were swift and agile runners. They were exceptionally nimble with their wings, using them to throw up dirt and dust to confuse their enemies. They had an incredible natural balance and could stand on one leg, using the other to slash and cut, with their barbed tails inflicting even more damage, usually killing their victims with one well-placed thrust. Their necks were long and very flexible so that they could spray their fire in one complete, semicircular motion.

All dragons, large and small, had two vulnerable points where one could dispatch the unnatural demons with an arrow, or spear, or their sword, with a single, well-placed blow—if they could get close enough. One area was directly under the jaw, where the narrow head of the beast, like that of a cobra, joined the neck with one protective scale missing; the other was just behind its front leg, where the upper wing joint met the body. It would take great courage for heroes to position themselves close enough to strike the fatal blow, the author warned. Sam got the unmistakable impression that there was no glamour or romance in dragon-hunting as she had read in her storybooks about knights fighting the winged monsters. It was hard, dirty, nasty work, and according to the book, many great warriors had died trying.

As Sam read on, she learned how to hunt the creatures, what weapons to use, and what magic spell and herbs would protect her from their throaty, liquid flames. Of particular interest was a recipe for an ointment that seemed as if it could be made from the roots and plants that grew in the meadow, around the pond, and along the creek bed where Jo grazed. All of which, if mixed correctly, could protect Sam's skin and Jo's hide from dragonfire. This was exciting information, and the more Sam read, the more she wanted to know; and the more she knew, the more she wanted to see a dragon for herself and stand up to it in battle.

There was one passage that seemed more like pure myth than fact. The author explained that after a dragon was killed, if one were to take just one tooth from the fallen beast and break it into many pieces, the fragments could be used as seeds to bring forth dragon warriors that stood eight feet tall, walked on two legs, and could fly. One could throw the broken shards on the ground during a battle and they'd take root, and dragon soldiers would sprout from the earth, dressed in armor, with weapons in hand, to fight for the one who had sown the seeds in the soil. And when the conflict was won and there were no more enemies to kill, they would return to the dirt from which they were born. At the end of the chapter on dragons, there was a note slipped in between the pages, written by the author's own hand:

A hero it will take to vanquish the great dragon during the reign of the wicked witch who controls such a menacing beast. And if you be that hero, I tell you this with all candor: carry with you more than a hope. May the Great Head be at your side and the Wizard of Oz in your heart.

—The Ozma, Princess of Oz

Sam's eyes became wide with surprise. The note was a stunning revelation. Her mother told her about the Ozma, Princess of Oz, the first ruler, and also about the first Wizard of Oz and how the two of them were such close friends. One of her favorite stories was about when her mother and the Ozma, along with Dorothy, had fought together during the engagement to rid Oz of the Wicked Witch of the West.

The image of her mother, Ozma, and Dorothy, the three of them standing alone on top of a hillside overlooking the bloody battlefield and raising their weapons in the air while screaming their war cries, was one of her favorite parts of the story.

She remembered too how brokenhearted her mother was when Dorothy used her ruby slippers to go back to Kansas and how her dear friend Ozma had disappeared soon after that. A sad moment for her mother, indeed. But this book gave Sam some hope that maybe she could actually do something to find out if a new wicked witch was alive and using her dark magic to take over Oz. Now all Sam had to do was make the fireproof ointment and find dragons—something she knew was not going to be an easy task, but one she knew she had to do.

Sam and Augie had been sitting under the grove of trees by the pond where Jo would cool himself and drink from the water when Sam read the chapter about dragons and found the note left by the Ozma.

When she looked up from reading, she could see the wind stir the treetops, making the trees sing their soft, delicate, healing music. The surface of the meadow grass seemed to ripple in rhythm to their song beneath the soothing, blue sky. The breeze, when it brushed across her face, made her thoughtful and she asked Augie, "Do you think my father is alive?"

"I don't know, lassie," Augie said, treading carefully. "What do you think?" They walked around the pond. Jo and Vail followed them, and when Sam or Augie stopped to grab a tall blade of grass to chew on, the two horses moved a step or two behind them and dropped their noses to the ground to sniff and nibble at the soft, wet grass. And when Sam and Augie moved on, the horses continued their leisurely pace, not far behind.

"I think," Sam said, after a time, "that Father *is* alive, stolen from us by demon-magic."

"You are a smart child, and you might be right."

Sam was silent for another moment and then asked, "Are dragons real?"

"Where did you ever get such a thought about dragons?" Augie questioned, raising an eyebrow in surprise. "Is it from that book you've been reading?"

"Yes," Sam said. "So, is it true? Are there dragons in Oz?"

They had walked the full circle around the pond and sat back down on the blankets. Sam handed Augie her book, opening it to the chapter about dragons. She shuffled on her knees over to the picnic basket and took two apples, placing them in the grass for Jo and Vail. Augie slowly turned the pages, reading carefully and listening to the crunch of apples. After a few moments, she said, "From what I can see, the book is truthful. But we don't have dragons now."

"Do they speak, like most animals?"

"They do not. They know only death and destruction."

"Is it true only wicked witches can control them?" Sam asked.

"Yes," Augie said, closing the book and setting it aside. "We have lived in a time of peace for many years with no foul and despicable wicked witch to take it from us and no dragons to cause us harm. When your mother fought in the war against the black witch Mombi, she fought a most terrible battle with a great red dragon that Mombi controlled. Your mother pierced its heart and then chopped its head off with one swing of her sword."

"I want to be like Mother," Sam said with a devilish grin. "I want to be a wicked witch hunter and dragon slayer."

𝕬 ♦ 𝕭

As days turned into weeks, and the weeks rolled into months, the horse became stronger.

Augie brought Jo's currycomb and his brushes with her each day. When at first Jo was standoffish and wouldn't let them groom him, they groomed Vail instead, coaxing, cooing, and pampering her with soothing sounds. Sam would sneak a peek in Jo's direction, and although his head was down, acting as if he were eating, she could tell by the look in his eyes and the soft stomping of his hoof that he was a little jealous.

Every day, Augie and Sam, and sometimes Elle, would do the same routine. With brushes in hand, Augie would pass Sam an apple, and Sam would hold it in her left hand, waist-high behind her back so Jo could see it, to entice him while they groomed Vail. Then one day, she felt the warm air coming from his nostrils as he sniffed the apple before taking a bite. She carefully turned around and moved slowly around his neck, keeping the apple steady at his mouth, and ran the grooming brush in her right hand along his neck. Augie slowly walked Vail off to the corner of the stall and then carefully went over to the other side of Jo.

Together they brushed his coat to a beautiful gleam, *oohing* and *aahing* and using pretty words to keep him calm, just like they did when they groomed Vail. It worked. But Jo was a warhorse with an overabundant sense of pride and too much dignity to admit how thoroughly enjoyable it was to be groomed again. It was undeniable, though, that he had been—and still was—addicted to their loving on him. His ears would flop down and his eyes would glaze over and shut halfway, as if he were about to doze off each time Sam, Elle, or Augie rubbed the brushes over him. He loved it, despite his arrogance.

"Augie, do you think he'll be lame?" Sam asked. "He does limp a bit still, but it doesn't seem to hurt him."

"We'll know as soon as you start riding him again. He's getting stronger each day," Augie said as she put the brushes into her grooming rucksack. "But he's gotten into the habit of favoring that leg. The muscles are soft and still stiff from the scarring." She kept her voice neutral, seemingly worried that she might make Sam feel there wasn't any hope that Jo would improve. "You should start exercising him soon."

"Yes, he is getting fat," Sam said with a giggle.

Jo sighed and flicked his tail, swatting Sam as if he heard the insult.

"It's doubtful he'll ever be up to having the weight of a man like your father ride him again," Augie reluctantly said.

"You really think so?" Sam questioned.

"I do." Augie paused as they walked Jo back to his stall. "And, I think if your father were here he would want you to keep Jo for your own."

"I would like that," Sam said with a smile as she brushed Jo's mane. "So how about it, Jo? Are you going to let me ride you?" Jo's shoulder muscles twitched, and he shook his head and stomped his hind leg, which Sam decided was Jo's way of inviting her to try.

The next day, with Augie's supervision, Sam rode Jo bareback for the first time since the accident. When Jo noticed Sam carrying his saddle, he had turned a beautiful orange, which they thought was his color for happiness. Augie felt the horse wasn't ready to handle a saddle on his back yet. But before they did anything, they brushed him first, and when they were done, they dropped the grooming tools together in a pile. Augie ran her fingers along his broad right cheek, then gently held Jo's face with both hands. He nosed her in the stomach wanting a little more attention with the grooming brushes. "Sam's going to get on your back," Augie said with a soft, reassuring voice, rubbing him between his eyes. "We're going to go for a little stroll, that's all—just around the pond." Augie carefully took a couple of steps to her right to stand next to Sam. "We're not going to use the saddle. Grab a good handful of his mane with your left hand," she instructed, "and use my locked hands as a stirrup. But before you mount, smooth his back three times with your right hand."

Sam did as Augie asked. She looked at Jo and said, "Well, here goes." She brushed his back with her right hand three times, put her foot into the makeshift stirrup of Augie's hands, pulled hard on Jo's mane, and hoisted herself up onto his back. Sam felt Jo settle appreciably under her weight. He was larger than most fighting breeds and stood quietly as she did so. And because he trusted Sam and was so well trained to having a soldier on his back, he didn't rear up or jolt. Only his shoulder muscles and withers twitched, and he took a small step back to compensate for the slight shift in balance when Sam swung her leg over his back as she was seating herself.

Sam had held her breath when mounting Jo, and now, with her back straight and taut, she let it out in one long, rippled, anxious exhale. She was excited. It was just like the rush she felt before she'd jump off her bedroom roof.

Jo cocked his ears back toward Sam, his head bowed just a little as if he were waiting for directions, as if he felt the bit in his mouth. Augie gently held him at his jaw as they moved forward and walked around the pond at a slow, relaxing pace. Sam looked undersized on the back of a war stallion, but it fit her well, and she loved it. Thereafter, Augie let Sam ride him without her help. And each time after Sam dismounted, they brushed him, groomed him, and checked the wounded leg for swelling. There was no heat, no tenderness. A good sign.

One time, Augie gave the ugly scar a firm pat, no different than when she'd slap him to say good day, to see if he'd flinch any more than he did with slaps for good behavior. And he didn't—another excellent sign.

"Within a couple of months, I think any sign of a limp when Jo breaks into a shuffling trot will be nonexistent," Augie said with a smile as she and Sam walked back to the castle. "Soon, the old sod will be galloping like a newborn." This was what Sam was hoping for. She needed Jo healthy and robust if they were going to battle wicked witches and hunt dragons together.

෨ ◆ ඦ

S am rode Jo every day without fail. At first, it was always once around the pond, starting and stopping and then eating some apples as they had done when she first rode him bareback. Then it was around his pasture, and soon after, long rides throughout Quadling (and more apples, of course). When she was sure Jo was strong enough, she practiced executing flying mounts and dismounts, which Jo responded to quickly and easily. He was no stranger to having a warrior on his back and other warhorses at his side. Hence, a flying soldier was not uncomfortable for him at all.

Sam and Elle practiced their sword fighting and their flying mounts and dismounts together. They set up targets for their bows and arrows and an obstacle course with jumping fences to improve Jo's agility. It became a daily affair that Jo and Vail anticipated eagerly.

In the beginning, when Sam was first allowed to ride Jo, they didn't use her father's saddle. They used her own saddle and she had gripped the reins as tightly as she could, wishing she'd thought to put on her riding gloves. But she'd been so anxious and excited with the prospect of actually being able to sit in a saddle that she left the gloves in the shed. By the end of that first ride, the tips of her fingers were numb, her palms raw and reddened from the rough leather of the reins, but it was worth the discomfort to be able to have Jo running and jumping around the pasture like the warhorse he was meant to be.

But the saddle didn't fit Jo and rubbed his hide raw. They decided it was best not to use leathers and only ride Jo bareback until the time was right. And for Sam, it didn't matter how long it would take. All she cared about was that the horse made the choice to live so one day when her father came home, he'd know that she had taken good care of his loyal steed and cherished friend.

☙ ✦ ❧

Now, years later, it was the same for them—hard practice and grandly galloping anywhere they wanted to go.

"Do you remember," Sam said one day to Elle while they were grooming Jo and Vail after a full morning of practice, "when I was very young, old enough to walk and run, and you were first learning to handle a sword, how you would show me what you learned?"

"I remember," Elle said with a giggle, teasing, "that you followed me around with your wooden sword and cried like a little baby until I showed you."

"I never cried," Sam replied with a grin. "If it weren't for you and Saran, I would not know how to fight. I thank you for that, but I want to learn more. I want to fight like you."

"You are amazing with a bow and sword, and your magic is getting much better," Elle said. "But not as good as me, of course." Then she continued reassuringly, "You know how to fight, Sam. Saran has taught you well. Trust your instincts."

Five

On Sam's sixteenth birthday there was a banquet for her, as there had been for Elle when she turned sixteen. But this time there were no arguments between the sisters, only excited chatter and hurried preparations.

Elle shot Sam glances with a smug, sisterly smile that said, I know what you're going through, and, better you than me.

Relax, Elle said inside Sam's head.

I'm trying, Sam returned with a closed, forced smile.

It was a party that her mother, Augie, and Elle had spent weeks preparing, making decorations, and sending out invitations—just for her. So Sam knew there was no way she could avoid it and that she had no choice but to attend, mostly since her mother was the queen, which added even more weight to the celebration. And that weight made Sam want to fly off to the barn and just be with Jo and forget about it all.

"Why all the fuss?" Sam kept saying to herself all day long. But she would never want to disappoint any of them, especially her mother, and act like a spoiled brat in front of the suitors and guests, although she knew it would take all her willpower not to do so. Plus, she knew if she didn't put on a happy face, Augie would be the first to bat her ears and shake her finger and say, *"Glinda Goodwitch might be the queen, but she is still your mother, and if she wants to give you a lavish reception on your sixteenth birthday, you will be there whether you like it or not, and you will smile and be a lady about it!"*

☙ ◆ ❧

It was a grand affair with many guests, some of whom had traveled from other towns and villages from the four corners of Oz.

A large band of minstrels played, and thousands of candles lit up the entire grand hall. It was an impressive fête that Sam had not expected—nor truly desired—and standing next to her mother and sister when greeting all the guests as they arrived seemed to last the entire night. But Sam did what was expected of her. She was a lady about it, despite the overwhelming urge to run away to her room and hide.

Lillith made witty remarks at Sam's expense when she gave Sam a toast in her soft, light tenor that always sounded kind when she was willing to speak. And Saran had given her a bullwhip, promising to teach her how to use it during their combat practices. Her mother gave a toast too. Elle pinched Sam's side, and the faces around the tables in the great hall glittered with smiles.

Sam took it all in with a thoughtful courtesy—she was in many ways delighted with the attention but hated it at the same time. And her one wish that she used when she blew out the candles on her cake was that her father could have been there with them. If he had been, she would have celebrated with much higher spirits and would not have been so inwardly dour.

Glinda watched her daughter and thought how beautiful she had grown. Sam was wearing a pale orange tunic over a long, lime-green skirt. The tunic had embroidered leaves and flowers that wound around the hem, like the grapevine crown Sam always wore, and pearls of many colors running up and down the long sleeves. And across her forehead was the silver strand with the small, oval-shaped piece of black onyx her father gave her—the day he disappeared—resting above the bridge of her nose. When she spun through and around the dancing figures, the colorful taffeta scarves that adorned her wings shifted and swirled softly with each movement, like a rainbow floating across the dance floor.

When Glinda saw Sam shy away from the courtiers' smiles, she shook Augie's elbow and whispered in her ear. Sam noticed the two of them conspiring with each other and returned a look that made them cover their mouths to hide their laughter. Sam knew what they were up to, and she had no intention of granting their wishes and being a party to their grand schemes. Being courted was not something she had any inclination to delve into. Dragons were all she cared about pursuing, not some dreadful courtship. But the funny thing was, all the attention did create a tickle in her stomach, especially when she saw her mother and Augie having so much fun at her expense.

Elle walked over to Sam and took her hand, bowing her head. Sam curtseyed in return, smiled, and then they danced together.

"So," Elle said with a sly grin as they twirled around the dance floor, "I think Geoffrey Giggins is looking rather dashing tonight, don't you?" Dark, loose, choppy bangs spilled across Geoffrey's broad face, emphasizing his pallid complexion as he smiled at the princesses.

"He's all right," Sam replied, not taking the bait, but taking a quick glance back at Geoffrey as he watched her spin past him. She winced. "And I have nothing against Munchkins. But I'm into taller men."

"Oh." Elle's smile widened. "So you're into men?"

Sam cut Elle a sour look. "No. That's not what I meant."

"I see," Elle teased. "Then what did you mean? Either you're into men, or you're not."

"Well, Geoffrey, he's . . . different," Sam said with a smile. "Let's just say that right now, I'm after something with a lot more fire in its belly."

"Really?" Elle replied, happily surprised. "I never thought I'd see the day my little sister would be such a saucy witch."

"Just following in your footsteps, *Sister*."

❧ ✦ ❧

After the banquet, Sam went to her bedroom and stood by the balcony railing, staring out into the darkness and down into the keep. She had said good wishes to all the guests, her mother, and Elle, and was now so tired she was fighting to keep her eyes open.

The torches that hung around the perimeter walls of the keep left great pools of light, like stepping-stones one could use to hop across the courtyard. Her bedroom was dark as well, and Augie had not yet come to make sure Sam had hung her clothes up properly instead of leaving them on the floor to be stepped on as she usually would do. But Sam loved her gown, and Augie had spent so much time making it for her that she would never have been so inconsiderate. She'd hung it in her wardrobe the second she took it off and put on her bedclothes.

As Sam looked deeply into the thick blackness of the night, her skin prickled. She felt a chill roll up her spine and her shoulders shivered. A waking dream edged into her thoughts, and she did not know if she had dreamed it only once or many times, since it seemed so familiar. She closed her eyes, squeezing them shut, shaking her head to escape the trance and push the dream out. But she couldn't.

It was a brief and disturbing vision. She was standing with her back to the water's edge of a lake the color of silver. The water was so reflective; the surrounding mountains with their snowcapped peaks seemed to float silently upon it. Somehow, she knew those mountains. She was sure she'd seen them before—in another dream, perhaps? She wasn't sure. But she knew they were important.

Her arms were outstretched, and in her left hand she was holding a beautiful sword that was on fire with a blue and white flame. The air was freezing. Her body shivered from the cold but for some reason, even though she wanted to run away and find shelter, she knew it was necessary that she keep standing exactly where she was, without movement. She had no jacket on, no winter clothing. She was wearing only her thin, silk bedclothes, and snow was blowing and clinging to her hair and eyebrows. Then, like dreams do, it shifted, and she was watching herself from a distance, watching the wind ruffle her silk pajamas like a fluttering flag. That's when she saw the frowzy crow perched on her arm, black as pitch, feathers broken and missing. The feeling she had was unsettling, and without question, she knew it was imperative not to move. So she didn't.

The crow had wraithlike, bloodred eyes and five pieces of straw held in its beak. And as the snowflakes danced frantically around her, she fell backward very slowly into the silver lake, as if in slow motion, splashing the water up on all sides of her body until it completely covered her, encasing her in silver, leaving only ripples behind. The scruffy, unkempt crow spread its wings and took flight and she heard a deep, hollow, echoing voice speak to her.

"Find the Crow."

The dream shifted again, and she could see herself floating underneath the silver water, slowly sinking to the bottom, her arms, her legs, and her hair suspended, shifting and drifting. The dream altered once more, and she was back in her body. She saw a fuzzy, enormous shape, with a long neck, broad wings, and a long, barbed tail, flying above the water. Flames spewed from its mouth as its neck and head reached around and sprayed the water with dragonfire. The roar of the beast and the hissing fire overwhelmed her. Her spine arched and her head snapped back. Then her breath went *oof*, and a bubbled, muffled scream burst forth. She felt the sword leave her hand. She turned her head and watched it drift away. Beyond shock, she reached for it in panic. More air escaped her lungs. More bubbles. But the sword was too far away, the blue flame spitting and sputtering, flickering on and off. Her eyes stung and a single tear escaped, only to mix with the silver water and become part of the lake as she watched the sword with the blue flame vanish into the murky abyss.

There was a knock on the door, waking her abruptly. Sam turned away from the balcony railing, losing her balance for a moment.

Another knock on the door, but lighter this time. Her eyes refocused and she slowly stumbled into her bedroom, supporting herself with one hand on the sitting table. For a second, she thought about remaining silent and letting the visitor leave, thinking she'd already gone to sleep, but she changed her mind and softly said, "Come in." She was shivering, and her head still felt spongy from the dream, queasy and unbalanced. She touched her forehead. It was sticky and wet. She wished only to decompress after the excitement of the birthday banquet, the food, bright smiles, and one curtsey after another, and her mouth was sore from all the smiling. Now was not the time to have a visitor. In reality, all she wanted was some private time and to let sleep find her and give her some much-desired solitude. And because of this disturbing dream she desperately felt a greater need to be alone.

Her bedroom door opened a little. More gentle knocking. It was her mother. Sam could see her mother perfectly outlined in the light from the hallway, since she had been standing in the dark long enough to be able to see clearly. But Glinda had to force her eyes to adjust to the dark. All she could see was a faint, inky figure that seemed part of the heavy curtains that hung at the opening of the veranda next to the sitting table. When Sam stirred, her mother saw a small flicker in her eyes and knew instantly it was Sam.

"Why are you standing in the dark?" her mother asked in a gentle, soft tone, speaking as a mother and not as a queen.

"Too much excitement for one night," Sam said, wiping sweat from her brow and rubbing her wet hand on her nightclothes. "And the dark is relaxing for me." Sam started walking over to her bed but still felt a little fuzzy from the vision, and placed her hand on the sitting table again to steady herself. "Why are you here, Mother?"

"Can't a mother visit her daughter anytime she wishes? In particular," she sighed, "a queen's daughter." Glinda gently raised her hand and pointed it at the sitting table in the alcove next to the balcony, next to Sam, waving at it with a soft flick of her wrist. A lit candle materialized on the table. A breeze made it flicker, and the shadows it cast made Sam's face become visible. For a brief instant, Sam's countenance looked to be that of an adult woman after years of living, her mother thought. Glinda smiled and waved her hand again with a swift motion, extending her arm above and across her face. The entire round room was instantly filled with lit candles hanging in midair just below the vaulted wooden ceiling, where they illuminated the beautiful, ornate painting of women on horseback charging into battle.

"You look troubled," Glinda noted.

Sam was quiet for a moment, deciding whether she should say anything. But the vision or the dream she'd just had was so strong and so frightening she thought it best to tell her mother. "I've been having visions."

"Good ones, or bad ones?"

"I'm not sure," Sam said softly, furrowing her brow and rubbing her eyes.

"No need to be anxious," her mother replied. "All the Goodwitch women have visions. The trick is not to grab onto them forcefully, but to hold them in your mind lightly, like they were alive. And then, the truth is revealed." She looked at Sam and smiled while candlelight danced across her daughter's ice-blue and green skin.

"I want to go with you and Elle to Rumpart's castle. To help protect you," Sam said, folding her arms across her chest. "To ferret out the demon-magic."

"We already talked about this. Not this time. Saran says your skills are improving, but I—"

"Oh, *Mother*," Sam blurted out sharply, frustrated, interrupting her mother and raising her voice. "Improving?" Sam felt her temper begin to rise. Her mother had scolded her many times that a wild temper was unbecoming of a princess and something a ruler could never afford. So Sam bit down hard on her lip, something she had taught herself to do whenever her anger ran away with itself. But her frustration didn't go away, nor did it lessen the forcefulness of her tantrum. She fell back on her bed, pressing the palms of her hands to her eyes and then slapping her arms on the silk comforter with a soft smack, muttering loudly to herself, "*Improving?*"

"A princess does not raise her voice when speaking with her mother," the queen said firmly but kindly. "And you have already made a promise to me."

"Please, Mother, why can't I go?" Sam scooted to the edge of the bed and pulled her knees up to her chest.

"It's not that I think you are not ready. It's because . . ." Glinda paused and took in a quiet breath before sitting down next to Sam. She touched her daughter's shoulder with her own, gently nudging her, and with a soft and loving tone, continued as Sam rested her chin on her knees and closed her eyes. "It is because, my dear daughter, I am afraid that you are."

"It's not fair, Mother."

"I agree. But being a princess comes with—"

Sam jumped in before her mother could say another word, knowing she could not win this battle. Her mother was never mean or cruel, never without compassion. Sam had felt the pinch of her mother's iron will often enough that she understood the shape of her resolve in this matter, almost felt it as her own, and knew better than to pursue it any longer. "Mother . . . I know, I know. Being the daughter of a queen comes with specific responsibilities and expectations." Sam turned her head to look directly into her mother's caring eyes, smiled, and continued softly, apologizing for her rash behavior. "I'm sorry for raising my voice. It's just that I've been feeling strange lately. I'm not sure if it's the visions or something else. Something dark. Something dangerous." She looked at her mother's soft, loving face and noticed that her eyes were compassionately swimming in a pool of tears. "I am worried you will disappear like . . ."

"Like your father? These are worrisome times, indeed," her mother said as she gently stroked her daughter's beautiful auburn hair and placed her warm hand on Sam's cheek. "Do not worry so, my dear daughter." Then Sam saw that she carried something over her shoulder—a long, narrow something in a decorative, soft leather satchel.

"What is that you are carrying?"

"I have brought you your birthday present—privately."

Sam watched with rising excitement as her mother stood up in front of her and pulled the something out of the satchel, holding it carefully in both hands. She unrolled the silk wrappings and from within, a soft gleam from the candlelight fell upon a sword, giving a bluish tint to its patina. "This is to replace the battered relic you use when you spar with my Consola. I think you'll find it easier to wield and its swing swift and sure."

Sam reached for it with great surprise, her mouth partially open. She slid it into its scabbard, and then slowly brought it out again. The blade was thin and elegant, so smooth as to shimmer, but on closer inspection, Sam could see the faintest runes inlaid up and down the metal. When the graceful designs caught the light, they shimmered like tiny diamonds. Its edge was sharp and strong, and the hilt was packed with elfish cord to make the grip sure. It felt light and true and perfect in her hand, and she trembled with the pride of it. She put the sword back into the scabbard, letting its point touch the ground.

Holding the hilt, Sam kneeled, then kissed her mother's hand. *With this sword,* she thought, *I can really protect you.* For a moment, Sam felt she could persuade her mother to let her go and stand by her side. But a moment later, Sam knew it was best not to ask again. "Thank you, Mother," she said, and when she looked up at her mother, her eyes pooled.

"At dawn, you can try it out. Saran is looking forward to judging how it suits you," Glinda said, holding her hand as Sam rose. Sam kept her eyes fixed on her mother and listened with wide, loving eyes. "I had Merrick Oslo, the renowned Quadling blacksmith, forge it for you. There is no other like it. You will need it to protect the castle and the people of Quadling when I am visiting with Rumpart."

"I look forward to showing Saran and my sister my amazing gift," Sam said excitedly, trying to speak as if their swordplay would be like any other, but she knew it wouldn't. "This is ever so much better than a pair of socks," she said with a gentle lilt in her voice and was pleased to see her mother smile.

Sam stood and pulled the blade out of its scabbard again with a metallic twang and sliced it back and forth quickly so that it wrinkled the air around it and cut through it with a *whoosh*.

"I will bid my daughter happy wishes on her sixteenth birthday and say good night." As her mother slipped out the door and was walking down the hall, Sam heard her say with a disappearing echo, "Don't cut yourself before tomorrow, young lady."

Sam smiled and gazed at her incredible present. She held it up in her left hand, looked at her reflection rippling across the sparkling metal, and sliced the air back and forth in front of her. Without waiting a beat, she twirled the sword and set her stance, bending low on her right knee to support all her weight and stretching her left leg out in front for counterbalance. Her eyes narrowed as though she were staring down an imaginary foe. She slowly raised her elbow above her shoulder, with the sword following a straight line horizontally along her right ear and cheek. In her right hand she held the scabbard, extending it to a full arm's length behind her along the same path as her sword, ready to thrust and parry her attacker.

She thrust forward with the sword, and then let it sweep around her head, as she slashed the air to the left, then right, then left again, like a windmill. She danced around her bedroom, thrusting and moving, fighting an invisible foe, and then vaulted onto the foot of her bed. She returned the sword to its scabbard and fell back, letting her head fall into her pillows, holding the sword against her chest with her hands clasped around the hilt. She took in a deep breath and let it out, and then another. Her heart was racing, her cheeks and forehead warm. She swallowed and took in one final breath, filling her lungs. Her rib cage expanded, and when she couldn't take in any more, she let the air out slowly. Then the thought about her waking dream hit her hard, like a slap across the cheek. It was a disturbing vision, and the sound of the man's dusty voice echoed in her head again.

"Find the Crow." And then again, *"Find the Crow!"*

She had no idea what to make of it or what it could possibly mean. *Augie could interpret the dream*, she thought. She told herself she'd tell Augie about it in the morning before she took a spin around the castle and did a quick flyby at the guards. But the dream was so familiar to her. She was sure of it. And then she remembered something. Once when she was twelve, she had ridden into the woods and gotten lost, finding herself in an unfamiliar part of the forest. She didn't know the trees or the stream she'd crossed. As the hours passed, the forest had closed in on her, and she ended up riding in circles. She was about to give up and cry when she heard the cawing of a crow sitting on a tree branch. It was looking down at her as if it knew she were lost. Moving close to it, the bird cawed again, flapped its wings, and flew to another tree, resting on another branch. And like before, it stared straight at her. Each time she moved closer to it, the crow flew to another tree and waited for her. She continued to follow the bird, when suddenly it flew out of the forest, cawing loudly as it flew away. The next thing she realized, she was back at the castle. Two days later she went back into the forest trying to get lost on purpose this time, intending to see if the noisy crow would return and help her find her way. But halfway there, she gave up. For some reason, she knew it wouldn't work. She felt something, a presence perhaps, telling her it would not work. The back of her neck tingled, and her horse became agitated. So she rode back the way she came. Sam never told anyone about that day, never giving it any weight, until tonight.

She looked up at her painted ceiling then flicked her wrist, just like her mother, and the candles vanished. She closed her eyes and her mind drifted, fantasizing about her beautiful new sword and how she would tangle with Saran in the morning.

But the vision kept haunting her. So she held her sword firmly against her body, concentrating solely on the wonderful gift, and listened to the soft, gentle rhythm of her breathing to help clear her head. And as difficult as it was to do, with determined effort, she pushed the voice and the image of the disheveled crow to the back of her mind and held it there until it slowly turned to a harmless vapor and vanished. Sleep took hold, and Sam slipped away, letting go of the dark and disturbing images that tried their best to keep her awake.

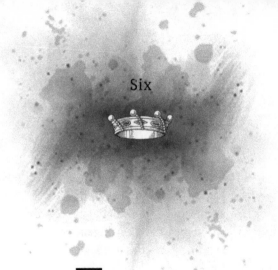

Six

Perhaps it was actually having a real sword of her own that made Sam feel she'd finally become an adult. Or maybe it was turning sixteen, or that sixteen years of being stubborn made her feel grown-up. *One thing is for certain,* she thought, *everyone would disagree with the growing up part.* Lillith, on the other hand, being a warrior who never had a lot to say, wouldn't say a word. She'd give an all-knowing smirk, or roll her eyes a little, or nod her head *yes* in agreement, or shake it for *no*. Nevertheless, sparring that morning with her new sword had proven to be more exhilarating than Sam had ever expected. Even Elle was surprised by her sister's newfound energy and concentrated effort.

The sword felt like it was a part of Sam, an extension of her arm, separate, yet connected. It moved through the air as if it were alive, as if anticipating each and every move she made. She loved it, and each time she blocked with a countermove warding off a blow, she thought of her mother and how much she loved her for trusting her and for giving her such a remarkable gift. But all day long—she couldn't shake it—having a real sword really did make her feel different. And as the new day had started out well, the rest of it had become even better. She was confident, absolutely sure, that she could figure out how to make the ointment on her own to protect her from dragonfire.

After her workout that morning, she snuck off to Jo's barn, making sure no one knew where she had gone. She placed a table against the wall on one end of Jo's shed to work on, away from where he slept.

᠅ ◆ ᠅

S am was sure the rumors of a dragon sighting at the western edge of Quadling, where Winkie Country and Quadling shared a border, were not merely the ramblings of frightened villagers. Or maybe it was the dream that had convinced her. She didn't know. But something was telling her that she needed to find out and be prepared in case the rumors *were* true. The dragon in her vision had seemed real and terrifying. So she also decided, while she mixed and tested her dragon potion, she would practice the protection spell she found in the book that would repel a hot blast of dragon breath. *If one fails*, she thought, *the other might not*. Although, when it came to magic spells, they often didn't last all that long and having a fireproof ointment to protect one's skin from dragonfire would be a decisive advantage.

Once her work area was ready, she took her time gathering the roots and herbs from around the pound that she would need to make the fireproof brew. But she couldn't find all of what she needed. She knew it was essential to follow the recipe word for word, ingredient for ingredient. No shortcuts. And as hard as she tried searching all through the meadow and the nearby forest surrounding the castle, Sam wasn't able to find some of the most critical ingredients she needed for her ointment. So for the past few weeks, she'd been raiding Augie's cooking supplies and her mother's personal stash of medicinal herbs for the odder elements. But Sam knew she couldn't keep that up without raising suspicion. Finding small apothecary shops in the city would be her next choice. But because she was the queen's daughter, that too might raise an eyebrow or two and most certainly cause a lot of gossip.

At first, she thought about using magic to create a disguise, but using magic in a deceitful way, no matter the intention, was using it in the wrong way, and according to her mother, abusing it. *"It will only corrupt the soul,"* her mother had told her once when she was first learning to use magic. Plus, she was sure Augie would see right through any disguise—spoiling everything—and throw a fit if she caught her royal charge sneaking around as someone or something else. Augie was no idiot. Sam knew trying to trick her would go over like a ton of stones. She could hear Augie ranting and scolding her, saying, *"Aye, lassie! What in tarnation are you doing? Turn yourself back this instant before I throttle you good and hard!"* Or words to that effect. Most assuredly, Augie would tell her mother. There was no point in conjuring an illusion and changing her appearance—it would inevitably end badly. Probably she'd be sent to her room and not allowed to fly for a week. Or worse, she wouldn't be permitted to see Jo.

So she didn't use her magic and decided to go into the village in search of herbs for her dragon-proof balm as herself. She'd been in town before, many times in fact, but it had been a year or so since the last time she'd gone shopping in the city. She kept saying to herself, *What would it matter, and why would the townsfolk really care if I were out and about?* And then she'd pose the question, *Surely, they would accept me like any other shopper? Surely?*

When Sam first strolled into town, it was alive with people traipsing about, talking, eating, laughing, bargaining. The town square was a melting pot of activity, a hive of comings and goings, the atmosphere electric, and she felt a thousand eyes were buzzing all around her and gazing at her with whispered muttering.

The first visits to shopkeepers made her stomach gurgle and do flip-flops. After that first shopping spree, some talk did roll around the city, but luckily not into Augie's ear. However, in the end, gossip did spread throughout the village. Augie would have been pleased to hear that the thread of gossip that was running through the streets was about how the queen's daughter, like her mother, had a smile for everyone and that she'd make a good queen herself one day. If Sam had heard the talk, she would have laughed. She never thought of ever stepping into her mother's silver slippers. Even though she wanted to be as strong and courageous as her mother, the thought of one day being the queen was not a desire of hers in any way. Elle was more suited to sit on the throne than she was.

Much to Sam's relief, the store owners were accommodating and didn't ask questions; they didn't seem to pay any mind that she was the queen's daughter, as long as she had coins to spend. They always had a kind smile and were wonderfully helpful. If they didn't have the herb she was looking for, they'd point her in the right direction to another apothecary.

The things Sam bought were harmless cooking herbs, even if some seemed odd, and she never bought a large quantity of them. So all in all, there would be no cause for anyone to think she was up to any kind of mischief. And most in the city knew Sam was taking care of Jo, so perhaps they assumed she was making an ointment for his leg to ease the pain and help heal his scar.

Somehow, oddly enough, that tale got around too, and all the townsfolk did remember her way with Jo and how easily she could calm him, so it was natural she'd need to make a soothing balm for him. What surprised her about the experience was that she truly enjoyed being in the city, with all its spirited hustle and bustle. It was a nice change of pace from the duties of the day-to-day life as the daughter of a queen, which, according to Sam, came at a heavy price—*specific responsibilities and expectations*, she constantly reminded herself.

On the day her mother and sister were leaving, it opened gray. The clouds hung heavy, low, and rippled, and the morning air was heavy with the threat of rain. The low ceiling of dark clouds held back the sun and hid the view of the snowcapped mountain peaks, but no matter how bleak it seemed, Sam's mother and her entourage were heading out in all their splendor, all dressed to the hilt in their glimmering battle armor.

Sam watched, cloaked and hooded, high above on her bedroom turret roof. She was dressed in deep green from her hood down to her tan-colored boots. The black onyx gemstone her father gave her dangled from its pure silver chain around her neck. The stone glimmered merrily from the morning light, casting intermittent flickers across her pupils. The jewel always had an annoying habit of popping out of Sam's tunic minutes after she had tucked it in. It was a friendly reminder of how much she felt lost without her father. She smiled involuntarily as the image of her father one day returning to her and holding her in his arms, squeezing her with all his strength, jumped into her head. But reality slapped back hard and stiff, covering that delicious and desired wish. Her mother was leaving. And the thought that she might lose her too became the overpowering, nagging alarm of worry clouding any hope of her father's return. *What if the rumors of an evil fairy witch were true, and Mother going to meet with Rumpart was a ruse somehow concocted by this witch to trap her?* she thought. *What then?*

As she watched the royal procession line up, horse by horse and carriage by carriage, she shook her head to rid her mind of such helpless thinking because as it stood at that moment, she was bound by a promise she made to her mother to stay behind so the good people of Quadling would take comfort in knowing at least one Goodwitch was still in the castle to see to their needs. But in her own mind, Sam didn't feel worthy of being the queen's substitute, her mother's stand-in, hiding behind dark, velvet curtains on a make-believe stage waiting to prove herself. Untested. Unsure. *I'm just a little girl who teases the guards and plays around in her castle*, Sam thought. *I'm a royal token. Nothing more.*

There were fifty-one soldiers on horseback, three in a row in the front. A carriage of courtiers. Then twenty more soldiers on horseback, with another passenger carriage, two supply wagons, and another full complement of fifty-one mounted soldiers guarding the rear, with outliers on each corner, all dressed in the orange and gray of the royal guard. It was an impressive sight, but from the top of the castle, everyone seemed so small to Sam, so vulnerable, like little toy soldiers, so open to attack. When she saw her mother on her white warhorse, Elle next to her on Vail, and Saran riding just behind, her stomach fluttered. They rode into the courtyard and took their place in the front of the cavalcade.

All the horses and their riders had full battle gear on. It was done on purpose as a courtesy, so when the procession rode through the town square, the citizens, Glinda's subjects, would know that their queen was keeping her promise to meet with King Rumpart and secure peace one way or the other, with or without a fight. But once they were out of sight of the town and its people, they would stop and repack their trimmings for the long journey ahead.

Elle looked so stately, Sam thought, like their mother, a ruler, a real queen. When they'd been out riding and running and jumping the obstacle course the day before with Jo and Vail, Elle had said, "One day, you will take off that earthen-crown you always wear and replace it with the real thing." Sam's crown and its grass shoots took an aggressive posture at the comment, ready for a fight, hissing back at Elle.

"On that day, my dear sister," Sam replied, "I will be six feet under the ground with celandine poppies growing above me." Her crown relaxed and rubbed Sam's cheek, grateful for Sam's support and love. "You are the one to sit on the throne after Mother is through with it—may the Great Head forbid—as I am most suited to be your First, your Consola."

"Well, Sister," Elle said as she straightened her back and lifted her chin to sit tall in the saddle and look as queenly as she could, "then we shall rule together."

It had been a nice ride with her sister, and she wished they'd go riding again soon.

As Sam stood up, one hand holding the flagpole for balance, she gazed across the countryside whispering to herself, "I love this land and its people." The wind was chilly, blowing gusty breaths. Sam looked over at Jo's pasture and watched him anxiously prance back and forth along the gate, letting out a strong bray, changing from a passive, pale blue to an irritated, dark gray and nodding his head. He could not see

Elle and Vail, but it seemed he could sense his companion was about to leave him. Sam pulled her hood down. The clouds had thickened, and Sam felt the first bit of cold, as misty water prickled her skin. She opened her wings just a little and let the wind fill them. She lifted slowly off the roof, rolling into a slow-moving back dive, down to the courtyard. She spiraled around her bedroom tower, making a smooth, careful descent, and landed in front of, and facing, her mother. Sam was wearing her new sword. She curtseyed, then stood tall, relaxed her wings so they would lay flat against her back, and said, "Wizard speed, Mother. May the Great Head look after you." She walked over to her mother's horse and held onto the cheekpiece, patting the beautiful white warhorse on its neck firmly, and looked into her mother's eyes. "I will miss you."

"You be nice to Augie and Lillith," her mother said with a soft, gentle voice and a kind smile, "and the other guards too. No flybys. Let them have at least one peaceful morning while I'm away." And then she added, "The sword suits you well."

"Thank you, Mother."

Sam stepped back. Her mother looked straight ahead. She gently pushed her heels into her horse's sides, and clicked her tongue. Her horse obeyed and walked forward, and the procession followed.

"Do as Mother says, be nice to the guards," Elle said as she rode past Sam.

"If the Great Head is willing," Sam said back with a sly grin.

The sword does suit you, Sam heard Elle say in her head.

See you soon, Sister, Sam replied.

And you, Sister.

Lillith and Augie had walked up next to Sam, and Lillith put her hand on Sam's shoulder. Saran and Lillith were extremely protective of Sam and Elle, as it was their duty, but it was more than that. Everyone who was part of Glinda's army or worked in the castle felt like they were family. And when it came to protecting the queen's daughters, the royal guards were always at the ready, Saran in particular. She had known both girls since they were children, and Sam as a newborn.

As Saran rode past, she said with a stern voice, aiming it at Lillith, "If I find one scratch on this child when I return, you will lose an arm." Lillith gave her famous smirk and nodded her head once for yes. The dark orange and gray cloaks the women soldiers wore swayed as they rode, revealing their costly weapons: their hand-forged swords and sword breakers, their decorated leather, and their chest, arm, and shin guards. All of them were wearing their leather and metal headgear, and colorful feathers that reached to the sky from the top, like a plume of water streaming out of a fountain. Many carried maces that Sam could see protruding from their saddles. The way they were seated, with straight backs and heads held high as they guided their horses out of the castle, made it very clear to anyone watching that they were proud to be the escorts for their queen.

But now that her mother, Elle, and Saran were on their way to Winkie Country to seek out Rumpart's allegiance, or lack thereof, Sam could think of nothing else but to start working on the dragonfire recipe.

Lillith and two other seconds, along with the rest of Glinda's army, stayed behind to keep order in the castle and provide security for the townsfolk. Her mother and her troupe would be gone at least a month, if not longer.

Sam turned to face Lillith; she put her hand on Lillith's shoulder and spread her wings, flapped them once hard and fast, then winked and lifted straight up about twenty feet, where she stopped and hovered to watch the procession. The grass tendrils on her crown were nipping at her ears, alerting her of something. What it was, she didn't know, but it was an unmistakable warning. Sam flew up a little higher and looked around, past the entourage toward the lower hillside and saw nothing out of the ordinary. But she could feel a distinct wobble in the air around her. Something wasn't right. Sam watched her mother for another moment, wishing she were riding by her side, and in that moment, the air moved again. A slight shift in the light. The hair on the back of her neck stiffened. She closed her eyes and listened, thinking she heard someone calling her name. Her crown poked at her again. Then, just as suddenly as it came, the distant voice was gone and the air around her returned to normal.

Sam shook her head and brought her thoughts back to the task at hand. She had no desire to fool around with nonsense and wrested the strange feeling loose from her mind, brushing the nipping shoots from her crown off her ear with her hand. "It's nothing," she scolded forcefully, and flew up to her bedroom to have breakfast with Augie and get apples for Jo. She figured one month was plenty of time to make her fireproof salve and test it, and perhaps to scout around for dragons. *Yes, plenty of time,* she thought. And as it turned out, a month was a lot more time than she needed, for it was a lot easier to make the ointment than she ever could have anticipated.

S ome time ago, Roman had turned the makeshift shed they made for Jo when he was first injured into a beautiful, small stone barn, which made it cooler in the summer for Jo at night when he slept and warmer in the winter. Most importantly, though, it gave Sam the perfect place to work in private, away from the castle, away from curious eyes, to mix and experiment with the dragon ointment.

On her first try at mashing and mixing the herbs and roots in her marble mortar, she made a thin paste that came out clear, malleable, and odorless. She made only a small amount so as to not waste the ingredients, in case it didn't work the first time. She made just enough to cover her finger, but thought it much wiser to test it on a piece of wood or stick before she put flame to her own skin.

She put a candle in the candlestick and waved her hand to light the candle. She then smoothed some of her mixture over the tip of a broken, bare branch and slowly moved it into the flame. The pointed yellow teardrop of the fire parted and surrounded the stick. It did not smolder or ignite. She pulled the stick out of the flame and touched where she had placed the balm. It was cold, as if nothing had scorched it. She thrust it back into the flame and kept it there for a long time. And still, the stick did not burst into flame.

Sam pulled it free from the fire and touched it. It was cold to the touch, as it had been before. She put it back into the flame and still nothing. She moved it past where she'd placed the ointment on the piece of wood, and instantly the branch began to smolder. If she held it any longer, the stick would have caught on fire, this she was sure of.

So, she took in a deep breath and greased her finger—her right index finger, in case the candle flame liked the taste of skin better than the flavor of wood and because she used her left hand to fight with her sword. The last thing she wanted was a burnt finger when sparring against Lillith—or battling with a dragon. And to her surprise, it didn't take much—the balm quickly dissolved into her skin, leaving only the slightest bit of film on her digit. She held her finger steadily in the flame and watched as the pointed yellow fire did exactly as it had done with the branch. It parted smoothly around her finger into two separate, yet connected, bright points, until it found itself above and rejoined to a single yellow glow, spitting and sputtering to stay alive. It was as if the dragon balm were sucking all the oxygen from the flame.

She felt no heat, no pain, nothing.

She withdrew her finger and touched it. It was cold to the touch, just as the branch had been. Sam stared at it in awe, then put her finger back into the flame. Once again, the flame didn't singe her. She pulled her finger out from the fire and touched the ointment, finding it wasn't greasy—in fact, it had completely disappeared and dissolved into her skin. She had a bad cut on that finger that had healed but had left a scar. The dragon balm felt cool and soothing, so she smeared more on her finger, rubbing it in deeper. As before, it dissolved into her skin.

She walked over to Jo, who enjoyed eating his oats more than watching Sam set fire to herself. "Well, I did it," she said softly to him as she stroked his cheek, as did the slender, flexible, grass-like tentacles on her grapevine crown. "I made a fireproof salve to protect us from dragon breath. Now, all we need are dragons."

Sam had an apple in her left hand and brought it around from behind her back so Jo could see it. He shook his head and nuzzled her arm, almost knocking the apple from her hand, then he sniffed the finger with the dragon salve on it and took the apple from her. She was pleased he didn't shy away from the ointment, a good sign he would adjust to it when she had to work it into his hide. And based on what happened to her when the balm quickly absorbed into her own skin, there wouldn't be any greasy ointment on Jo's hide to snare flies and insects that she'd have to brush off him.

Soon, she would make enough to cover Jo and herself, and plenty to have on hand for when they needed to use it—*if we need to use it*, she thought. She wondered what it would be like to stand against the torrid heat of real dragonfire and if the ointment would bear out. Or would the blaze of a dragon be so much more intense than that of a tiny candle and its flame that she'd be burnt to a blackened statue, ashes for the wind and nutrient for the dirt?

She let those musings go because she knew they would consume her, and if she gave them weight, she would lose her nerve. But what better way to demonstrate one's mettle to her mother than to kill a dragon and prove that she too could fight the good fight and help protect the Quadlings and the land they loved. Battling a dragon would surely show her mother, Elle and Saran, and all the royal guards that she was worthy of being a soldier in the queen's army. But what it really meant was that dragons were the precursor of something far more sinister. Seeing a dragon would show beyond doubt the rumors to be true, and that would mean that this wicked witch, or enchantress, or some evil demon, was real. Now was not the time to panic, but the time to react and prepare for her trip west.

She had kept her father's saddle in a dry, safe place and made sure to oil it and keep it shiny and ready for him on the day when he returned. She had Roman repair the frayed ends of its leather straps, as well as the front cinch and skirt, and the knee roll. The leather on the bit, worn from years of hunting game and fighting many battles, was also replaced. She got out the oil and cleaning tools and sat on a stool in Jo's stall with the saddle at her feet. She opened the bottle of oil, pouring a small amount onto a piece of chamois. Jo sniffed the gear and rubbed Sam's cheek with his nose.

"Augie and Roman believe you're strong enough," she said as she pushed his face away and rubbed oil into the skirt of the saddle, "and so do I." This time, Jo pushed Sam's shoulder with his nose and blew hot air in her ear. It tickled, and Sam pushed his face away again, saying with a slight giggle, "It's time for you to wear Father's saddle again and for me to get used to sitting in it."

Early the next morning, before the sun even thought of breaking the horizon, Sam placed her father's gear on the ground outside of Jo's stall. She walked Jo to it. He sniffled the saddle and pushed the bit with his nose, inspecting the equipment slowly with enthusiasm and dancing with impatience while Augie and Roman supervised Sam as she tacked him up. "You must pull the cinch much tighter on him," Augie chided. "He's a powerful horse, larger than most warhorses, and he will unseat you without any hesitation if the saddle is loose." Sam did as Augie told her, the best she could and with no argument. She stepped into the stirrup and hoisted herself up and onto the saddle. Roman could tell right away the saddle didn't fit her, as expected. It had been custom-made for Lucius and Jo, since a horse of a different color has a much sharper spine and withers than most horse breeds.

"The saddle does not fit you well," said Roman as he walked Jo out of the barn. "And yours rubbed his hide raw."

The eastern sky showed only a thin line of cornflower blue against the shadow of the hills. And the rose-pink of dawn was barely touching the edges of scattered clouds, promising a bright and peaceful day.

"Can you have your saddler make one?" Augie asked.

"Yes," Roman replied. "I'll ask her today."

They continued to walk with Sam and Jo, making sure Sam remembered all that she'd been taught before letting her go on her own, because a warhorse is a strong-willed animal and will take control if it knows the rider is weak. "Show him you are in charge," Augie reminded Sam, "and don't let him for an instant think otherwise."

Sam looked at Roman and Augie, their faces confident and supportive in the ashlight of the morning. She nodded and gently prodded Jo with her heels. Jo moved off proudly obeying each of Sam's commands at once. She stood and pulled her sword from its scabbard and swung it expertly while they trotted around the pond. She replaced the sword, sat back in the saddle, and dug her legs into Jo's sides and kicked him in his ribs. Delighted to feel the signal to gallop, he bolted without a thought and tore off across the pasture, nearly jerking the reins from Sam's hands. Behind her, she heard Augie call out, "You'll need to be tougher than that, lassie! You're not playing with dolls!"

Roman was right, though, and so was Augie—Sam could tell immediately that her father's saddle was too big for her, and she needed to be as tough as nails. When Jo raced for the first obstacle, she fell out of it when he leaped into the air and sailed over the jump post. Instinctively she unfurled her wings, caught the wind, and lifted up and over into a backflip, landing right back onto the saddle as if she hadn't been thrown from Jo at all. Her wings retracted and she grabbed the reins, slowly bringing Jo down to a canter and then docilely to a walk. "Good boy," she said reassuringly, and patted him on the neck. "Well done, Jo. Well done."

She realized at that very moment while she felt Jo's warm, sweaty hide and heard his heavy but steady controlled breathing, that she had just reacted from a fearless gut. Sam smiled and believed perhaps that being with Jo was helping her find her inner strength and that, perhaps, she could channel that strength, and instead of trying to conquer fear, she could shake its hand and ride alongside it.

She readjusted her foot in the stirrup, but Jo was still overwhelmed with the excitement of wearing his master's leathers and feeling the weight of a rider on his back again, and was anxiously stepping back, shaking his head up and down, not ready to call it quits.

Then, without warning, his color metamorphosed quickly to a coal black. His head and tail came up, and he reared. Sam clutched him around the neck and he neighed, striking a war stance, sticking out and waving his forelegs. She pulled back as hard as she could on the reins, forcing his nose to his neck. Jo fought back, jumping and kicking in the air like a pugnacious Gillikin bronco trying to buck off its rider.

Her crown quivered, terrified, and grabbed onto Sam's ears and hair like a blacksmith's jaw-post leg vice. Sam shrieked. Her wings popped out, but she held firm, pulling Jo's reins sharply to the left when they landed back onto the ground after the third buck. Then she immediately leaned her body over, while at the same time arching her back around in the direction she wanted the horse to go, forcing Jo to turn in a tight circle to slow him down and remind him that she was in control. Sam remembered seeing her father and other soldiers of the cavalry out in the field practicing this maneuver to build a fire in the horses' bellies before galloping into battle. She almost lost her balance, but braced herself and kept Jo under control until his excitement settled.

Slowly, his black color turned to orange and then back to cream. Now she knew for sure she would need a saddle that fit her and Jo, if they were going to charge into battle and fight dragons. Using her father's saddle was so different than riding Jo bareback. For now, though, she would use her father's seat until her new saddle was made.

They made their way back to the far side of the meadow again, to the place where Jo had made his leap. Sam dismounted and walked Jo along its length. He sniffed the jump bar, a fallen cedar that Elle and Sam used when building the practice course. He shook his head, huffed, and slapped the ground twice with his front left hoof as if he remembered how good it felt to jump and wanted more.

"Ah, I see," Sam said with a sly grin, stepping quickly into the stirrup and mounting, "you want to go again." Jo cocked his ears and wrinkled his nose at her in a quiet whicker. "Oh, you agree." His ears flicked back as if saying yes. And as soon as they were far enough away from the jump, without hesitation Sam pulled the reins back hard and kicked his ribs at the same time with all her strength. Jo raised up into his war pose, neighed—instantly turning black again—and then, the very second his feet touched the ground, he shot off toward the cedar hurdle. There was nothing but speed, a pure, clean speed that Sam had never achieved with any other horse she had ever ridden. The wind screamed in her ears, and she tasted the bitterness of adrenaline in the back of her throat. Augie's voice thundered inside her head, *You're not playing with dolls!* Sam clamped her thighs more tightly against Jo's sides and urged him to go faster. This time, Sam was ready. She anticipated the leap and stayed with Jo when he soared over the barrier—the *rush* came fast and strong. "*Just like flying,*" Sam said to herself, and she smiled as they rode back around and jumped again.

When Sam and Jo returned to the barn, Sam and Augie took off Jo's gear and walked him to the pond with a bucket and brushes in hand to wash and groom him. "Where's Roman?" Sam asked. "Jo was amazing!"

"He had other chores to do," Augie replied, picking up a brush.

"How soon do you think the saddler can make a saddle for me?" Sam asked with excitement, not wanting to hold any of it back.

"Roman said he'd have it for you in three or four days," Augie told her. "We'll continue to ride and practice wielding your sword and using your bow as you and Elle have been doing without a saddle. In battle, you'd have to drop your gear with a slashed cinch or rein and ride bareback. You have improved so much and are better than all of your mother's soldiers. Saran would be hard-pressed to beat you sword to sword, especially while on Jo's back."

The corners of Sam's mouth lifted at what Augie said and made her appreciate Augie all the more for her support. She had an almost irresistible urge to confide in Augie and show her the discovery she had made with the recipe for the dragon lotion. But she didn't because she knew precisely how Augie would react, and she had no intention of being lectured or scolded. Sam was unconsciously rubbing the finger she had put the balm on, the one she had tried to burn. But when she looked down at it, she noticed the scar was gone, and she stared at it with awe.

Augie asked her twice, sharply, "Sam, what's wrong? What's wrong?"

The properties of the dragon salve seem to have a bit of magic of their own, Sam was thinking to herself, ignoring Augie. Then she thought about Jo's ugly disfigurement and the other smaller blemishes from the hacker bush thorns, and wondered if the miracle ointment she had made would heal his wounds like it did her scar—what a great gift to give to Saran, Lillith, and all the guards to rub into their battle marks. *The salve could be used to help so many people*, she thought.

Augie sighed and walked over to Sam. She touched her arm softly. "Sam—are you ill?"

Sam came back to herself with a visible jerk. "Augie—oh, I'm fine." Sam was so overwhelmed with excitement about the healing aspects of her balm that she had the impulse once again to tell Augie everything, but as before, she quickly changed her mind. "Truly, I'm fine. Just excited about Jo and the ride. He's really feeling strong." Sam smiled and moved her brush over Jo's back and his hip, looking at his eighteen-inch scar, still heavy with the thought of the added bonus her ointment had given her.

Augie gave Sam a look, as if wondering what ailed this poor child, but said nothing. Finally she asked Sam, "Should we braid his mane today?"

"Yes," Sam agreed, rubbing her finger thoughtfully. "That would be nice."

Seven

The next day opened with bright smiles and sunshine. But after dithering awhile, and much worrying and muttering to herself about whether or not she had enough herbs and roots to make the quantity of ointment she would need to use on Jo and herself, Sam decided to mash and mix all she had. She could always fetch more ingredients if she needed to make another batch.

After her workout with Jo and practicing riding bareback from the lessons she had been receiving from Augie, she spent the rest of the morning and the better part of the afternoon making the dragon salve. In the end, when she had finished and used all the herbs and roots, she still thought it wouldn't be enough. As she looked at the shallow trough filled with the clear goo, she wondered how long it would last on her skin and Jo's hide and still repel fire. And then another troubling concern found its way into her thoughts: When she made the trip to Blackwood Village, where the rumor of a dragon sighting began, would she have to drag along a wagon full of the stuff?

She looked at her healed finger, where once a scar had been. Her eyes widened. Because, where her greenish-blue skin had discolored and turned a dark blue because of the injury, it was now as if her finger had never been cut. No one would ever know that she had injured that finger. Her skin was soft and supple, the coloring perfect. She wondered about something else and lit the candle on the worktable, scrunching her eyes in anticipation of pain and thrusting her finger into the flame, where she held it firmly in place.

Nothing happened. No fiery pain. No smoke.

No acrid smell of sizzling flesh.

Nothing.

Sam pulled her finger back from the flame and touched it. It was as cold as ice. She was amazed that the ointment still protected her. She decided she'd need to test it every day to find out how long it would keep her from burning, but at least now she knew she wouldn't have to make as much of it as she first thought. She had plenty for her trip. *Now the big question is*, she thought, *what do I do next, throw myself into a bonfire?* "No," she said out loud, slapping Jo on his shoulder. "I'm going to listen to Elle and think before I jump into the flame." She held Jo by his head with both hands. She looked at him straight in the eyes and repeated what she was thinking. "What do we do next? We have our fire ointment and my protection spell." She scrunched her forehead, kissed Jo on his, and said in a softer tone with determined eyes, "All we need now is a dragon." And for a second, she truly believed that Jo understood what she was saying. "Let's do one more test before we head west."

Sam walked Jo out of the barn and slapped him gently on the hind end to urge him to graze in the pasture while she gathered wood to make a small fire by the pond. When the fire was good and hot, she rubbed the ointment over her entire hand, past her wrist, and a few inches below her elbow.

Once again, she was amazed at how quickly the salve absorbed into her skin and that it didn't have the feel of something unguent in any way. If she shook someone's hand, they'd never know it was on her, only that her skin felt smooth and soft. Then she thought about the antique book she'd read that had given her the dragonfire recipe. Since the author knew how to make the fireproof salve, and it had worked, it was likely the story about a dragon's tooth would also be true.

Jo was nibbling close by, waiting and hoping for her to place apples on the ground and watching her out of the corner of his eye without much interest. She held both of her hands close to the fire, trembling slightly. The other hand, the one without the ointment, could feel the heat from the fire wrap around her fingers while the other felt nothing. She slowly put her hand into the heart of the fire and again she felt nothing, only the heat working its way up her arm where she hadn't rubbed in any cream. She let her hand cook for a full minute, turning and clenching it, and then removed it. She locked her hands together, intertwining her fingers. Her hand was cool to the touch—no scorching, nothing. It felt like she'd never thrust it into the flame.

Sam brought Jo into his stall, brushed and groomed him, and rubbed the fireproof goo all over his hide. Then she lathered her hands and rubbed it on his ears, his face, his mane, and his tail, paying careful attention when rubbing it over the large scar. Jo did not like the feeling of the ointment being smeared into his skin at first. He pranced and shuffled and flared his nostrils, snorting in little rolling huffs. "It doesn't have a smell," she said, letting him smell her hand. "It will do your hide good, and it's no different than the oil Roman and I use on you to make your coat gleam."

She continued to knead it deep into his muscles, ignoring his small display of dissatisfaction as he continued to kick and sidle away. Sam said through clenched teeth, "I'll tie you up if you don't behave," giving him a healthy slap on his rear end. But she could tell he was only playing with her, trying to be the boss, and was actually starting to enjoy the massage.

After she finished, she rubbed it all over herself, and Jo watched and sniffed and pushed her with his head as if he were jealous she wasn't still rubbing it into his own skin. "This will be good for us both," she said as she carefully worked the ointment onto her face and forehead. It made her skin tingle, a sharp, cooling sensation. It was soothing and absorbed quickly, leaving no gooey, mushy film, and leaving her skin with a soft and silky feel. "It will make our skin shine."

She dropped an apple on the ground to try to stop Jo from goading her and massaged the ointment on her legs and feet. "We'll do this every day until we find the dragons, and we'll do your saddle too . . . all your gear, my armor, and the clothes I'll use for battle." When she was done lathering the fire ointment over all of Jo's gear and her battle clothes, she walked up to her father's warhorse and put her forehead to his. She rubbed his neck with both hands. "It's time to leave the castle and head to Blackwood to see if dragons are real. I wish Father were with us."

She knew it would be a long trek.

But how to convince Augie and Lillith was the big question that confronted her.

Sam didn't like to be deceitful in any regard, but she had to make up a story they would believe, one that would allow her to leave the castle for a camping trip that might last as long as two weeks. It made her nervous thinking about the deception, but she knew she had to try. But two weeks was a long time, and Sam knew Augie and Lillith would never agree to such a long junket. *Don't be a fool,* her mind snapped. *Better to just say camping trip and leave it at that.*

ॐ ✦ ॐ

Later in the morning, Sam confronted Augie with her desire to leave the castle grounds. Augie did not like her idea in the least. "It wouldn't be for very long," Sam insisted. "Plus, Jo needs to know he's strong again and fully healed. It will do him good to go on a camping trip."

"I don't think he's ready for a trek just yet," Augie declared.

"If not now, then when? He's as ready as he's ever going to be. Surely you can see that," Sam said a little too strongly, and quickly lowered her tone. "But if you truly believe it isn't a good idea, I will obey."

"You surprise me," Augie said. "In the past, you'd rant and cry and cause such commotion when I would disagree with you, but this time you aren't. I'm proud of you." Augie changed her stance, continuing, "You might be right, though. Jo will have to venture out at some point. And if not, soon he will have no desire to leave the comfort of his pasture and will be no good to anyone, as fat as he will become."

Sam's eyes made it clear this was more important to her than just a whim. Augie begrudgingly gave in with a sigh and sternly said, "Okay. You can go. But only if Lillith says you can." Sam knew it took a lot for Augie to agree with her. It surprised Sam, but ever since she'd turned sixteen, the grouchy old Munchkin had been a lot more understanding and forgiving. "Yet, still, it worries me for you to leave," Augie said, a smile touching the corners of her mouth. "But I suppose you are an adult woman now and can make your own decisions. Good or bad, right or wrong, it is your choice to make. Your father was the same, taking off on a whim for a fortnight to sleep under the stars. Why would I think you're any different? I'm sure your mother would approve, but you still must ask Lillith."

"I'll ask her right now," Sam said, smiling and giving Augie a long, robust hug.

Sam let go of Augie and ran out of her bedroom to find Lillith. As she was running down the stairs, she immediately began to agonize over the best way to approach Lillith. She figured it would take at least two days to travel to Blackwood, maybe three days or more to look for a dragon, and at least two more days for the return. Plus, she wanted to give herself a couple of extra days, just to be safe, in case killing dragons turned out to be a lot more complicated than she thought. Lillith was unpredictable and very difficult to read. She had the best poker face of any of the guards, but Sam knew Lillith liked her, and she hoped Lillith would allow her to go. Coming with Augie on her side was a decisive advantage because Lillith knew how protective Augie was of her.

She found herself worked up and nervous not only about how to ask Lillith, but questioning why she was going to do what she was doing at all—slathering an ointment that she'd found in a book all over her skin and Jo's hide to hunt for and kill dragons. *Why? Why take such a risk?* was a question that kept jumping around inside her head. And then she answered it. *To prove that I am not a child anymore. That I am my mother's daughter, the queen's daughter, and worthy of the royal blood that runs through my veins.*

⁂

Lillith was in the main hall, having breakfast with some of the top lieutenants and discussing the day's schedule. They were almost finished eating and about to practice their morning swordplay. Her face lit up with a smile when she saw Sam. Sam thought this rather out of character, but maybe being in charge had given Lillith a boost in spirit, for it was not often that Lillith was the one to make the important decisions on her own.

Sam smiled back, and Lillith poured orange juice in a cup and pushed a tray of hotcakes and honey bush-berry jam toward Sam. "Lillith," she said carefully, spreading jam on a hotcake and rolling it, "I think it might be time to take Jo on a short trek to see how he fares. If you would allow it."

Lillith looked at Sam thoughtfully, her deep calculating eyes lingering. She had been impressed by how well Sam and Elle brought Jo back from the brink of death, but Sam could tell there was hesitation glazing over Lillith's eyes. "No one will miss me," Sam added. "You have everything under control, and . . . Augie is in favor of it. She thinks it would be a good change for Jo."

"That horse is looking a bit chubby," Lillith said in her soft, quiet tone with a gentle smile. And then, without any more prodding from Sam, she added, "Yes, I think you and Augie are right. It's a good idea to get him out of his pasture."

"Thank you," Sam said through crumbs, then downed her orange juice in one gulp. "I will leave tomorrow."

"No more than a few days," Lillith demanded. "If you're not back in a timely fashion, I'll hunt you down myself, and there will be hell to pay. And not just from me. You would not want that grouchy old Munchkin to be the one to fetch you, of that I am sure." Lillith paused and swallowed the last of her drink, adding, "Now get your sword—you have to practice like any other royal soldier who defends this realm."

Sam stood up, nodded, and spread jam on a second hotcake before rolling it and taking a bite.

"I recommend going south and following the creek from Jo's pasture, which will give you water and prevent you from getting lost. There is little to the south of the castle that will harm you. Still, you must be on your guard. Set your campsite at the edge of the Great Sandy Waste. It is a vast expanse, where the skies are wide and open, and the stars brighter than you've ever seen."

"A good idea," Sam said, holding her hand over her lips and swallowing. "I'll meet you in the yard." She stuffed the rest of the hotcake in her mouth and quickly ran out of the dining hall, out into the courtyard, and flew up to her bedroom to change into her sparring togs and retrieve her sword, with only one thing on her mind: dragons.

Even though dragons were predominately the main thing running through her mind, the new saddle still hadn't arrived yet. Sam heard nothing from Augie or Roman about it and dared not ask so as to seem too anxious in her desire to leave on her quest.

The day moved forward slowly. When daylight was failing, there still wasn't any sign of Roman and the new saddle. Sam made up her mind that she'd leave late in the afternoon the next day. She couldn't wait any longer. She knew she was ready to face a dragon eye to eye, nose to muzzle. *It's not the saddle that makes a dragon slayer*, she told herself.

The next day, Sam decided to leave earlier than she had first planned and arrived at Jo's pasture before noon. The day before—because she was going on this trip whether or not she got permission, and whether or not she had her new saddle—Sam had taken the large leather satchel that held her dragon-proof balm and hidden it a mile away from the castle, south, close to the creek. She was going to follow the creek, as Lillith had suggested, and once she reclaimed the ointment, she would turn west toward Blackwood and the Winkie border.

Augie had insisted that she be with Sam to help pack and see her off. Together, they groomed Jo to a spit shine, which he loved; he preferred being fussed over, but not as much as he liked eating apples. As they were just about finished brushing Jo, Roman arrived with Sam's new saddle.

"It's gorgeous!" Sam said with delight. She picked up her new saddle and shrugged it onto her shoulders before she put it on Jo. Its fresh new leather smell hit her hard and made her smile. Together, Augie and Roman helped her attach the saddle. The new leather creaked and groaned as they cinched it up as tight as they could. She could barely stand still and pranced around, just staring at it. Jo looked spectacular. She had never seen a saddle that was so beautiful, so perfect. A true warrior's saddle for a great warhorse. *All I need to do now is become a great warrior*, she thought to herself.

Roman cupped his hands for Sam to use to put her leg over Jo. When she stepped up onto the beautiful saddle, she could tell instantly it was the right fit for both of them. It had intricate scrollwork on the skirt, down the flap, and along the outer edge of the knee roll. It reminded her of the antique dragon book she found in the castle library.

The second she had settled into the seat, she could tell Jo approved too. She instantly took Jo and the new saddle out for a quick run, and it felt as if she were riding bareback—as if the saddle weren't even there at all. It was absolutely beautiful, and when Jo leaped over the jumping bar, Sam stayed right in place without any extra effort. They felt like they were one together. When she was ready, she walked Jo back to his barn and jumped off, handing Augie the reins and giving Roman a hug. "Thank you," she said softly in his ear.

"It is a saddle fit for the queen's daughter," Roman said with a wide smile, showing all his teeth. "I had it made with extra leather to make it stronger. Jo can handle the extra weight. If you will excuse me, I have other duties that need my attention. Ride it well, milady."

❧ ◆ ❧

S am couldn't have been happier. The saddle was perfect and made her feel that she was ready.

"A beautiful saddle," Augie said, inspecting it and rubbing her hand thoughtfully along the cantle and seat. Then suddenly, Augie's face momentarily hardened as she thought about the queen confronting King Rumpart. She thought about the gossip of dark magic and another wicked witch skulking about in shadow. It filled her with apprehensiveness, giving her second thoughts about letting her charge leave the protection of the castle. "I am worried and—"

Sam interrupted, seeing concern etched across Augie's brow. "Don't fuss. Help me with the saddlebags and my gear. I'll be fine."

"I don't know why, but I have a feeling there is more to this trek than you are telling me," Augie asserted, concern and uncertainty rolling across her eyes.

Sam blushed. "It's been . . . quite a while since I've slept under the stars. Do not torment yourself so. Jo will protect me, and I will protect him. We can do this."

"You have plenty of apples, but might need more," Augie said as Sam stepped into the stirrup and threw her leg up and over the saddle. "There is an orchard in the direction you're going, in the middle of the Enchanted Forest. Just ask the tress first, and politely, before taking any apples—even the ones that have already fallen on the ground. They get real cranky when you don't ask before you pluck them off their branches."

"I promise to be polite," Sam replied, smiling and looking at Augie. "I'll see you soon."

"Not soon enough," Augie insisted, her voice tinged with disapproval, still feeling unsure about letting Sam leave the castle. She let go of Jo's cheekpiece and rubbed his nose, then looked up at her charge and smiled a weak, worried smile.

Sam pulled Jo's head around, walking him carefully around her worrisome nanny, and turned her head back to give Augie a reassuring smile before they jogged away. "I'll be back before you know it."

❧ ✦ ☙

Augie stayed until Sam dissolved into the tree line and slipped into the forest before she headed back to the castle. All her Munchkin intuition was pushing hard against her thoughts. There was something more to this little slog Sam had decided to go on than Sam was telling her. She was certain of it. She could feel the dull ache in her old bones warning her something wasn't quite right. And if a war were truly coming, to have her charge caught in the middle of it, unprepared, did not sit well with her. Not at all.

❧ ✦ ☙

As soon as Sam rode into the forest, she looked back and saw Augie still standing by the barn and watching. It bothered her a great deal that she was hiding her real purpose for her expedition, not telling Augie the truth. She was feeling upset with herself but thought it would turn out right in the end once she brought back a dragon's tooth to show what she had accomplished: that the rumors of dragons and an evil witch were true. She was sure Augie would understand then. But she was aware her conscience believed otherwise.

Sam looked toward the gray clouds that silently covered the sky from horizon to horizon. Where the day had begun with sunshine, it now drizzled. Sitting there on Jo's back, the gentle, light shower drifting down from the clouds formed droplets on her nose, trickled down her cheeks, and beaded and rolled off her new saddle. She felt another momentary pang of guilt. She was fooling herself. Sam knew deep down that Augie would be upset with her no matter what evidence she might bring back that would prove dragons are indeed alive.

She looked over her shoulder again, back at Augie, regretting her deception and pulling her hood over her head against the cool breeze and misty rain. *This is no time to let emotions get in my way,* she thought. Then she softly kicked Jo with her heels and clucked her tongue. He sauntered forward. She swallowed hard and her face became rigid, steadfast, her eyes became slits. Ignoring the chill that was seeping into her bones, she kicked Jo harder, and they quickly disappeared into the forest with loping strides. They raced through the deepest heart of the woods, moving in and around trees at a fast pace. Then, after about a mile, they settled down to a canter and then into a comfortable, steady walk, but Sam still felt the edges of guilt nipping at the back of her thoughts. Sam's crown stroked her cheeks and rubbed her ears, gently trying to ease Sam's feelings of doubt.

Sam rode for about an hour. From time to time, she blinked the rain from her eyes and stuck out her tongue to catch the drops. When they arrived at Sam's hiding place, she hopped off Jo before he had a chance to stop. But before she tied the two large satchels filled with the fireproof balm to her saddlebags, she took a little of the ointment and rubbed it on Jo's scar. It had already begun to heal. Where it was once dark, bloodred, and ragged around the edges, it was now a pale yellow and disappearing.

The rain had stopped, but the thick, washboard-gray cloud cover remained. They rode for a few more hours, and as the day began to slip away, Sam pushed Jo along rather briskly so they might have enough time before twilight, before the day turned to night, to set up camp. They had already turned west and had been riding for some time when they found a small stream that bisected the forest—a good campsite—so Sam unpacked and made a fire. She filled her cooking pot with water from the nearby stream, cutting up an onion, carrots, and bits of dried meat for her soup.

"We'll get a good night's sleep," she said to Jo while stirring her soup, "and get an early start in the morning. I'm anxious to see what we will find in Blackwood." She poured some soup in a cup and sipped. Steam touched her cheeks like soft, warm hands. Her crown poked her on her ear and her neck. She tensed, then heard a slight rustling. Jo heard it too. His ears cocked and he let out a soft huff. Then the rustling stopped, and only the sound of spring peeps and crickets could be heard. Sam's crown poked her again, but she brushed the shoots away and whispered, "Quit. It's nothing. Perhaps a snake, or a mouse." She sipped more of her soup. Her crown nipped at her again. "Quit, I said! There's nothing there."

The spring air still had the scent of winter on its breath at night, and she took her blanket and put it over her shoulders, watching the flames of the fire sputter and dance. *Dragons*, she thought. *What will they be like?* Sam took another sip of soup, trying to decide how to track down any signs of the dangerous, bloodthirsty beasts and found herself thinking the same thoughts over and over without comprehension. She was waiting for her mind to settle itself so she could let sleep take hold, but the anticipated dragon hunt was so alien to the patterns of her life that she kept thinking of it as a kind of charade, a game she had agreed, too hastily, to play. So many questions with no answers: *Will I find dragons? Will the fireproof salve protect Jo and me from their fiery breath? Will I have the courage to battle the beasties?* All these questions and more rattled and shook her worries back and forth.

And even when sleep finally took her by the shoulders, she tossed and turned the entire night, dreaming of fire-breathing monsters and once again finding herself standing by the silver lake with the flaming sword in her hand and a crow standing on her shoulder.

Eight

When Sam woke the next morning, the dream hit her hard, like a slap. It was so detailed, so real—the mountains, the lake water smooth as glass, and the feeling of drowning. But hearing the dusky, enigmatic voice calling out in the front of her mind, *"Find the Crow,"* made her spine tingle. All of it rushed back like a sharp razor and made her skin break out in gooseflesh and shoulders shiver. She sat up, wiped the sweat off her forehead with the palm of her hand, rubbed her eyes, and pulled her knees to her chin. Her crown stroked her cheeks softly, consoling her, and rubbed the tips of her ears. Jo sidled up to her, hoping for a treat.

"I'm fine," she said to him. He pushed the satchel sitting next to Sam that held the apples and snorted. "Oh, I see. It's not me you're worried about." She reached over and opened the bag, taking one out and cutting it in half. Jo sniffed it and grabbed it with his teeth, crunching and spilling pieces on the ground. But the dream had changed. This time, as she fell into the silver lake, she saw a man in a dark, rusty red, ground-length robe, ragged in appearance. His yellow, gold-flecked eyes peered out from the dark shadow that shrouded his face in the hood of his robe. His right arm was stretched out in front of him, reaching for her; his left was stretched out just above his shoulder, bent at the elbow, and in his hand he held a gnarled wooden staff. But he wasn't reaching for her, he was pushing her, pushing her into the lake with an invisible force. And the bedraggled crow that had been standing on her arm as she fell into the water had settled itself on the hooded man's arm, cawing as it landed.

She shivered and looked at Jo with soft eyes, then used her knife to cut another piece of apple, palmed it, and rubbed his nose as he took the juicy fruit from her. She ate the last bit for herself, wiping the juice that rolled down her chin with the back of her hand. "Do you dream, Jo?" she asked him as she put her cheek to his jaw. "You wouldn't like my dreams," she whispered. She patted him on his neck and opened the satchel of fire goo. Jo moved his head up and down, anticipating the rubdown.

Sam stuck her hand deep into the satchel, scooping up a large glop and slapping it on Jo's back. She rubbed it along his ridge and hindquarters, causing Jo to shake his head up and down in delight. "We'll be near Blackwood before nightfall tomorrow," Sam said thoughtfully, "and make camp close enough not to be seen. In the morning, we'll go into the village and see what people will tell us about the dragon sighting." She rubbed the ointment on his scar and was amazed that it was almost completely healed and the hair on his hide was growing back. The long gash that reminded her of that awful day when her father disappeared, and when Jo had thrashed and screamed in pain, looked as if it would soon be gone forever—though never the memory. She rubbed his legs and neck and finished gently with his face. Then she kissed his nose and started massaging the ointment on herself and her grapevine crown, and the grassy shoots scooped up the ointment and rubbed it on Sam's back and her wings.

The weather had turned murky and the clouds hung heavy, filled with the promise of more rain. The air had lost its icy feel, but now a thin eerie mist clung to everything, wrapping around tree trunks and moving over the ground in visible tides.

Thunder could be heard off in the distance, and as they rode along the creek, Sam kept thinking about her dream. Why the same dream again? It felt so real. So powerful. And who was the raggedy man wearing the dark red robe? What did it all mean? And the mountains? She knew those mountains, looked at them from her bedroom balcony every day, but not from where she stood in her dream. She was sure of it. She had never heard of a silver lake nestled somewhere in a valley hidden up in the snow-clad peaks.

Her crown slapped her on the cheek, jolting her out of her thoughts. She listened and heard a rustling in the brush behind her. But when she stopped and pulled hard on the reins to turn Jo around, there was nothing there. Her crown was now softly pinching her cheek, still warning her. This was the second time she'd heard something, and her crown had warned her. Her crown was never wrong—someone or something was following them. Now she suspected this must be what her crown had been trying to warn her about ever since her mother and sister left the castle to meet with Rumpart.

She felt the first drops of rain. Tiny droplets. She looked deep into the marsh grass, then closed her eyes and tilted her head, listening again for any sound that wasn't part of nature. All she heard was the gentle rustling of the grass from the cool breeze and the sprinkling of rain softly tapping on the leaves of the trees. As far as she could tell, there was no sign of anyone or anything tracking them.

She pulled Jo back around and continued toward Blackwood. But her crown continued to gently tug Sam's ears to make sure she kept a watchful eye out for possible danger.

The rain had turned into a cold spring mist, and the water on Jo's hide and her skin, instead of wetting them down, beaded and rolled off. Another remarkable attribute derived from the fireproof emollient.

It was midday, and they had been riding through the Enchanted Forest for the better part of the morning. Mature red and white oak trees were scattered everywhere, most of them one hundred to two hundred feet tall, forming a canopy of green that overspread her head. Much of the forest had not been thoroughly explored, where animals and all kinds of unknown creatures were yet to be discovered, and those that could speak had not yet been given proper names.

The woods were growing thicker each hour, and there was some low underbrush too, unfamiliar to Sam. Their branches looked like creeping roots that twisted and spiraled around each other, and they had long leaves, yellow and curling, with a reddish tinge that warned of a poisonous variety. Sam tried to avoid putting Jo through the foliage, but in some places, it couldn't be helped. And as they rode, Jo stepped over a crackling, golden carpet of discarded oak leaves. Sam felt as though the entire world could hear their passage. What clouds she could see looked a little less threatening but still laden with the prospect of opening up again and dumping more showers. At least for now, the misty rain had stopped. There came the occasional break in the low-hanging clouds as they continued along their path, and Sam could make out steep, rugged cliffs just beyond the edge of the forest. She hoped that they did not have to trudge through such uninviting terrain.

Sam and Jo forded a broad, long creek, crossed a field of tall, brown grass dotted here and there with blue-and-yellow wildflowers, and shortly thereafter entered a grove of thick, sprawling trees laden with juicy, ripe red apples dripping from their branches. She heard what she thought was the soft tread of that someone, or some unknown thing, trailing her. A small deer broke cover. It was young, still showing its white spots on its back. It leaped over a fallen moss-covered log, up a slope, and disappeared into the brambles.

Sam pulled back gently on the reins, Jo responded, and they stopped. As it was a natural occurrence for all blooming trees in a magic forest to bloom whenever they liked, it didn't surprise Sam in the least that apple blossoms drifted lazily by, glittering as they flew, and gathering on the forest floor like snowflakes from heaven. "So many apples," Sam said, the corners of her mouth lifting to a soft, pleasing smile. "This is your paradise, Jo."

The ground gradually flattened as they rode down a sloping

ravine, and a few minutes later apples littered the landscape. The majestic, ancient woodland apple trees hummed, buzzing with honeybees, mingled with the ceaseless, peaceful chatter of chipmunks, squirrels, and birds. The great trees were sturdy, their proud, woody trunks thicker than one could put their arms around. Here, there was a vast sea of the wildflowers, thousands upon thousands of the blue, white, yellow and pink blossoms flowing in and around the magnificent trees and rolling over the entire forest floor, filling the air with the sweet perfume of nectar and early evening dew.

Sam swung her leg over Jo's neck and jumped off. The horse lowered his head to the ground and nibbled on one of the large, bright red apples. She took hold of his cheekpiece and pulled his head away from the apple, scolding him. "No, Jo. We haven't asked yet."

"Not to worry," the apple tree said. "Nonspeaking animals have the right to indulge any time they wish."

"Yes, it's fine," said another tree.

"Absolutely fine," said another.

"Would it be all right if I picked some fresh ones to take with us? Our supply is getting low." Jo thrust an anxious nose into her cheek, and she patted his neck. "My horse, as you can see, has a passion for your juicy red fruit."

"The best apples this side of the forest," all three trees voiced in unison with pride.

"I have no doubt," Sam bubbled with delight.

"Pick all you need, Princess Samantha Goodwitch, daughter of our queen, the Good Witch of the South. Our protector," the first tree said, as it and all the others in the orchard bowed at the waist, creating an ocean wave of canopies throughout the forest, creaking branches, and rustling leaves.

"You know my mother?"

"Of course we do," the three closest trees said in chorus, lifting their branches and standing upright.

"Why would you think otherwise?" the first tree said. "I am Red, and at my left is Hedge." Hedge bowed again. "We are grounded to this realm like any other creature and will do as our queen commands."

"We know of you as well, Your Highness." Hedge added.

"And I am Hodge," the third tree said standing to the right of Red. "We won't introduce you to all the trees. As you can see, we are many."

"How do you know of me?" Sam asked.

"Tree-speak," Red replied. "It starts at one end of the forest and ends at the other. We have known of you since you were a seedling and your branches barely green."

"Yes, tree-speak," said Hedge. "Some of us speak plainly, as we apple trees do. Others move their branches and jostle their leaves to convey their thoughts."

"Oh, we talk a lot," Hodge added. "And listen."

"We are excellent listeners," Red said. "We know you're on a quest in search of dragons."

"Have you seen dragons?" Sam asked.

"We have."

"Then the rumors are true," Sam said softly as she picked a ripe red apple from one of Red's branches and placed it in her satchel. "Evil has returned to Oz."

"Yes. I'm afraid the rumors are true, Princess. There is darkness brewing in the west. Another wicked witch has clawed her way out of the dirt, a most powerful and dangerous enchantress. She is building an army."

"War is coming," Hedge warned.

"Yes, war."

"Where have you seen the dragons?" Sam asked.

"There is a goat farm that sits slightly north of Blackwood," Hodge explained. "Across the border in Winkie Country. The dragons come at dusk to feed on the goats."

"There are also reports of farmers' crops being destroyed and chickens being eaten," Red said, "and a child badly burned who had accidentally discovered their lair. Thankfully, the child was rescued in time to save her life."

"How many dragons?" Sam asked.

"Three."

"Yes, three."

"We're sure it's three," Hodge said. "But we must warn you, Princess. There has been tree-speak of a bloodred dragon ten times the size of the ones we have seen. More vicious and dangerous than the smaller ones."

Sam reached for another apple, and the grass shoots on her crown touched the leaves growing from one of Red's branches. Red shivered as Sam's crown spoke to him through its touch. "You're being followed," Red said. "We aren't sure what it is. But something is following you. Your crown has been trying to warn you since the moment you left your home."

Sam's crown softly slapped her on the cheek as punishment for not listening to it. But Sam ignored her crown and brushed the grassy shoots away, promising herself she'd be more attentive to her crown's warnings from then on. She picked more apples and tied the satchel to her saddle, then mounted Jo and asked, "Have you heard of the Crow?"

"We have," Red replied. "He is a powerful and fervent mage. Nestled in the middle of the great Quadling Peaks is Silver Lake Valley. The Crow lives there."

"Thank you for your kindness," Sam said. She gently dug her heels into Jo's ribs to urge him forward. "And for the apples."

"It has been our pleasure to serve you, Your Highness," Red said, and lowered his branches with respect, as did the other two trees.

"Yes. Our pleasure."

"Our pleasure, indeed."

᷎ ◆ ᷎

Sam and Jo had descended onto a large, open meadow surrounded by a dense forest within an hour of riding after saying their fare-thee-well to the apple trees. They had been making good progress and moving further west toward the village of Blackwood. Here the lush, green grass grew to Jo's knees, and he had to wade through it with a rustling sound like dry leaves pushed by a stiff breeze. "One more night," Sam said to Jo. "We should see the village tomorrow." She patted his neck then arched her back, rolling her shoulders to sit straighter in the saddle, as it was easy to slump during a long day of riding. She felt her spine shift and heard it crack.

In front of them, the grass was thinner. Sam's crown grabbed her ear pulling it firmly. Sam switched the reins from one hand to the other and turned her head to look behind her. She noticed that the grassy green shoots were the deepest where their trail had been, and ocean waves of grass rippled out in long, curving swells. She turned forward and rubbed Jo's neck, speaking softly. "I believe my crown is correct. We have company after all, but it chooses to be hidden from us." Jo cocked his ears back to listen, then gave a short huff in agreement.

Soon, they came to another forest, and there the light had more trouble following them since the trees were thick and tightly packed together so that the uppermost branches formed a continuous layer of foliage. As they ventured deeper in, the light became so dim it was difficult to tell the time of day and felt more like it was the middle of the night. The low, leaflike branching of lichen on the trees and rocks had a soft, fluorescent white, pink, and bluish glow to them. Butterflies of all kinds glowed as well—shimmering, fluorescent orange, yellow, blue, and pink dancers fluttering everywhere, all around them, almost as if guiding them. Lightning bugs popped on and off like tiny sprites playing a game of hide-and-seek. Ferns and plants all had their own colored luminescence, making it easy for Sam and Jo to gaze into the murkiness.

Jo huffed and shook his head each time a glittering butterfly tried to land on his nose. "Amazing," Sam said in a hushed tone, and dismounted. "I've never seen anything so beautiful." She stood in front of Jo and smiled, stretching her arms out from her sides shoulder-high as she watched the butterflies one by one land on her arms. "What a magical place this is," Sam said quietly, looking at her warhorse. "Now I know why they call it the Enchanted Forest." But it seemed that her words were sucked away from her, sucked into shadow, echoing in some distant and faraway place from where they stood.

She raised her chin as if someone might be watching and looked back where they had come from, then carefully opened her wings and slowly lifted off the ground, trying not to disturb the butterflies that now covered her arms and entire body. As she flapped her wings a second time, the butterflies gently lifted off and followed Sam as she slowly flew a few feet off the ground and remounted Jo. As they carried on, Jo did not huff or snort or shake his head when a butterfly landed on his nose. Soon, hundreds were resting on his mane, his ears—any part of him where they could find a place to rest and soak up the warmth from his body.

The feeling of being watched increased as they went on, though Sam saw nothing, except perhaps that there seemed to be more rustling, and her crown kept warning her to stay vigilant. And every now and again, maybe, she thought she saw quick glints of what might have been eyes. She pulled Jo forcefully to a halt. All the butterflies flew off him. She lowered her head close to his ears and speaking softly, said, "Did you hear that?" They waited, listening, and Jo snorted. "Quiet," Sam said firmly, pulling hard on his mane. She cupped her ear, but whatever it might be, it was not willing to show itself just yet—of that, she was sure of.

The trees thinned as they came to the edge of the forest. It had taken them the entire day to travel that distance, and now they could tell how late it was in the day as the sun was below the horizon, scattering a pinkish glow in the western sky. They made camp, and Sam did the same as she had the night before. She made a fire, chopped onions, carrots, and celery, and added dried beef for a much desired and inviting stew.

⚜

S am sat on her blanket, savoring each sip of the hot stew. She closed her eyes and let the steam from the stew warm her face.

The green shoots on her crown tugged at her ears, warning her yet again. Sam listened to her crown's alarm and once again heard a gentle rustling in the grass behind her. She didn't move; she opened her eyes and took another sip, looking out into the shadows. "If you're hungry, come then, and sit and have some stew." Her own voice was trembling ever so slightly, but she managed to keep it under control, for it sounded as if she knew what she was doing, and she was quite certain she did not.

Sam took another sip from her cup and then said, "Please, join me, and you can tell me why you're following us." Sam closed her eyes again and listened carefully. But now she heard nothing, no movement, no rustling through the undergrowth. She only heard the sounds of the forest—crickets and spring peeps singing to each other, releasing their night songs.

She sucked in a frightened breath when, after a few moments, something did come, and it pressed gently up against her, up against her back. It brushed past her slowly, then turned around and pressed up against her back again, this time with more of its weight. She counted her heartbeats thrown hard against her sternum—*one, two, three*. The creature was warm and had an earthy, musty smell, and when it took in a breath, it let out a deep-throated purring and she felt the creature's warm breath on the back of her neck. She did not move. The air pulsed with apprehension. Her neck shivered, and her crown stood motionless. With reluctance, she unbent her left elbow and let her hand holding the cup of stew rest on her knee. She closed her eyes and then opened them with a jolt, as a very rough tongue dragged over the side of her arm, almost making her spill her stew, and a large, round, furry black head three times the size of her own with yellow, beady eyes, rubbed into her leg. The great black cat looked large and powerful, and when on all fours, the cat could easily stand shoulder to shoulder with that of an average cow. Sam thought it was strong enough to carry off a whole ostrich or bring down a raging, wild bull if it had an inclination to do so.

After a moment, the great cat—acting as if Sam or Jo didn't even exist—slowly strolled over to sit on its haunches next to the fire, curling its tail around its four paws. The creature lifted one of its front paws and licked it, and said in a warm, unhurried female voice, "Pleased to make your acquaintance." Then she smiled. "I'd love some stew."

Sam stood up, eye-to-eye with the great cat.

The furry thing had short, sharp ears with a pronounced fringe of white hairs around each and down her neck and back, where white splotches and stripes rolled over her shoulders and covered her haunches. She carried a travel pack that held a sword and spear.

"Pleased to make your acquaintance as well," Sam said shakily, "I think." She saw a flicker in the great cat's piercing yellow eyes and braced herself just in time as the cat sprang up on her hind legs and put her forepaws on Sam's shoulders. The animal's breath was soft and warm against her face, and the ends of her whiskers tickled her cheeks.

Jo laid his ears back flat to his skull and rolled his eyes until the whites showed. He shuffled his feet and turned an angry red, ready to fight. "No," Sam said firmly. "I think we're just saying hi." She hesitated and then said to the cat, "Or maybe—I'm your dinner?"

The great cat huffed and pushed out air on Sam's face and looked rather pleased that Sam had stood her ground and stared back at her with little fear. Two slender grass tentacles from Sam's crown reached out and brushed the cat's fur, pushing her ears down and rubbing behind them softly. The great cat dropped to all fours again and circled Sam twice before letting her tail skim across her cheeks, then padded silently over to the fire and settled back onto her haunches.

"I like your wings," the great black cat said as she took off her backpack and placed it on the ground, the spears clanking as they settled onto the dirt.

Sam took another cup and poured some stew into it, then cautiously took guarded steps over to the great beast, and handed it to the cat. "Do you have a name?"

"I do," the great cat said as she took the cup with her forepaws, sniffing first before taking a drink. "*Mmm* . . . you make a delicious stew, Princess."

Sam walked over to Jo and rubbed his face, giving him an apple to reassure him that she wasn't in any danger. "You know who I am?"

"I do," the great cat replied. "The apple trees told me. It seems we are on the same quest, you and I." The cat paused and took another drink from her cup.

"They do talk a lot," Sam replied, and walked back to the campfire to sit on her bedding that was lying unrolled and ready near the fire, while keeping a wary eye on her new visitor, unsure of her true intentions.

"They do indeed," said the cat. "May I have more?"

"Help yourself," Sam said, gesturing politely with her hand, palm up, pointing it toward the pot of stew bubbling by the fire.

The great creature filled her cup. "You have every right to be dubious, Princess. I see it in your eyes when you look at me and hear it in the tone of your voice. I assure you, I mean you no harm. I only wish to help."

"What makes you think I need help?" Sam questioned.

"My name is Akasha. I am a mountain warrior cat from the Shadow Mountain Kru. Our village lies near the westernmost ridge of the great Quadling Peaks, what we call Shadow Mountain. It is a rich, verdant valley with plenty of game. We are a sizable kru, a clan of more than two hundred. Six weeks ago, three of our hunters went out and never returned. When we found them, one was dead, and one was still breathing enough to tell us what had happened, but burned so badly she didn't last the night. The third had been taken by the dragons—for food."

"Once again, more proof that the rumors are true," Sam said, staring deep into the flames of the fire.

"Yes, Princess. Darkness has returned to Oz. The villagers I have met in search of dragons have the same fear that war is coming. Their panic dislocates them from hope and has left them unmoored from their purpose, from the destiny they must serve, to band together and prepare."

"I too am worried," Sam said softly. "My mother and sister are on their way to speak with King Rumpart, to ferret out what might be concealed in the darkness."

"Yes, Rumpart," the cat said. "A weak man and a weaker ruler."

Sam put two more sticks on the fire and watched them blaze to a fiery passion, their edges erupting into a bright orange. The campfire sputtered and spat, and sparks lifted up and were taken by the breeze. Sam knew, with dreadful inescapability, the great cat was right—the raucous voices, the fearsome gestures of the forces of darkness, were once again trying to bleed Oz. They would take the country to the brink, to war, for sure. To change the subject and quell her anxious thoughts, Sam asked, "I thought all talking animals wore clothes and walked on two legs?"

"I do," Akasha replied. "I don clothes when it's appropriate. Visiting a queen, like your mother, or going to the Emerald City and congregating and debating to my heart's content with the Big Head himself about the future of Oz, or religion, or revolution, politics, or the poetry of war . . ." The great black cat licked her paw and smoothed down her fur before she continued. "It is just as natural for me to wear clothes as it is not to. And it is just as natural for me to walk on four legs as it is on two. But not when I'm hunting. I maneuver quicker on all my paws when running and cornering my prey, and I use two legs when fighting an enemy with my sword or throwing my spear."

"So then, I am not your prey?" Sam asked with some trepidation. "I am not your dinner?"

"Only if I want you to be," Akasha said with a sly grin as she took the last sip from her cup and placed it near the fire. She unrolled her bedding and batted it with a forepaw until she'd disarranged it to her liking, then circled it three times before lying down full-length upon it. She let her cunning smile broaden her cheeks, watching Sam through slitted eyes.

Sam stared cautiously back, then looked at Jo, who had settled down, somewhat accepting their new guest. "Do you know of Silver Valley," Sam asked, "and a mage called the Crow?"

"I do, Princess," Akasha replied.

"Do you know how to get to Silver Lake?"

"I do, Princess."

"We should sleep," Sam said as she took her sword and laid it close to her. "Tomorrow, we hunt dragons." The silence was broken only by the great warrior cat's purring and the little snaps and hisses of the fire, and as campfires do when left unattended, its sputtering voices soon subsided and real darkness fell.

Sam's eyelids became heavy, even though her mind was still churning. *I should keep the fire going,* she thought. *Who knows what else is lurking out there and waiting. Who knows . . .*

But she fell asleep quickly and was suspended in nowhere. But nowhere was lit with a foggy, gray, cold light from an overcast sky, and a voice off in the distance was calling her name—or at least she thought it was her name—urging her once again to find the Crow.

PART TWO

DRAGONS
AND
THE CROW

Nine

Sam didn't sleep well and woke at dawn with an ache along her spine. Another restless night. Akasha was gone, but her backpack and bedding were still there, and Jo was dozing peacefully, leaning against a tree. Sam sat up, rubbed her back, and rubbed the sleep out of her eyes as she asked herself softly, "Where did that cat go?" No sooner did that thought come and go than Akasha roved out of the forest with a lagomorph between her teeth. She approached like a cat of any size would do, as if stalking, trying to stay hidden, and dropped the fresh kill by the fire.

"Thought we should have a good breakfast before we go hunting for the real prey." Akasha placed dried leaves and kindling on the campfire and blew onto the leftover coals until they turned a bright orange, igniting the leaves. When the kindling took hold, she added a few larger sticks on top. Then she took out her knife, gutted and skinned the cony, skewered it, and held it over the flames.

Sam was rubbing the fire ointment on Jo, and the enticing smell of cooked meat quickly permeated the cool morning air. "What are you rubbing on your horse?" Akasha asked.

Sam looked at where the large gash had been on Jo's hindquarter and was still amazed at how the balm had healed his hide so perfectly. She rubbed her hand over the spot, remembering how at one point, she'd thought for sure Jo would always have a scar. "It's a fireproof salve I've made," Sam said as she finished Jo's rubdown. She massaged what was left on her hands and on her arms as she walked over to the campfire and kneeled down, taking in a strong whiff of the roasted rabbit. The meat was sizzling, and the hot coals spitting from droplets of fat made the flames leap and jump. The delicious smell of cooked cony was impossible to resist and made Sam's stomach gurgle and groan.

"A fireproof salve?" Akasha said. "What do you mean, a fireproof salve?" Sam put both of her hands into the middle of the campfire and held them still, letting the flames flicker and flow around them, as if trying to avoid them. The cat stood up and stepped back. Her eyes widened, and she almost dropped the rabbit meat. "Magic?"

"Herbs," Sam replied. "I made the ointment from herbs. I've also been practicing a magic spell to guard against fire, just in case my fireproof ointment isn't strong enough to hold back dragon breath. But the ointment is not magic. It has healing properties too. Jo had a bad injury that left him with a large scar. After using the balm, the scar is gone."

Sam pulled her hands out of the fire and showed them to Akasha. Akasha held one hand in her paw and sniffed, and her eyes became wide. "You're not burned?" Then she looked at Sam, simply astonished.

"I've been saturating everything for days now. Me, Jo, his saddle, his war gear, my war gear, arrows, my sword. Everything is fireproof."

"Do it again," Akasha said with a purring giggle. "Put your hands in the fire."

Sam put her hands slowly back into the fire. As before, the flames circled around her hands as if her hands weren't even there. "I found the fireproof recipe in an old book about the history of Oz that had an entire chapter concerning dragons," Sam said. She made a fist with both hands and opened and closed them as she watched the flames dance and sputter. "The author, I think, was Ozma, the Princess of Oz." Sam removed her hands from the fire and Akasha held them with her paws, checking to see if Sam's hands had any burns, but there was nothing. No blistering at all.

"If your fireproof recipe was from Princess Ozma, then that's why it works. She was a great and kindhearted good fairy witch who used magic and herbs to heal. You've rubbed the dragonfire ointment all over your body and didn't use any magic?"

"Yes," Sam replied, pulling her hands free of Akasha's paws. "As I said, I rubbed it all over Jo, over everything, and no magic."

"Do it again," Akasha said, giggling again. Sam did, and Akasha smiled a sly cat smile. "We should test it completely. We should make a bonfire, and you and your horse should walk into it. It is the only way to know for sure you won't be burned to cinders."

"On one condition," Sam said. "We rub the ointment all over you, and you dance with us in the flames."

Akasha agreed, and Sam massaged the dragonfire salve deep into Akasha's fur down to her skin. She rubbed it on Akasha's tail and paws, over every inch of the great cat. "It's not greasy at all. It feels as if my body has consumed it and it has soaked deep into my hide," Akasha declared.

"Put your paw into the fire," Sam told her.

Akasha slowly placed one paw into the fire, and as it did to Sam's hand, so it did precisely the same to the great cat's paw. She pulled her paw out of the fire, examined it, and then thrust it back into the flames.

In a small meadow close to their campsite, they built a large bonfire. The three of them, Sam, Jo, and Akasha, stood and watched the flames leap over their heads, shooting up to the clouds. As the breeze spurred the fire on, some of its flames spiked and swirled like miniature fire funnels, lasting for only a brief moment, then vanishing. Sam listened to her heart beating quickly, swallowed, and said to Akasha, "Are you ready?"

The cat nodded in agreement. "Ready."

Sam slipped into the fire like creeping into a lake of cold water, first her fingers, then her hand, and then her arm. She took a deep breath and stepped directly into the flames as Akasha followed with the same wariness and stood beside Sam. Jo stayed back, skirting the edge of the fire and snorting anxiously while the fire tapped at their faces and bodies like lighthearted and playful spirits, buoyant and ebullient. It murmured and snapped in their ears and wrapped its flames around them like a quilt in winter, as a clement and warm embrace. Instead of burning them, it almost seemed as if it were protecting them.

They moved around as if floating in a dream, looking at their hands and arms, amazed that they were not being burned; but instead, they felt nothing more than gentle pricks on their skin.

Sam turned to look at Jo and stepped out of the fire. The fire burned on, unconcerned that Sam and Akasha had invaded its province, and she took hold of Jo's reins. "Your turn," she whispered in his ear, and patted and rubbed his face. "Jo, you can do this." He thrust a worried nose into her neck but trusted her completely, and as Sam gently tugged on the reins to coax him into the fire, he resisted only slightly. After another gentle tug, Jo yielded, letting Sam lead him into the flames. His color changed to a bright yellow, then to orange and back to yellow, fluctuating back and forth, mimicking the color and movement of the flames, becoming one with the fire.

Akasha gently massaged Jo's back. "You're a brave horse, Jo. A powerful and brave warhorse." She purred in his ear to help crush any apprehensiveness he still might be struggling with. The cat turned to Sam and smiled. "Looks like, little dragon slayer, we're ready for the hunt." Sam smiled back, eyes wide open, amazed, but in the back of her mind, something was tugging at her. Something dark, making her chest feel heavy.

The sun was shining and the birds singing, the sky cloudless and bright, and Akasha had picked up the pace as they made their way through the thick forest on their way to Blackwood. There was a break in the dense growth of shrubs and other plants, and Sam prodded Jo into a canter, making him run for a while. Ever since they had stepped into the bonfire, Sam didn't feel quite right. It was an uneasy feeling, an eerie ghosting playing with her mind. Perhaps the disturbance that chased her thoughts was from their test in the flames, or maybe it was merely restlessness. This she wasn't sure of, but as they moved closer to the dragon-infested village, Sam thought of only her mother and sister and what might be going on at the gathering at Rumpart's castle. What had they found? Were they greeted well, with respect and honor? Or did they find that evil mischief did indeed control the Winkies once again? This, Sam thought, would surely be the case, given the talk and sightings of dragons the apple trees had told her about, and the account from Akasha. All of this evidence made it indisputable that a wicked witch was indeed on the march to war.

Akasha stopped at the top of a ridge, a little distance from Blackwood Village. Sam dismounted and stood by Akasha's side, looking down at the small town. "We should prepare," Akasha said, "and you should rub more ointment on me, since I have had only one round of it, and you and Jo have been drenched in it for days. And I can do a better job on your wings than your crown can." The grassy shoots stood stiff and took a defensive stance, pointing at Akasha as if to strike and sting her. "I mean you no disrespect," Akasha said to the crown. "Just trying to be helpful." The crown relaxed, except for one tentacle that snapped to show its displeasure.

Sam rubbed the ointment all over Akasha, over her long tail, face, eyelids, and then did the same with her battle armor, including Akasha's weapons. Together, she and the great cat massaged it into Jo's hide, face, mane, legs, and tail. And with the help of Sam's crown, the cat rubbed the fireproof balm deep into Sam's back and carefully on her wings.

"In the book you read about the dragons," Akasha began, while scooping up a handful of the fireproof goo to finish rubbing it on Sam's wing, "did the Ozma tell you how to kill the fire breathing beasts?"

"With a lot of courage," Sam joked.

"Funny," Akasha replied, not all that amused. "Any help would be great, since I've never fought a dragon before."

"The book said the dragons have two vulnerable kill spots. One place is under the jaw. There is a missing scale, only flesh, where the head meets its neck. The other is just behind its front leg, where the upper wing joint meets the body.

"Good to know."

"But I'm serious about the courage."

S am tied the satchel of ointment to her saddle bags. There was a silence that stood between them as they dressed in their battle armor. Sam truly hoped they would be brave enough to accomplish their task; she was a little doubtful, but pleased to have Akasha as a comrade.

When Sam mounted Jo she held her head high, with Akasha striding close to their left side on all fours. Sam looked down at her newfound friend and said, "I fear my courage would be stuck in my throat if you were not here with me now." Sam's bluish-green skin glistened in the sun, and the sunlight danced off her and Akasha's armor. It felt good, comforting, to have Akasha by her side.

It felt right.

As if it were meant to be.

Jo was fresh and inclined to bounce, and did not pay any attention to Akasha's dragon spears attached to his saddle, for he was accustomed to such weapons from the battles he'd fought with Sam's father on his back—Jo was no stranger to armed conflict and what was expected of him. It was a silent stride and they went at an even, steady pace so as to keep their strength, since Sam wasn't at all sure how effective their first encounter with a real dragon was likely to be. It was one thing to carefully plan a strategy and play with it in her head, but she was quite sure it was an entirely different matter when confronting a fire-breathing beast in the flesh, staring at each other eye to eye. Sam pulled gently back on Jo's reins and stopped. "I'm going to take a look above the trees," she said to Akasha. Sam stood up on her saddle, opened her wings, and with a great *whoosh* flapped them twice, lifted into the air, and flew above the treetops. She hovered, and there she could see them, or thought she could see them. Off in the distance, a few miles northwest of the village—just small black specks, they were—three flying beasts circling like vultures over the dead. She squinted, adjusted her eyesight, and zoomed in on the creatures. Sam's neck shivered. Her shoulder's tightened. The rumor was true. Dragons. Real dragons. Three bloodthirsty, fire breathing dragons.

Sam floated back, softly landing on her saddle. Without missing a beat, she placed her feet in the stirrups, took hold of the reins, and nudged Jo's ribs, urging him to move swiftly. "They're about a mile northwest of the village," Sam said to Akasha. "Three dragons."

When they rode into the village, they slowed their pace. Jo always stood apart and made a grand entrance. He was unmistakable as a warhorse. And with Akasha by their side, black fur, large size, dressed in battle armor, they were fearsome strangers indeed. An old man stood up from his stool in front of his doorstep and bowed his head, staring at them in helpless fascination from beneath the shelter of his hood. There was an indefinable air of despair about the man. Sam stopped and asked kindly, "Why do you bow to me, sir?"

"I mean no offense, milady," he said as he looked at Sam. "Only to show respect for the daughter of my queen, Glinda Goodwitch. You look much like her, and your father too." He removed his hood and bowed again. His white hair, what was left of it, was oily and matted and his eyebrows were the same white, as though life had leached the very pigment from him. Hard lines etched his cheeks and forehead. His deep-set, dark eyes were rimmed in red, but they spoke of kindness and a hard life lived when he looked directly at Sam.

"You know my mother?" Sam hesitated. Something caught in her throat. She swallowed and asked, "And my father?"

"Yes, Princess. I have met your mother, and I am her faithful servant. I fought alongside your mother and your father in the last great war over talking animals' right to speak freely and stand as free creatures of Oz." Then once again, he bowed his head to Sam and turned to Akasha and did the same. "I know of you as well—"

"Thank you for your respect, old man, "Akasha broke in sharply. Sam gave the cat a stern look, thinking it rude of her to cut the old man off when he was just being friendly. She was about to make a remark when suddenly, there were a dozen folk following them. Then two dozen or more started lining the street, coming out of storefronts, standing on balconies, and standing on wagons. Children were climbing lampposts, and others were opening windows on the second stories of their homes to gaze upon the two warriors. Most of the buildings were poorly constructed of cheap wood, and they leaned haphazardly every which way. *One good blast from a dragon*, Sam thought, *and the entire village would burn to the ground.*

Along the street there were rows and rows of stalls, where merchants displayed everything from simple fruits and vegetables to exotic birds. Sam and Akasha worked their way along the street and came into a small open-air market in the center square. Around the edges of the square, specialty shops lined the cobblestone circle, each with a gaily-colored placard out front. Sam saw a tailor, a baker, a healer, a hairdresser, even a haberdasher, and wondered what sort of vanity supported a hat shop in such a small village as Blackwood.

"There is much fear here, Princess," murmured Akasha. "People with little hope."

"I agree." Sam's gaze roved over the worried faces of the people. And the crowd gazed back at the two visitors with hope. They all looked worn, the young as well as the old. It made Sam sigh deeply. Many appeared to have scars. She didn't want to imagine what they must have been dealing with living under the threat of dragons, but she couldn't help it. But this wasn't at all how Sam had pictured this moment. Some of these people were weeping, but not the happy tears that someone had come to save them as Sam had imagined. All of these people looked as though they had been living with terror and hadn't known a peaceful night's rest in years.

Sam had grown up in a castle, raised in that privileged life, never giving a thought to the land or the people her mother ruled. Her mother's kingdom was vast, and the people living on her land were her mother's responsibility. At least that was what she had always believed. But seeing the sight of the men, women, and children staring back at her with fear laced deep within their eyes seemed to turn something over inside her. All these people were her responsibility too.

She suddenly remembered standing by her bedroom balcony as a child, crying, staring out over the landscape, certain that this was the day when her father would finally return and rescue her from the ache she felt every day so that she could sleep without nightmares. Sam remembered her certainty completely: her father *would* come, he would hold her in his arms, and she would never be afraid again.

She knew exactly how the villagers were feeling, and it made the heartache in her chest pound all the more for them.

ॐ ◆ ॐ

S am looked around at all the frightened people and swallowed hard. Akasha stood to her full height, light gleaming off her war armor, and the crowd stepped back.

The crowd began to murmur, a buzzing that grew louder with each passing second. Sam's attention caught and held on two women looking at her as if questioning why one of the queen's daughters, the youngest daughter, had come to their village. "We have come for the dragons," Sam said, her hands shaking slightly on the reins. Sam had no desire to explain that she was here without her mother's permission. If she did, she knew her courage would fail her, and she feared that the people of Blackwood would not believe she was (or could be) a dragon slayer. Sam was determined to prove to her mother—and to herself—

that she was brave enough and strong enough to protect the people of Quadling Country, her mother's realm, and all of Oz.

Her fears were misplaced. From the way the villagers were acting, they didn't see a spoiled princess disobeying her mother. Sam could feel from their gaze that what they saw was royal pride, the confident daughter of a queen, not a frightened, disobeying child. She could tell that they believed instantly when they saw her riding her mighty warhorse, striding into their village with her head held high, that she was a courageous woman who was willing to give her life to save them from the evil that had descended upon their town.

Without trepidation several spoke at once, offering to show the way to where the dragons had made their lair. "About eight miles northwest, milady," said one villager, a mother holding her daughter's hand as she pointed the way and curtseyed. "On the other side of the Tessa Green Forest there is a bridge that spans the Rockenteer Gorge and separates Quadling Country from Winkie Country."

Another villager jumped in, wanting to be helpful. "Cross the bridge, but keep a sharp eye out. Keep the Yip Mountain on your left. Less than a mile from the bridge, you'll see a cave."

Even though the villagers were eager to point Sam and Akasha in the right direction, they had no intention of getting anywhere near the scene of the battle. They knew they would be more of a hindrance than any kind of help, so they said their prayers and bade them Great Head speed. The villagers stood at the edge of their small town and watched Sam and Akasha head off in the direction of the Rockenteer Gorge, then returned to their homes to wait and see how events would unfold, with hope and a prayer in their hearts.

The clouds began to part and the sun edged toward the horizon, painting the sky and surrounding forest a brilliant gold. The trees shivered in delight, longing for a good night's rest. Soon, a crescent moon would grace the night sky and dance with the stars. They rode until the long shadows of dusk turned to the black shadows of night, and decided to stop and make camp and continue in the morning.

Ten

They had gone perhaps seven or eight miles after they broke camp in the morning, when the ground began to rise very rapidly. In a short time, they arrived at the foot of a small mountain. After traversing a narrow, curvy, rocky trail along the vast Rockenteer Gorge for an hour, a wooden bridge the villagers had told them they would find came into view, spanning almost two hundred feet across the great chasm. The bridge was old, but still sturdy. Moss and vines had found a place on the railings, hanging over and growing downward with tiny white flowers sprinkled over the green shoots like powdered sugar.

On the other side of the bridge, a sheer cliff that was part of another mountain range rose up to meet the clouds, and a narrow trail like the one they had just traveled upon followed the edge, which was large enough for one horse and a small wagon. Sam dismounted to walk Jo. He was hesitant at first to step onto the bridge and pulled back, shuffling his front hooves. She rubbed his face to calm him and pulled him gently to follow her onto the bridge. Still, he pushed back.

Akasha moved in front and walked onto the bridge. When Jo saw that the great cat wasn't afraid, Jo carefully moved forward and followed her. Sam looked over the railing. It was so deep she couldn't see the bottom, only the rock face descending into nothing but black. When they reached the other side, they were no longer in Quadling Country. They were in Winkie Country.

Once off the bridge, they turned to the right and continued along the narrow trail. They followed its snakelike path back and forth until it opened into a small meadow, with the Yip Mountain on their left and the Tessa Green Forest on their right. A runnel was gently flowing into the woods, water coming off the mountain. The villagers had said that a mile from the bridge, there would be a cave. The dragons lair. And there was.

∾ ✦ ⌁

Sam hung her sword around her waist and had her bow and quiver settled over her shoulder. Akasha stood on her two legs and settled her spear into the crook of her arm. Jo walked with his ears sharply forward and he snorted—Akasha noticed it too—when she smelled the smoke and the stench of burnt flesh. And there was something else. It was the unmistakable odor of death. It didn't matter to these creatures if their meat was cooked or raw. This was the redolence of dragons, with the entrance to their cave littered with the bones of their victims—animal or human, speaking or nonspeaking, it mattered not.

Jo, after his warning snort, paced closer to the cave, cautious, twitching, and nervously shaking his mane. Sam's grapevine crown held the tips of her ears and pointed toward the black hole in the mountain. There was a hillock twenty feet before the cave and a clearing. The rock ledge that surrounded the opening was rimmed with greasy smoke and the litter of past meals; bones and uneaten flesh spread out from the entrance into the once green and lush clearing, the ground now scorched and blackened. Here and there, a few branches of burnt-out trees still smoldered. Other than the crackling of the burning embers, it was deathly quiet.

Akasha stood still. Jo halted and lost his footing, but regained his balance quickly. Sam gazed into the black opening, and it occurred to her that the ground would be slippery for Jo's hard hooves, but not so for a dragon's sinewy claws. She patted Jo on his neck and quietly said, "Move carefully, Jo. Slow and easy."

A minute or two went by, and then Akasha asked, "How do we

get these creatures out and cleanse them? Do we yell? Throw a rock at them? Or yell, 'C'mon out and play'?" Just as the cat's spearpoint touched the blackened ground with doubt they heard rustling, clicking, clawing, deep-throated growling, and the heavy thudding of dragons tromping toward them. The sounds were approaching from the cave entrance and echoed all around them. The very ground came alive; dirt and small rocks, dead leaves and fallen branches jittered and danced. Sam's hair pricked up along her arms and Akasha's fur bristled.

One dragon raced out of the cave and moved quickly to their right, bloody quick on its yellowish, clawed feet. The next nimbly moved to their left, and the final dragon took flight and settled on the ground behind the dragon slayers. Sam and Akasha were surrounded.

Without hesitation, the demon beasts lifted their long-horned heads and scaly necks up to the sky and sucked in large amounts of air. They made a deep, rippling, throaty, gurgling sound. Then they abruptly dropped their heads low to the ground and let out powerful blasts of dragonfire, completely enveloping the trio—just like when they had stepped into the bonfire. However, this fire was different. It was hotter, different in color—reddish-orange and white—and smelled heavily of sulfur, which hurt their throats when they took a breath. As the three of them were bathed in the white-hot, blast-furnace dragon breath, they felt only a little warmth, but it pulled at them, seeking their lives. It washed over Akasha's spear, down the shaft to the handle, and fought to stay alive on her elbow, then flickered and slowly went out. Sam watched the fire on her arms and legs as small, individual flames danced along her skin, trying to find a spot to stay lit and burn her, then sputtered and vanished.

The fireproof ointment held.

She had no need for the magic spell she'd been practicing to ward off a blast of dragon breath if the fireproof balm didn't work. The miracle ointment was doing precisely what it was meant to do, and that knowledge gave her courage and cleared her mind. And like when she would fly, she felt the *rush* and lost her fear to the cry of battle.

But the dragons were a lot bigger than she'd expected. The book had said the smaller dragons were no bigger than a horse. But these scaled, vicious, and destructive monsters seemed as big as elephants. The dragon on the left closed its mouth and reached upward again to take in another deep gulp of air. It was a little smaller than the other two, maybe the youngest of the three. The scales on its snakelike neck shuddered, and a mean growl rumbled up from deep within its throat. Akasha ran forward, leaped into the air, and thrust her spear deep into the soft spot just below the dragon's jaw, on its neck—the weak spot that Sam had told her about.

As Akasha watched the creature wither and spout and cough up puddles of fire, it rolled on its back. Akasha yanked the spear from its neck. Dragonfire oozed out of the wound like molten lava, sputtering and spitting in all directions.

The cat spun around and jumped high into the air, twisting around into a back scissor-kick somersault, and landed with one bent knee on the dragon's stomach and the other wedged tightly on the monster's wing joint. Akasha stood up, leaned forward, pulled her elbows back hard and quick, and with one solid thrust, pushed the spear through the dragon's scales deep into its chest, cracking bone and perforating one of its lungs. Akasha jumped off the dying dragon as it let out a deep, rolling, pitiful-sounding squeal. It rolled over, coughing up more fire and trying to escape, but after only a few strides it began to weave and stagger, its hindquarters collapsing, its breath coming out in a harsh, wet wheeze. Then the vicious beast stopped, unable to do anything but lie there and watch the cat coming to kill it, panting as molten fire dripped from its lips.

Akasha's eyes were hard, without hate or pity, the eyes of a predator. She thrust the spear into the dragon's heart. The dragon thrashed, twitched. Then lay still.

➤

Sam kicked Jo hard in the ribs. His color turned a reddish orange with splotches of white, the same color as dragonfire. He reared up and shuffled his front legs, then raced toward the dragon on the right. For when that dragon saw that its companion had been pierced by a spear, it stopped belching fire and turned to look at its dying sister. It raised its wings and let out a horrifying cry of distress that harrowed Sam's very soul, prickling the back of her neck.

She had her bow and arrow poised and aimed at the point where the dragon's wing joint attached to its body. Her mind was clear, focused, determined. She closed her right eye and rested the other on her two fingers at the nocking point on the bowstring and looked down the arrow's shaft. The bowstring was so tight it bit into her skin, but the pain kept her alert. She took a breath, held it, and let her body move to the rhythm of Jo's gallop. Then she let the arrow fly. Her aim was perfect.

The arrow flew true and was sent with such force that the entire shaft went through the soft place where the dragon's scales were their thinnest, into the chest, slicing through the heart and exiting the other side. It was so quick the dragon instantly dropped to the ground with a sickening thud and was silent. Its mouth lay open and its tongue hung out as liquid fire slowly foamed and rolled onto the scorched earth. Sam could see the life leave its yellow, reptilian eye as it turned a cloudy, lifeless gray.

There was an angry scream from Jo, a warning that came too late for Sam to react. The other dragon slammed its huge tail into the side of Sam's face. Sam's head exploded with white light and pain, and the next thing she knew, she had been knocked off of Jo and was tumbling backward. She hit the ground hard, and everything went blurry. Her bow flew out of her hand and her quiver broke loose.

She tried to suck in a breath, but her mouth was full of something wet and warm. She coughed violently, spraying the ground with her own blood. The side of her face had gone numb. She reached up to her left temple and felt more blood. The sky was moving back and forth, and she thought she saw stars twinkling off and on. She tried to stand and couldn't, but instead fell into a sitting position, holding her whirling head. She sat frozen for a moment, her breath coming quickly. She was sweating in thick drips that trickled down her neck and back. The third dragon had lashed her and caught her squarely with its tail when it spun around. Sam spat repeatedly, trying to clear her mouth of blood, and saw a blurry figure moving toward her. She smelled the sulfur-laced flame before she felt the heat. She cleared her eyes in time to see the dragon coming at her. Dizzily and slowly, she made it to her feet. The dragon clawed at her. She tried to twist out of the way, but one of its talons raked across her arm, leaving behind a fresh, deep gash. The dragon slashed again with its claw. She ducked, then collapsed to her knees, clutching her arm, her face clenched tight with pain.

She saw Akasha out of the corner of her eyes, coming for her. When the dragon whirled around to face Sam and spray more dragonfire, the cat threw her spear. It stuck in the dragon's neck, but missed the soft spot under its jaw and lodged itself where the neck attached to the body. The hit slowed the dragon down enough to give Akasha time to leap over to Sam and help her stand as the dragon thrashed its neck to rid itself of the spear, stumbling and lumbering away.

"Are you okay?" she asked Sam quickly, keeping an eye on the wounded monster.

"Never better. Let's finish this."

The dragon's lips peeled back as though it was actually grinning. Its eyes laughed at Sam and Akasha, taunting them, daring them, with the promise that it would like nothing better than to tear their throats open and roast them to embers and ash.

Sam swallowed loudly, her mouth suddenly dry. Saran had taught her there was only one way to master fear: *to attack it head-on*. Sam took hold of the hilt of her sword and pulled it from its sheath. Akasha's spear hadn't struck a mortal blow, and the dragon twitched and lashed its tail, roaring in fury. It bent its head around to the wounded shoulder and grasped the spear with its teeth, wrenching it from its flesh and throwing it to the ground. Then it snapped its long, narrow neck back and spat fire at Sam and Akasha. Sam could tell that the dragon was surprised it hadn't killed them the first time with its flame. Its blazing breath had always dispatched its prey, and for an instant, it seemed puzzled, unsure how to kill these creatures.

It cautiously circled the dragon slayers. Akasha took a dozen steps forward with lightning speed and slid under the dragon's chest and front legs, kicking up blackened dust and dirt. Then she grabbed her spear as she slid in one quick movement and thrust it into the dragon's stomach. Red-hot dragon blood and steam gushed out of the wound. Akasha rolled out from under the dragon, ripping out her spear as she ran free. The dragon roared and swung around, breathing fire, to face Akasha. As it did, its tail lashed at Sam and brushed past her face so close she could feel and hear the *whoosh* of hot, rancid air rush across her forehead.

The dragon lowered its head and began to circle the princess. Sam knew if she took her eye off the dragon, even for a second, it would attack. Then, the dragon charged. *Now!* Sam screamed to herself. *Kill the beast!* She arched her back and felt the wind push against her skin as its tail whizzed past her again, inches above her body. She jumped up, slashed her sword up and down with all her strength, and chopped off the tip of the dragon's tail.

Quickly, the princess spun around and leaped back into the air and opened her wings. The dragon screamed, snapping its long, narrow neck around and gnashing its razor-sharp teeth. Sam flew directly under its snout, flipped up and over, flying past its eyes, then hovered directly behind its ears. The monster spread its wings out and lifted up a short distance in the air. Without any hesitation, holding her sword with both hands, Sam raised it above her head and in one fluid motion, slashed straight down hard and fast, cutting off the dragon's head with one mighty swing. The dragon's body went limp, its head spinning in the air and throwing globs of fire as it fell and then crashed to the ground. Its severed neck twisted violently back and forth, belching liquid fire until it too slammed to the ground with a heavy thud that shook the earth.

Then Jo raced up and bit the dragon's head above its eye socket, locking onto its ear, and the muscles of his heavy warhorse neck that ran with sweat and smudges of ash swung the dead dragon's head back and forth. He let it fly and Jo's hide turned coal black. He kicked the dirt with his back legs and shuffled his front ones in a victory dance, neighing and snorting loudly.

Sam walked over to a scorched and blackened nearby tree, reached down to the ground and sat with her back to the tree for a few minutes, knees drawn up, her head between them. Her head began to clear and Akasha walked over and sat next to her, dropping to all four legs and curling her tail around her body. Sam heard Jo's hoofbeats move toward her. She put her hands out and he nuzzled them with his nose, then pushed gently against her face.

"I know what you want," Sam said with a dusty voice, sore from inhaling hot air and smoke. "First, we rest." Jo snickered and shook his head, and the three of them remained there for a few more minutes.

When Sam's head cleared, she stood up and held onto Jo's reins. Akasha watched Sam and blinked her eyes to rid them of ash and dust. "Let's head back to the bridge," Sam said. She picked up Akasha's spear and threw it to her as she walked over and picked up her quiver, arrows, and bow, and then mounted Jo. "There was a brook with fresh water running out of the mountain back the way we came. Not far from here. I need a drink, and Jo wants an apple."

"He deserves two," Akasha said with a smile.

When they came to the rivulet, Sam took off Jo's saddle and bathed him. Then, after guiding Jo out of the deep stream and cutting up two apples for him, she returned to the water and splashed some on her face, washing the dried blood off. She then took off all her dragon-tainted clothing and battle gear and submerged. When her head breached the surface, she gasped for air—the water was cold and inviting. Her skin felt the comfort from it, and her heart was beating rapidly in her chest, still pounding in her ears from the excitement of the fight.

When it came to water, in this regard Akasha was not like any domestic kitty. Her kru, her breed of feline warriors, loved bathing. She did exactly the same as Sam and took off her armor and jumped right in, splashing and rolling around to wash away the dragon blood and the filth of the fight. Together, they brushed and rubbed Jo hard until his hide was gleaming and turned his calming cream color, and when they were warm and dry from tending to the horse, they dressed.

"We need to go back to the battlefield. I need one dragon tooth from each head," Sam said as she threw her saddle onto Jo's back.

"What in the Great Head's name do we need dragon teeth for?" Akasha asked, frowning.

"The dragon book said if we throw fragments of a dragon's tooth into the ground, dragon warriors will instantly sprout out of the dirt and fight by your side."

"And you believe that?"

"Not sure," Sam replied. "The book was right about the fireproof ointment. If it's right about dragon teeth and there is a war coming, I'd rather have dragon warriors fighting for us instead of against us."

With much reluctance, Akasha returned with Sam to the battleground and helped pull all the teeth from the jaws of the dead dragons. The dragons' eyes were glazed and jellied, staring back at them, the agony of their death plain to see. Other than a slight tightening of her jaw, Sam showed no emotion. She thought the horrible creatures looked smaller now that they lay motionless on the burnt ground, but no less menacing and dangerous. The dragons were vicious and cunning animals, and the battle could have turned out entirely different, especially if she had tried to fight them alone. Sam was sure that if Akasha hadn't been fighting alongside her, she would be lying in the dirt as fresh meat for the dragons' dinner instead of standing there unharmed and gathering the teeth of the three deceased monsters that lay there before them.

❧ ◆ ☙

Without warning, the sun disappeared and the sky turned black, and they felt the explosion of more dragonfire. So powerful it was, it knocked them to their knees. Sam and Akasha covered their faces with their forearms. The flames were so much more intense than the scorching breath from the dragons they had just killed, white like lightning, hotter than a blast of scalding air from a Quadling forge. It was a sizzling, searing hand of heat that pushed them backward toward the dragon cave and burned them.

"*Tobash-norku-turah,*" Sam spoke in a quiet but firm voice, focusing on the torrent of flames, her eyes turning bright orange. "*Tobash-norku-turah.*" A bluish, transparent light sparkled and shimmered and shielded them from the sizzling heat. But the fiery breath of this dragon was more potent than the magic Sam brought forth, and it bulldozed through the protective spell. *A fourth dragon!* Sam thought.

Akasha planted her claws into the ground but as hard has she tried, she was shoved back by the force of the inferno leaving deep furrows in the dirt. Sam spoke the words again with more force to give the spell greater power and keep it alive. But this dragon's fire seemed indomitable, much stronger than her incantation.

Jo had been quick enough to scramble away from the conflagration, and galloped to the edge of the forest. He paced and stamped at the tree line. His eyes showed white as he glared back at the massive dragon, his hide turning a blazing scarlet. *All our battle gear!* Sam thought to herself. *Akasha's spears, my bow—packed and tied to the saddle.* The only weapon they had was Sam's sword. She pulled it from its scabbard and held it with a firm grip. Akasha's claws were extended, ready for a fight.

The enormous dragon threw its gigantic head to the sky and roared, spewing dragonfire into the clouds. For a brief moment the sun returned, and that was time enough for Sam to see that this was no ordinary dragon. It was immense and shimmered red in the sunlight, and then she remembered that the book said there was always one large dragon, the alpha dragon, that controlled the smaller ones.

It lifted its mighty wings and darkness fell on the dragon slayers once again. A gale-like storm from the vast wingspan howled and rushed toward them. It made them take two steps back, but Sam and Akasha stood their ground as the hot air ruffled their hair. They had to squint their eyes to just slits to keep the dust and dirt from blinding them. The great beast was the apex predator.

The monstrous red dragon bowed its long neck to the ground and pointed its tapering snout directly toward them. Its half-lidded yellow eyes glared and scowled at the princess and great cat that had murdered its kin. Then it closed its eyes. It shook its head, lifting it to the sky, and made a thunderous rumbling along its long neck that shuddered and shook the earth. The deep-throated echoing sound rolled across Sam's skin and ruffled Akasha's fur. The monster turned away and pushed its nose into the side of one of the motionless dragons, hoping to coax it back to life. It sniffed and snorted and smelled each companion, but it knew the smell of death.

The great dragon turned back to its prey, yellow eyes opened wider, and then it began to grin. Smoke seeped out between its fangs, which were longer than Akasha standing straight and tall on two legs. The caustic smoke crawled in all directions along the ground and curled around Sam's and Akasha's feet, and then coiled up their legs and around their bodies, covering them entirely. They both coughed and gagged from inhaling the acrid smoke, which had a metallic taste that sat heavily on their tongues and reeked of sulfur that stung their eyes. It burned their throats and scorched their lungs, sucking away the clean air. And the dragon grinned even wider.

The smoke from its breath was so dense, the day had turned to night. Akasha and Sam couldn't see even a foot in front of them. The dragon swung away from them faster than any creature of that size should ever have been able to move, and the wind of its movement pushed so hard at them that Sam and Akasha stumbled. The gigantic, scaled monster threw its head hard and fast to the side and then to the sky with a sound like a mountain landslide. It lashed its long snout down and toward them, once more spitting out a long, searing stream of white-hot fire. Akasha's fur crackled, the tips bursting into flames, then burning away down to her hide. The skin on Sam's forearm, when she held it up to protect her face, instantly bubbled from the intense heat, as did the right side of her body and right thigh. The ointment wasn't able to hold back the fire anymore—not this kind of dragonfire. They both knew that another blast of this great dragon's breath could very well be the end. The great beast shook its head violently and they heard the hiss of rushing air as it inhaled to let loose another bout of fire. As it pulled in air, it also sucked in most of the smoke that surrounded them, and they could see the monster standing only a few feet away. The dragon's eyes were wide open, but each time it was about to send more fire their way, its eyes would close. Akasha crouched on all fours and ran forward past the dragon, ducking under the dragon's tail and running to the woods where Jo was still pacing and rearing on his hocks.

Sam unfurled her wings and shot up, straight along the dragon's long neck, and when the monster finished filling itself with air, it dropped its pointed head to let out its flame. Just before the beast closed its large, yellow eyes to release its burning breath, Sam let out a warrior's cry and plunged her sword into the center of its pupil. The force of the blow had all her weight behind it, carrying the sword deep into the eyeball, and as she pulled her sword free, she slashed it back and forth. The dragon's deft motion completely caught Sam off guard. It was quicker than she had anticipated. It clawed at its eye, slicing Sam across her left hip and thigh, knocking her hard to the ground. The great red dragon then opened its wings and took flight, retreating to lick its wound.

When Sam saw a great shadow looming over her, she was sure it would be the last thing she'd ever see, and for a split second she was certain she saw the dragon's jaws opening to devour her. The sun broke free and bathed her in soothing light, but the pain of her scorched lungs and the throbbing of her burnt skin was so intense, it almost made her forget about the gashes on her arm and leg. The wound on her thigh was bleeding freely. Her pant leg was soaked, turning the tan legging to a scarlet pool, and she felt wet rivulets dripping down her arm. Sam could smell her own blood, a coppery odor like the old pennies she kept in her keepsake box at home: dull round copper coins with the Great Head on the face. She was surprised and thought it strange that the smell of blood could trigger a good memory during a time of distress. But her mind was whirling, and nothing was making any real sense.

There was a red haze hanging before her eyes and she could not see clearly—when she blinked, it stung from the dragon's acid smoke. *I'm still alive*, she thought. She blinked again and saw in the distance two familiar but fuzzy shapes walking toward her. All her senses were in riot.

She tried to speak, but couldn't. Then the sun disappeared again, and the world went black.

Eleven

Akasha dreamed that she woke up, lying with her left arm curled around her head and Sam's head resting on her right paw. In her dream, Akasha noticed that her own arm and face were completely healed and Sam's terrible life-threatening gash along her hip had been cured, along with the horrible burns on the princess's face and left arm. She gently moved her paw away from Sam, careful not to wake her and sat up, paws falling easily into her lap. The moment reminded her of the languor and warm happiness of golden afternoons with her friends and family.

Every movement she made was slow moving, like she was underwater struggling against a stiff current. Akasha rubbed her cured arm to make sure it was whole and healthy, and it was. She touched her face and thought cheerfully that she had had the most remarkable dream about an enormous red dragon that she and Sam fought, and they had won the battle. She was standing in front of the lair of the dragons. A little gust of burnt-smelling breeze slid across her cheek, ruffling her fur, and the sound of her pawsteps became the crunch of ash and cinder. Small patches of fire littered the blackened earth. The red dragon's snaky neck lay stretched out along the ground, the long red snout looking like a barrier of burnt-red stone. Ash lay heaviest against the enormous red beast in spite of the breeze, and around the monster the gentle gusts lifted grayish clouds that swirled and swelled and dwindled so that it was hard to tell where the fiendish fire-breather ended and the earth began.

Then Akasha suddenly realized that her fur wasn't its lustrous coal black with gray markings anymore, but now was fingerprinted with white and black markings. Panic seized her; she was confused, unsure, maybe not awake and possibly stuck in a dream that seemed real. She was sure she was not herself, but something new, reborn, and the dream of the red dragon had not been a dream at all, but real. She remembered everything. And instead of winning the battle, they had lost. And the dragon was still alive.

As the dream continued, Akasha was finding it difficult to breathe and slow her heart from pounding out of her chest. She sat down, resting her back against a tree.

"I can help the princess," said a dark and chalky voice that reverberated all around her and inside her head.

But where Akasha was at that very moment, she did not know, and she still was not sure if she was awake or in a dream, so she could not be sure that the words spoken could be trusted. She looked up from where Sam lay sleeping peacefully on the ground and saw a tall man in a dark red, ground-length robe, ragged in appearance, his yellow eyes piercing through the shadow that covered his face from inside the hood of his robe. Akasha stood to face the raggedy man and fight him if he made the wrong move. He kneeled down and touched Sam's forehead and examined her burns and the inflamed gash.

"Akasha," he said with a kind but anxious voice. *"Do not fear me. I am here to help the princess."*

"This is not real," Akasha said, more to herself than to the man kneeling before her. *"This is nothing but a dream. It's the dragon smoke that has choked my mind."* Akasha circled the man, taking a fighting stance, and then said, *"You are not real. Begone, you ghost."*

The raggedy, hooded man stood up and the sky instantly went dark. Swirling gray-and-black clouds formed above him. His yellow eyes flared and when he spoke, he spoke in a powerful voice that echoed in every direction, *"AKASHA, OF THE SHADOW MOUNTAIN KRU . . . ,"* then his voice slowly softened and his eyes settled. *"I mean you no harm."* And just as quickly as the thunderous, black clouds had formed, they waned to a purple-gray and swirled and shifted, then rolled into each other, gradually turning a dull, washed-out gray. A rent formed in the overcast, a bright shaft of sunlight sneaked through, birds began singing, and the deep, throaty voice became gentle and kind again. *"You have need of me. I am the Crow. Bring the princess to me so you and she can aid her mother, the Good Witch, in a battle that has already begun."* He reached one hand out to Akasha and touched her shoulder and said, *"You know where to find me."*

The great cat's body shuddered from his touch. *"Silver Lake,"* Akasha replied, and then she broke free of the dream, repeating what she had just said. "Silver Lake."

S am woke screaming—or would have screamed, if her ravaged throat had been able to do so. She moved to sit up, but couldn't. It was like a long, sharp, double-edged knife ripped through her and cut her in half. Sam lay back down, put her hand on her forehead, looked up, and saw the early morning light filtering through leaves being gently pushed by a cooling breeze. She listened to the soothing rustle and then heard the unmistakable huffing and snorting of Jo.

Sam turned her head and there was her faithful horse, inches away, dipping his head down to get a better look at her and nuzzle her. She reached over and slowly rubbed his nose. Jo shivered, and he whinnied eagerly but uncertainly. "What happened, Jo?" she said with a muted voice, and discovered that her voice was not entirely gone—she could at least speak. But her throat was throbbing. She put her hand down and felt her crown and sword on her sleeping blanket next to her side and turned again to rub Jo's face.

"You've been asleep for three days," Akasha said as she poured hot tea in a cup and walked over to Sam. She put her large paw behind Sam's head and carefully lifted it to help her sip some tea. "I had to tie you to Jo so you wouldn't fall off." Sam swallowed the tea and winced. Her throat was swollen and sore. She took another drink, but it burned and she coughed. It was difficult to swallow—the liquid wouldn't flow easily down her throat, and she had to persuade it with much effort. She moved her wounded leg to try and sit up again, but the feeling reawakened to horrible life as though shards of glass were being driven into her thigh.

"What happened?" she croaked, and coughed again.

"After you sliced the dragon's eye, the beast hit you squarely in the leg with its wing-talon. You hit the ground hard. Really hard." Sam sipped more tea. This time, it was easier for her to swallow.

"Where are we?"

"On our way to the Crow," Akasha answered.

"The Crow?"

"The dragon must have knocked your hearing out of whack too," Akasha said, her smile spreading to her furry cheeks. "Yes, the Crow. You've been having nightmares and calling out for the Crow. So, I'm taking you to the Crow."

"To Silver Lake?" Sam asked, slurring her words. She felt beads of sweat on her forehead despite the cool morning breeze and knew she had a fever.

"Yes, to Silver Lake. And yes, you have a fever." Akasha took the cup of tea from her and walked back to the fire to fill it. "I'm worried about the gash on your leg. The villagers helped dress your wound, and we put a lot of your fireproof ointment on it and wrapped it as best we could. The ointment is working well on your burns and the slash on your arm, but on your leg wound . . . if we don't get it treated soon . . . The villagers also sent a messenger to your castle to warn them of the giant red dragon and to tell them of our battle."

Sam looked at Akasha through a foggy haze, then to Jo, and then at the sunlight peeking through the leaves. It all began spinning back to her: the three dragons they killed, the heat of the flames, the red dragon, the *pain*. She briefly thought with apprehension that once the messenger delivered the news to Saran, there would be hell to pay, and she would never be able to leave the castle ever again. The scolding from Augie would last a lifetime and beyond. This, she was sure of. Then the realization overcame her hot and fast and full of disconcertion. She became dizzy. Her eyes rolled to the back of her head and her lids closed. She had been wandering in and out of consciousness for the past three days, drifting back and forth within the ambit of the living and the dead. Each time she woke, her mind was walking through dark shadows. She'd ask the same questions, and Akasha would tell her the same thing over and over. She opened her eyes once more, tried to focus, but couldn't. She let the soft sounds the breeze made as it pushed through the leaves, and Akasha's voice, hold her. Once again, her eyes rolled to the back of her head, but this time she slept, or fainted.

Akasha listened to the gurgling rasp of Sam's breathing, and even the most shallow of breath rattled in her lungs. "Soon," Akasha said to Jo as she poured what was left of the tea onto the fire, "if her fever doesn't break, the red dragon will have won. Our only hope is the Crow." Jo nodded his head and huffed as if he understood the alarm that resounded in Akasha's voice and the anxiousness in her eyes. But this worried Akasha, so she used a softer tone and more positive words, hoping to ease the horse's distress. "She'll be fine, Jo. I'm sure of it. Your princess is a strong cub." Each time they stopped to make camp or rest, Jo would stay close to Sam. And as he did now, to show his concern he'd blow down along her cheek, touch his nose to her shoulder, and stand by her side to guard her. And when sleep took hold of him, he'd rest his nose on the ground near his folded knees and Akasha would lay Sam against Jo's side to keep her warm. The horse would stay still to keep her protected and let her sleep, not moving a muscle or even swatting at insects with his tail.

S am wasn't looking as good as Akasha had hoped. The fire ointment had reduced the inflammation, but Sam's leg was still very swollen. Her face was red with fever, and she continued to drift in and out of consciousness.

The dragon had scorched Akasha severely. She had looked only once at her own injuries and felt so sick from the sight she dared not look again until they were healed. But, now, on the fourth day, Sam's fire ointment had healed her almost completely. She even saw that some of her fur was actually growing back.

Oddly, like in her dream about the Crow, her fur was coming back white instead of her luxurious black. Her first thought was the burn marks on her coat looked mismatched, different, unlike her clan. It took a strong will to acknowledge that once she was healed, she would look different than her own kind and not be ashamed or embarrassed because of it, but rather use it as a sign of strength and bravery in a battle well fought. She was a determined and self-willed Shadow Mountain Cat, proud of her heritage, something that had always been evident throughout her life, especially when she had taken up arms in the war to give talking animals the same rights as all citizens of Oz. The cat had been an outcast before, subjected to incarceration for speaking her mind. Akasha knew what it felt like to be different than the crowd. She told herself after the war for the right of speech that the most inalienable of all animal rights—to speak their minds freely among all the peoples in the great land of Oz—had been honorably won in battle. She was proud that she had successfully done a great deed and had been heroic. She felt exactly the same now as she did then, even though she and Sam had not won their battle with the great red dragon. But they had fought a good fight. "Things will be different the next time we stand paw to talon with the great red beast," she said out loud to herself.

But Sam's injury from the dragon's talon worried her deeply. It was a nasty, festering gash. And where the princess had been waking from her deep sleep a few times during the daytime and evening hours, she now rarely opened her eyes, and when she would gain a moment of clarity, her eyes would quickly ghost over and she'd fall back into the shady recesses of her subconscious.

⊰ ✦ ⊱

They had been traveling east, back to the crest of the great Quadling Peaks—mountains always on their left, the Enchanted Forest on their right, and the Forest of Fighting Trees to their front. There was no trail for Akasha to follow, but she knew her way to Silver Lake, as it was a place where her clan had laid claim as sacred ground, made for prayer and meditation.

They came at last to a large hummock in the shape of a roaring lion; it looked over a pocket valley in the lower hills of the mountain range, near the largest of three lifeless volcanos that had once spewed lava from their bellies. Their crowns were rimmed with snow, and the wind pushed clouds that rolled over the edges and down their faces. The middle volcano was their destination, and the rays of the late afternoon sun cut across the tips of the pines growing along the ridge. The shadows began to deepen and Akasha cupped a paw across her brow, shielding her eyes from the light as she looked out across the landscape. She gazed at the small, undistinguished basin at the foothills of the mountain. It was well-furnished with thick grasses, flowers, and groves of trees, and she smiled because she knew they were close to their destination. This hollow was unique, only because from the mouth of the roaring lion rock there was a deep coulee that cut the dale in half.

Seeing the lion's head was as if the cat had been kneed into moving on and not stopping. But the sun was falling quickly. Soon it would set. Akasha paused, thinking it might be best to stop here, a perfect place to set up camp for the night and give Jo a chance to graze on the delicious grasses that filled the valley.

As if listening to Akasha's thoughts, Jo shuffled his hooves and kicked the ground, uninterested in the lush green grass that covered the vale. He nudged Akasha in the back and snorted. She looked back over her shoulder at him and said, "All right, big guy, we'll keep going."

The sun walked below the tree line; the light turned a vibrant pink and quickly thinned, and then a few minutes later, disappeared completely. Because Akasha could see just as well in the dark as she could during the day, she had no issue with walking the steep, narrow, rocky path to Silver Lake that began directly behind the roaring head of the lion rock. With the sun below the horizon, Akasha put a blanket over Sam's shoulders to keep her warm from the night chill. Sam was unconscious, and it made no difference to stop and set up camp—it was far better to reach Silver Lake as soon as they could, to find the Crow and hope that he would keep his word and help them as he'd said.

The only sound Akasha heard the entire night was the clomp, clomp of Jo's hooves stepping on hard dirt and rock along the path. By dawn, they were both exhausted and found their breathing much more difficult due to the altitude, but they were close. Still they toiled on, sweat running down Jo's shoulders though the air was crisp, making their final steps all the more difficult to tread. When they came to the crest of the volcano, they looked down at the peaceful lake sleeping silently in its center.

They had arrived at Silver Lake, and the air was filled with the sweet, wet aroma of pure, fresh water. It lay heavy on their tongues and made them thirsty. The water of the lake was so crystal clear it looked like silver and reflected the sky above, making it appear as if the clouds were floating on the earth itself.

As they followed the short path down close to the edge of the lake where the ground leveled off abruptly, Akasha could feel the magic pouring out from the water of the lake and surrounding the entire valley. It was a powerful feeling, to the point of making her a little lightheaded. For hundreds of years her kru regarded this vale as sacred ground.

Two rows of hundreds of pine trees held the trail on both sides, and at the end of the short path they came to a small, open glen at the far extremity of which, no more than a couple acres square, was a low tableland upon which they beheld a plaza. Akasha mounted Jo and held Sam around her waist. They galloped toward this large, open, man-made structure, entering what appeared to be a ruined roadway of broken cut stone leading from the plaza to the edge of the tableland where they had been standing, and ending abruptly in a flight of broad steps.

Akasha carefully nudged Jo up the stairway and walked him slowly across the courtyard to the entrance of a magnificent edifice. She had never rested her eyes upon anything like it before. It was cut directly out of the very wall of the volcano. Two massive pillars stood at attention on either side, holding up an archway that was some hundred feet in width and projected from the building proper to form a huge canopy above the doorway that opened into the heart of the mountain, with another flight of steps to gain entrance. The building was enormous, constructed of gleaming white marble inlaid with polished onyx stones that sparkled and scintillated in the sunlight.

Above the doorway, etched into the stone, were words written in an ancient language unknown to Akasha.

Δεν Υπάρχει Μέρος Σαν Το Σπίτι

And standing in the shadow of the portal was a tall dark figure.

Jo showed no sign of alarm, and Akasha recognized the man from her dream, with his piercing yellow eyes hidden by the shadow from the hood of his ragged, rusty-red robe.

It was the Crow.

Twelve

The Crow scooted past Akasha without looking at her and walked over to Jo.

He moved quickly, shoulders slumped, forgotten for the moment his normal strong, straight-shouldered posture and careful gestures. It was a controlled body language designed to match the flowing robe he always wore, but now was replaced with concern for the princess. His boots were soft-soled and his footsteps silent. Even with rolled shoulders he was tall, taller than Jo by a good yard, and he scooped Sam up as if she were made of straw. Fear crossed his face. He brushed past Akasha again, who looked in awe at this giant of a man. Without glancing at her he marched up the six steps to the entrance—in two strides—and said in a commanding yet kind tone, "Are you coming?" Then he disappeared into the blackness of the doorway.

೧ ♦ ೬

Akasha hesitated, but only for a second, before following the man. Inside, the steps faded into a gentle incline, which turned into a long, wide, arched, stone hallway. Hundreds and hundreds of candles floated in the air, layers upon layers reaching thirty feet. The soft candlelight illuminated a massive fresco on the ceiling depicting the Tin Woodman, the Cowardly Lion, the Scarecrow, and Dorothy Gale skipping together arm in arm through the Enchanted Forest along the Yellow Brick Road, with hope etched upon their smiles and wonder glinting in their eyes—cheerful, oblivious times. Then the painting faded into a vicious battle where the happy-go-lucky foursome donned their ornate battle armor, held swords and pikes high in the air, and screamed for blood as they stood alongside Sam's mother and the Princess Ozma. Hundreds of warriors were engaged in battle, exchanging blows with the Wicked Witch of the West and her winged monkeys, fighting and dying in the middle of a vast poppy field that was in full bloom. Such beauty, mixed with such horror and the cruelty of war.

The entire scene knocked the breath away from Akasha, and the cold stone floor sent shivers up and down her spine, making her fur bristle. The great hall opened into an enormous chamber, encircled by gallery insets cradling sculptures of famous people of Oz from the beginning of time, many who Akasha could not identify. Scattered about the chamber, there were at least eight large tables and maybe seven cabinets filled with papers and books, and along the walls were rows and rows of bookshelves.

There were so many candles sprinkled about that it was impossible to count them all. Dozens of the books were haphazardly strewn on the floor, open and tossed around, resting on worktables or on chairs, and some very large ones were chaotically arranged on a large, ornate wooden writing desk. Quills, manuscripts, single sheets of paper, and vellum were laid out in every direction. Some had found their way to the ground, while others rested peacefully on two tapestried wing chairs that sat on either side of the enormous fireplace. There were numerous potions and flasks filled with colored chemicals and herbs of all kinds. Large and small pestles for grinding, test tubes, various burlap sacks filled with minerals, and jars of rare and exotic oils were sitting on the tables and on the ground.

The amber flames burned evenly in the immense walk-in fireplace, bathing the room in their soft, caramel glow. The design of which was easily big enough for ten grown women and men to stand in shoulder to shoulder in the opening with its elaborately decorated mantelpiece that stretched twenty feet from end to end. It had been carved directly out of the igneous rock wall with figureheads of the Scarecrow, Cowardly Lion, Tin Woodman, Dorothy, Glinda, and the Princess Ozma. The fireplace was ablaze with tree-sized logs that spat and sparked and crackled, with a stack of logs piled six feet high on each side, waiting for their turn to be thrown into the blaze.

And standing by the fireplace were the Tin Woodman and the Cowardly Lion. Akasha could not believe her eyes. She rubbed them. *Ghosts*, she thought, *a trick of the light*. She looked again, and still, she could not believe what she was seeing. It was not a trick, and they weren't ghosts. Two of the greatest warriors for animal rights, and the rights of all the citizens of Oz, were literally standing before her, in the flesh. She rubbed her eyes again, and there they were still, bowing their heads to her as if she were royalty, as if they knew exactly what she was thinking—knew that she *was* royalty, something she'd kept hidden from Sam. Akasha had only seen drawings of the famous duo. And actually seeing them now, in the flesh, was beyond belief; it made her legs feel like melted butter and her fur prickle.

The Tin Woodman stood straight and tall at over six feet, with piercing green eyes that sparkled as he gazed at Akasha. His skin was silver in color, and he wore his tin can funneled hat; the red heart-shaped clock the Wizard of Oz had given him was riveted to his tinplated chest. And the Cowardly Lion, standing to the Tin Woodman's right, was at least a foot taller than the Tin Woodman, if not more. He was dressed in a red-and-black plaid kilt and had the same twilled cloth draped over his shoulder with medals of honor pinned to it. He was well-groomed, his blond, bay-colored fur neatly brushed and combed, curling at the ends, and he looked stately, powerful, in control, courageous. But he also looked tired, his large, dark brown eyes ringed with hollows that suggested he hadn't slept in some time.

The Crow carefully set Sam in one of the high-backed tapestried chairs by the fire. She opened her eyes but saw only hazy, indistinct shadows of movement—a man, she thought. The Crow picked up a goblet, poured a reddish liquid from one of his flasks, and glared at it, waving his hand over it. He closed his eyes and muttered over it, saying softly to himself, "This should help." The liquid bubbled and foamed up to the rim but did not roll over, then fizzed and settled back down.

He placed Sam's hands on the goblet while he held the stem to keep it steady. His hands were rough like sackcloth, but warm like cuddling against Jo during a cold night. The haze covering Sam's eyes lessened. The man was beginning to come into focus. "Who are you?" she asked with a weak voice, looking at the glowing yellow eyes of the hooded man.

"Drink," he said. "And rest. We have much to accomplish, you and I."

Sam took a sip obediently, without hesitation, as she had obeyed Augie when Augie had her drink the remedies she made for colds and fevers when Sam was a child. She knew this man from her dreams and was not afraid. She felt his good-natured spirit instantly and took another sip, a stronger gulp than the first. Then she reached for the man's hood. He did not move, letting her do as she wished. Sam slowly pushed the hood off his head. The man's face was tightly pulled burlap and was painted with such remarkable human-like detail it was impossible to tell if it was painted on by an artist's steady hand, or if it was real. His painted dark-red lips turned up at the corners, showing a warmhearted and understanding smile, and his eyebrows, stitched in thick lines of dark brown embroidery, were wrinkled with concern.

Sam gently touched the Crow's cheek to make sure she was not in a dream. His burlap skin was rough on her palm like the morning stubble on her father's face. "You're the Scarecrow," Sam said with a languorous surprise. The Scarecrow nodded his head in agreement and removed his pointed, wide-brimmed felt hat that had patches stitched on it covering tears and torn edges from years of use. He placed it over his heart, revealing his bald, burlap head. Sam blinked twice to fight the haze, then held her eyes down with force before she opened them again. "I know you," Sam continued dreamily, her hand relaxing and falling to her side. "At least, I think I know you. I mean, you . . . you were in my dreams. Yes, in my dreams, and you watched me drown. You just stood there and did nothing . . . just watched me fall into the lake and let me . . . no, wait. You pushed me . . ." Her words floated on the air like loose strands of spider silk, and the Crow became two scarecrows as Sam's tired eyes refused to focus. Her eyelids were tingling and quickly grew heavy, and once again everything around her turned to black.

Sam woke startled, pressed down with many blankets in a simple, narrow bed. She sat up, though the movement brought a sharp warning twinge from her left leg. Exploring the area with her fingers, she reached down and felt a large bandage wrapped around her leg. She wrestled with the enshrouding blankets, shedding them one by one, then worked her way to the edge of the bed and dangled her feet off the soft feather mattress. The air was cold around her ankles. But sitting up was painful, her hip and thigh muscles seeming to peel away from the bone. She felt her left arm, where another bandage was wrapped around a sticky poultice, and she could feel stitches.

She put her hand to her forehead, and it felt normal. Her fever was gone, yet she felt frail, though somehow safe, with a seamless, transparent comfort, like when she woke on Sunday mornings in her large velvet-curtained bed at her mother's castle, knowing that Augie would be bringing her a breakfast tray of pancakes and trussleberry syrup. She blinked drowsily and rubbed her eyes, trying to look at her surroundings and get a grasp on where she was. It was difficult to focus. She noticed the pillows on the bed were wrapped in smooth, dark cloth, and above, there was a large circular shaft that had been cut into the ceiling, directly through the mountain on a slight angle to let the light sift in. The bed she was sitting on was one of many that hugged the walls of the large bedchamber. All were neatly made except for hers, with the same soft blankets and pillows.

There were two other shafts cut high into the lengthwise wall opposite the one her bed rested against, where more natural light filtered into the room, the walls themselves high enough that if it weren't for the hundreds of candles that floated in midair, the arched ceiling would be all but covered in darkness. Chiseled into the gray stone walls above the headboards of each bed were beautifully carved reliefs: dragons, the talking apple trees, the Wicked Witches of the West and East, one of Mombi, and one of Locasta, the Good Witch of the North, and all the hidden witches of Oz. There was one of her mother and her father with his wings spread out in all their splendid glory. There was another with her father wrapping his arms and wings around her mother, pressing his forehead to the woman he loved, while Sam and her sister Elle played sword-fighting at their feet.

A short distance away there was an open doorway, and beyond it was the Scarecrow's main chamber—she could see the fire in the fireplace blazing brightly. Her stomach grumbled. She was certain she smelled freshly cooked bacon. She rubbed her eyes again and slowly, she realized four figures were walking toward her. Sam tilted her head just a little to one side and squinted. She was beginning to see clearly. She recognized the people standing before her—Akasha, the Tin Woodman, the Cowardly Lion, and the Scarecrow. The Scarecrow was holding a goblet and stepped forward, handing the cup to her. "You're still weak, Princess. Drink this."

"Who did my bandages?" Sam asked.

"I did," the Scarecrow replied. "I used some of your ointment. And a healing poultice of my making."

"Thank you," Sam said sheepishly, then realized that she wasn't wearing her own clothing, but a gown of soft, gray cotton; someone had washed her hair and given her a bath. She looked up at the Scarecrow, her cheeks reddening.

"Yes, me as well," he said as his eyes ignored Sam's embarrassment.

"I feel I've been in and out of a bad dream for days," she said in a throaty voice as she took the goblet and held it in both hands, looking directly into the Scarecrow's eyes. "Some of it was beautiful.

But most of it was terrifying. There was a great battle . . . and . . ." She took another sip, keeping her eyes on the Scarecrow. With a shaking finger, she pointed at him and each person standing before her. "You, and you, and you . . ." she smiled and looked at Akasha, and said with a loving heart, " . . . and you were there." Akasha sat on one side of the bed by Sam's feet. "It was so real. I can still hear the screams of the injured and dying and the smell of death." Then she hesitated and continued, "But that's impossible, isn't it? You couldn't have been there. It was just a dream." The liquid from the goblet was fresh and sweet, and lay lightly on her tongue. When she swallowed it rolled down smoothly, like soothing spring rain.

"Dreams are the foretellers of what might become," the Scarecrow said.

"What happened to you?" demanded Sam, curling her lips. "My mother thought you had died when you disappeared . . . you, you broke her heart. She loved you. My bedtime stories were about you, all of you. But you, Scarecrow . . . you were her favorite."

"I am truly sorry for that," the Scarecrow said with a regretful sigh.

"The citizens of Oz thought you to be a great Wizard," Akasha added curtly, wrapping her tail around her waist and gripping it firmly. "So did I. So did my kru. You ruled with dignity and fought for our right to speak freely. I was there when you gave your proclamation of passion for all Ozarians to rise up and fight the old régime and tear down the detention centers. Everyone was lost for so long without you. The Great Head we have now is nothing but a figurehead of little worth, and easily swayed. He has ignored the signs of evil that again threaten our freedom."

"Don't be hard on our brother," the Cowardly Lion said.

"Yes," the Tin Woodman quickly added. "Don't be harsh. When Jinjur's army took over the Emerald City we were given a choice, leave the city, or stay and be slaves."

Sam tilted her head back slightly, taking the last sip from the goblet and then handing it back to the Scarecrow. When he reached for it, she held his burlap hands in hers, and with a softer, kinder voice, asked again, "What happened to you, Crow?"

"All I had ever wanted was to have a brain. And when the great and powerful Wizard, the Great Head of that time, gave me one, well, I thought about everything I could possibly think of, and couldn't think of anything more . . ." He paused, took in a breath, sighed, and continued. "I knew everything about everything. I thought the Wiz gave me an ordinary brain, a simple forty-eight ounces of gooey, gray matter, but he didn't. He gave me so much more. Then I realized anybody with half the brain I had could be the Wizard. I had to rethink everything I knew. And when General Jinjur took the throne from me, I came here and built this sanctuary. I carved the history of Oz on its walls and painted it on the ceilings and I stopped thinking and just let my mind wander. Now I know more than I ever thought I could possibly know." He kneeled to let Sam see his face better, so she could look directly into his gleaming, yellow-painted eyes and know of his steadfast sincerity. "Like you, Sam," he said. "I know you. I know what you are capable of. It's the reason I called you here."

"How long have I been asleep?"

"Two days," said Akasha, purring as she spoke. "Five, if you count the ride here. The Scarecrow healed the wound on your leg with herbs and magic. He was impressed with the dragonfire ointment you made. I thought you were a goner for sure."

"You still need to rest," the Scarecrow cautioned her.

"I've rested enough. I'm fine." But when she set her feet on the cold stone floor, her body winced and her breath shot out in a quick painful groan. Then she lost her balance, closed her eyes, and began to sway, leaning against the Scarecrow. Every muscle in her body screamed as though it was being shredded, and her wounded thigh felt like raw flesh, like a seam had peeled open all the way down her leg. She took in a slow breath, regained her balance, and stepped forward, releasing her grip on the Scarecrow but stumbling. The Cowardly Lion and Tin Woodman caught her arms and held her by the waist. She crumpled her brow, trying to work past the pain. Then her stomach rumbled again. "Is that bacon I smell?"

"Yes," said the Tin Woodman. His eyes twinkled. "Fresh bacon. A boar slaughtered and smoked a few days ago."

"It's very good indeed," the Cowardly Lion said with a hungry smile, then added, "There is plenty waiting for you."

"My crown?"

"On the bedside table, Your Majesty," the Lion said as he picked it up and handed it to Sam. "Waiting patiently for you to wake."

She put it on, and immediately the grassy green shoots started prodding and poking her nose, pinching her cheeks and pulling at her earlobes, pleased to have her back.

When she looked at the fire blazing away in the fireplace, it seemed a very, very long way from the sleeping chamber to where the plates of food sat on the table by the hearth. At least, it seemed long to Sam. Her eyes were still playing tricks on her, still working to find focus. She could see the Scarecrow close his hands on the high back of one of the tapestried chairs he stood behind next to the table of food as he watched her. He pulled the chair out as a welcome gesture for her to come, to sit and eat. Akasha had already seated herself in the other chair at the opposite end of the table, grabbing two large, thick chunks of bacon and placing them on her plate.

Sam shuffled her feet slowly along the cold stone floor with the help of the Tin Woodman and the Cowardly Lion, and leaned up against the chair the Scarecrow was holding for her. She looked up at him and smiled as she sat down, though he felt her eyes were studying him in a way he did not like, as if Sam's smile were more a question of his motives than a display of kindness. He returned her smile with a concerned, questioning frown of his own, and Sam chortled—a gentle, subtle sound like the wisp leaves make when a gentle breeze pushes through them. She tilted her head, giving him a soft, kind, knowing grin. "I may not have a brain like yours, my dear Crow," she said, taking a cloth napkin and putting it in her lap. "Though I am smart enough to see a scowl hidden behind that smile and trepidation etched upon your brow."

"You and your sister are the keys," the Scarecrow said. "You, Sam, have waited too long to come here. As has your sister. But it is she who I am the most worried about, now that you have arrived and are safe."

My sister, my mother, she thought to herself. Her mind echoed busily with worry when the Scarecrow mentioned her sister. Sam looked around the room. So many books and papers. The long walls full of leather-bound volumes caught her eye.

One Christmas when she was six or seven, she found a present from her mother and father in her bedroom: a built-in daybed next to a tall wooden bookshelf filled with books, fiction on the right and nonfiction on the left. The daybed was covered with pillows and quilts made for cozy nights of reading. The memory of collapsing onto the daybed and reading a book with her sister while sharing a quilt made her eyes pool. She placed both hands on the table and closed her eyes. The heat from the fireplace touched her face. Her smile ebbed away. The image of her mother and sister meeting with King Rumpart instantaneously became vivid, as if she were standing there with them in the great hall of Rumpart's castle, pushing the happy memory of reading with her sister to the back of her mind.

In the next instant, a snapshot of the dragons she and Akasha had dispatched slapped her hard; the acid flames from the monstrous, vicious red dragon and the sting of its claws slashing her skin and cutting deep into her thigh reignited; the Crow, now the Scarecrow, in her dreams, the silver lake, drowning, the evil descending upon Oz— everything came back to life, glaring and bold and knocking her mind back and forth. And now, the dream of the horrible battle that raged for days struck her with dreadful force.

She inhaled deeply and let it out slowly. She could hear the squeaking joints of the Tin Woodman as he sat down at the table to her left and she thought he should be oiled, which made her grin. She heard the soft, padded gait of the Cowardly Lion's paws as he walked over to a chair and scooted it across the stone floor. She knew the Scarecrow was sitting next to her, close and to her right, with his musty smell and rustling straw. She felt the coarse but gentle, warm touch of his burlap hand as it covered hers to confer his understanding, as if he knew what she was thinking at that very moment.

She slowly pulled her hand away from his, opened her eyes, unsure of herself, "My mind seems somewhat lost, yet set in its way. I see only the eensy-weensiest speck of light where dangerous shadows loom . . . so many strange dreams of late . . . no thanks to you, Crow." She raised her hands to her face to cover her fear, tilted her head forward, and rested her elbows on the table. "It was easier, Crow," she said through closed fingers, "not to believe the visions you placed in my dreams rather than to accept them as truth." There was a silence that sat between them. Sam stirred and dropped her hands, but her face remained forlorn and she looked straight at Akasha, alarmed. "Jo?" she abruptly asked.

"Smacking his lips to his heart's content in a luscious meadow filled with tall sweetgrass," Akasha assured her. "He's having the time of his life filling his belly and getting fat."

Sam groaned and rolled her eyes in approval. "That pleases me more than you know," Sam said, wiping away tears. "I don't know what I would do without him," she smiled. "Or you, Akasha."

Akasha rolled her eyes as well. "Please don't get all mushy on me. Eat some bacon."

Thirteen

Many days had passed. Precious healing days for Sam—resting, getting to know her new friends, laughing, riding, grooming Jo, talking to him and convincing him that everything would be fine, and stretching her wings with lots and lots of soaring through the air. *Flying! The greatest healing power of all, better than any herb or magic*, she thought. *Catching the wind and playing tag with the clouds*. She had flown all over Silver Lake, from one end to the other, skimming its glassy, glacier-cold waters, leaving snowflakes behind in her wake. She was beginning to feel like herself again, a little wiser and a little happier, yet troubled and worried for her mother and sister.

She'd traverse the entire volcano and let the updraft take her to the top of the great Quadling Shadow Mountain Peaks, where she'd watch the sunrise in the morning. And there were moments she wanted only to take long, directionless walks through the crater's pine forest. But if she were absent too long, Akasha would always find her without any trouble, and on many occasions they hiked together, soaking in the beauty of their surroundings and the close bond that was growing between them.

Once when they went out hunting for game, Akasha's skill, cunning, and quick, merciful kills reminded her of how her father taught her to hunt. Akasha had just caught a rabbit, and as she pranced up to Sam with the cony between her teeth, time had suddenly slipped backward. Sam saw her father, heard his voice as clearly as if he were beside her, his fingers cleverly weaving reeds through a series of holes punched in a piece of sanded wood. *"Now Sam, we purposely make the reeds just tight enough that the rabbit cannot escape the trap, but not so tight that the poor thing suffocates before we find her. We have to hunt to survive, but a good hunter makes sure the animal suffers as little as possible."* The pain of not having her father often found its way back to the front of her thoughts, and each time it did she'd hold on to the necklace he'd given her, closing her eyes and saying a prayer. Special memories of her father cut deeper than a knife—that was the Great Head's truth. And each time she clutched his gift, she could see him vanish in the sky in a radiant green flash and then nothing, just gone, gone from her forever. She never wanted him back so badly as she did right then at that very moment, after everything that had happened to her since she left her home.

Akasha held the rabbit in her mouth, her large, winsome, almond-shaped eyes smiling back at Sam with pride. She dropped it at Sam's feet and then without waiting a beat, rushed off to hunt for more game.

Sam sat down and leaned her back against a tree and watched the sky slowly turn from a dark purple, to blue, to pink, then to a glowing orange reaching across and gently touching the ragged edges of the snow-capped mountain peaks.

Another day, another chance to find herself, and she wondered what new insight would touch her and give her hope. *So much depends on what happens next*, Sam thought grimly. *The Great Head plays a hazard with us all.*

S am's leg was on the mend, as were her lungs. The burns on her arm were healed entirely, and her skin was now soft and supple. As she smiled and inhaled the sweet mountain air, she was grateful at the sight of things. Simple things: the leaves on the trees, or the way Jo would sidle up to her and nuzzle for an apple, or when he would tear across the meadow, kicking and bucking like a colt in its first year of foaling. She felt little pain; only a thin, whitish scar was left as a reminder of the nasty gash the red dragon had sliced into her leg. Soon, she hoped, that too—using her dragonfire ointment—would all but vanish, but of course not the memory.

She was beginning to become Sam again, ready to fight, and as each day opened and closed, her thoughts loosely tumbled between the needs of the present and the uncertainty of what was to come.

The cold nights had been filled with cozy fires, good food, and good conversation. It was early evening, and the sunset had faded swiftly toward twilight and turned into celestial darkness, lacking any moonlight. Everyone was enjoying the evening feast together. The Scarecrow sat wearily down at the dinner table and said to Sam, "I have wasted away up here for far too long." He took a sip from his goblet, and when he set it down on the table, he stared deep into its center. "It is so pleasant here, this sanctuary I've created. No politics, no ruling the people, just alone with my own thoughts." He looked at Sam, narrowing his eyes and then said, "Perhaps after so much time by myself, it made it easier for me to ignore the turpitude brewing in the west."

"You and my mother were very close friends?" Sam questioned.

"Yes, very close."

"Then why did you leave her when she needed you the most?"

The Scarecrow tilted his head, taking a moment to think before he responded. Sam watched Akasha as she reached fluidly for a piece of bread and meat on the table. The Lion and Tin Woodman did the same, placing their food on their plates and putting the cloth napkins in their laps. There was a familiarity in watching them eat, talk, and laugh with a crackling fire and its warmth. Though she missed her family terribly, she was quickly beginning to love this one, and felt comfortable enough to speak her mind. Sam picked up a handful of grapes and began to eat them one at a time with a satisfied grin, waiting for the Scarecrow to answer.

"You are so much like your mother," the Scarecrow said after Sam finished the last grape and started on a piece of bread, ignoring

Sam's question. "The burden of the great battle with the Wicked Witch of the West was more than your mother could carry. And after Dorothy went back to Kansas and the Princess Ozma disappeared, well, it pressed down heavily on your mother with a powerful force. So much so that she lost herself." The Scarecrow paused. "Forgot who she was for the longest time."

Sam's thin figure leaned over the table and placed more grapes on her plate. "I can't imagine my mother ever feeling sorry for herself, for any reason."

"I agree," the Scarecrow said, his voice level. "But it was a brutal engagement. She had lost many friends, people dear to her. Years later after that terrible war, she came to me when I was still the ruler of Oz. She seemed to have forgotten joy until she met your father and your sister, who I believe gave most of it back. But when you were born, it certainly all returned."

The Scarecrow smiled sincerely and reached for a piece of bread. His eyes softened as he gazed at Sam. He thought how much she looked like her mother and father and how beautiful she had become. He had watched her from afar ever since she was born, knowing what lay ahead for her. Now, the Scarecrow had a choice to make that had to be made then and there, a choice he did not like. He could see into the future, and knew he must give Sam and his friends a small glimpse of what that future might become. But he could not see far enough to know for sure of its true nature.

He smoothed some butter on the bread and took a bite, and quietly sighed as he watched Sam eat the grapes and listened to his friends' soothing talk and laughter. Sam's destiny played heavily on his mind, but in truth, he knew the decision he had to make had already been made. He, along with everyone around the dinner table, had a vital role to play. Even though he was in no hurry to play it out, he knew it was time.

"I think I'd like to stay here forever," Sam said in a quiet voice, reaching for more grapes and a piece of bread.

"Your destiny lies elsewhere, Princess," the Scarecrow said softly.

"There is something I must show you."

Somber murmurings hummed around the table, and all began to speak at once.

"What is it you need to show the princess that we don't already know?" the Lion called out, his words slurred from drinking more of the ale than he should have.

"Has the evil spread? Have you been holding back on us?" the Tin Woodman demanded.

"What are you all talking about?" shouted Akasha.

"There is something I must show all of you." The Scarecrow spoke, his voice commanding, not loud yet somehow rising above the ruckus. He came to his feet, eyes gleaming and his shadow growing tall, darkening the room. Silence rolled slowly across the dining table. He looked both kind and dangerous, and for a moment Sam was afraid. "We must all know the truth." He looked from face to face and saw fear in their eyes. Then he spoke in a softer, gentler voice. "It is time to face what's waiting for us in the shadows."

The Cowardly Lion stiffened, and the Scarecrow set a hand on the Lion's shoulder to ease his tension. The Scarecrow let out a doleful sigh and sat back in his chair. His eyes drifted away as though he were somewhere else. He looked very sad to Sam, and she wanted to do whatever she could to cheer him up. His eyes found her, and he smiled. Sam smiled weakly back, worried about his troubled heart.

Then the Scarecrow held out his hands, palms up, and spoke again. "Everybody hold hands." When Akasha, the Lion, and the Tin Woodman turned to look at the Scarecrow, they saw a dark shadow of regret settle over his face, as if it had been there his entire life. The Scarecrow looked at each and every one, one at a time, and then back to Sam. "I'm going to use your power of sight, Princess. Something you haven't yet learned how to control."

The corners of his painted mouth lifted slightly and he grinned lovingly. Sam looked directly into the center of his golden, sparkling eyes and nodded her head. He closed his lids and quietly mumbled words, and when he opened them, his yellow-painted eyes flashed to a brilliant orange.

꘎ ◆ ꘎

Suddenly there was a deep-throated roaring around Sam and everyone sitting at the table. She flinched, and it seemed that the cold, gray stone walls of the large chamber, with its inviting fire warming them all, burned away like the bright orange embers burning the edges of a piece of paper—the food on the table, the table itself, the chairs they were sitting upon—all of it burned away. She blinked hard, trying to keep from getting dizzy, and when she opened her eyes again she felt as if she were falling into an endless flume at the bottom of a great ocean floor, frightful and silent. In the next instant, they were standing outside on a small, open grassy knoll under a storm-tossed, overcast sky. It was an oppressive, dark grayness—not the pale gray of the stone walls of the Scarecrow's home, but a blackish gray—clouds mixed with smoke and the stench of burning flesh.

They followed the trail of smoke with their eyes and turned toward the screams and fierce war cries of a great battle. In the distance lay a desert of warriors. The sky was clouded with flying monkeys. And the two massive stone monoliths that marked the gates of Glinda Goodwitch's castle lay broken on their sides, large stones strewn across the burned and smoldering grass.

Sam's eyes widened in horror when she saw that her castle was in flames as the red dragon flew over it and spewed its dragon lava, swinging its head back and forth and screaming its war cry at the sky. Her lungs were on fire again, just like when she and Akasha had fought the red dragon. The scar on her leg throbbed and stung, biting deep into her muscles. She leaned over, grabbing her thigh with both hands. She opened her mouth to scream but couldn't. And there, on a distant hill in the middle of the battlefield, she saw her. She saw her mother all in white, fighting for her life sword to sword with a tall, slim figure wearing black, with skin as red as blood.

"*Sam,*" came a voice from very far away. A voice she knew but ignored. She heard it again.

"Sam."

Still she ignored it. Standing on the opposite side of her mother and the figure in black was her sister, Elle, holding her own sword with both hands level and above her head. Her fighting stance Sam knew so very well. As the figure in black stepped back, Elle jumped in and slashed her sword at her mother, but her mother blocked it from striking a devastating blow.

And there, to her wide-eyed astonishment, standing next to the dark, evil, black-cloaked sorceress, was her father. He was pointing his pike at her mother, protecting the black witch, ready to strike her mother when an opening appeared. Sam screamed inside her head, *Mother, Father, Elle!* and tried to unfurl her wings and take flight. She had to fight. But each time she tried to open her wings, she couldn't. She tried again, slowly, hopelessly. Again and again she tried to force her wings to open. She strained and groaned, but her wings did not obey her.

Then, the unthinkable happened. Elle struck a blow that knocked Sam's mother to her knees, and she watched her father thrust his pike deep into her mother's chest. The queen's face clouded, and Sam could feel and hear her own breastplate crack and splinter from the blow. A sharp pain arrowed through Sam's chest, and she pressed a clenched fist between her breasts.

When her father pulled the pike free, her mother fell to her side. The witch in black with the bloodred skin stepped forward and kneeled, then took her mother's crown and stood and placed it on her own head. The pain of it all dropped Sam to her knees.

Peeking beneath her shirt, Sam saw that her father's gift, the black onyx gemstone, was glowing a bright, angry, effulgent green. She held it as tightly as she could, making a fist as her knuckles turned white, sweat pouring down her forehead and stinging her eyes. The stone burned her hand, but the pain was nothing compared to the burning inside her chest, which continued, deepening with each passing second, until it began to change, moving toward something else, something out of control. She bit her lip as hard as she could, and could only stare mutely at the scene in front of her. The world tipped crazily around her, and she dug her fingernails into her palms, drawing blood until the haze disappeared. In its wake came fury, a terrible, cheated anger that threatened to overwhelm her.

The voice again. Sam closed her eyes, and heard her name aggressively nipping at her ear.

"*Sam.*"

Her heart thrumming. Her skin clammy. Her chest aching.

The voice again: "Sam!" It was a familiar voice, a voice she trusted. She stood up and whirled around to confront the voice and saw the sad, painted face of the Scarecrow holding her shoulders. All at once, the entire chamber seemed to darken for a moment, and the Scarecrow's head and face looked four times life-size. His mouth was moving, but she could not hear what he was saying. She shook her head and blinked her eyes to shake away the dizziness—then she could hear his words.

"Sam, I'm so sorry," he said softly, and sighed. "So very sorry." Tears gushed down her cheeks and she placed her head on his chest and moaned a deep, cutting groan that went straight through him.

Blackness was descending on her, filling her gut with cold, dreadful grief. Her inner voice ascended to a terrible eldritch wail that became so strong she had to clap her hands over her ears. She tried to force it out, but only moaned again, deep and dark. She struck out with one fist and pounded the Scarecrow hard, then again much lighter, and yet again. She let her tears pool and stream down, blurring her vision. Everything was shrinking, shrinking to a single bead of light, and then the light dimmed and wavered, growing darker and darker—and then her body went limp.

☙ ◆ ❧

S am woke with an aching head and a parched mouth. She was back in her bed, like when she'd first arrived at the Scarecrow's sanctuary. Everything was out of focus. She gulped in air and let it out slowly and her throat burned. Then she sat up and gulped again, and the world slowly started to sort itself back into order: the carved reliefs on the pale gray stone walls; the soft feather mattress; candles floating in the air; her crown sitting on the bedside table; her friends standing around the bed, looking at her with concern and love. All the pieces were fitting back together in her mind: the red dragon, the bloodred skin of the evil black witch fighting her mother, the smell of battle, and her mother being impaled by her father's pike while her sister watched, doing nothing to stop it.

Sam put her hands to her face, pulling down on the skin along her jaw, savagely pulling, saying nothing, thinking, *This was only a dream. This was only a dream.* She closed her eyes, unconsciously grabbing the blankets and clenching her fists. The itch of tears grew behind her eyes once more, but she didn't let them pool. In her heart, she knew it was more than just a dream. It was too real and too powerful to be only a dream. She pulled the covers up to her face, shaking, looking at the Scarecrow for comfort and understanding.

The Scarecrow sat down on the bed next to her, as the others had already gathered around Sam.

"It was a dream, right?" Sam asked hopefully. "Not the future?"

"A dream? Yes," said the Scarecrow, "and no. More like a spark of what could be, but not always things that will be."

"It was so real," Akasha said, closing her eyes to revisit what she had just witnessed.

"We all saw it," said the Cowardly Lion. "The smells and the screams of battle."

"Yes, we all saw it," added the Tin Woodman. "It felt real. I could smell and taste the sulfur in the air from dragonfire. We were all there, I'm sure of it."

Then the harsh, discordant mixture of the sounds and images of the vision rushed back to Sam. Her mother's death, the red dragon, the Wicked Witch. "But my mother, my father, my sister, the red dragon, the castle, they were—"

The Scarecrow interrupted. "The future hasn't been written, and it is your destiny . . ." The Scarecrow paused. "It is *our* destiny to write it the way we wish it to be."

"And the red-skinned Wicked Witch?" Akasha asked with trepidation. "What of her?"

"Yeah," said the Tin Woodman, "what of her?"

"Yeah, what of that ugly, red-faced sorceress?" growled the Lion, with a bit of fear rattling amidst his roar.

The Scarecrow paced once around the table before he said anything. He placed his hands on the Cowardly Lion's shoulders and squeezed gently to help the Lion compose his solicitude. "I'm afraid this new Wicked Witch is very real and very dangerous."

"What of a future with hope?" asked the Lion. "Is there not one that still has hope?"

"That future," the Scarecrow replied, "is all but gone."

"But it is not lost," the Tin Woodman added firmly, banging his tin fist on the bedside table. "By the Great Head, tomorrow hasn't happened yet. There is always hope for tomorrow."

Sam reached over and put her hand on his clenched, cold tin fist to loosen it and ease his anxiety. She examined him with soft eyes and then turned her gaze to the Scarecrow. "And my mother, Crow?" Sam asked with apprehension. "She is not dead?"

"No, she is not," said the Scarecrow. "She is very much alive and well and on her way back to her castle to gather her troops for war. It is your sister that I am worried about. She has been taken prisoner by the Wicked Witch and Rumpart."

"And my father," Sam asked. "He is alive too? Why did the witch take him? For what purpose?"

"Your father is alive. He was stolen from you, and now you know by whom. As for the why—because he is a powerful warrior and under the witch's spell—he will do whatever she asks of him, as will all the Winkies and the flying monkeys. She carries with her at all times, cinched around her waist, the golden cap that controls the Winkies and flying monkeys." He paused, took a breath, and sighed.

"And I must add, the witch controls the red dragon, too. Fortunately, you and Akasha have done everyone a great service by killing the other three."

Sam sat back into her pillows, staring at the Scarecrow. "My destiny lies elsewhere, you said." She looked at him sternly. "Is it my destiny to kill this witch?"

The Scarecrow's face softened. "Yes, but not quite the way you might think. Come, get up and bathe, then let's sit by the fire and have some tea. I will help you as much as I can with what you need to know, and we'll hope it will be enough."

"It will have to be enough," Akasha said fiercely looking at her companions for support. "All the way, or not at all."

Sam, the Scarecrow, the Tin Woodman, and the Cowardly Lion nodded in support. And as Sam looked at her friends, her warrior friends, she could see golden flames dancing on their eyes from the vision they had shared, each and every one willing to die for the others, for the land that they loved, and the freedom they cherished above all else. Sam threw off her covers and said, "We must leave immediately."

"No, not just yet," the Scarecrow cautioned her. He paused and smiled faintly. "There is a small task you must do before we go." Sam stood on the bed, her feet sinking into the feather mattress, and put her hands on the shoulders of the Scarecrow. She looked him square in the eyes.

"What then?" she asked.

"A baptism of sorts," he replied.

"Really?"

"Yes. To help balance your power and control the fire within you. It's in your royal blood, passed down from your mother. Now you have it. Your mother is stiff with it, and so are you."

"You must be joking, Crow."

"Time to wake up, milady."

The Scarecrow extended his hand to help her down from the bed. Sam accepted, trusting the Scarecrow completely. She placed her hand in his, and jumped.

Fourteen

T he lake water was gently lapping on its pebbled shore. They were all standing at the water's edge except for the Tin Woodman, who stood only a couple steps behind, worried he'd rust and need his oil can. Jo had followed them too, and the Scarecrow turned to put his hand up, palm facing forward with closed fingers, almost slapping Jo's nose to stop him. But Jo snorted and stomped his hoof and shook his head. *Horses choose one true master for life,* the Scarecrow thought. *This one is very rock-ribbed.* "Fine," he said to Jo, giving him half an apple. "You can stay."

"Have there always been good and evil witches in the world?" Sam asked the Scarecrow as she gazed upon the cold, clear waters of the lake.

"I suppose you can't have one without the other," the Scarecrow answered. A small, outthrust finger of water reached out and splashed his feet and then moved up his ankle, grabbing and tugging his robe, anxious for the Scarecrow to hurry up and do what had been asked of him. The Scarecrow looked down at the water and muttered something under his breath, and the water that had touched him receded quickly, swirling off in a broad, rippling circle to the middle of the lake.

Sam listened to the soft crash of the curled waves rolling up to her bare feet. They quickly disappeared into the pebbled sand squishing between her toes. She sank down where she was standing, and Jo crunched up beside her and lowered his nose for Sam's hand, giving

Sam a gentle nudge of confidence. There was a dark, gray, overcast sky that made the water look black instead of silver. A stiff breeze played with the tentacles of her crown and pushed at her braids. She stood up, looking at Akasha and the Cowardly Lion. Their fur waved like meadows of tall grass in the moving air as they too, like her, were mesmerized by the awe-inspiring beauty of the lake.

The Scarecrow had on his long, ragged red robe with the hood up to keep the chilliness at bay. "When the first Great Head of Oz, the first great wizard," he said, "built Emerald University, the world became obsessed with learning, inventing, and creating great works of art. That's where your mother met Mombi, the first wicked witch. But Mombi wasn't an evil tyrant then. She was just like everyone else— thirsty for knowledge, and full of hope about the future."

"Your mother was her best friend," the Lion said. "They went to the university together, had classes together, practiced magic spells together, laughed together, and competed in athletic events against each other. They were inseparable."

"But your mother always won. She was better at everything," the Tin Woodman added from a distance. "This made Mombi jealous. When they graduated, Mombi became the Great Head's First Consola, and when she didn't believe in the Great Head's policies, she tried to convince your mother to build an army to rebel against the crown, take down the throne, and put the Great Head on trial."

"Glinda would have nothing to do with it," the Lion said, "and she warned the Great Head, telling him as much."

"Do you know why?" The Tin Woodman looked across the faces and then directly at Sam. "Because your mother knows what it means to fight for freedom, and none fought harder to keep wickedness at bay than Glinda. No voice rang louder to rid this land of its stink. None hungrier to do what needed to be done."

The Scarecrow pushed his hood back, his faint smile bleak. "At that time, Oz was in its golden years and had known a thousand years of peace. When Mombi didn't get her way, her anger consumed her, turned her skin green, and she used her magic for evil. Her malevolence ripped a seam across Oz so deep it didn't heal for hundreds of years. Some believe it has never really healed." He walked up next to Sam and stood by her side. "Ever since that time, there has been a lineage of vicious, wicked witches. They don't seem to last very long because, in the end, their wickedness is their undoing."

"Your mother was fortunate not to have to place a verdict on the Wicked Witch of the East. Dorothy's house did a fine job of that," the Tin Woodman said with a clever smirk. "But Glinda would have been the first to take up arms and put an end to that witch's duplicity, just as she did with Mombi and the Wicked Witch of the West. I am proud to be of service to your mother. There was nothing like fighting alongside her, the Princess Ozma, and Dorothy. They were unstoppable warriors. And I will serve her now in this time of need."

"Your mother is a good, powerful witch fairy. The first of her kind," the Lion said to Sam. "And you are the second Goodwitch to bless us and protect the good people and talking animals of Oz."

"Well, we can't always rely on a house falling from the sky, now can we?" Akasha said with a large, wry, cattish grin, hoping to lighten the somber mood.

The Scarecrow paused and took a breath. "As I already told you, Princess, when your mother fought the Wicked Witch of the West, it pulled her away from life. But it was your father and your sister—and you—that brought her back. Now, she needs your help, your strength, and your courage."

"I never read about that in any history book."

"Ah, well, historians are a fickle bunch," the Scarecrow noted. Sam reached out and hesitantly put her hand on his arm, and he covered it with one of his own. "They care not of the emotional scars of war."

"Why are you telling me all this now?" Sam asked. "Is it part of the task you are asking me to do?"

The Scarecrow smiled and patted her hand. "No, not really. Think of it as . . . my way of trying to beef up your courage. How'd I do?"

"Needs work," Sam said with a kind grin.

"I thought if you knew more about your mother, it would be easier to take the next step."

"And what *is* the next step?"

He closed his eyes, but his hand stayed on hers. "To walk into the lake and let it take you." Sam eyed the Scarecrow with an inscrutable look that settled over her face as if it had been there her entire life.

"What will happen to me?" she asked. The Scarecrow opened his eyes and looked down at Sam. He could see that her beautiful, innocent eyes were searching for an answer, glowing brightly with their golden flame, and their strength shook him. He fell silent and dropped his hand from hers, but his breath stirred her hair as it fell across her forehead.

"Even I don't understand everything. This, I do know . . ." He paused. "You will become something more than you are now." Then he pulled Sam's sword from his robe and held it for a moment before handing it to her. Her eyes wavered and dropped. She grabbed the sword at its hilt, watching the reflection from the ripples in the water wash along its glimmering length. Then she lowered it to her side and let the tip touch the water. As if she needed reassurance and his protection, she turned to face him and slowly rested her head against his shoulder. He gently placed his arm around her and held her close, then stepped two paces back. Then he flipped his wrist at her and shooed her forward. Finally, he said with a soft, kind, but firm voice, "Go on, Princess. Into the lake. It's waiting for you."

Her neck bristled. Her crown touched her cheeks to spur her on. She heard Jo snort and shuffle behind her. The inscrutable look etched across his face faded, and she quietly chuckled to herself. She looked up into the sky and remembered the carvings on the walls in her sleeping chamber and the fresco on the ceiling of the Scarecrow's main hall.

Sam turned and faced forward and took three steps into the lake. The Scarecrow raised his voice a little and said, "You must be willing to let the lake take you." He moved a step forward. "The lake will know if you are not sincere, and if you are not, it will take you forever."

"Oh, great," Sam said softly to herself as she looked down at her feet and wiggled her toes. "He could have warned me sooner." She looked over her shoulder and met the Scarecrow's yellow, smiling gaze, wrinkled her brow, and smiled back.

Sam walked further into the lake until the water was above her knees. Every hair on her body puckered from the ice-cold water. Her stomach tightened, her mind racing. *I must show that I am not afraid,* Sam's mind whispered. She turned and looked back at her friends once again. The Scarecrow stood there, just like in her dream, but this time she wasn't afraid—suddenly she knew and understood the kindness in his eyes.

The chilly water started to swirl around her legs, moving with purpose. Then it crept slowly up, and as it did so, it felt in some way personal, warmer, and soothing, like the loving arms of a mother holding her newborn child. Sam stretched her own arms out from her sides, holding her sword firmly in her left hand, and thought she heard the haunting cawing of a crow off in the distance.

Then she closed her eyes and fell backward and let the lake take her.

The water splashed up on all sides of her body until it covered her, leaving only ripples, and for a moment, she imagined herself soaring high above the lake as she watched the small wavelets circle outward, lapping against the shore and across the Scarecrow's boots. But just like in the dream the Scarecrow had sent her, she was floating underneath the silver water and sinking to the bottom. Her arms, her legs, and her hair were suspended, shifting and drifting with the gentle current of the lake water, slowly pulling her deeper and deeper to the bottom. She saw a fuzzy, enormous shape flying above the water, with a long neck, broad wings, and a long, barbed tail. She knew instantly it was the red dragon. Flames spewed from its mouth as its neck and head reached around and sprayed the water with dragonfire. The roar of the beast and the hissing fire overwhelmed her. Her first thought was, *How could it have found us?* And her second was, *My friends, and Jo!* Then panic shook her. Still, she kept her eye on the terrible beast. It turned and flew up into the dark clouds and was gone. Or so she thought. Suddenly, it burst through the canopy of dark gray with great speed and plunged headfirst into the water directly above her with a thunderous crash.

Her spine arched and her head snapped back. Then her breath went *oof* and a bubbled, muffled scream burst forth. She felt the sword leave her hand. She turned her head and watched it drift away. Sam reached for it.

More air escaped her lungs.

More bubbles.

But the sword was too far away, and it soon vanished into the murky abyss. Her eyes stung, and a single tear escaped only to mix itself with the silver water and become part of the lake. She looked for the dragon, waiting for its fire to consume her. She flailed her arms, clawing her way to the surface for air, but something gripped her left ankle. *The dragon*, she thought. She kicked her legs to rid herself of it and fought harder to reach the surface, her lungs screaming for air, burning. Then the creature latched onto her other ankle and pulled her deeper, down to the bottom of the lake. Her lungs were on fire, her body convulsing, her head pounding.

Then, she had no more strength left to fight. Her mouth opened and the last bubbles escaped, floating slowly past her eyes and up to the surface, and she swallowed water. But the liquid was faintly sweet somehow, warm and calming. It rolled down her throat smoothly and filled her lungs, coursing through her entire body. Her eyes widened, and to her amazement, she could breathe; breathe as if she were standing on the pebbled lakeshore next to her companions. *There is no dragon*, she realized. Sam relaxed, and just as she had done only minutes before, she once again gave herself to the power of the lake. Then she shut her eyes and inhaled a deep breath of water. It was sweet to the taste, filling her lungs like a breath of spring air.

When she opened her eyes, she was no longer in the lake. Three women stood before her, floating like spirits, identical in every detail.

One was reaching forward, offering her a goblet.

The ghostly forms wore long gowns of such a lightweight fabric that they floated around them. They hovered above the ground, huddled together before a circle of three tall, wide, black, leaning stones. The stones appeared much older than the surrounding rocks. She took in a deep breath and the musky smell of damp earth filled her nostrils. Mold and moss and vines that held hundreds of tiny white flowers laced the surface of the large stones, and all manner of strange white symbols ran up and down their four sides.

"Drink," the woman said.

Sam could see the tips of their pointed ears poking out of their hair. Their feet were bare and clean, their flesh so smooth and white as to be blue, yet almost translucent, and she could see the spiderwebbing of green veins just beneath their skin.

Sam looked around, wiping the lake water from her face, inhaling and exhaling heavy breaths of air. The air was cold but not uncomfortable, with a robust, sugary fragrance of butterberries. She was standing on a bed of orange, moss-covered rocks inside an enormous cavern filled with trees and flowers. Hundreds of feet above her on the rocky ceiling, luminescent lichen stretched out in all directions, their algal cells like the branches of a tree illuminating the entire expanse, giving everything a bluish and yellow tint and setting the thin, flowing ground mist aglow. She looked down and wiggled her toes. Her feet tickled from the soft, spongy, mossy ground. There was so much to see, she didn't know where to look first. Thick, knobby tree trunks twisted their way upward to the ceiling into a canopy of vivid, colorful leaves, their branches—dripping of vines dotted with orange flowers—reached out, intertwining with one another. The chunky, gnarled roots of the trees crawled through the tangled undergrowth, and red-topped mushrooms spotted with white dots surrounded every inch of the underwater cave amid ferns of all sizes that seemed as if someone had dipped each one into a colorful fluorescent dye. Some were as large as Jo, and others as small as Sam's fingernail. They were scattered all about, mixed in with thousands and thousands of vibrant, variegated flowers, each trying to outdo the next in color and brilliance. Many of them were growing on the trunks and branches of the large trees.

But it wasn't just the incredible beauty of the hidden wonderland that held her spellbound, it was also the little creatures. Some were strange, small, impish, pointy-eared, chameleon-like creatures no bigger than a forest bantam or small cat, and they disguised themselves as rocks and moss. Others were barely the size of bees or little birds. Many of these puckish, elfish, humanlike creatures had wings, all kinds of wings—bird wings, insect wings, butterfly wings, bat wings— and were as diverse in their appearance as the colors of the flowers. They buzzed and giggled and chirped in every corner of the cave. A thousand gentle and soft songs formed a gleeful symphony as they flew in and around the trees and flowers, chased each other, and danced among the toadstools.

Sam looked back at the women, puzzled, for she had never seen such beauty before and had never been in such a place—never knew a grotto this unique even existed in Oz—and yet, there was something familiar about it all. Her crown was not warning her to tread lightly, but instead, its grass-like shoots appeared calm and also excited; it reached out to touch and talk with the flowers on the vines that dangled from the tree branches like so many strands of beautifully woven thread.

Sam was calm and felt welcomed. The flowing gowns the three women wore were made of many strips of fabric, dripping from them in ropey strings. Each piece was made from different shades of light to dark gray and shimmering spider silk was sewn into their clothing that reflected the bluish-yellow glow from the lichen. The pieces of cloth floated and shifted in slow motion, defying gravity, directed by an invisible current as if they were connected in some veiled way to the lake, like tendrils that trailed out behind the women as though in an underwater ballet. Their hair—long, red, and flowing like their clothing—twisted and turned and moved like the quiet motion of tree branches being pushed by a soft breeze. Their white, almost translucent skin reflected all the colors of the flowers, and the fluorescent lichen on the walls of the cave rolled across the surface of their skin like gently lapping waves on the pebbled shore of the lake.

But hidden just underneath their skin, barely noticeable, were darker etchings, umber in color, more like symbols. They swirled along the smooth features of their arms, their shoulders, and up one side of each of their faces. But it was their eyes that surprised Sam the most—hypnotizing. They were large, bright blue, and almond in shape—penetrating yet soft, and filled with hope. The ladies were tall, narrow-waisted, and childlike, yet seemed somehow ancient, blessed with long life (Sam was sure) and overflowing with wisdom.

One of the women held Sam's sword in both hands. The other was holding a round shield in the shape of a full moon with a cut, as if something had taken a bite out of it. She spoke into her twin's ear, and then that twin spoke to the other. They nodded at Sam and smiled. Welcoming smiles.

"*Drink,*" the girl with the goblet said softly and stretched out her arm as she slipped across the ground, stopping a short distance in front of Sam. The girl smelled sweet, like the glacéed scent of an early spring morning just after a misty rain when the air has been washed clean. Sam reached to take the goblet, and as she did, she noticed with mild surprise that her left arm had the same drawings as were on the three women, except hers were grayish green and not umber. She touched her face with her fingers and wondered if the markings were there as well. Sam looked at the girl and the girl nodded yes, as if she had just read Sam's mind. Sam paused before she took the goblet. *Ah,* she thought wisely, *I'm dreaming . . . surely, I'm dreaming.*

"*No, Princess,*" said the girl, reading her again. "*This is not a dream.*"

Sam froze.

"*Drink,*" the girl said, her voice soft and reassuring. "*There is nothing to fear.*"

"*I am not afraid,*" Sam said hesitantly. "*Well, maybe a little.*"

"*Curious, perhaps?*" the other asked.

"*Yes,*" Sam replied.

"*Drink,*" the other answered. "*And find out.*"

"*What will happen?*"

"*Drink. And find out,*" all three girls repeated together. "*You've come this far. Take one more step and drink.*"

Their deep, rich voices blanketed Sam, comforting, soothing, chasing away all her fears. Sam brought the goblet to her lips but smelled it first, then smiled and cautiously took a sip. The liquid was white, a little sour and cold, wild somehow, and sharp. It had a taste she could not put a name to. She took another sip, and after she swallowed, she drank it all. Sam looked up and met the girl's smiling gaze as she drifted back to her sisters.

Then the girl holding the shield floated within arm's reach of Sam and held it out as a gift for her to take. The shield was tarnished green and speckled with gold. The red dragon was stamped in the center, along with three smaller dragons placed evenly apart, surrounding the mighty beast. Along the rounded edges of the shield were the words *Dragon Slayer.* Sam reached out and took the shield and nodded to say thank you. It was surprisingly light, and felt as if it were a part of her when she placed her hand through the arm straps. And when she moved it from side to side, the shield sliced through the air like a knife through butter.

Sam smiled at the girl.

The girl returned her smile and said, "*May this shield protect you, Princess.*" She bowed her head and floated back to her sisters.

The girl with Sam's sword threw it into the air, where it spiraled end over end toward Sam. Sam caught it with her left hand, grabbing its hilt. She stretched her arm up as high as she could, pointing the sword to the ceiling of the cavern. Suddenly, the drawings on her arm and face started to glow, and then from her shoulder a bluish-white flame crept down her arm. Her hand pulsed with warmth, and the ghostly fire worked its way along the sword. When it covered the sword, finger-like bolts of bluish, white-hot lightning exploded from the tip and arced over to the shield, setting it on fire. Sam caught her breath at the sight and the intense feeling of the flame pouring out from within her. She gazed upon the three women, her eyes dilating and her breath quickening, and then with an odd little laugh that brought roguish dimples to the corners of Sam's mouth, she shook her head and tears rolled down her cheeks. She nodded to give her appreciation for the marvelous gifts that had just been bestowed upon her.

"There will always be natural causes tending toward the diminution of a population," the first girl said softly, the one that held the goblet. She moved closer to Sam, and then wiped the tears from Sam's face with her red hair, her breath the sweet scent of jasmine. She whispered in Sam's ear, *"but nothing contributes so greatly to this end than that of wickedness."*

All at once, an overpowering gurgling sound filled Sam's ears. She looked at the three spirits—they smiled, but it seemed that they were dissolving into a misty smoke. They had glided into the very center of the symbol stones where one large, rounded, white marble stone lay flush to the moss-laden ground. They floated above it, and their bodies began to sparkle. One by one, they swirled and shifted into each other, and then faded effortlessly into one hazy cloud and drifted away. The winged wee folk followed the wispy trail of the three maidens and skated around the landscape, zipping about the flowers and trees. Then the entire cavern became a foggy mist. Still the roaring continued on, only now it was louder, like ocean waves crashing hard against a distant, rock-strewn shore.

Sam could also feel her heart pumping and hear the swish of blood through her own veins and arteries. She closed her eyes and felt the cold water of the lake once again touch her, hold her, take her, and she heard the faraway smoky voices of each of the sprites speaking softly in her head, barely more than a whisper. Yet she heard them well, as though they were beside her, all three together repeating the same words over and over in her ears: "*There will come a time when everyone you love is all that matters . . . There will come a time when everyone you love is all that matters . . . There will come a time when everyone you love is all that matters . . .*"

Sam opened her eyes and the roaring she heard was that of thousands of water bubbles encircling her, attaching to her arms and legs, her entire body, forcing her to rise to the surface.

Fifteen

They stood on the shore of the lake, staring at the spot where Sam had fallen into the water and vanished. The Scarecrow was standing very still; he looked stiff as a statue, worried for Sam. He searched for a moment—a splash, a ripple, a sign that Sam was okay and coming back. *It's taking too long*, he thought. *Could this be too much for her?* And then he had a terrible thought. *Maybe she's not the One?* For a moment, he wondered if he should dive in, try and find her before it was too late, before the lake took her. She was part of his life, an essential, ineradicable piece of a long past now washed ashore by magic waters, standing together in his world to protect it and save it from evil. Ever since she was born, he had been watching her from the shadows, guiding her, protecting her, and waiting for her. Now there was a strange certainty about it all, a total belief that everything would work out the way it was supposed to. The world had no need to break apart with any huge, dramatic flash and bang as it had when he and Glinda, the Lion, the Tin Woodman, Dorothy, and the Princess Ozma had fought and won the vicious battle with the Wicked Witch of the West.

The Scarecrow filled his lungs with the fresh, moist air and thought he heard a ripple, but the surface of the lake was smooth as glass and strangely silent. All he heard was the distant screech of a mountain hawk and the occasional whisk of Jo's tail and the shuffling of his hooves on the sandy, pebbled shore.

"No one can be underwater that long," voiced Akasha.

"Patience," the Scarecrow replied.

"I agree with the cat," the Lion said. "The princess has been under far too long."

"Yes," the Tin Woodman agreed, weeping in a way most dangerous to his joints. "She's been under far too long."

"Stop your blubbering," admonished the Cowardly Lion. "You'll rust."

"Shush," the Scarecrow reprimanded, putting his finger to his lips. "Listen . . ."

A strong breeze rustled the Scarecrow's straw, pushing the hood of his robe off his head and playing with the fur on the Lion's and Akasha's backs. Bubbles formed on the water in the exact spot where Sam had fallen in. Tiny bubbles at first, then larger bubbles, until the water looked like it was boiling and foaming over a scalding pot. Unexpectedly, a bluish hot-white flame shot out of the middle of the bubbling brew, igniting the low-level black-and-gray clouds above. Blue lightning lit up the sky, flashing out in every direction, with the thunder crashing almost simultaneously.

In the next instant, Sam's sword broke through the water, then her hand and arm, until she was walking out of the lake. She was glowing as if she'd been set on fire. She moved her sword quickly, slashing from left to right, slicing through the air with tremendous speed, water dripping off her, and when she placed her sword in her scabbard, the bluish-white flames that surrounded her and the shield she held ceased to shine. She dropped to her knees, then fell face forward into the water. She bent an elbow to prop herself up, and then she saw her friends splashing across the lake to help her.

The Scarecrow ran to Sam, the others following his lead, splashing through the water (except for the Tin Woodman). The Scarecrow knelt down beside her. He was soaking wet, but it mattered not to him—all he cared about was that the princess was all right.

They helped Sam up and walked to the water's edge, where she fell again to her knees. Then there was a familiar stomp and whiffle on her right side. She reached out without looking and touched Jo's nose and rubbed his chin. She staggered to her feet and stood shakily beside her friends, wrapping her arms around Jo's neck to steady herself. "I could breathe . . ." Sam said, and inhaled the sweet taste of the air, coughing before she spoke again. "Underwater—I could breathe underwater. It was amazing."

"And the shield?" asked Akasha. "Where'd you find a shield?"

"And the blue flames?" asked the Lion. "How in the Great Head's name did you do that?"

"They were given to me," she said, out of breath, "by three spirits, or fairies, or ghosts . . . I don't know what they were. But they were beautiful, ageless."

"The Sisters of the Lake," the Scarecrow said under his breath and he smiled, knowing that the Sisters of the Lake gave Sam exactly what she needed. If they had found her to be unworthy, not pure of heart, the lake would have taken her forever.

S am sat down on the beach and crossed her legs. She realized she had a stiff neck and rubbed it, and then found she was stiff all over. "Did you know this would happen?" she asked the Scarecrow.

He bent down on one knee and looked at her, and she looked up at him. "No," he said. "But I had hope. Even I don't understand everything that happens in the lake. There are stories that the Sisters of the Lake are the spirits of truth, giving only those worthy the gift of what's hidden under their skin. Your true self."

"The shield?" Sam asked.

"The shield? Well the shield, I believe, is just that, a gift."

"And the fire?"

"The blue-and-white burning flame—that, my princess, is from you and has been with you since you were born. Every witch fairy has a different kind of magical power. This one of yours, the blue flame, it's been yours all along. You just didn't know how to use it. The Sisters of the Lake helped bring it forth. You can use it for good to fight the nefarious or for your own self-aggrandizement. It is up to you to decide how you will wield it."

The Scarecrow held out his hand to Sam. She took it, and he pulled her up. Sam put her arms around him. His body was shaking from fatigue, and Sam suddenly realized how emotionally tired he'd become from his concern for her well-being, and that it had taxed most of his energy. His thick arms tightened about her for a moment, and then he pulled away, his yellow painted eyes glowing with kindness. Sam reached for Jo's reins, and the Scarecrow boosted her onto the horse. "This way, Jo," he said over his shoulder as he clicked his tongue.

Jo pricked up his ears and followed the Scarecrow, excited to have his master riding again. The Scarecrow's long legs covered the ground quickly, and Jo had to stretch himself to keep up.

It was comforting to feel Jo's gait under her, and Sam leaned forward and rubbed his neck, whispering, "I do not know what I'd do without you."

They soon came to the Scarecrow's sanctuary. "We should all eat," the Scarecrow said, stopping at the steps of the doorway.

Sam nodded her head in agreement as her stomach roared at her. She had been unceasingly hungry since the moment she'd hobbled out of the lake.

Once inside, she walked along the great hall and sat at the table near the hearth, warming her hands and body by the fire.

"Sam," the Scarecrow said as he put a towel around her shoulders so she could dry herself, "are you all right?"

Sam didn't reply or even say thank you. She took the towel and aimlessly rubbed her arms, looked past the flames sputtering in the fireplace and let the heat warm her body. Her thoughts moved rapidly, replaying all that had happened to her since she left her home.

Then she saw the shadows of the perfect life she used to have dance in front of her, living without worry or fear in the castle with her mother, her sister, and Augie. She missed that life, which now almost seemed nothing more than a dream to her. How pleasant and straightforward her life had been with her family, waking early in the morning to sit on top of her bedroom turret, waiting for the sun to rise and a stiff breeze to carry her off. She missed the morning sparring games with Saran and Lillith; so simple and lovely it all was.

She longed for the days spent with her sister, following deer trails and creeks, hunting game, listening to the bird calls and the whining cries and chirps of insects that sounded so close to speech. She missed not knowing where she and Elle were going, only knowing how exciting and peaceful it was. And then, near dusk, how jubilant she felt when they carried their kill through the castle gates with such pride. Sam's eyes pooled. She had been away for so long, so much longer than she thought she'd be gone for. She was certain that Augie must be thinking she'd had a terrible accident, maybe even died. She sniffed and rubbed her eyes with closed fingers, pressing hard to lessen the tension and apprehension.

"Sam," the Scarecrow asked again, this time a little louder, "are you all right?"

The Lion was carrying a plate of food and set it down on the table. The others sat down too and began eating. Supper had become a time of reflection, filled with talk, debates, and questions.

"I'm fine," she replied as she reached for some bread and cheese, not looking at the Scarecrow, avoiding him, tears growing.

He sat down next to her. He cupped her chin with his hand. Her golden eyes flickered from the fire. His other hand covered hers and she placed the grapes on her plate and brought her hand to join his.

Once again, gently, because she needed his comfort and reassurance, she leaned slowly forward and rested her head against his shoulder. "I'm sorry," he said, "for throwing you into the lake without any warning of what might happen."

"When I was under the water . . . I thought I was going to die. But I was not ready to die. Then I heard your words, 'Let the lake take you,' and I did. I let it take me." She leaned forward and put her forehead on his and said softly, with deep sincerity, "Thank you."

"I'm sorry," he said.

"When you came out of the lake on fire, with that blue flame covering you," Akasha said, hoping to lighten the mood, "it was so crazy, you lit up like that, like a blinding, sizzling blue ball of lightning. I was paralyzed, stunned!"

Sam laughed a whisper of a laugh, sitting back and wiping tears from her eyes, and reached to Akasha. "No more stunned than I."

"What did it feel like?" Akasha asked.

"Did it feel hot, like you were burning?" asked the Tin Woodman.

"Did everything look blue?" asked the Lion eagerly, almost before the others had finished.

"I felt the same, and yet—different. Like I didn't know myself. It was as if I were outside, looking in."

"A good witch on fire," Akasha said. "And I was afraid of you." Her sly, broad grin stretched across her face and her slanted, golden-flecked, almond eyes sparkled with laughter. "But only for a second."

Sam smiled back. "Yeah, I held back. Didn't want to turn the heat up all the way. Not yet." She reached for more grapes and bread, then turned back to the Scarecrow. She was about to ask him a question but hesitated, ate a grape, and after she swallowed asked, "Do you have a plan? What's our next move?"

The Scarecrow turned to look at all his friends. His face seemed tired, worried. He settled his elbows on the table and folded his hands as if in prayer and said, "Yes. I have a plan." He reached for a piece of bread, cut it in half with a knife, and placed two thin slices of meat on one half and a bit of cheese on the other. "The Lion and Tin Woodman and I are going to meet Glinda at her castle and join her army. You," he said, pointing at Akasha with his knife, "are going to take the princess and go to Rumpart's castle and rescue Elle."

Just hearing her sister's name made Sam stiffen. She had been so consumed with the experience of the lake, she had pushed Elle to the back of her mind. "And the Wicked Witch?" Sam questioned.

"It's not Rumpart's castle anymore," the Scarecrow warned her. "It's the witch's castle now." He took a bite from his sandwich and sipped some ale.

"And how do you propose Akasha and I will do that alone?"

"I don't know," he said. "You have your new power and your wits. You are a Goodwitch. You'll know what to do." He paused and took another sip of his drink. "I'm sure of it."

"You overestimate me," Sam said. "I may be all you think I can be, but I have been nothing—nothing but a silly child, relentlessly teasing my mother's guards and doing only whatever pleased me and only me. Particularly because I had been born to a queen and felt I had the right to do whatever I liked, without consequence."

"That may have been true in the past," said the Scarecrow. "But not now. Your mother would be proud of you. You will make a great queen one day."

"No," she replied, somewhat stung by the thought. "Elle is strong, powerful, and responsible, and she will make a far, far better queen than I ever could since she is flushed with queenly manners."

"The queen's blood runs through your veins, not your sister's."

"I do not believe," Sam replied, raising her voice, "that royal blood has anything to do with anything. Only actions can be a test of such character."

"Then you'll make a good queen by your deeds," the Scarecrow insisted. "Of that I am sure."

A silence stood between them, and after a second the Tin Woodman raised his goblet and said, "To the queen, and into the fray." He paused, smiled, and winked at Sam. "I mean your mother, not you, Princess." They put their cups together as one and repeated, "To the queen, and into the fray!" A group cheer echoed throughout the chamber and the mood grew into something serious, yet noticeably buoyant and optimistic.

The Scarecrow took a drink from his goblet, set it on the table, and poured more drink into his cup. Then he looked at everyone with a happier face, and said again, but with a softer tone, "To the queen, and into the fray."

❦ ◆ ❦

E veryone had gone to bed early. But it was difficult for Sam to release the energy and images running around in circles inside her head. It was a restless sleep, filled with tossing and turning, and nightmares of war.

In the morning, Sam crept out before the others woke and flew to the top of Shadow Mountain. She looked east, where she could see the faint pink glow of the sun reflect off the clouds. The chilled air sat sharply on her skin, making her shiver. She opened her eyes, bringing the clouds into a clear and fine focus.

The *rush*.

She was waiting for the rush.

It was only minutes before the sun was going to rise.

Her sense of the passage of time had been uncertain since she'd left her mother's castle and fought the red dragon all those many months ago. As her health returned in the Scarecrow's hidden sanctuary (along with the new presence, the power she'd been granted by the Sisters of the Lake), she now believed that the months of recuperating had significant meaning and had been placed before her by some mysterious cosmic force. When one season had passed and another was just beginning, she was now stepping forward, head-on, with the knowledge that she had finally found her resolve and that this moment was meant to be. She wasn't a child anymore, and life had become a lot more complicated, but she knew what needed to be done and what she must do (had to do), for she now understood what the Scarecrow had told her about her destiny.

As the air grew warmer, the currents and pockets were becoming restless. It was coming. The *rush*, she felt it. Strong and steady as always.

The grass in the meadow was turning a vibrant green and the flowers were starting to bloom. The blue sky. The trees. Her friends. Sam noticed these things with so much more wonder and appreciation. The instant she'd broken the surface of the water in the middle of the lake, she had experienced a shift, a metamorphosis of a profound nature. She was the same person she knew before, yet someone entirely different—reborn in the right way.

She could feel it coming. The *rush*. Her heart was pounding in her chest and her blood was sprinting through her veins, making that telltale sound like the rhythm of war drums in her ears, the warning before the rush—the music she loved. She inhaled deeply, feeling her chest rise, her ribs expand. The stiff breeze wrapped around her and she extended her wings, letting them grow full of air, and she slowly lifted off the top of the mountain, then turned and faced the sun burning through a cloud. Then she turned again and flew off, spinning and diving, letting the rush take her away.

The rush never failed her.

It kept her wanting more.

Kept her alert.

Focused.

Connected.

She was ready to fight.

Ready for anything.

She would follow the Crow to the very end.

PART THREE
TO WAR

Sixteen

Sam flew along the rim of the volcano beneath the silvery glow of the low-hanging clouds, pushing over its steep-sloping, tapered edge; she angled down into a long, gentle glide over the Scarecrow's sanctuary before landing softly on the ground by the low barn and the meadow where Jo was quietly grazing. The Scarecrow and the others were in the barn preparing their horses, except for the Cowardly Lion. He had taken his horse to drink the fresh cold water of the lake with the hope that the Ladies of the Lake would grant them good fortune.

Sam took in a deep breath of the early morning air and let it out slowly. She looked up at the rain clouds that were full and ready to break open. *It's so beautiful here*, she thought. Leaving such a place of peace and making preparations for battle made Sam's spine shiver as she walked up to Jo.

She held out her hand, holding a much desired and anticipated treat, and said in a soft, singing voice, "And how are you this fine spring morning, my dear friend?" The horse's hide turned from a pale, sandy, yellowish-brown color to an excited yellowish orange. He trotted up to Sam and snatched the apple from her with a delicious crunch, while Sam stroked the side of his face. She looked into his eyes, thinking of her mother and wishing her father was with her. "Hard to believe I'm a year older. You too, you old nag. Seems like it's been a lifetime ago since we saw our home and our family."

Sam guided Jo into the barn, slapped him gently on the neck, scratched him behind his ear, ruffled his forelock, and whispered, "I bet you miss Vail . . . and I bet that old nag misses you." Jo snorted, shaking his head up and down as if he agreed with her. "Soon. We'll be home soon." Sam stared directly into his beautiful cornflower blue eyes wanting desperately to believe the words she had just spoken. She spent a good amount of time currying him while the last bit of colorful winter hair rose in clouds around them, and Jo made delightful faces of ecstasy and relief. Everyone was quiet while they saddled their horses. No one felt like speaking. The mood was somber, lacking color, the air filled with apprehension. Sam threw Jo's blanket over and onto his back moving with practiced motions, putting on his bridle, saddle, and all the gear needed for the trek. She performed these things automatically with her thoughts far away from the safe home the Scarecrow had provided for her. An inviting, soft, morning spring rain began dancing on the roof of the barn. Something that always brought serenity to Sam's soul. But this time the sound of comfort was a sad reminder of what lay ahead of them. Their days of peace and tranquility with the Scarecrow were soon to become a mere wispy memory placed on a dusty shelf, but it was a memory she would always treasure and never forget.

The Scarecrow watched Sam with apprehensive eyes and had a suspicion of what she might be thinking, but had no comfort to give her; all he could offer her was his friendship, his allegiance, and his knowledge of magic and her place in the history of Oz.

One day during that winter, she'd offhandedly asked the Scarecrow, *"Why do you teach me so much? So much of what you know?"*

It was one of those perfect wintery mornings when she'd asked the Scarecrow that question. The morning had opened gray. Clouds hung heavy, low, and rippled, foreshadowing the colder days and more snow to come. The ground was already covered in a thin blanket of white. The snowflakes floating down, one by one, were the fluffy kind, spinning slowly like miniature pinwheels, perching on branches and resting on the ground like soft, white, flaky dust. The type of day Sam so dearly loved. And for Jo, he spent his days at the barn at the edge of the meadow with the other horses the Scarecrow owned. Sometimes a few deer would be brave enough to join them, mainly for some fresh hay and oats—but perhaps happy to have the company as well.

When Sam asked the Scarecrow her question, he considered it in silence. Then he swung his sword sharply left and right, attacking. Sam backed away, deflecting his advance sword-to-sword, her hands vibrating from the power of each strike and the clanging metal pounding in her ears. Sam turned around—blocking and protecting her back by throwing her sword over her shoulder—and stopped a deadly hit that would have surely sliced through her spine.

The Scarecrow raised an eyebrow. "Good block," he said gruffly.

Compliments were hard-won from the Scarecrow, and Sam was surprised how much his approval meant to her. She couldn't help but smile, but it was a brittle smile that cost some effort. "Why do you teach me so much?" Sam's temper kindled. *Why does he not answer my question?* she thought.

"You must focus on using the edge of the sword more," he said, taking in a heavy breath. They stopped and repositioned their stances, never once taking their gaze away from each other. "Not as much stabbing." He slapped her hard on the hip with the flat of his sword. Sam scrunched her eyebrows as her anger continued to boil, ignoring the sharp pain shooting down her leg. Then the Scarecrow pointed his sword at Sam and continued. "The enemy you will fight can take many stabs and keep coming." The Scarecrow found himself amazed by how much Sam's speed, dexterity, timing, and even endurance had improved, and he smiled to himself, proud of how focused she'd become.

"Why do you teach me so much?" Sam demanded, her forehead and shoulders gleaming with perspiration. She was amazed by the Scarecrow's mastery of sword fighting, but found she could now see the technique beneath his speed, could often recognize his form and his tricks for what they were. And even at times predict or read his moves before he even acted upon them. She slowly scooted her left foot directly behind her right, bent her knees, and placed both hands on her hilt, wrapping her fingers around the elfin cord with purpose to make sure her grip was firm.

"It's best to make quick, strong strikes," the Scarecrow coached.

Sam moved her shoulders and twisted her waist to her left side slowly, so her blade was slightly angled down, ready to attack or defend. Keeping her eyes focused on the Scarecrow, she tried to anticipate his next move, looking for his tell, a slight movement in his eyes or shoulders that would give her a split-second warning of how he might slash and jab. The Scarecrow set his stance precisely as Sam had just done, relaxed his shoulders and lowered his sword, and said, "To answer your question, my queen . . ."

"Don't," Sam said harshly, releasing her stance, then standing and squaring her shoulders, but staying rigid and alert. She bit down on her lip, hard, to keep a rein on the temper that had grown to its full strength inside her. And before the Scarecrow could blink, she flipped her sword up with great speed and pointed it directly at him, only inches from his nose. "My mother is the only one who deserves that title, not me." Her eyes narrowed, and she cocked her head as though hearing something in the distance and turned away.

"I'm sorry, Princess," the Scarecrow said, unfastening the clasp on his cloak and letting it fall to the ground. "I meant no disrespect."

Sam seemed to pull herself back from the edge of an inexplicable irritation with the Scarecrow. In one quick movement, she turned back to face him, slashing her sword back and forth, slicing through the air with lightning speed—*whoosh-whoosh*—and once again the sharp tip pointed directly at his nose. The Scarecrow, did not try to defend himself, and took two steps back as Sam moved forward. He held the point of his sword to the ground and behind him, using it to steady his balance.

With tight eyes, quivering, closed lips, and beads of sweat rolling off her temples, Sam tilted her head, studied him, and asked again, resolute in getting an answer, "Why do you teach me so much of what you know?"

"There are moments when I still see fear behind your eyes."

"Aren't you ever afraid?" she questioned him.

"Yes. But I have learned to be the master of it, as should you."

"You still haven't answered my question." She inched forward, wiggling her sword in small circles as if she intended to poke him and slice him. The Scarecrow stood his ground and let the point of her sword touch the tip of his coarse canvas nose. Sam's tattoos began glowing and the fire within her ignited, bluish-white flames engulfing her body and sword.

"I do not bleed, milady," he said with a wily smile. "If you cut me, you will draw only straw."

"Why do you teach me, Crow?" Sam asked once again, but this time speaking in a softer, pleading way as the flames covering her body subsided, and faded away.

"So that you believe. But . . . ," he hesitated, taking his index finger and carefully moving Sam's sword away from his face. "I haven't taught you everything." Then he smiled. "Only what you need to know for now." He put his sword in his scabbard and raised his hands, palms forward, forfeiting the match. Then he crumpled his painted eyebrows and looked solemn. "Also, because I want you to come back and learn more, and sit by the fire at my dining table with all your friends, and be happy. Read books with me, take long walks with me, talk of simple things like the age of the trees and all that is dear to both of us, all things contentious and mystifying."

"I would like that," she said, relaxing her stance and lowering her sword.

"As would I," the Scarecrow said softly, as a ghost of a smile crossed his face again. He reached down, picked up his cloak, and threw it over his shoulders. "Enough practice for tonight."

The pale winter moon gleamed on his yellow, straw hair and glinted in his glowing eyes. His burlap face had no wrinkles, and he had told her once it would never show age. His narrow shoulders were straight and square, but he looked old to her just then, as timeworn as the Shadow Mountains, as ancient as when the earth made its first flight around the sun. He had taught her eagerly, and eagerly she had learned, each of them preparing the other for something they each did not want to face but knew they must.

Sam's lessons had grown longer and longer as the days and weeks progressed, and as she healed from the battle with the red dragon and became stronger, her thirst for perfection also became insatiable. Some of the things she learned made her afraid of what she had transformed into, but for the most part she was adjusting well to her new skin. The days would open with training with her new shield, and sparring with Akasha, the Tin Woodman, and the Lion. Each was skilled in a variety of different fighting styles and weapons—they were seasoned and deadly warriors. Then at night, she'd spar with the Scarecrow, and they'd practice spells together or read from his magic books, and when they could, they would take long walks just for the company. Sam was becoming extremely proficient with her shield, and quickly found that without it, she felt slightly off balance. Together, they all helped the princess control the flame that was now a part of her. And each time she used it, each time she let the fire from within run freely, her tattoos would flame on, turning a fiery blue, igniting her arm, then her hand, and finally, the sword. Little by little, with trial and error, she learned to control the fire inside her and was able to generate a power blast, like a small ball of hot-white lightning from the tip of her sword.

But mostly, she had instantly fallen in love with the learning and the physical endurance of their workouts, and found it unsettling to think that soon they would end. Her newfound love for perfecting her abilities wasn't about her *destiny*, as the Scarecrow had said, and it wasn't because the Sisters of the Lake had shown her the flame that had lain dormant inside her, nor the fact that she had royal blood. It was because she was waking up and finding the person she was meant to be. Royal blood or not, she knew when standing toe to toe with the enemy on the battlefield, that blood and its color mattered not.

❧ ◆ ❧

After the day of that conversation with the Scarecrow, winter seemed to move forward too quickly. The snow had melted too rapidly, and the first tight-knuckled buds were pushing themselves out from the trees. Sweet tasting purple shoots of sweetgrass were popping out everywhere—all things sleeping beneath the dirt were waking up. There was a heavy, rich, loamy smell in the air, and Sam kept seeing things in the shadows just beyond the edges of her vision and hearing the faraway, joyous laughter of her sister.

Often when she allowed herself to drift away with the feelings of all she missed about her sister, she would whip around to find the Scarecrow eyeing her from a distance with that silly but cute painted smile on his face, as if he knew exactly what she was thinking. It was something Sam had never gotten completely used to, but a hallmark of his that she was at least learning to appreciate.

She mounted Jo and looked at her new friends—at Akasha, the Cowardly Lion, the Tin Woodman. She smiled and then thought about that one wintery day when she had gotten so upset with the Crow. It seemed like ages ago, as if she were just a silly child banging wooden swords as she had with her sister. *When my mother sees me next, she will not recognize her daughter,* she said to herself. *She will be proud of the woman I've become.* That thought was what made Sam practice all the harder, and she looked directly at the Scarecrow. For a moment, she worried that they might never see each other again.

"Something on your mind?" the Scarecrow asked Sam while he mounted his horse. His was a Percheron—a stunning, powerful draft horse, eight hands taller than Jo, with a dappled-gray and black body and a bright white mane.

"No. It's nothing," Sam replied. "Just a wisp of a thought."

"Please," the Scarecrow said, turning his horse around to face her. "This is no time not to say what's on your mind." He looked at her with supplicating eyes. "The crater trail is long and tedious. We have plenty of time left to talk before we part and go our separate ways." He gently kicked his horse in the ribs with his heels, urging her forward at a relaxed pace. The path was narrow as they walked side by side. Sam felt a need to be close to him—yes, perhaps to speak her mind, but mainly to be close.

The others followed behind, each with their own steed, two by two as well. The morning was bright and inviting. A cool, gentle breeze worked its way through the evergreens, casting its strong, fresh, minty pine scent as the trail snaked back and forth through the forest and out of the crater, leaving Silver Lake at their backs.

At last Sam said, "I fear I'll never see you again."

"Nothing is certain, Princess," said the Scarecrow. He knew her concern and understood how she felt because he felt the same, but wisdom and his ability to think beyond the disquietude made it easier for him to deal with the uncertainty of the future. "You might be right. We might not see each other again. I might fall in battle, or tumble over the edge of this cliff along this narrow path, or a house might fall from the sky and squish me like a bug." Then he smiled, an honest, sincere smile, and said, "Then again, it may not."

"Still, I worry," she replied.

"You are right about one thing," the Scarecrow said. "There is much to worry about. Your mother, your father, your sister, the Wicked Witch, the fate of all of Oz." He pulled back on his reins and stopped his horse. "It is a lot to deal with, especially when it involves life and death."

Jo took a couple steps forward before he halted, and Sam turned to look at the Scarecrow. "Yes, I am worried about my family," she said with a frown and a heavily furrowed brow. "And my friends, the ones back home—Saran, Lillith, and Augie—and all of you here." She turned her head away from the Scarecrow and nudged Jo in the ribs and moved ahead of him. "And you, Crow; I worry about you the most."

The Scarecrow was concerned for her. He knew he wasn't quite ready to send her away, but he knew he had to. He had done all he could do to help her. The rest was up to her. "If we worried about everything, Princess, then we'd be too exhausted to do anything about it, now wouldn't we?" He tilted his head and smiled, even though he knew she was looking away from him. But in truth, he knew she understood. Then he said, "You were born to quell the wickedness, to vanquish this evil witch. It is your destiny to go back into the dragon's den."

There was silence that sat lightly between them, and after a moment Sam said, "Thank you."

"For what, Princess?"

"You have given me many kindnesses, my new power not the least of them."

"By the grace of the Ladies of the Lake, not by my hand."

"You know what I mean," Sam replied. "I will be forever in your debt. If we both survive, is there anything I can do to repay you for your counsel?"

"Nothing comes to mind, milady. But if it makes you feel better, I'll collect on the debt someday. And my price will be steep."

The corners of Sam's mouth swept up into a playful smile. "Whatever the price may be, I will gladly give it to you without argument."

The Scarecrow let out a low, quick chuckle. "That, milady, I am not so sure of."

"It is because of you, Crow, that I found my place," Sam said. "I will master my fear as you have taught me." Then she asked, "The Wicked Witch . . . does she have a name?"

"She, the one who sends the mischief across Oz? She, the one who controls the flying monkeys, King Rumpart, and the Winkies? She, the one who means to destroy our way of life? The one who, even now, infiltrates Quadling Country with her army of minions, decimating village after village, and harries your mother's castle and the Quadling city it protects? Does she have a name?" he replied. "She goes by many names: the Dark One, the Destroyer, the Unholy. But a name like you and I have—no, that I do not know. She was born from the tar of the earth and seeped forth unnoticed from the back side of hell."

Then without warning, they eased out of the pine forest, and the narrow path suddenly opened up into an expansive valley, rolling down and along the foothills of the mountain—an open, majestic sea of waving spring wheat and grass that began at the shifting feet of their horses and ran to the edge of the horizon. The Scarecrow spurred his dappled horse and blasted off in a powerful gallop, shooting past Jo and Sam, his pace shaking the ground beneath each planted hoof, kicking up clumps of grass and dirt in his wake. Sam smiled and the Scarecrow yelled back as he zoomed past, "I just call her the Wicked Witch."

The Scarecrow was right, and she knew it. Action was what was needed, not wallowing in the muck and embracing fret. She watched him ride into the valley and smiled again, admiring his imposingly deep and full character.

Jo didn't need any prodding. He wasn't about to let any horse take the lead from him or his master, deep character or not. Sam could feel his muscles tighten and grabbed his mane in anticipation. He reared up, kicked his front legs, turned a bright red, and took off to catch the Scarecrow. The others did the same, hooting and hollering, all racing across the grassy valley to purge Oz of demon scum.

To war and fight for freedom for queen and country.

To war and into the fray to the very end.

To war.

Seventeen

T he sunlight was dimming, the day almost over, and the dark blue sky was slipping down against the orange bar of sunset, narrowing it to a thin red line.

They had decided to camp for the night, somewhat for the fact that they were simply tired, but more because they wanted the company a little longer—to at least have one more meal together before going their separate ways in the morning and running headlong into the unknown. It had been a long day of riding down from the mountain. When they made a campfire and cooked a hardy meat stew from the food they had packed, the rich aroma lifted their spirits and excited their taste buds. Having her merry band of compassionate and fearless souls together for one last meal gave Sam a sense of well-being. She had come to look upon their nightly gatherings and conversation as a much-desired part of her life—an indispensable part of her life. One she wished would never end. *We'll sit by another fire once again soon,* she said to herself. *May the Great Head guide us and protect us.*

When the last bit of sunlight passed from sight and the shadows deepened, nightfall came to the forest. It was a peaceful evening, crisp, with a full moon rising, and Sam wondered as she looked at her friends sitting close to the fire to warm their weary bones if this would be the last time they'd know peace. But she was going to heed the Scarecrow's advice and not let worry occupy her thoughts. It was best to just enjoy the time with her new family, for in fact, if this was the last time they would ever see each other, then it should be a moment filled with peaceful talk and hopeful spirits.

She had been quiet most of the night, staring into the flames of the fire. She missed her mother, and she had only a small amount of hope that her sister wasn't being tortured or killed. And then there was her father. Knowing that he was alive was unbelievable, and yet, it was frightening at the same time. Since he was under the vile witch's devilish spell and had no control but to do the old hag's sinister, dark bidding, could he be saved? Could he be turned back to the light, or would he remain forever in the dark, never knowing how much she loved and missed him? Those thoughts and more made her skin shiver, even with the warmth of the fire to comfort her.

Akasha sat beside her, resting her arms across her knees and said, "You've been staring right through that fire all night. What's on your mind?"

"Nothing, really," Sam replied.

"I know it's something," Akasha said, nudging her with her shoulder. "It's your mother and sister, isn't it?"

"And my father."

"Well, I'm up for a fight to save them. Are you?" Akasha picked up a stick and tossed it into the fire. The flames kicked and sputtered and crackled, shooting sparks up into the air.

"Yes, of course," Sam replied, also nudging Akasha firmly with her shoulder. "Not sure I could do this without you, though."

"Not sure I could do this without you either," Akasha said with a smile, nudging Sam a little harder. They laughed, and Sam picked up a piece of kindling as well and threw it into the flames.

☙ ◆ ❧

The Cowardly Lion asked the Scarecrow, "I heard you say that the witch has no history. Is that right? So she has no parents or family—just born from the dirt?"

"Is it true?" asked the Tin Woodman. "She is the spawn of pure evil, a true darkling?"

"How do you know this?" Akasha asked.

"Was it from a vision?" asked Sam.

The Scarecrow filled his spoon with stew and held it over his bowl as if talking to himself. "The evil mark on her is so bright it will blind any simple folk into submission if they look upon it," he said as he swallowed the stew, pointing the spoon at the fire and wiggling it up and down. "I knew long ago that this day would come, but paid no attention to it, ignoring the signs, just brushing them away. Didn't want to believe it. If I had listened to the warnings, then maybe I could have prevented the witch's awakening." He scooped up more stew, swallowed, wiped his mouth with the sleeve of his robe, and continued. "And now, at great cost to my friends, I ask you all to ride to a doom like the one that is coming. One that I believe we have little chance of averting, but with my friends by my side, I feel there is hope—without it, we are lost."

The Tin Woodman and the Lion exchanged a look, and Sam saw within them a ghost of many battles they had fought together. Theirs, she believed, was a powerful bond. An unbreakable bond. It took no extraordinary imagination to see that they would fight to the death for the right cause. The Tin Woodman had the heart of a thousand warriors, and the Lion, once a coward, was as brave, if not braver, than anyone in all of Oz. "I would not wish to be anywhere else but by your side," the Tin Woodman proclaimed.

"Nor I," agreed the Lion.

"I know I cannot defeat her alone," the Scarecrow interjected. He took off his wide-brimmed, floppy hat and flipped it upside down. He plucked a few strands of straw that were poking out from the sweatband and stuffed them into his chest. Then he looked at his friends and put his hat back on, shaping it to fit his head as he always wore it, and continued. "She has tried to creep into my brain and control my thoughts many times. Although I have been able to hold her off these many years, she keeps pecking away at my straw bit by bit; and she is getting stronger every day, much stronger. If we don't act now, it will be too late for me—for all of us."

"What of the princess?" asked the Tin Woodman.

"She's strong," the Scarecrow said. He blinked and smiled at Sam. "Very strong indeed."

"Strong enough?" asked the Lion.

"We can only hope," replied the Scarecrow. "And as I said—without it, we are lost."

Sam smiled back and lowered her eyes. "Then call me hope, because hope I will be."

"I have watched you grow up," the Scarecrow said, pointing his spoon at Sam, "knowing some special but dangerous destiny awaited you. And when your father was stolen from you, I knew then you would be the answer. That is why I sent you the dreams."

"I am pleased that you did," Sam said. "Because now, Crow, you have opened my eyes." She had been feeling numb since her battle with the red dragon. The old, practical sensitivities she'd held before she let the lake take her had seemed like a dream out of control. And the new emotions that had been awakened by her experience with that deep dive into the magic waters of the lake—and her lessons from the Scarecrow—had made her feel like a newborn trying to walk for the first time. But it was the Scarecrow who had pushed the numbness away and helped her see clearly and showed her how to unravel her new identity. "Do you truly believe we can put an end to this madness?" Sam asked.

"I believe in you, Sam. I believe in you, Akasha. I believe in all my friends. I believe that all things have a way of ending up in the right place. Maybe believing that it will all work is no greater or less than believing in the Great Head—a wizard who watches the plight of every sparrow and is rumored to have a plan so comprehensive that he allows wicked witches to claim Oz for themselves, even to allow slavery and suffering, and war. I don't have all the answers, but one day it will all be made clear to us." The Scarecrow looked at Sam again, a more profound gaze than before. "There is someone I have sent for, someone who will help you and Akasha accomplish your task."

"Where do I find this someone?"

"He'll find you."

"Can he be trusted?"

"Yes," the Scarecrow said without hesitation. "We have a long road ahead of us. We'll need to get an early start in the morning. I am weary, and my brain is tired of thinking so much." He stood up and walked over to his bedroll, which was lying on the ground a reasonable distance away from the campfire so as to not let any sparks ignite his straw. Then he lowered himself and stretched out on his blanket and closed his eyes, muttering something to help him fall asleep, a prayer of sorts, while the others lay upon their own blankets, also waiting to let sleep take hold of them.

꙳ ◆ ꙳

It wasn't long before Sam fell asleep, too exhausted from the day's ride. But it was a restless sleep, full of anxious, haunting dreams.

After few hours, she opened her eyes and sat up, sweat laying heavily on her skin. Sam rubbed her face with the palms of her hands and wiped the moisture off her forehead. It was the middle of the night. The bit of silvery moonglow that found its way through the low-hanging clouds glistened off the dewy leaves.

Their campfire had lost its flame, but the orange and red embers smoldered, and smoke drifted up like ghostly figures floating away and vanishing into the chilly night air. A cricket was chirping to the light of the moon, perhaps hoping to impress a potential sweetheart. A couple of bats whooshed back and forth across the black, looking for unsuspecting insects. Off in the distance, Sam could hear the bleating song of a night crooner calling to its mate.

She looked out across the shadows of the trees and spotted a few fireflies sparkling like tiny dancing fairies. She remembered her father watching her dance and run after the flashing bugs, and then laughing as she flew up to chase them into the night.

Help me.

She snapped her head toward the voice, but saw only her friends sleeping soundly.

Sam, help me.

Again, she snapped her head toward the voice now floating through the air from a different direction, the words coming from a soft patch of tall grass where Jo had been sleeping. His head was up, alert, ears pricked. He was looking directly at her. When she walked over to him, he huffed and quickly stood up, shaking his mane in agitation.

She grabbed his jaw with both hands and asked softly, "Did you hear that? It was Elle's voice. I'm sure of it." She put her cheek to Jo's and rubbed his neck, listening . . . waiting for the voice again.

Suddenly, everything around her shifted, and Jo vanished. Time became elastic, stretched out in all directions; sounds turned into muted echoes, and colors changed to gray. One second she was rubbing Jo's neck, and the next instant, she found herself standing in the great hall of King Rumpart's castle. And sitting in a chair in front of his throne was her sister, Elle, held by a spell-induced yellow strand of glowing magic twine that was binding her arms and legs.

"Elle!" Sam tried to scream. But her voice was silent, caught somewhere between the abode of the souls and the place of the living.

She ran to her sister and dropped to her knees in front of the chair, cupping her hands over her mouth. Elle's cinnamon scent was strong, almost overpowering. Her spicy fragrance always got stronger when she was angry or afraid. Sam reached over to rip off the glowing magic strand, but instead, her hands brushed through her sister's body and the chair as if they were smoky ghosts. She tried touching Elle's face, but again, her hand moved right through her.

"It's me, Elle," she said out loud, looking deep into her sister's eyes, pleading with her sister to hear her voice. But Elle didn't hear her, didn't see her, and Sam realized she was caught in abeyance, suspended somewhere in between her own reality and that of her sister's. It was a compelling manifestation that allowed her to be in another world, unnoticed and not really there. After watching her sister shift restlessly in the bindings for another minute, Sam's anger

built, and she bit down on her lip as hard as she could.

Her crown tugged at her ears, warning her of coming danger. Her skin rippled with goose pimples. The hair on the back of her neck stood straight up, and her whole body shivered. Then she felt the inescapable compulsion to stand and turn around. When she did, standing before her was the Wicked Witch—with glowing, orange eyes, skin the color of blood, and one bony finger pointing directly at her.

Sam straightened herself up and pushed her shoulders back to face the witch, setting her fighting stance. Then suddenly her eyes widened, and her breath caught in her throat. Standing off to the left and behind the witch was her father. His eyes were glowing orange too. He stood like a statue, glaring at nothing, just staring into a deep and dark void and breathing heavily. His beautiful, mighty black wings were unfurled, stretched out to their full length, and he held the very pike she'd seen him use to kill her mother in her vision. And on the witch's right was Rumpart with the same glowing orange eyes and the same vacant, baleful gaze as her father.

At first glance, Rumpart looked both flamboyant and silly, but she knew he was as slimy and toadish as she remembered him. He was a small, lurid man with bad posture and a watermelon belly, animated in manner, idiosyncratic in speech—the perfect candidate with the right mindset to be easily seduced and manipulated from spells of any type. He was a nervous man with mannerisms unbecoming a ruler— tugging at his hair, pinching his nose, pulling his earlobe, biting the edges of his fingernails. He wasn't a gentle king, nor humble, nor self-deprecatory, never concealing the pleasure he felt when ordering more taxes or sending citizens to jail for nonpayment and confiscating their property. His only concession to any independence of thought was a drooping pistolero mustache, shades darker than the thin orange hair that he combed back across his bare skull and glued in place. He was a simple man to read, greed and gluttony rolled together. She remembered he smelled of cigar smoke, and even in this in-between place, he reeked of it. He was wearing bright green trousers and a brilliant blue vest over a shirt in faded pink with oversized pearl buttons.

Soaring high above them—some perched on window arches— were dozens of the witch's flying monkeys, swishing back and forth, clapping and growling with a low, deep-throated thrum. Rumpart walked over to Elle and gently, slowly, took a small handful of her hair, rubbed it with his stubby little thumb, and leaned forward to sniff it. Then he pulled his dagger from its scabbard and cut it from her head and sniffed it again.

"Tell me what your Glinda is planning," the Wicked Witch asked in a slow, controlled voice, shooing Rumpart away with her hand.

"My mother will destroy you," Elle returned, her breathing raspy and heavy. She shook her head to rid herself of the greasy touch of Rumpart's hand. When Elle took in a breath, Sam could feel her do so, and she knew that Elle's lungs burned and it was difficult for her to pull in air, and that Rumpart's touch made her sick to her stomach. Sam could feel everything Elle was feeling, physically and emotionally.

"Your mother can try," the Wicked Witch said as if talking to herself, tapping her finger on her cheek and carefully deciding what to say next. Her orange eyes flared for a second, searching, questioning, unrelenting. Then the witch furrowed her brow as if the words she'd formed in her head finally found their place. She pushed her thick black eyebrows closer together, and the wicked old crone stepped closer to Elle, bending down only inches from Elle's ear. Sam could feel the evil witch's warm, pungent breath on her own neck. The witch's words sent shivers down Sam's spine when she spoke to her sister.

"There is no shelter your mother can hide in, no armor to protect her, no spell to stop what's coming . . . I will send out an army in the middle of the darkest night and destroy everything you hold dear, and your father will lead that army. You don't know it yet, but your mother is a dead witch walking, just like you and your silly little sister, too."

In the Wicked Witch's left hand, the evil hag held her broom. She was a narrow-faced, narrow-bodied woman, wearing a tight-fitting black blouse that puffed at the shoulders but was skintight on the long sleeves, which came to a point at her wrists, covering most of her hands. Her skirt was pleated at the waist and fell to the ground, hiding her pointed ebony shoes, and her hair was coal black, bushy, and unkempt, with kinked strands shooting out in all directions. The Wicked Witch's black, venomous look danced on her pupils, bristling from her so palpably that one might have cut it with a knife. She cupped her right hand and rolled it back and forth until a ball of red energy emerged, flickering and spitting small shoots of lightning, and without any hesitation she threw it at Elle with all her strength.

Sam flinched, putting her hands to her chest expecting to feel its burning force, but instead, the red energy ball passed right through her, hitting her sister with a terrible force. Elle screamed as the red lightning coursed all over her body, electrical fingers snapping and pinching burning flesh, and that's when Sam felt it too. The pain struck Sam so fiercely she doubled over and fell to the ground, and noticed red blistering marks appearing on her arms.

Elle's head snapped back. Her mouth opened wide, and she cried out. Using what strength she had left, she clenched her teeth, scrunched her eyebrows, and looked directly at the Wicked Witch with strained, but steadfast resistance. Her breathing was rapid, and she growled until the electrical charge faded away. Beads of sweat were rolling off of Elle's face as she shook her head. She let out a weak snicker, and with labored breath, she mumbled, *"Is that the best you can do?"*

"What is Glinda planning?" the witch demanded as she paced back and forth, ignoring her words. *"And where is that silly sister of yours?"*

"You leave her alone," Elle voiced strongly.

Sam's vision blurred with sudden tears as she watched her sister fight back.

☙ ◆ ❧

The Wicked Witch made another ball of lightning and threw it at Elle with all her strength. Like before, it slammed into Elle's chest and exploded, covering her with electrical sparks. Elle let out a horrifying scream and her body shook from the shock.

The Wicked Witch closed her eyes, slowly moving her head from side to side, tilting it back as she sniffed the air, curling her hands into fists. *"There is evil in you. I can smell it. There's a dark aura that surrounds you. Its aroma is strong and heavy. It percolates out of your pores like a black cloud of delicious, sweet-tasting, beautiful, barbarous lawlessness. Join me, and together we'll be unstoppable."*

"Never," Elle said, her strength ebbing. The witch looked directly into her eyes and Elle managed to endure the penetrating directness of the witch's poisonous intent without looking away.

As Sam watched the Wicked Witch aggressively interrogate her sister, she felt alarmed, as though she were alone in a room with an animal and had no idea what its next move might be. She knew at that very instant there would be a day soon when that bleakness she now felt, that feeling of fury and outrage she was trying to hold in precarious control, would shoot forth and show itself with uncontrollable ferocity toward this fiendish witch, this necromancer of cruelty. She could feel her sister's pain, feel the strength systematically being ripped from her.

But there was something more. Something Sam saw in Elle's eyes. Something hidden deep within. *She's going bad,* Sam thought. *Slowly. Like something rotting away under her beautiful, shiny green skin.*

Perhaps it had been festering, waiting ever since Elle was born? Perhaps not.

Sam just wasn't sure, but if it were true, Sam knew she'd have to make a deep cut into it to find the rot. And Sam was sure the witch was doing just that, bit by bit, cutting a long, deep gash into the soul of her sister to let the bad out. But more than just that, it was the innate suggestion from the witch of her sister's destructive madness that also made Sam so worried about the future of the Quadlings and for all the kind, innocent people of Oz.

ॐ ♦ ॐ

T he Wicked Witch's piercing leer left a sharp, bitter aftertaste that was appalling. It made Sam feel as though her mother's entire empire of good, which had been so carefully rebuilt out of the chaos caused by Mombi and the Wicked Witches of the East, and West, was now an unsteady castle of playing cards on Sam's bedroom rug. And this corrupted, dark soul of a witch played there like a destructive two-year-old—willful, devilish, destructive, and unpredictable.

Sam turned to face the witch and closed her eyes, focusing all her energy to one central point in her mind, attempting to bring on her flame and kill the wicked creature where she stood, to put an end to the nightmare here and now. But she was unable to ignite the fire inside her. She tried again, but to no avail.

Sam paced around the witch, taking subtle notes, studying every inch of the evil tyrant. *"She may be a formidable and ruthless adversary, having no pity or compassion for others,"* Sam quietly mouthed to herself, *"but she is mortal, of that I am sure. If pricked, she will bleed like anyone else."* There was nothing good hidden beneath the witch's skin, only evil, a terrible, murderous evil and nothing more, with a black heart as cold as the water in an ice-covered lake. This, Sam was sure of. But there was something else: the way the witch's eyes seemed to swallow the light. An undeniable feeling rolled over Sam's spine, that this evil creature would stop at nothing to achieve her goal, no matter the cost.

"I was born of the downtrodden, the suppressed," the Wicked Witch said, shaking her hand in the air as if waving to a crowd in a parade, keeping a close eye on Elle. *"I am the dark threads of all who've been caged."* Then the wicked old crone hesitated. There was a subtle disturbance in the air, a pale shift in the light that made her abruptly stop, and she wrinkled her forehead and tilted her head to one side as if eyeing a ghostly shimmer. She turned her head and looked over her left shoulder, then a second later snapped her head back to the right, as if,

for an instant, she could feel something, a shadowy presence gliding around her. Then it happened again, another wobble in the air, but this time there was the delicious faint odor of sweet innocence.

She grabbed her skirt and forcefully swished it behind her. She abruptly turned to the side and sniffed the air. Then sniffed again, but the scent was gone and she let the notion go. She turned back to her captive and pointed her bony red finger at Elle once more and curled her hand into a fist, like she was squishing a bug. *"All those who can't face the darkness, those poor, tortured souls who try to deny me, who will try and suppress me, they're frightened of the truth that darkness is more fundamental than light, cruelty more powerful than kindness, evil more primary than good—more deserving of existence than the light could ever be. I am the black, viscous mixture, the bitumen of truth. I, and I alone, deserve to rule Oz."*

This Wicked Witch had a wily, sly, pernicious perspective of the world and a presence that placed fear in your bones and made the hair on your neck prickle. This rage, this evil that was oozing out of her, actually made Sam step back a couple of paces and look down at the ground and tremble.

But her sister remained strong. *"You're wrong,"* Elle said, looking away from the witch and closing her eyes hard to keep from fainting. Tears seeped out of the corners and rolled down her cheeks.

The witch whispered a low and dusty laugh, then rolled her eyes and waved her broomstick in the air, dismissing anything that her captive might say. *"Oh, please tell me."* The Wicked Witch reached down and picked up her wide-brimmed, towering, pointed black hat that was sitting on Rumpart's throne, and put it on. She walked over to Sam's father and rubbed her hand along the edge of his wings, then placed her hand on his shoulder and took her razor-sharp black fingernail and slowly scratched his cheek until a trickle of blood seeped out. Elle's father didn't move, didn't make a sound, his red-stained eyes holding steadfast, void of life, filled with evil.

"You see, your father completely understands me," the witch said glibly, with an insincere smile. Elle looked directly at her with a hard stare and then rolled her eyes and looked away. *"What? Why do you look*

away?" the witch asked in a raspy voice and smiled even wider. She rubbed the brim of her pointed hat, dipping and turning like she was dancing at a ball, and then speaking in a sarcastic tone, she continued. *"Oh, it's my hat, isn't it? You don't like my hat? A bit much, perhaps? I like it. Makes me look taller."*

Elle spoke in a quiet, hopeful tone. *"Empathy and kindness are basic to all forms of life. Nothing would exist without compassion and tolerance. Good far outweighs evil. Light always conquers the dark. Our existence would have fallen apart without it. You . . . ,"* Elle stopped, coughed, and glared at the witch, peering deep into her sinister orange eyes. She licked her chapped lips, which stung when her tongue moved across the dead skin. Then Elle said, *"You—you are just an afterthought."*

The witch scowled, rolling her shoulders and bending slightly forward. *"And you are a stupid, ignorant child."*

"I am not afraid of the dark," Elle said bitterly. *"And your hat is a bit much."*

The Wicked Witch quickly walked over to Elle and dropped her head, which made her drawn-out chin disappear into her neck as she leaned down. Her long, pointed nose pressed into Elle's cheek, and her cold red hand with its long black fingernails cupped her chin. The witch's hot, sour breath fell across Elle's ear as she whispered, *"You should be afraid. You should be very afraid."* The Wicked Witch stepped back, raised her broomstick with both hands, and aiming its prickly straw toward the ceiling, swirled it around twice, bringing it to rest and pointing it at Elle's face.

Dark gray and black clouds crawled and billowed outward, creeping along the arched ceiling above the witch, and rolling thunder echoed throughout the castle. Wind thrashed at her skirt. *"Oz will have a queen, and all will love me!"*

The flying monkeys flew out of the large windows that stood like sentries along the towering stone walls of the great hall. In unison, her father and Rumpart bent their knees, turned their shoulders, and pointed their long pikes at Elle. Then the witch said in a powerful, deep booming voice, *"I am the dark that has come. I am the darkling that dances on your soul. I am the endless shadow that surrounds your heart, the black ink that runs through your veins. You come from a long line of wickedness. You are the spawn of the last great Wicked Witch of the West. There is pure evil in you, child, hot and heavy, boiling and bubbling, and I shall have it."*

"*I will never let evil control me,*" Elle said with labored breath, working hard to fill her lungs with air.

Sam could feel her sister's rib cage rise and fall, and she felt the burning each time her own chest heaved. It was maddening to feel all that Elle felt and not be able to do anything about it. Sam paced back and forth, watching, listening, trying to remain calm—trying to figure out if there were any way she could intervene, to push through this reviling and frightening apparition and stand before her sister to whisk her away from all the madness.

The Wicked Witch ignored what Elle had said, waving her hand in dismissal. "*You will know evil soon enough, my dear. I am going to give you the existence you were denied. The child who never had a chance to know the pleasure of being wicked because her mother was murdered by some goody-two-shoes country girl in a pretty little blue plaid jumper and a stupid little dog.*" The witch smiled and once again pointed her bony finger at Elle and continued. "*Oh yes, Princess, I'm going to give you back what was stolen from you.*"

"*Nothing was stolen from me,*" Elle whispered under her breath, *expect for my father.*" Her tongue felt like one large cotton ball rolling around inside her mouth, and when she had tried to look at the witch directly, the monster had become a blurry mess, shifting in and out of focus. Wind roared in her ears, and Sam covered her own to keep the horrible sound at bay. Everything around Sam—the Wicked Witch, Rumpart, her father, Elle—they were all turning gray. Sam watched Elle's chin drop to her chest, and the witch's voice became nothing but a confusing, distorted jumble, stretched out like an elastic band slowly being pulled to its limit.

"*But how?*" The Wicked Witch said, tapping her finger to her cheek and turning away from Elle. "*But how to do it? That's the question. These things must be handled delicately.*"

"*I . . . am not . . . evil,*" Elle said, slurring her words. Her eyes rolled to the back of her head, as did Sam's, and then everything went dark.

≈ ◆ ≈

The next thing Sam knew, she was lying on the ground and Jo was nudging her face with his nose, blowing into her ear. She was light-headed and stood up, then leaned forward, using one hand to support her weight on her knee, rocking her upper body side to side, hoping the rhythm of the rocking would be of some comfort. She put her hands on her hips, straightened her back, and tried to swallow. When she couldn't, she tried again. She gagged, doubled over, then retched, though nothing came out. She straightened herself up once more and took one step forward, but her knees were spongy.

Then the image of her sister bound to the chair and the ugly old wicked witch of a hag torturing Elle engulfed Sam, smothered her, and slapped her with a force beyond physical. Spasms tore at her body again. Sam braced herself. Once more she had to bend forward and put her head down, hoping she wouldn't faint. She closed her eyes and held her lids as tightly closed as she could to push back the black.

Then another wave of spasms struck her. Harder this time. She sank to her knees, pounding her hands on the soft grass, clutching and ripping the green shoots out of the earth and thinking, *This isn't happening*. When she opened her eyes—the ground, Jo, and the dark night sky shining with stars seemed to shift and swirl around her. She shut them once again to stay the swirling, to push back her anger, but the blackness descended upon her anyway, filling her gut with cold, dreadful pain. Her inner voice ascended to a terrible, eldritch wail inside her head that became so strong she had to clap her hands over her ears. Sam gulped air in—cold, invigorating air—and with it, the world started to sort itself back into order. She noticed that her friends were still asleep. They had no idea what she had just experienced.

Sam was beyond exhausted.

Her stomach muscles ached.

Her head was pounding.

She prodded Jo to kneel and lie down so she could find a cozy spot next to him and let sleep take her away from the dreadful vision she'd just witnessed. And as soon as she placed her head on Jo's warm body, she fell into a deep, dreamless sleep.

＊

Morning came too quickly. The sun was barely showing itself; a beautiful morning in its early stages with a slight cast of pink that touched the edges of the clouds that were scattered across the sky. Sam heard the soothing, chirping songs of birds and rubbed her shoulders to push back the chill. She inhaled deeply, taking in more of the refreshing, crisp early morning breeze, pulled her blanket over her shoulders, and gradually opened her eyes. Immediately, when her eyes focused, she noticed that her friends were standing close to her, four big heads in a circle with worry written across their faces, staring down at her.

"I heard you cry out last night," Akasha said. "It was only a whimper. But when I saw you sleeping with Jo, I thought nothing more about it."

"What happened?" asked the Lion. "A bad dream?"

"No. I had a vision," Sam said. "It was so real." She took her blanket off and stood up.

"Ah," said the Scarecrow. "The Sisters of the Lake have given you more than just the flame."

"A vision of what?" the Tin Woodman asked.

"My sister," Sam began, as she walked over with her blanket to pack up her gear. Then she tied her scabbard around her waist and pulled the sword out and looked at it. After seeing her reflection and her tear-soaked eyes in the shiny metal, she put it back into the sheath. "My sister is being tortured by the Wicked Witch, trying to turn her to the dark."

"That may be a good thing," said the Scarecrow.

"A good thing?" Sam said fiercely. "It's my sister. She might die!"

The Scarecrow sighed. "That's not what I meant. It means the witch has used up the three wishes from the golden cap to control the flying monkeys. The same cap she used to control your father and all the Winkies." He continued, a little vexed from having to explain everything and calm Sam's nerves. "It's worthless to her now unless she gives it as a gift to someone else. Then that person will have three wishes. For now, it means she doesn't know the power of the golden cap. But your sister is in serious danger, and I don't know how long she will be able to keep the darkness at bay."

The Scarecrow refocused his eyes to look at Sam gravely and added, "Be prepared, Princess. You might have more manifestations. This Wicked Witch is cunning, and she might sense this ability in you and turn it against you."

Sam put the blanket saddle on Jo's back and said, "Let her try."

He walked over to Sam and placed a gentle hand on her back, softened his eyes, and looked at Sam with hope and determination as a father would his daughter, giving her thoughtful and vital advice. "Don't allow reliance on your weapons and your skill as a warrior to impair your mind, Sam. You have grown into your wits; see that you don't lose them along the way. It is easy to do when holding a sword in your hand and staring evil directly in the eye, knowing your sister is in peril."

A distant voice rang out.

"The day waits for us, Scarecrow," The Tin Woodman called. "The morning light beckons."

Eighteen

E veryone had mounted their horses except Sam and the Scarecrow. The Scarecrow kicked dirt over the campfire. "You must head west," he said to Sam, "for one day. Then north for two. Akasha knows the way."

Sam was leaning up against Jo and rubbing her left forearm. She was listening to the Scarecrow, but not really paying attention to him as she inspected the red scorch marks on her arms that were slowly fading away. She was trying desperately to put the vision of the Wicked Witch out of her mind, but it came back to her in heated flashes. The sour, rancid taste of the witch's breath. The witch's cackling laugh with her beastly grin, smirking while she tortured her sister. The red flaming ball of lightning. And then . . . the pain . . . the red-hot, searing pain, and the smell—but worse, the sound. She'd never forget the sound of her sister's flesh sizzling or her nightmarish screams.

Then the thought jumped into her head that perhaps it hadn't been a vision at all—that it had been real, and she had been in Rumpart's castle, actually there, watching the witch interrogate Elle. That this was all part of her evil plan. That the witch had intended her to be a witness to her crime so she would try and rescue Elle. *If this is true*, Sam said to herself, *it worked, because I will get my sister back and will do anything to do so—anything!*

Jo stood still while Sam tied the last bundles behind his saddle and rechecked the flank billet and cinch. Still, his ears spoke of restlessness and concern that he was leaving the rich meadow of mouthwatering, succulent sweetgrass. She heaved herself over the saddle and swung her leg a bit too hastily behind, thumping her bedroll with her boot in the process and wondered why she suddenly was so clumsy. But she knew it was nothing more than the rumbling of discontent, of not knowing how the days ahead were going to unfold.

She settled herself into her saddle and tugged on a strap, then turned and looked straight at the Scarecrow. Sam stared fixedly at the open neck of his ragged robe, so she would not see his worried eyes staring back up at her, but she found herself eyeing a rapid pulse beating in the hollow of his throat. She felt her heart sink, but she kept looking at him anyway, despite the desire to look away. "When I see you next, I'm bringing you a new robe."

"I could use a new one," he replied, smiling and letting his eyes shine bright yellow. Sam reached in one of her saddlebags and pulled out a large leather pouch and tossed it to the Scarecrow. He caught it and opened it. "Dragon teeth splinters," he said. "Keeping secrets from me, I see."

Sam and Akasha had already turned their horses away, leading them west, but Sam turned back at that and said, "If my mother is engaged in battle with the witch's army as you say, she'll need them more than I will, I think." Then she fastened her most steadfast and resolute stare on the Lion and Tin Woodman, scrunching her brow. "Lion, Tinman, I charge you with the Crow's protection. Fail me, and you will know my sword personally." She smiled, unable to hold the tough façade.

The Scarecrow mounted his horse, and the three of them turned to face Sam and Akasha. "Once you rescue your sister, ride as fast as you can to your mother's castle. We'll be there waiting for your return."

"May the Great Head protect you," said the Tin Woodman.

"And give my regards to the witch," the Lion added.

"With the edge of my sword," Sam said over her shoulder. Then she and Akasha shook their reins, dug their heels into their horses' ribs, and trotted briskly along the trail. Sam wanted to look back at her friends but dared not, certain that if she did, her eyes would water, so she kicked Jo harder in his sides, spurring him on into a full gallop. But a moment later she couldn't help herself. She turned around just before she and Akasha rounded the bend and found the Scarecrow, the Tin Woodman, and the Lion still standing as small specks on the hillside. Watching them go was like a scene from a tale written in a storybook she'd read as a child. Then the trees hid them from view.

The Scarecrow raised his right hand, palm facing forward, and held his thumb to his index finger like a priest giving a blessing; he softly said under his breath in a low, reverent tone, "Δεν υπάρχει μέρος σαν το σπίτι. Come back to us, Princess." The last he saw of Sam was a momentary sun flash reflecting off her shield, as she rode into the tree line. He waited only a moment more, and then he and the Lion and Tin Woodman turned and headed to their queen's castle to join Glinda the Good and her army.

He'd seen this day play out in a vision years before and prayed daily for it to never happen. It was a mental image of what the future would—or could—be like, and it burned through him with great angst. His heart was heavy because the vision never showed him how it would end, and he feared he'd never see the princess again. Then he remembered what the Tin Woodman had said: There is always hope for tomorrow. And even though that should have kept his fears at bay, he could not rid himself of the sense of uncertainty nesting in his old, straw-packed body. A twinge of worry pricked at him, hounded him, and made him question if he'd done everything he could have done to help the princess in this moment of great need. Even with the gifts graciously bestowed upon her by the Sisters of the Lake, he wasn't sure if his princess had enough fight inside her to confront such wickedness.

He knew this was not the time to be doubting himself. What was done was done, and done for the right reason. That alone, he had to accept. But it was difficult not to question his motives, especially when he found that he was so connected to the princess and duty-bound to protect her. And as he rode with his companions, he thought back to all the good that had happened during the past year and how much the princess had grown. That made him smile, and if he could have shed a tear, he would have. For now, he could only wait and see how the days ahead would unfold. Once again, he recalled his friend's wise words, but this time he said them aloud, "There is always hope for tomorrow."

Spring seemed to be bursting out much stronger everywhere around Sam and Akasha, as they moved lower and away from the mountain valley. It was as though each step their horses made added more greenness to the land, as if the last hairs of their steeds' winter coats conveyed a spell of vibrancy to the plants they touched. When they slept, they slept in a small glade, hidden by trees where leaves had uncurled and lay heavy with sap, providing cover. Jo seemed to be enjoying the trip more with each day they traveled, his color changing to meet his good cheer—brilliant white, yellow, orange—and capturing the colors of the flowers on his hide, tirelessly jogging mile after long mile.

"I do believe spring is giving a show just for us. A welcoming nod, perhaps?" Akasha remarked one morning. "The birds are following us and the flowers open as we pass and cast their perfume upon us. It's as if they support our cause, helping us along."

Sam had noticed this too, and thought she had been imagining what she saw. Now she knew it wasn't her imagination because certainly she and Akasha would not be visualizing the very same thing. It was so beautiful—amazing, in fact. But when she felt the hard steel of the sword her mother gave her for her birthday and the sun told her that they were heading due west, as the Scarecrow had told her to do, she scowled at the thought of her sister being held captive. Tomorrow they would turn north to Rumpart's castle and know the truth.

Thinking of the Scarecrow now reminded her of why they were going on this dangerous adventure and the seriousness of their mission. She already missed his companionship and didn't realize until that very moment just how much.

Sam and Akasha had descended far from the mountain valley and the forest plain where they'd left their friends and now were far below the foothills. The country was no longer covered with trees; they were riding through a gentle, slopping valley with hills surrounding them. Here, the weedy grass, parched yellow by the sun, grew to their horses' knees, and they had to wade through it like water rushing along a gentle stream, a sea of rolling yellow. Akasha slowed her horse, falling slightly behind Jo and Sam, and looked back to where their trail had been, noticing the grass rippling along the path they had just cut in. Odd, since there was no breeze to make the yellow shoots move and sway as they were.

And then, suddenly, the rippling stopped. Akasha nudged her horse to catch up to Sam, then looked back again. As before, the grass moved and stopped. Akasha laughed quietly to herself and said to Sam, with the same hushed voice, "Company is following us. We are being tracked hard. And if they are trying to mask their hunt, they are not very good at it."

"How do you know?"

"In the grass behind us," Akasha said, smiling. "I've felt someone following us since we left the Scarecrow. At times I got a whiff of something sour, but I wasn't sure until now. "

Sam turned her head to look back at their trail and noticed a hint of movement in the tall grass. Her crown touched her cheek to warn her, and with a soft giggle of her own, she said, "Reminds me of when you were slithering through the grass, stalking me."

"Yeah, well, I let you hear me on purpose," Akasha replied with a muffled gruffness.

"Maybe this stranger is doing the same," Sam suggested.

"Why don't we gallop hard and fast toward our unknown foe and shake the reeds to see what kind of snake we find?" Akasha said as she came to a halt and turned her horse around to face the intruder. She waited and watched the grass behind them suddenly stop its gentle swaying.

Sam turned her head, bringing Jo to a complete stop. "No. Let's not ferret out our guest just yet. I think you're right; she might be purposely letting us know that she is following us. If she had wanted to do us harm, she would have attempted to already."

"What makes you think our goblin is a she?" questioned Akasha.

"I'm just saying, let this nosey ghost make the next move."

They continued forward climbing back into the mountains again, but always keeping a vigilant eye on their not-so-stealthy stranger. Farther along, after the sun rose over them and was behind, halfway over their shoulders, the ground underfoot was no longer the loamy and soft dirt of the lower terrain, but full of medium pieces of flat, smooth rock and small pebbles. Jo's hooves rang loudly when they hit the stony, uneven ground, striking a hard warning sound.

It was not a trouble-free path for either horse to follow, as it would be easy for the steeds to lose their footing and tumble to their doom. Akasha's horse seemed to have the most trouble keeping a steady foothold on the slippery landscape, while Jo appeared more adept at dealing with the smooth rocks and loose stones, but still, he too had moments of insecurity. "This won't do," Sam said, and she and Akasha dismounted. Sam knelt, picked up a handful of pebbles, and threw them to the side. "We'll walk till dusk and then make camp. Let's head lower for better footing for the horses."

"And what of the outsider who tracks us?" Akasha asked.

Sam smiled and said, "We'll invite him—or her—for dinner, of course."

Akasha smiled and dismounted, pulling the reins over her horse's head. She held onto the noseband and cheekpiece and started walking. Sam did the same, patting Jo on the neck as they headed for firmer ground.

When they had traveled far enough down the mountain, the horses' hooves sang out merrily with the heavy tread on solid ground. The feeling of being watched increased as they remounted and went on, with quick glints of wispy, shadowy movements: a small sapling wiggling, or a group of ground birds taking flight for no apparent reason. Sam and Akasha would smile and nod at each other, knowing that their traveling companion was still on their trail.

The sun was now hitting the top of the tree line and sinking rapidly. The light was fading, dusk deepening, and the spring wind was still icy with the coming night. Sam knew they should be smart and stop soon to set up camp and rest. But she was willing to freeze in her saddle to reach the witch's lair if she felt they had to ride through the night. But despite her desire to carry on and confront the witch, her thoughts played with her curiosity so much so that she couldn't help but want to find out who, or what, was following them and why.

They found the perfect place to set up camp, hidden amongst a small island of trees. They dismounted, unpacked, made a fire, and cooked a robust meat stew from the fresh meat the Scarecrow had packed for them, hoping to entice the one who was stalking them. Sam had seen deer and plenty of birds, rabbits, and squirrels on their ride, and the greenery was very lush; there was no lack of game or water. It was a pleasant treat not to have to hunt for their dinner for a change.

The sun finally slid below the horizon and then the shadows crept in—and so did their shadowy guest, skulking behind a tree, waiting for the final darkness. When the stew was hot and its aroma just right, Sam and Akasha poured a good helping into their bowls, and Sam placed another bowl filled with the hearty stew by the fire with a spoon, steam rising from its center. Sam caught movement out of the corner of her eye. A boy-sized shadow climbed straight up a tree and disappeared into the branches. She sat down next to Akasha and filled her spoon full of the delicious stew, and said loudly enough for their unknown guest to hear, "Come, eat. Warm your bones and tell us why you're following us." Her voice was lusty, but not threatening, and sounded more like an honest welcome.

As if this were a signal, a white flag of truce, the interloper poked his head out from a clump of leaves up in a tree a little ways away, with a smile as wide as his pudgy face could hold. "I am a bit hungry," he said, showing a large crop of teeth as his smile widened. "Wouldn't mind if I had a taste of your fine-smellin' cookin'." He jumped down from the branch and walked toward the campfire, on alert, his tread nearly silent—a gnarled, bowlegged Munchkin with the swaggering stride of a town ruffian, with two swords in crossing scabbards attached to his back. He rubbed his hands together, smacked his lips, and without missing a beat, picked up the bowl and slurped down a healthy gulp of the hot stew before plopping himself down. "I've excellent ears, as you can see from their size," he said, wiping his mouth with the back of his hand. The Munchkin slouched forward as he sat, inhaling a hearty whiff of the hot stew, and let a sly smirk drift across his face. "If I wanted to do you harm, you would have never known I was there until it was too late."

Sam eyed the squat, thick-boned Munchkin suspiciously. His swarthy skin glistened from the light of the fire, deeply scored with weather wrinkles and frown lines that melted into each other, which reminded Sam of the tuck and folds on the hide of an old, lumbering hound dog. He had big, oversized teeth, which looked false but were his own, and a rim of lustrous purple hair cut short, which looked like a hairpiece but was also his own. The whiteness of his teeth was not that of ivory, but of the snowiest and most gleaming of china. Against the dark background of his saturnine skin they stood out most strikingly, giving the Munchkin a comical but formidable appearance. The irises of his eyes were bright orange, and the pupils an ink black. The eyeballs themselves were very white. And on the top of his head, mixed in with his purple hair, was a long, tufted patch of curly-green hair that also ran down his arms all the way to his ginger knuckles. He had a mild farmer's voice from the southwestern tip of Quadling Country, and a look of chronic suspicion and amusement.

"Then why," Akasha asked, "did you follow us and not make yourself known if your reason for doing so was not malicious?"

Sam's first impression was that the overall manner of the stocky Munchkin and the way he looked made it difficult to tell if he was good at what he did.

But unknown to Sam and Akasha, he was an assassin—a perfect killer. He had known his entire life that it was his special ability, much like being born an athlete, singer, or musician. He was proud of the fact that he could move from one shadow to the next with total obscurity, and with no hesitation when it was needed and when it suited him. He could blend into a grove of trees or melt into a crowd without ever being noticed. So stealthy he was, his victims never saw or heard his approach, and he was gone before their hearts stopped from his poisoned needle. He was able to see the entire shape and scope of his attack clearly in his mind and recreate it in slow motion, ferreting out any unseen detail. He had purposefully let Sam and Akasha know they were being followed. But at the moment, he decided not to tell his true nature. Not yet.

"I am on the same quest as you," he said, scooping out a big spoonful of stew, stuffing it into his mouth and sucking it down in one hefty, satisfying gulp. He then pointed his spoon at Sam but licked it first, and then with a wily smile spoke again. "And you, my dear princess, yes, I know who you are."

"Oh, really?" asked Sam.

"You need my help."

"And why is that?"

"I saw you and your cat fight the red dragon. You are both lucky to be alive," he said with another wily grin, his left eye narrowing to a curious slit.

"I can't disagree with you there, you funny, arrogant little goblin," Sam said, snickering and looking at Akasha. "I ask you again, why do you think you can help us, especially since you were cowering behind some tree watching us fight the red dragon and not willing to give us aid?"

"Point taken," the Munchkin replied, scooping up another large spoonful of stew, eating it, and licking the spoon as he slowly pulled it free of his mouth.

"A very good point, I might add," Akasha quickly added.

The Munchkin wiggled his spoon at Akasha and continued.

"Because, milady, the witch that you and your <u>cat</u> are tracking down is much harder to dispose of than a dragon," he said, showing a broad, toothy smile. "She is a sadistic spawn of evil, a hellish abomination that should be put to death by any means possible, and I am a born killer. You need a born killer."

"What makes you think we are looking for a witch?"

"Not just any witch," the Munchkin said, spooning in another mouthful of stew and swallowing. "She is the Dark One, the incarnation of pure evil. She is the temptress of vengeance. The harbinger of death. The wrecking. She is the enchantress who controls the flying monkeys and the Winkies. The one who has kidnapped your sister and your father."

"We know, we know," Akasha voiced with irritation.

"No, I don't think you do," retorted the Munchkin. "She is the one who has her sights on the Great Head himself." He paused and took another mouthful of stew and continued, "You are a fearless warrior, Princess. And so is your cat. Having another, like me, fight alongside you, will be to your advantage. The two of you can't do it by yourselves."

Akasha's fur stiffened. She stood up, walked over to the pot of stew sitting next to the fire, and dumped what was left in her bowl into the cooking pot. Tapping it on the edge of the kettle to get all the last little bits, she growled deep and low in her throat, thinking that Sam was right. She said to herself, *This Munchkin is certainly full of himself.* Then she looked straight at the Munchkin with narrowed eyes and said, "I am not anyone's cat." She sat down on her blanket, clawing it with her front paws, scrunching it into a comfortable mess, then curled up and pulled her sword out of her scabbard, placing it close to her, turning her back to the Munchkin before she spoke again. "Why should we trust you? Maybe you are under the witch's spell and one of her spies."

The Munchkin laughed out loud at that, showing all his teeth. If he had been grinning any wider, his face would have split in two. "If I were a spy, we wouldn't be having this conversation. I'd be sitting here alone, looking at your cold bodies as I slurped down every last tasty morsel of this delicious stew."

"Enough," Sam said firmly. His wide grin seemed as if it were permanently stitched to his large, broad face and puffed-out cheeks. Sam believed he was undoubtedly an expert at his craft. No question in her mind about that now. And up close, Sam couldn't help but notice all the scars on the Munchkin's body, and she wondered how many challenges and battles he'd been in and won. There was one particularly nasty-looking scar that was impossible to ignore; it snaked lengthwise down from the top of his forehead and stopped between his squinty, unflinching eyes. "You are the one the Crow told me about. The one he said would help us."

"Yes," the Munchkin said, as he scooped up more stew and put it in his bowl. "The Crow saved my life. I owe him a debt."

"What is your name, assassin?"

"Utherain Gresswolld Thorn, milady."

"That's a mouthful," Akasha mumbled with a huff, aggressively swishing the tip of her tail back and forth.

"My friends call me Thorn," he offered, ignoring Akasha's remark.

"Suits you well," Sam said, giving Akasha a stern look to mind her manners. "We will take any help we can get. And because—and only because—I trust the Scarecrow, I will trust you. We are grateful for your companionship." She glanced again at Akasha, who still had her narrowed and stern look, and continued, "Aren't we, Akasha?" Sam nodded her head to prod the cat, and Akasha relaxed her face, but only a little.

"As you wish . . ." Akasha said to Sam. She paused, sighed, and turned around to look Thorn directly in his eyes and spoke with an edgy tone to her voice that held only a small trace of sincerity, but was mostly filled with uncertainty. "Thorn, we are grateful for your help." Then she rolled back over onto her side with her back to the fire, facing away from Sam and Thorn, and let out a low guttural, *umph*. She stared wide-eyed at the writhe of a tree root planted close to her, while she rubbed her paw along the cool, flat surface of her sword, and added, "But you're not riding with me. You're on your own, Munchkin."

Thorn whistled—a loud, earsplitting whistle. Akasha and Jo's ears flicked toward the sound, and out of the dark trotted a horse, half the size of Jo, coffee-colored with a cream mane. Thorn got up and clicked his tongue and his horse slowly walked up to him. The Munchkin reached into his pocket and took out a couple cubes of sugar, palming them in his left hand. The little, half-sized pony—a roan mare—shook her head and her full, lustrous, cream-colored and black mane. And with her lips and tongue, she quickly took the sweets from him. Thorn rubbed her cheek, patted her neck, grinned, and said, "Billy is a good horse. She's been mine since she was born."

"Even allies must know their place," Sam said, and was surprised at how decisive her voice sounded, "even if they call a female horse Billy. If we can't work together, then we work alone. Your choice, Thorn." Sam got up and walked over to Billy, opening her hand to show the horse an apple in her palm. Billy sniffed it first, but happily took it from her. Sam patted Billy on the neck and looked at Thorn, then said, "I will not let my sister die in the hands of such wickedness. Nor my father." Sam extended her hand down to Thorn and they shook, sealing a promise that they'd work together for the same cause. "Get in my way, and you'll know my sword firsthand."

"Understood, milady," Thorn said, as he stood up and bowed to Sam with respect.

Akasha turned back around, leaning her weight on one elbow, and said to Sam, "I am with you, Princess. To victory or death."

"As am I," said Thorn. "To victory or death." The Munchkin unpacked his bedroll and lay down, covering himself with a blanket.

࿈ ◆ ࿈

Sam sat on her bedding and pulled her blanket over her shoulders. Reaching for her travel pack, Sam dug through her clothes, looking for a small leather purse. She kept a small amount of the fire ointment in her pack so she could rub it on the thin scar on her leg. Every night before bed, she would use a tiny amount of the ointment's healing powers, and tonight for some odd reason, her thigh was throbbing more than it had in months.

Something unfamiliar shifted and scooted lightly inside her pack. She found an envelope of white vellum, one that the Crow used for all his writings. Sam held it up and stared at the letter, willing it to be filled with wisdom and encouraging words from the Crow. Sam gazed at the envelope for another long moment, watching the amber glow from the campfire dance across its skin; then, she broke the Crow's seal.

Out slid a simple braided leather bracelet with bits of straw woven into the decorative band.

Sam opened the envelope wider, rolling her finger around the inner corners, looking for a letter. She tilted the envelope up, peering inside against the sputtering firelight, and saw a single word scrawled in the Crow's writing beneath the seal.

Believe

She chuckled to herself. There were no great words of wisdom, but she loved the thoughtful gift. She smiled and put the bracelet on her wrist. She stretched out, covered her body with her blanket and looked up into the night sky. The stars dotted the blackness overhead, shimmering quietly, unconcerned with the events unfolding all around her. After a moment, she could hear Jo and the other horses shuffle and shift to find a spot for sleep.

Sam inhaled and let her breath out slowly, feeling her rib cage rise and fall. She was exhausted from the ride, and her thigh still ached. She closed her eyes and turned over on her side. Her crown gently stroked her cheeks, sensing her gloomy mood. "It will all work out," she said in a hushed, sleepy tone, as she placed her crown on the blanket close to her, letting its grassy shoots rub her hand for comfort as she gripped the hilt of her sword. Despite having Akasha by her side, and now the interloper, this Munchkin thrown into the mix, Sam felt isolated. For the past year, she had spent her days practicing swordplay with the Crow, the Tin Woodman, and the Lion. And at night, they sat around the long dinner table by a warm fire, talking, debating, and laughing. Now her friends were miles away, riding to join her mother's army.

She heard more shuffling and snorting from the horses. Once they finally calmed themselves, the silence was broken only by the small snaps of the fire, and even those at last subsided and real darkness fell. Sam wondered, *What else is out there waiting for us?* And then she repeated in her mind, like a monk's meditative chant, *Believe. Believe. Believe.* But when she fell asleep, her nightmares claimed her, and again she was suspended in a frightening fog, with only a dim, ghostly glow of her sister's face reflecting from it.

S am woke with a cramp in her side and a root resting under her, wedged in the hollow between her last rib and pelvis. Jo and the other horses were wide awake and anxious to start the day, and Akasha had already packed her gear and saddled her horse and was giving Sam a wide-eyed smile. Jo's ears were turned back as he eyed the newest cast members to their troupe. Sam thought how tired a horse like Billy must be—and so small—to carry an oversized Munchkin like Thorn, and she instantly felt sorry for the tiny horse.

Thorn had restarted the fire, and Sam's stomach gurgled from the meaty aroma of the leftover stew. "We added a plump cony to the mix," Thorn said without looking at Sam. "Your cat was up early and went hunting."

Sam grinned and got up and rubbed her hands by the fire. "I would suggest that you call her by her name and not my *cat.*"

"I like *cat,*" he said with a wink and wry grin as he poured some of the stew into a bowl and handed it to Sam. Sam took it with both hands and held it close to her nose to let the steam warm her face.

"Smells good," she said.

ॐ ◆ ॐ

After eating and dousing the campfire and covering it with dirt, Sam gathered up her gear, saddled Jo, and tied her bedroll behind the cantle. She moved slowly as if all her joints ached, and then decided she was willing enough to ride at a comfortable pace for the first part of the morning to help ease the dull pain in her joints. She pulled an apple from her saddlebag, took her knife from its sheath that was attached to her chin guard, and cut it in half, holding one piece out to Jo. He sniffed and snorted and immediately gobbled it down. When she gave him the other half, she put her cheek to his and closed her eyes, listening to the sound of his chewing. But the chewing sound turned into the jabbering voices that were growling and whimpering at the very ragged edges of her mind. And there—suspended, it seemed, in a cold and uninviting fog—were those voices, trying their hardest to overpower her thoughts. The nightmares that haunted her sleepless nights were now tormenting her during the day. It had been happening ever since she had the vision of the witch torturing her sister. To lift the fog and quell the devilish voices echoing back and forth in her head, Sam murmured the words the Scarecrow had taught her, but the image of her sister crying out in agony claimed her. Sam was not able to keep the weeping flow from coming and felt hot-wax tears roll down her cheeks. She tried again, but this time with conviction. She chanted the Scarecrow's words over an over until they replaced the fogginess of her mind with something bright and definite, something real.

She recalled one weekend when she was seven, when Elle had been given a real sword and was allowed to train with Saran, and she wasn't. Sam had been so jealous she honestly thought she would die if she weren't given a real sword too. Her mother and father had no patience for theatrics; they tried to reason with Sam, but she ran out of the castle and threw a full-blown tantrum in the storage barn, filled with tears and screaming. She grabbed an ax, hacking her wooden sword to splinters. It was Elle who'd wiped Sam's face and sat with her on the straw floor of the barn until she cried herself out.

"I will find you a real sword, and you and I will practice here in the barn," Elle had told her. "I will teach you everything Saran teaches me."

"Mother and Father won't approve," Sam replied sobbing, as more tears seeped out.

"It will be our secret."

"You swear?"

"I swear."

That had been enough to dry Sam's tears and calm her anger. Elle had kept her promise. In the years that followed, they secretly practiced their sword fighting in the barn whenever they could sneak away together. And now with her sister being taken from her and held captive by the Wicked Witch, it was more than Sam could stand and something she wouldn't accept. She bent forward to press her face into Jo's mane and dry her eyes, and then she felt the pressure of a heavy paw on her shoulder and whiskers tickling her neck. She looked up to see two large, almond-shaped, yellow eyes swimming in a black face that had a soft and sympathetic smile.

"We will save your sister," Akasha said confidently, and with a fervent look and great care, she reached out with her other paw and held Sam's shoulders in a firm, reassuring grip. "And your father."

With an inward wince, Sam asked, "And if not, what then?" Sam took the palm of her hand to rub her eyes clear and looked hopefully at her friend.

"That I cannot answer," Akasha replied, removing her paws from Sam's shoulders and taking the reins of her horse. Then she mounted her steed and looked back at Sam. "Let us worry not about the future, but ride straight into it and bend it to our will."

They did not make camp at the end of the long day, but instead only stopped for a moment to rest their horses and let them drink the cold running water of a gentle, peaceful stream. They had decided they would ride through the night. The sooner they arrived at Rumpart's castle, the better they would feel—or so they hoped.

With the sunlight almost gone, the shadows twisted and crowded together, layer upon layer where the darkness claimed the forest. The full moon was slowly rising and peeking through the tree branches with its shimmering yellow glow, casting long, eerie, wraith-like tree shadows across their path.

There was nothing to talk about, only riding and wondering about what might happen once they were standing eye to eye with the Wicked Witch. Night sounds were the only noises that broke the silence of the ride, and worried thoughts crowded their minds.

The clear, whistle-like call of the oblong-winged tree beetle, smooth and without vibrato, sang out in a loud chorus from every part of the forest, and the rasping lisp of an argyle mud hornet buzzed for a while and then stopped, rested a bit, and then buzzed again. They heard the occasional haunting, echoed hoot of a great horned night owl and the hurried rustling of larger creatures scurrying through the undergrowth, and they flinched each time their horses snapped a twig as they marched along the forest trail. These were the sounds that kept them company while they rode to confront the witch and save Sam's sister. Or die trying.

Sam inhaled deeply and let her breath out slowly, rubbing Jo's neck. He was warm to the touch, and she gently patted him with the flat of her hand. "Everything will turn out fine," Sam quietly said. "I can handle it." She reassured herself by rubbing Jo some more, because doing so helped her convince herself that what she had just said out loud was the truth—that everything, in fact, would be okay. She leaned forward, putting her ear against his neck, and listened to the rhythm of his breathing, closed her eyes, and whispered to herself, "Elle, I am coming."

Nineteen

The mountains were now far behind them but still visible, standing like proud, wise wizards guarding the world.

Their horses were anxious, shifting from side to side and shaking their heads. Sam rubbed and patted Jo on his neck to calm him.

They stood on a hillside looking over an ugly, uneven plain where no living plant or animal could be seen, only the gnarled carcasses and broken stumps of trees that had been blackened and scorched by dragonfire. Gray and black saturated everything, dull and rutty, like the skin of something long dead. The landscape laid out before them was comprised of barren, sooty, useless soil and the skeletons of once-mighty trees. Sam's tiny army stepped off and glided down from the butte.

"We are close," Sam warned, and Jo heaved a great sigh and stopped. "This devastation is from dragons." Sam unslung her sword, as Akasha and Thorn did the same. She felt the comfort of its shank in her hand, but there was nothing for the sword to do in the bleakness of the land that had been destroyed, where no spring could ever again come to the trees that had been charred to smoldering ash.

Sam's eyelids closed. She tilted her head and listened, and the memory of the Wicked Witch's fierce and angry eyes slid through her mind, leaving a fetid residue, a taste of staleness. The unappealing thought ended when she heard the fluttering of a single bird flapping its wings overhead, chirping in distress as it flew, and Sam opened her eyes to once again gaze upon nothing but destruction and hopelessness.

As soon as they rode upon the desolate landscape, Jo was on alert, nervous, and his hide had turned a grayish black mixed with orange, the colors of burning charcoal. Without a word, they traversed in utter silence, like some small phantasmagoria across the blackened waste of scorched earth, leaving only ashen hoofprints behind from the slow gait of their odd-toed ungulates, the only sign left for the next travelers to know that other riders had been there to be a witness to such reckless destruction.

They might indeed have been the wraiths of the departed dead upon a dead sea of a dying land. There was no joyous birdsong, not even the occasional trill and churr of an insect, and the silence hammered at them, except when the stillness was broken by one of the horses snorting or shaking its head, or the creaking of the leather saddles. The nightmares were still trying to invade Sam's thoughts, and the voices could barely be heard, as if they were locked behind a thick steel door. But she did hear them, quietly somewhere far off in the distance, muffled, snarling, and sniveling—patiently waiting for her to let her guard down.

"The sun will set soon," Akasha said. "Maybe we should make camp here and continue in the morning?"

Sam looked at Akasha and shook her head, nudging Jo to walk forward, leading the others. There was nothing to see but the heavy gray sky above and the bleak, charcoal-blackened, parched landscape under their feet. The slate-colored thunderclouds that were rimmed with dark edges concealed all the sun's light, and there was no visible horizon in front of them except for a dense, white and dark gray fog that moved and shifted as if it were alive, traversing the entire length of the valley, hiding—or perhaps protecting—what lay behind it.

֎ ◆ ֍

Her troop followed her because they believed in the same cause she did, and they were all too aware of what lay ahead of them. Just as the Scarecrow had said, the voices inside her head pushed harder along one side of her skull than the other, and so she went toward them and listened to their cries. She lost track of herself, didn't know where she was, but kept marching forward toward the voice, toward the fog.

And then without warning, she could see right through the dense, auguring mist.

Standing in the middle of it was Rumpart's castle, but it had been altered, for it had in the middle of it an enormous tower made of black stone, an impossible, looming minaret of such height that it seemed as if it could be easily ripped apart and turned into a pile of rubble in the next great storm. At its peak were huge windows, two times Sam's own height, and in one of the windows was the Wicked Witch, standing, staring, waiting.

Akasha trotted alongside of Jo. "Sam!" she shouted, reaching down to grab Jo's reins to stop him before he blindly walked into the fog. "Wake up!"

"In front of us," she tried to say calmly, looking at the cat. "Rumpart's castle." Her crown tugged at her ears and pulled her hair, and Jo turned a fiery red as she lowered her head into his mane to control her breathing. After a few deep and even breaths, she straightened her back and looked through the fog. "The witch is waiting for us." Then she steepled her fingers, pressing them firmly to her lips, and closed her eyes.

Thorn pulled his swords from their scabbards, his unibrow forming a confused knot. "Where is she?"

"Not here," Sam answered in an anxious whisper, with a frown that was bleak. "There."

When she pointed toward the ominous, misty cloud, it parted, but only enough for them to peer through its murky, nebulous wall. There before them, on the other side of the fog, was Rumpart's castle and the massive center spire with the large windows at its peak that circled the tower. The Wicked Witch, holding her broom, was standing before one of the windows looking down on them—a dark shape, a silhouette of evil.

Soaring around the tower like vultures hovering above a decaying carcass were dozens of flying monkeys.

The three dismounted and slowly walked forward. Akasha and Sam raised their swords and Sam gripped her shield firmly, her eyes fixed on the Wicked Witch. Thorn moved his two swords swiftly back and forth and over his shoulders, before holding them steady in front of himself. Thorn and Akasha looked at each other and shared numbed, perplexed expressions on their faces.

Sam tilted her head, closed her eyes, and just listened. "We're coming to the point . . . ," Sam opened her eyes, looked around, then lowered her voice, and continued, "We're coming to the point where there is no turning back."

Akasha interrupted Sam's reverie. "So, what's the plan?"

Sam tossed her braided hair back impatiently, and she gave Akasha a strange, flat, challenging look. She didn't know what her plan was, but one of the good things about being the leader, she thought, was you can sometimes get away with just winging it. "We wing it," Sam said in a faraway voice, as she focused her gaze all the more on the dark, evil shape standing in the tower window.

"Works for me," Thorn replied, slashing his swords back and forth quickly through the air.

Akasha flashed a look of irritation toward Sam and let out a low growl in agreement, then set her eyes on the Wicked Witch standing patiently in the window and felt a chill run up and down her spine. "Okay, we . . . wing it."

"I'll take the lead," Sam said.

The witch disappeared from the window and the window's yellowish glow brightened. The ebony tower seemed to change before their eyes and turn into the neck and head of the great red dragon; it snapped its neck toward them and opened its mouth, breathing out its deadly fire.

Akasha's left arm was suddenly on fire and the pain of the old burns returned, new and fresh, and she smelled her fur and skin burning as before.

Sam clutched her leg, and like Akasha, she felt the old pain as if it had just happened, burning and ripping down her thigh.

Thorn stood and watched as Akasha and Sam fell to their knees, writhing in agony on the blackened, scorched ground, watched them squirm and twist their bodies as if being tortured by an unseen foe. He did not understand what had crippled them so and why he was left unharmed, nor could he help them.

Then Sam stood up and fell against Jo and grabbed his mane. She smelled his scent, something familiar, something she loved, and her mind cleared, and she no longer felt the stinging claws of the red dragon ripping into her leg. She bent down next to Akasha, who was still thrashing on the ground; Sam grabbed her paws and yelled, "It's not real!" Then she firmly pushed Akasha's paws down hard to the ground. "Listen to my voice . . . Akasha!" she cried. "Open your eyes. It's not real!"

When Akasha finally obeyed and opened her eyes, she saw Sam hovering over her, and the smell of her burnt flesh had vanished. Akasha sat up fearfully, for her left arm still throbbed with memory. But there was no fire and no dragon, only Sam and Thorn, their horses, the fog, and the monstrous black tower standing before them.

Sam stood up and held her arm out to Akasha to help her up.

"It's the witch," Sam said in a thin and uncertain voice. "Made our wounds come alive again."

"That was quite a show," Thorn replied.

"Indeed," Akasha agreed. "Quite a show."

Sam looked again at the window where the witch had stood, with its yellowish glow, and she narrowed her eyes, for she knew she would not let the witch trick her again.

⌘ ◆ ⌘

As they entered the foggy veil, the breeze died and the air became stale. It smelled of old things, like rotting earth. The mist closed in on them and grew perceptually colder and brighter, as though glowing from its own radiance.

The moisture-filled haze seemed to actually touch them, caressing and slithering along their skin, the touch cold and clammy. The earth's surface had changed and was now soft and chalky—the same color as the fog—and they were surprised when they noticed each muffled clump their horses made as the chalky residue evaporated off their hooves, drifting away in smoking tendrils as though it too were somehow part of the fog.

When they cautiously moved forward into the mist, an odor permeated Sam's nostrils, every bit as offensive as the sour rot of garbage. It was the musky smell of decay and burning flesh—the gastric utterances of the dead. But it was the sound they heard that confused them, an eerie, brittle crunching.

The three horses faltered and stopped in midstride. Then the trio noted what their horses had tripped over, a white shape with two large dark holes. Sam squinted, leaned forward, and realized she was staring at the eye sockets of a human skull. Not just one, but thousands of skulls and bones of the dead were scattered about; and not just bones, they saw helmets, swords, pikes, and shields. The skeletons lay half buried in the toxic yellow dirt, wrapped in the last remnants of rusting armor and worm-riddled flesh, and there were nests of red, blond, and black-braided scalp still attached to the top of many of the dried and ashen skulls—rotting flesh stretched across silent screams.

"A killing field," Akasha whispered. "Planted with the crops of the dead."

"Of those unwilling to kneel to the wicked queen," Thorn quickly added loudly, his horse neighing and snorting.

To Sam's alarm, Thorn's voice and his horse's neigh had carried, not just echoed, actually rolled across the fog as though the fog itself were pushing it along. Sam snapped a finger to her lips, "*Shhhh!*" She looked at Thorn in surprise, then over to Akasha, and that's when they heard it—soft and far away at first, but quickly moving closer—low, deep, unholy growling and gnashing of teeth, of wild things foaming at the mouth. And behind this, or maybe within, they heard wailing, a pitiful, bloodcurdling keening. The hair on the back of Sam's neck stood up and her crown stiffened. Then Sam caught movement out of the corner of her eye. The mist had begun to stir, only shadows at first, mere shades of gray on top of gray that began to swim and fly through the etiolated air, the dull, shifting grayness swirling and boiling all around them. The shadows grew, became more distinct. Some of them turned into hulking and sluggish-looking beasts, almost lumbering, and some just furtively moved along, tendril-like wisps of indefinable vapor that flew around their heads and bodies and the legs of the horses. Some were small and fleet as sparrows, hovering around them, staring down at them with searing, pitch-black eyes. Some were no bigger than grasshoppers, while others were closer to the size of rats—thin, spindly, elfish creatures with silky gray insect wings and sharp, whipped tails, with their mouths opened into a gaping maw where Sam could see rows and rows of jagged little teeth.

"Shoo," Sam whispered, as her crown swatted at the vicious aberrations. But the small, gray, nebulous manifestations continued to stare back at her with their cruel, beady little eyes, unwilling to let go of their prey.

"Leave me alone," she said louder, waving her hand at them to shove them away. But her hand merely went through their smoky bodies, and they quickly coalesced into their original ghoulish shape. Sam watched Jo's color change, and could feel his coal-black hide shiver as a dark, bloodred color rolled across his body from one end to the other. She nudged him with her heels and clicked her tongue to make him move forward.

"Go away!" Sam yelled, swatting at the vile apparitions to no avail. The nasty little creatures became more aggressive, following them in tight circles, howling and hissing. They bared their needlelike teeth, shrieking like feral cats. Then the rest of the gray shadowy monsters began to growl. Their cries echoing from every direction seemed to crawl into their heads, wiggling and squirming and gorging on their gray matter.

Sam's breath quickened. Her crown screeched and thrashed at

the foul spirits. Sam gritted her teeth, balled her hands into fists, and clamped them tightly onto the reins as they marched onward at a quick, steady clip. She felt the mist was caving in on her like she would suffocate—like she was being swallowed.

The howling grew stronger. More gray shadowy phantoms came, dozens, then hundreds, all shapes and sizes, filling the air with their screams and wails. She felt their wispy fingers crawling through her hair, her clothes, over her mouth and eyes, nipping at her skin— poking, stinging, biting. Then suddenly, many of them gathered together, as though trying to build a wall to encircle them, to hem them in. Their horses became more agitated, turning and shifting, disorienting their riders. Each stinging bite left tiny, nasty-looking red bumps that dotted their skin.

"What kind of black magic is this?" Akasha cried out at the top of her voice.

"The kind that gets you dead," Thorn replied with his own anxious tone. Then raising his voice to be heard over the ghostly cries, he yelled, "Which way do we ride?"

Sam took in a slow breath, closed her eyes, and muttered words for a direction spell her mother had taught her when she was a child. It was a simple spell to cast, one she had used many times when she found herself turned around when foraging in the North Woods or hunting game. And since the trees always liked to move in search of better sunlight and firmer ground to root, it was easy to become confused and not know which way to go.

She repeated the incantation over and over, then opened her eyelids as each word grew louder and louder, echoing across the mist. "Estahowen, naweowen! . . . Estahowen, naweowen! . . . ESTAHOWEN, NAWEOWEN!" Her eyes turned a brilliant orange, glowing for only a second, and there on the chalky, powdery soil lay a thin, golden thread, sliding and shifting as though blown by a hidden wind, showing the way out of the fog.

But more and more evil spirits came, disembodied heads flying around, swarming around them, beasts of all shapes and sizes, their barks and howls, screams and growls rumbling back and forth, joined by the crackling wails and moans of those who had died, their tortured cries booming about the mist like thunder. "Follow me!" Sam shouted above the wails and screams. Then she kicked Jo hard in the ribs, triggering him into a run, and tried not to listen to the cracking and crunching of bones as she galloped, following the golden thread to get away from the creatures she believed would consume them, kill them, and add their skulls and bones to those already littering the ground.

Sam and her companions broke through the ghostly wall, out into the open, and raced forward. The horrifying cries stopped, and as the fog settled down, the sky returned to a state of placid, endless gray. Sam pulled back on Jo's reins hard to bring him to a halt only inches away from falling into a massive moat that was guarding the enormous, black stone walls of Rumpart's castle. She realized she was holding her breath and had to take a moment to breathe again and let out a gulp of air, like a surfacing swimmer, and held back her desire to scream.

Sam carefully stepped Jo back from the edge of the moat. As she leaned back into the saddle, pulling on Jo's reins, she looked back over her shoulder, back into the swirling gray mass. It was as if the instant they had left the fog's embrace, two giant hands had taken hold of it along their path and pushed it away like curtains being drawn apart, leaving only the dead behind to seed the earth.

"What was that?" Akasha wondered aloud between big, hitching breaths as she rode up alongside Sam.

Sam shook her head regretfully. "The witch's doing."

Still full of adrenaline, Akasha examined the high walls of the castle and its massive drawbridge and anxiously asked, "What do we do now?"

"We wait," Sam replied, as she too stared straight ahead at the castle with her eyes wide open, her heart caught in her throat. Atop each of the gateposts sat the head of a soldier, their mouths frozen forever in the silent screams of the dead, their hair blowing in a brisk breeze. The dark hollows of their eyes stared back at Sam, an ill omen of the fate of all of Oz if the warriors did not defeat the witch. Sam studied the drawbridge and gate entrance to the castle. It was a marvel of engineering: at least fifty feet high, cut from massive northern oak trees, supported by two enormous pillars that jutted upward from the ground, reaching another twenty feet above the drawbridge.

Jo was nervous, stomping and braying, and shaking his head. She relaxed his reins and patted his neck, making soft cooing sounds and hoping to reassure him and calm him, and in doing so, it helped her lower her own heart rate, which made it easier for her to breathe. Jo turned from his bloodred color to black, but was still keyed up, still on alert. All the horses were jumpy, anxiously dancing back and forth, wanting their masters to ride away and put the castle, that horrible place, to their backs. Sam felt her chest tighten, and she glanced back the way they'd come, thinking for only a second that she too wanted to run away from all this madness.

Then she heard a voice. A voice she knew. It was in her head, just a faint whisper, but it was clear enough. Sam called back. *Elle, it's me. I'm here.*

Thorn's horse, Billy, was extremely nervous, dancing back and forth, turning, shifting from side to side, wanting to bolt. Thorn held her reins in a tight grip, trying to calm her down and keep her from running off. "We should circle the castle and maybe find another way in," he suggested. But before Thorn could say another word, the enormous gate shuddered, and its heavy bolts clacked open. The massive wood-and-iron door creaked and groaned and clanked its rusty metal chains. They watched, pulling back on their horses' reins to keep them steady, as the drawbridge slowly came down, offering them passage over the moat. It hit the ground with a loud thud and shook the earth beneath them, rattling their bones and jolting their nerves.

Jo reared, neighed, and shuffled his front legs. Then he shook his head and turned coal black, holding his ears flat. Sam's crown yanked the tips of her ears and pulled them hard, more out of fear than as a warning of danger. "The witch is certainly sure of herself," Sam said, more to herself than to the others.

"I guess it's her way of saying, come on in. Let's have some tea," Thorn said sarcastically. "But you'll have to climb to the top of my big, hulking fortress of doom and eternal punishment."

Sam did not remember Rumpart's castle being as fortified and menacing as it looked now. The air that rushed out from behind the giant drawbridge was stale, heavy with the smell of death. The air was also burning—a burning of unclean things. Jo and the other horses shifted their feet from side to side, hides twitching out of apprehension. And when the trio urged their steeds forward, their clomping echoed loudly on the wooden drawbridge, for there was no other sound in the air but their own.

Sam looked up at the top of the tower and noticed that only a few of the flying monkeys were circling overhead now. Most of the vicious creatures were nesting on the slate roof of the tower, watching them with their sinister orange eyes, and the windows at the top were still glowing like beacons of doom, like the eyes of the red dragon. In the back of Sam's mind, there was a terrible bloodthirsty monster in a cage, hidden in the shadows, pacing tirelessly to and fro, showing only the glint of a savage eyeball, the shine of a predator's fangs. She knew if she allowed herself, the hinges of her knees would go weak from the memory of her first encounter with the great dragon. She reached down and brushed Jo's neck to help calm her rapidly beating heart and slow her breathing. Daylight was quickly disappearing. Soon, it would be dark.

They rode carefully across the courtyard, for the stones that covered the ground were slippery, not sound footing for a shod horse such as Jo and the others. When they came to the entrance of the great black tower, they dismounted. Sam stared at the top. It made her dizzy, and it forced her to look away. She put her arms around Jo's neck to steady herself, and quickly put her face in his mane, something she had done so often to ground herself, show Jo her love, and receive comfort from his warm body. He tucked his nose against her shoulder, which gave her great pleasure, and she stepped away from him to enter the tower. He bolted forward—rearing, neighing, and turning bright red, a warhorse going to battle. She looked back at him sternly, lowering her hand, and he settled, but only a little, snorting and stomping his right leg. He walked over to her, rubbing his muzzle against her body and nosing for an apple. Sam reached into her saddlebag and pulled one out, cut it in half, and gave it to Jo.

୧ ◆ ୨

Through the entrance they saw stairs winding up into the black tower, yellow with torchlight flickering over the steep staircase, and the horses had their eyes on the trio as they entered and set their feet on the first stair.

The limestone steps went up and up in a long spiral, and as the group moved upward, they circled round and round until it seemed to them that they must be climbing a tunnel to the heavens, and at the end they would step out and touch the stars. With the noiselessness of disembodied spirits, they moved stealthily up the tower. For a short while, they could hear their trusted companions snorting and neighing restlessly below. But when the last sounds of their horses faded away, all they heard was the soft sound of their own footsteps or the occasional sputter of a guttering torch. Daylight had abandoned them when they entered the tower, and now it had left them entirely. All that was left was the yellow reflection in their eyes from the burning torches that bounced off the black stone walls.

The air around them was tainted and foul. Their legs ached from climbing. Their backs ached with tension. Their necks grew painful from looking up as they ascended.

୧ ◆ ୨

L arge brown wood-and-iron doors were scattered every twenty feet or so along the staircase. The doors led into rooms they dared not enter, for there was only one room that Sam knew they needed to reach, and that was at the very top, where the Wicked Witch was waiting for them.

The silence grew heavy, crushing. It weighed Sam down. She recognized the fetid, repugnant scent, its sickening flavor. She had smelled and it tasted it only twice before.

Pure evil.

She'd known it when her father was taken from her and in the red dragon's fiery breath—its destructive flame had the foul smell of it. Reeked of it. And this place, this tower, the air all around them, everything had that nauseating stench of corruption, the odor of death permanently seared into its core. But they moved on, the muscles in their thighs and shinbones twisting and curling, tightening, and still they climbed and didn't stop, not for one second. The sooner they met the witch face-to-face, the sooner they'd be free of the evil that was trying to suck the life out of them. Their eyes burned from it; it rode on their shoulders. It whimpered and screamed from the doorways they dared not open, smelling like the scorched trees in the open plain and rising like oily smoke from the torches. The witch's foul scent was all around them. Step-by-step it watched them, watched them sweat and heave in heavy breaths of the rancid air, coughing and choking from its strong, repugnant smell.

Still, the stairs loomed forever upwards, and yet they continued their ascent with no rest. Sam wondered how many hours they had spent climbing, or was it her imagination, another of the witch's deceptions? She worried about the horses, and if they too, like her, could feel and smell the surge of evil that was pressing down upon them. She especially worried about Jo, and wished now that she had not brought him to such danger.

S uddenly the torches brightened, and in an instant, Sam could not see clearly, and she had to shield her eyes from an intense, white glare. Everything around her seemed to sway, and the world blurred before her for a second in a swirl of colors. When the haze dissipated, she was not climbing the staircase any longer. She found that she was standing on top of a large hill, looking out over a vast and beautiful green valley, trees healthy and full of leaves swaying in a gentle, sweet-smelling breeze. And off in the distance was Rumpart's castle and the witch's tower, now made of alabaster instead of black stone, shining like a beacon of hope. She heard her name off in the distance. It came as a muffled ripple, uncertain, worried.

Sam.

Then she heard the soothing rhythm of the outdoors—birds singing, trees breathing, flowers blooming, bees buzzing, all the peaceful sounds of life in harmony. Beautiful butterflies floated about, pollinating thousands and thousands of multicolored flowers blooming from every vine, tree, and bush from where she stood to the horizon. A chorus of birdsong drifted about on the gentle spring breeze. The bright sun touched her face, and she lifted her head to meet the light, letting the warmth bathe her whole body.

Sam drew in a deep breath, filling her lungs with the sweet aroma of flowers and the spice of earth. Jo was standing next to her, cream-colored and calm, his head down munching on new, sprouting sweetgrass.

She smiled and let out a soft breath with a soft sigh, and immediately took in another deep breath of the fresh, cool, clean air, which prickled her skin and brought color to her cheeks. Then she put her hand on Jo's neck and didn't feel his warmth; instantly she knew what she was experiencing could not be real. *Another trick by the witch*, instantly jumped into her mind. But everything was so amazing, so beautiful, and so peaceful that it was hard not to want to believe it was real . . . giggles caught her attention. A multitude of faerie folk danced and frolicked from one end of the dreamy landscape to the other. All different sizes, from that of a small bird to that of an insect. Many of them had wings and ice-blue skin like hers. Others were white and pink and yellow, which reminded her of the wondrous creatures in the cavern under Silver Lake.

As she looked out at the gorgeous scenery, she realized she was holding the red hand of the Wicked Witch. She did not feel the evil that had been pressing down on her, nor did she feel anger or hatred toward the witch. The witch's hand was warm to the touch, soft and comforting, and Sam looked up at her. *"Is this heaven?"* she asked.

"This, Samantha," the Wicked Witch said with a smooth, gentle motherly voice as she moved her free hand, palm up, from left to right in front of her in a gesture of peace and tranquility, *"will be the world we'll live in if you stand by my side."*

"It's beautiful," Sam said, dazed. *"And my sister?"*

The voice again.

Sam.

"Your sister is happy," the witch cooed. *"She is waiting for you, and she misses you. She wants you to join us. The day of the Wiz, the Great Head, the Great and Powerful Wizard of Oz, is over. Together, we shall rule over this land with a mighty and unshakable fist."*

Sam did not answer the witch, for she heard her name again, this time with much concern, and she paused.

Sam, wake up!

This was not the witch's voice, but another—one that was familiar to her. This was Akasha's voice, and it was frantic. The witch seemed to hear it too and whirled around, her black skirt spinning over the ground with a sinister *whoosh*. Dark, ominous clouds formed in the sky, and the alabaster tower changed to black stone. Trees burst into flames, turning as black as night, leaves curling and turning to ash, blown away by the breeze. All the flowers, one by one, burst into flame as though they were thousands of torches set on fire that washed through the landscape—hissing as it rolled—like an ocean wave, and the witch howled, *"You shall not have her!"*

Sam raised her hands to push the witch away, and that's when Sam's skin turned black. Right before her eyes, twisting splotches of darkness snaked along her arms, and scaly spots the color of bruises bloomed across the back of her hands. She watched, terrified, as her fingers twisted into jagged black claws.

"Sam!" Akasha shouted, grabbing her shoulders and shaking her. "Wake up. Wake up!"

The vision faded. "My sister?" Sam said, opening her eyes and seeing the two large, almond-shaped cat eyes staring back at her. Sam could feel the veins in her neck throb; she panted in rhythm with her pumping heart. Sweat ran into her eyes and her crown wiped them free, but they still burned from the saltiness of it. "By the Great Head," she muttered, "we shall be free of this evil." This lightened the malevolent cloud that was trying to invade her mind, press her down, control her and weaken her. But she felt her face grow hot and she felt faint, as if someone were trying to pull her back into the dream.

Sam buried her head into Akasha's shoulder to push back the dizziness, and she waited until her breathing evened out. Finally her pulse slowed, and her mind stopped racing. *How could this witch deceive me again?* she admonished herself. "Let's move on," she insisted.

"At your side," Akasha said, taking two steps at a time up the stairs. "It won't be long now. I am sure of it."

"And I have your back, Princess," Thorn said, as he gazed back at the staircase that seemed to spiral downward into nothing but an endless, dark, and malevolent void.

Sam was fighting not to shrink, leg muscles on the edge of collapse, face flushed, still on fire. They continued to climb. Up and up.

Having Akasha and Thorn by her side, and seeing that their determination was equal to her own, motivated her to fight through the pain and not let the witch creep back into her skull. But everything ached, and for a split second, Sam wished she had flown to the top of the tower instead of tromping up the never-ending staircase.

But it would have been foolish of her to have done so and met the witch alone. *Maybe I am maturing and using my wits, instead of jumping in first without thinking of the consequences*, she thought, as she gasped for air.

"You had another vision," Akasha said over her shoulder, "didn't you? The Wicked Witch?"

"Yes," Sam replied.

"And?"

"Nothing but a lie."

"Why am I not surprised?"

At first, when they reached the top, they were unsure, did not believe it, for they were looking at a doorway similar to all the others they had passed on their long, spiral ascent, except it was a double door, rounded at the top. Two torches were spitting and sputtering on either side, and as they approached, the ceiling blackened from the flames. The doors opened on their own by an invisible force, and as they did, the torches went out, although there was no draft to silence them. The tower chamber was brightly lit, with torches staged around the room, one on each side of the windows. Sam let out a quiet sigh, trying to overcome an awful premonition of finality. And although Sam's premonitions often came to nothing, this time she felt a throbbing ache in her bones that said otherwise.

The trio looked into the giant hall and had a choice as they stood before the threshold: turn around and go back, or cross it. The rational side of their minds briefly considered simply bolting back down the stairs—a bright and tempting fantasy that lasted less than a second before it faded.

The three intrepid warriors shot a quick glance at each other and nodded, accepting their choice and solidarity. Then they turned to look straight ahead and stepped forward, ready to face the Wicked Witch and fight to the death.

Twenty

he tower chamber was enormous, as big as a stable for fifty horses. The large windows were staggered twenty feet apart, like devilish sentries protecting their queen, and the blackness of the night was pervasively present. Between the windows and torches, large flags with a red border were seated on flagpoles. They were flapping gently in a stiff breeze and showed the witch's colors: black with a red circle in the middle, and in the center of that, a smaller black circle, and a smaller red circle within that.

☙ ◆ ❧

Overhead, the ceiling was elaborately decorated with a dramatic, colorful mural showing the Wicked Witch standing on top of a hillside, holding a red sword that was shooting out red lightning in all directions. Below her, all the different citizens of Oz were depicted— Munchkins, Quadlings, Gillikins, Winkies, speaking animals— everyone bowing their heads in obedience. And hovering above the good people of Oz was Sam's father, with his mighty black wings stretched to their full length, along with the red dragon and the flying monkeys blindly following the witch's orders.

The painted ceiling was breathtaking and frightening at the same time, but it had one depiction that was far more disturbing to Sam than all the rest. Sam raised an eyebrow, trying to hide the shiver that passed through her. On a furrowed hillside of corn, burnt and smoldering, only a short distance away from the witch, was the

Scarecrow. He was nailed to a wooden pole and was burning to death as the Tin Woodman and the Cowardly Lion were desperately trying to put the fire out.

The Scarecrow?

Sam had not thought of him, had not said his name even once since they looked upon the Wicked Witch standing before them at the top of her edifice, grinning her sinister grin, tall and proud like a queen. Sam wondered how he was. Was he safe? And the Tin Woodman and the Cowardly Lion too, did they make it safely to her mother's castle? She realized she was breathing hard, but when she placed her friends in her thoughts and knew how strong they were, how determined they were, the tension eased, and even the air seemed to taste a little less sour.

But when she saw Elle standing in a daze at the far end of the room, only a few feet away from the wicked old bat and holding the witch's broom, her breath was instantly stolen from her. She opened her mouth, but no words came out. Her sister's eyes had turned bright orange, just like her father's had. She was breathing heavily, and Sam could see her rib cage rise and fall. Her shoulders looked tense, coiled like a spring waiting to be let loose, and etched across her brow was a dreadful stare of eagerness to shed blood. *Elle*, Sam said in her head. *It's me, Sam.* But there was no response. And as what Sam most feared, that which had happened with her father, the witch had sought the dark from within her sister and now controlled her as well.

The witch wore a full-length, hooded, black cape and was standing with her back to the three warriors, gazing out one of the large windows, perhaps the very one where they'd first seen her. Sam had pulled three arrows from her quiver and held them firmly on her bow, low and to her right side, pointed at the floor. Akasha had an iron grip on her spear with her paw, ready to let it fly, and Thorn held four razor-sharp throwing knives, two in each hand. As Sam had said, they were going to wing it, but what they did next seemed as if they could read each other's thoughts and had practiced for this exact moment a thousand times over. She glanced at Akasha and Thorn; they looked alert, dangerous. Not a group she'd want to run into alone in the forest. She was glad they had her back, as she had theirs. *To the death*, she thought, and looked back at the witch.

Without missing a beat, in unison the three warriors took two powerful, lunging steps forward, leaped into the air, and unleashed their weapons at the same time. Then they landed with great force on one bent knee and watched as their weapons cut through the air, hard and fast toward the evil witch. In a blink, the Wicked Witch raised her arms above her head, throwing off her cloak. As if it had a will of its own, the cloak spun around with incredible speed, creating a round, impenetrable shield that deflected each weapon back toward them.

Thorn was quick as lightning, reaching for the two swords on his back and pulling them free. He slashed them like a windmill being blown by a stiff wind and knocked Sam's three arrows away. The throwing knives shot toward Akasha. She dodged to the right, then to the left, missing two of the blades, but one clipped off a small wedge of her right ear. Sam had just enough time to drop her bow and raise her shield as the remaining knife and Akasha's spear found their target, harmlessly rebounding with a hard ping and then rolling along the stone floor.

The Wicked Witch laughed, a deep, ragged sound with terrible echoes that pricked at Sam's skin and forced its way to the darkest recesses of her mind. The witch looked directly at Sam, placed her hand affectionately on Elle's shoulder, and said in a sarcastic but giddy tone, "Well, well, well. That's no way to treat your host." Then the witch put her hands on her waist, and when she looked at Sam, her eyes glowed a bright vulpine orange. Her voice was low and soft, a voice anyone might trust. Its tone was soothing and controlled, and Sam understood how it could sway one's heart to the dark. "We finally meet, Princess Goodwitch." Akasha slowly moved a little distance from Sam's right, and Thorn did the same on her left, inching their way closer to the witch. "I see you brought some friends," the Wicked Witch said with a sly, crooked grin, and then, slowly but deliberately, stretched out her next words. "*H o w   d e l i g h t f u l.*"

Sam stood motionless, probing, searching as deep into the Wicked Witch's evil orange eyes as she could. She bared her teeth at the witch. The glint of madness sparkled in the witch's eyes. *Someone*, Sam said inside her head, *needs to teach this witch some manners.* It seemed to Sam that she and the witch were no different than two bloodthirsty beasts on opposite slopes of a bottomless ravine, lifting their muzzles to sniff all aromas, no matter how faint. Sam was trying to take a cool measurement of the wicked hag, staying alert and aware, all of which mingled into vague awe and the curiosity about whether, somewhere in that black heart of hers, there might also be good mixed among all the wickedness.

But deep down, Sam knew that was reckless thinking. She felt her legs tremble ever so slightly. "Release my sister," she said at last in a strangled voice that seemed to cut ugly holes in the currents of air that lay between them. Hearing the sound of her own voice refocused her and revived her courage. "Release her now."

"No, I think not," the witch said, and grinned again. She rested her elbow on her hand and tapped her cheek with her finger. "You and your friends seem a bit upset. Would you like some tea? We can sit and have a little chat."

"You kidnapped my father, and now my sister . . . and you would also have Oz for your own and make slaves of us all."

"That about sums it up," the witch chuckled with a smirk. "And your father . . . what a good little soldier he is." The witch walked in a mocking way, dipping down slightly as she strolled behind Elle; she peeked her head around Elle's head and placed her hands on the princess's shoulders. She pressed her cheek up against Elle's cheek, sniffing the powerful cinnamon aroma seeping from Elle's skin, and said to Sam, "Right now, as I look at your pathetic, beautiful face with those big, piercing, gold-speckled eyes, your father is leading my army and advancing on your mother's castle." The witch paused and looked at Elle, using her fingers like a comb, running them through the princess's hair. "Soon, your mother's castle—and all the land that surrounds it—will be mine."

Akasha moved slowly toward the witch and kneeled down to pick up her spear. The witch moved only her eyes, and she looked directly at the great cat. The corners of the witch's mouth became broader, and she pointed at Akasha, wiggling her bony finger back and forth to warn her to stop, and then said, "Ticktock, the mouse ran up the clock, the clock ran down, and the mouse did frown. My, my . . . aren't you just *purrrrrfect*. I think you'd make a warm winter coat or perhaps a furry rug in my bedroom. And you." She moved her eyes and finger with blinding speed and pointed at Thorn. "I can always use another assassin, or perhaps a slave to shine my shoes?"

Akasha and Thorn looked at Sam. She gently shook her head at them, telling them to hold back and wait.

"That's right," the witch continued, "listen to your master. You wouldn't want to be too hasty now, would you? And you." She stared directly at Sam again. "I can see there is no hope for you, my dear. Too much Crow in you." The witch paused. "He has spoiled you, and made you his pet. Pity. Now your worthless to me."

She moved around Elle again, who continued to stand perfectly still, eyes glazed over, anger oozing from every pore, holding the witch's broomstick. As she walked in front of Elle, her black skirt rippled softly, then she clutched the broomstick firmly but did not take it, and when the witch turned to step back around, Sam noticed the witch's sword tied around her waist.

It's me, Elle, Sam tried again. *It's me. I'm here.*

As the witch pulled her sword from its scabbard, she slashed it from side to side. She spoke calmly and moved with a confident and easy manner. "She cannot hear you, child." The sword was made from the burning flame of the red dragon's breath and it glowed a dark, sinister red. "I get it. You care about your sister and your father. You miss your father and all the tender love and ministrations you could have shared." Her voice sank lower, a raspy purring, and she smiled a deep, sinister smile as she looked vacantly down the sharp edge of her flaming sword. "Yes, too bad for the poor, abandoned child. Too bad for the little girl who lost her father."

It's me, Elle, Sam tried once again. *Wake up.*

The witch rapidly blinked her eyes at Sam, grinning as she sarcastically mimicked Sam in an exaggerated, high-pitched voice while cupping her fingers to her pointed chin. "*Elle, wake up . . . Elle, it's me . . . Wake up . . . Wake up.*" The witch's eyes flared and then quickly settled back to their normal, piercingly intense orange color, and she laughed her cackling laugh, dismissing Sam as she spoke. "Begone, you have no power here." The witch waved her sword to shoo them out. Then she walked to the other side of Elle, putting her sword back into its sheath, placed her hand on Elle's shoulder, and then laid her head on it. The witch looked at Sam and grinned, her eyes flaring and then settling again. "I like your sister. I want to keep her."

Sam shook her head dumbly. The Wicked Witch's words buzzed in her ears like a bee wanting to sting her, and the terrible image of her orange eyes and black fingernails bit deeper each time she looked at the old hag's ugly face. The low, murmuring buzzing of that raspy voice drilled on and on inside her head.

"And your mother, Glinda." The witch paused for a second. "I met her recently." Even through the seductive melody of the witch's voice, Sam heard the malice when the witch spoke her mother's name. She was only too aware of the witch's hatred, for it was something she was sure of at that very moment, as she felt the same about the witch. "The Goodwitches have seen their last days. Soon, you will kneel before me."

"I kneel to no wicked witch," Sam shot back.

Princess.

It was as though she heard the Scarecrow in her head.

Believe.

And then she realized it was, in fact, the Scarecrow reaching out to her, and she knew from hearing his voice he was safe. She looked at the bracelet he had given her, and understanding landed in her head like a loud, satisfying splash of cold water and brought her back to herself.

"Ah," the witch said. "I see it mirrored in your eyes. You want to prove yourself to your mother. Prove you are a true blood, descended from a long line of Goodwitches. How sweet." The Wicked Witch quickly released her sword, and at the same time, yanked the broomstick from Elle's hand and held it up next to the sword, pointing them both to the sky. Red flames shot out of the sword like lightning, striking the ceiling and exploding. Bits of stone fell to the floor. There was a roar of thunder from such power—it howled like a banshee's scream, forcing the trio to cup their ears. The wind spun around them like twisting vines, pushing them backward. The flags whipped and snapped, and the torches were blown out of their guards. Now the only light within the chamber was the redness before their eyes: the witch in flames and the evil intent reflected in her pupils, glowing red and glistening.

Sam staggered forward, clutching her shield and sword, working her way closer to her sister, who was still standing, unaware, her hair whipping back and forth from the vortex.

"What is that joyous noise off in the distance?" the witch asked sarcastically, speaking loudly over the erupting squall. "It is the cry of victory, my army defeating your mother and her sorry band of worthless warriors!"

"That will never happen!" Sam shouted into the wind.

"The Crow!" the witch howled back. "I'm going to make a mattress out of his straw and a rain barrel out of the Tinman. And the Lion, well, he'll make a nice, furry pet to play catch with." Then she pointed her gnarled, wrinkled finger at Sam, and in a low and threatening voice, she continued. "And you, my little pretty . . . I will deal with you here and now."

The witch waved her arms again, and the storm cried out louder, lifting Sam, Akasha, and Thorn off their feet and then dropping them to the ground, hard. Thorn doubled over in pain, and Akasha landed on all fours, as cats almost always do.

Sam felt hard cold stone against her cheek and searing, white-hot pain that sent her reeling and fighting to get back on her feet. It knocked the breath from her, rattled her teeth and loosened a tooth, but when she got up, she shook it off and walked two steps forward, when yet again the air around her—as if alive, like a gusty invisible hand—grabbed her and lifted her off the ground. It hurled her into the ceiling, and then slammed her to the stone floor with great force, once more knocking the breath from her.

She held her sides and groaned. The back of her head had hit the floor hard, and it felt like a torch ignited behind her eyes. She tasted blood, touched her lip, and stood up again, hands gripping her sword with all her strength, lips pressed tightly together, eyes squeezed down to slits. Her heart began to drum, and she rolled her shoulders, forcing her wings flat against her back, ready to charge again.

Thorn had been thrown into the wall, hitting his head, leaving a cleft from the top of his forehead down to his eyebrow, deep and bleeding. His wind had been knocked out so completely that he could only chuff out small puffs of air. He pushed himself up, but his legs wouldn't respond. He tried to force breath in and only managed a hitching gasp.

Akasha was able to grab onto a flag to keep her balance, shredding it with her claws, but was not able to advance and help Sam. Each time Akasha tried to take a step forward, she was pushed back, time and time again. She crouched as low as she could, wound up like a spring. She let out a powerful, snarling growl and used every leg muscle she had to leap with all her might toward the demon witch. The witch simply put her hand up, palm facing out, and stopped Akasha in midair, hard and fast, the great cat's claws only inches from the witch's face. The cat felt her stomach jump to her throat. She was suspended, paralyzed, the witch's blazing-orange eyes burning into her. She used all her strength to try and slash with her claws and cut deep into the witch's neck, but she could only let out a frustrated snarl.

The Wicked Witch tilted her head, examining the great cat, and said, "Naughty kitty." She swished her hand back and forth, jerking Akasha violently to the left, and then to the right. Without missing a beat, the witch let go, throwing Akasha across the room like a big, furry rag doll. The great cat slammed into the wall with a horrendous, thick, resonating *whump*, tumbling down next to Thorn, groaning and holding her ribs with her paws. She hit the wall hard enough to crack the stone, and there came another moan from her, followed by a low growl that sounded more like an exhale of anger than pain.

S am had watched as Akasha slammed against the wall, and she heard all the air go out of the cat in a wounded *uuuff*. Sam turned her head to look at the witch, narrowed her eyes and scrunched her eyebrows, and at that moment she felt she had jumped from purgatory into Gehenna. The world seemed a spinning kaleidoscope of insanity, but Sam knew she wasn't insane—this was real, and she wasn't about to run away.

She put her weight onto one knee, wiped a trickle of blood from her lip with the back of her hand, and spat blood-filled spittle on the floor. "You will not take my sister from me," she said in a whisper to herself. Then she stood straight and tall, the gale force whipping her braids back and forth. Her crown clutched her ears to keep from being blown away. Then Sam braced herself, her sword point touching the floor, and she closed her eyes to concentrate on her inner flame. She took in a deep breath, and then everything around her went darkly silent. Suddenly, her tattoos began to glow and spark and caught on fire, releasing the bluish-white flame within. It traveled down her arm to her hand, along her sword, and then shot out in all directions from its sharp tip. She raised her weapon, pointing it at the witch. Blue lightning discharged and leaped out in sharp tongues that lit the entire room and set fire to all the flags hanging on the walls.

Akasha let go of the flag she was holding, as it burned bright orange and turned to ash. The cat leaned forward, lowering her head into the gale, and used her claws to dig into the stone floor.

Sam's powerful lightning bolt struck the Wicked Witch hard in the chest, throwing her back like a shot and slamming her into the tower's stone wall with a loud thud, cracking stone around her and forcing the witch to land on her hands and knees. She shook her head and stood, when another blazing bolt hit her in the stomach with blistering speed. But this time, the force of the blast only made the witch bend slightly forward, as she absorbed the blue lightning until it turned red, adding its energy to her own.

The demon witch lifted her head to look at Sam and grinned her evil grin—a grin of triumph. "Do you hear that sweet sound?" the witch hissed, her grin turning into a full smile. But Sam didn't hear anything except for the gusty roar of the wind, the burning hiss of flames, and the crashing thunder of stones falling around her. The witch glowered. "That, Princess, is the sound of inevitability."

࿇ ✦ ࿇

Sam shifted her weight, and with much effort was able to take one step forward. But the blistering wind was relentless in its push, knocking her to all fours. She stood up again, and the witch pointed her broomstick at her. Red fire shot from it, biting Sam on her hip before she had a chance to use her shield to protect herself. She dropped to one knee. Another red-hot flame blasted out of the witch's broomstick, but this time Sam was prepared and used her shield to deflect it. It bounced off and exploded on the ceiling, knocking out an enormous chunk of stone that fell with a thunderous thud just inches away from Thorn. The agile Munchkin rolled away just in time and tried to stand, but the wind knocked him backward, rolling him end over end, and he hit the entrance door so hard it splintered. Still, he tried to make his way back to help Sam fight the Wicked Witch.

"You are not strong enough to defeat me!" the witch howled at

Sam, and as she spoke, she grew twice her height, her wind-swept hair turning and shifting like black snakes ready to strike.

Sam raised her sword and slashed it high to low, then held it above her head, pointing to the ground. The bluish-white flame now covered her entire body and with both hands gripping the hilt with all her might, she slammed the tip into the stone floor, cutting into it six inches deep. Cracks instantly appeared, shooting out in all directions like hot, bluish-white, molten tendrils. The tower began to shake and moan, and pieces of stone were breaking away from every corner of the witch's citadel—the walls and ceiling tumbling and crumbling all around them. The witch flew at Sam with her sword leading the way, running her down as a bull might a wolf, but Sam held her own and flashed to stop the witch's swing. Where the blades crashed together, blue-white and red molten fire dripped and splashed around them, adding more cracks to the tower floor.

The witch and Sam were locked together in a dance to the death, face-to-face, inches from each other, and Sam could hear the thumping of her own pounding heart slamming against her ribs and could smell the sour breath of her evil opponent, as the witch scowled and hissed through clenched teeth. They circled without slashing swords but remained connected, and there was a curious bittersweetness that cloyed Sam's senses.

"You can't win," the witch barked.

But Sam saw one bead of sweat slowly dripping down the witch's forehead. *She's afraid*, Sam thought to herself. *The wicked thing is afraid.*

And Sam smiled.

The witch stepped back, and her red sword slashed at Sam again and again. Each time the witch's sword sliced through the air, Sam countered the blows. Back and forth they parried, one countermove after another, brilliant, burning swords ringing out upon the chaos as they crashed together. Yet even so close, what seemed like only seconds from death, Sam saw a shadow of fear walk across the witch's eyes, so quickly she thought she might have imaged it.

Sam's most transparent thought—even now, battling such wickedness—was still a desperate desire to save her sister. Her arm jerked once more, as the witch's red sword struck with tremendous force. Sam parried the next blow by using her shield and slashing her own sword with lightning speed from left to right. The witch countered each slash, then brought her sword over her head, striking from above, but Sam held her own sword vertically, only inches along her back, to stop the deadly swing. The red sword came down with an ardent crash, and more white-and-red fire splattered and spilled onto the floor, opening up more long, narrow, deep and blazing fissures.

The witch quickly struck Sam's sword again, which almost broke Sam's guard, and her arm seemed suddenly frail; the recoil was such that her sword twisted out of her grasp and fell to the burning floor. Sam fell with it, stretched out on the ground, vulnerable, with her cheek touching the cold stone. *It would be a pleasant thing to faint at this point*, she thought, exhausted from the battle. *Then I would not know if I were dead or alive, and would not care one way or the other about the outcome.* But she didn't, and instead, quickly reached for her sword and shield, jumped up, and held them more firmly.

Sam and the witch circled for some time without doing much damage on either side, glowing swords flashing, spitting flames and ringing loudly into the roaring wind, as they crashed together with each parry. The entire tower seemed to be coming apart from each thunderous crack of sword strike that echoed throughout the chamber, dislodging huge blocks of stones that continued to fall from above and widening the fractures that were zigzagging in all directions across the polished stone floor. One window violently shattered, exploding apart as the large stone lintel fell over the side and out into the dark, scattering fragments through the air. The witch laughed, and

Sam wavered at the sound, hesitated, and the red sword came for her again and struck deep into her shoulder.

Sam fell to the floor, resting her weight on her elbow. Her shoulder was on fire and a terrible scream came from her—or from the red sword, she was not sure—and then the witch came at her again, even more swiftly than before. Their two swords caught each other, then hurled apart. Back and forth they fought, Sam protecting her shoulder as best she could, but she twisted it when she turned to use her shield to block another blow while trying to set a new stance to defend herself. The pain was so great it once again dropped her to her knees. She was splattered in blood. A nasty slash ran across her shoulder. Her breath came hard and fast through clenched teeth, but her sword was still in her hand and the shield in the other. Her eyes were burning, her body worn out.

The witch, realizing Sam was tiring, decided to close in and end the battle in a final blaze of glory. The red sword came for Sam, swift and true, and again bit into her shoulder while she was still finding her footing. Sam's scream cut through the air from deep within her, sounding an almost inhuman rage and anguish. She slumped against her shield and the white-hot flame surrounding her flickered and sputtered. The Wicked Witch pulled her sword free, and Sam let out another agonizing, earsplitting wail, as her opponent stepped back three paces behind her, preparing for the final strike. But in that moment, Sam's sweeping glance to locate her adversary revealed an astonishing sight that paid her well for what the wound had caused her. She saw a slight smile on her sister's face. A smile of recognition.

Sam looked over her shoulder and she also noticed that Thorn and Akasha had found a foothold together, still trying to find a way to reach her and help her to her feet. But Sam shook her head, telling them to stand fast. She could see in their faces that they were weary to their very souls. As her fleeting glance swept past her companions, a little tableau was presented when her gaze returned to her sister, which Sam knew would stand graven in her memory to the day of her death. She saw the fury of a tigress beaming from Elle's tortured eyes, which were no longer orange, but now were her sister's shining green orbs.

"Foolish child!" the Wicked Witch cried, and instead of striking Sam with her sword, she leaped into the air and away from her. The witch held her red flaming sword and broomstick above her head, slammed them together with a blazing, resounding crack, and glowing flames jumped all around her, scorching and brilliant red. Thick, reddish-black smoke bellowed forth, and the witch sheathed her bloody red blade. With her free hand she made a ball of fire, rolling it in her hand over and over in her palm until it grew to the size of a large rock, and just when she was about to throw it, Elle sprang to life.

She leaped for the witch's sword, pulled it from its scabbard, and slashed at the witch's neck but missed, falling to her knees. Elle then staggered to her feet, bloodlust in her eyes and ready to kill, her face livid with hatred and baffled rage. Elle's eyes went wide with horrified understanding, and then they turned orange and evil again—as evil as the Wicked Witch.

Elle! Sam said inside her head, near tears. Sam heard a low moan and realized it came from Elle. *It's me, Elle.* "It's me!

With a blood-muffled shout Elle slashed again, pushing the witch back. And then quickly swirling, she slashed the red sword through the air with all the strength she had left in her and chopped off the witch's hand that was holding the ball of red fire.

An inhuman scream went out from the Wicked Witch, high-pitched and terrified. It was a scream sharper than any sound imaginable. It cut across the thunder, the roaring wind, the crumbling tower, and the sputtering flames. Sam's eyes went wide, but not wider than the witch's, as green blood began to spurt from her severed wrist. The witch held her stump away from her, as though afraid of it, and watched in numbed astonishment as her hand tumbled across the cold stone floor and fell into one of the many erupting fissures. The flaming fireball she had held exploded with such force that when it punched into the floor, it opened an enormous seam that split the tower room in half. Elle dropped the red sword and it rang out as it hit the ground, metal clanging against stone. Its red flame sputtered, then fizzled out as it scooted to the very edge of the flaming cleft. The tower shook, and the red sword fell into the burning abyss.

The Wicked Witch leaped out the window, pressing her wound firmly against her side, hard against her rib cage to stop the bleeding, and flew off on her broomstick along with a small band of flying monkeys following close behind, protecting their evil queen.

Elle had fallen on her side from the shaking floor but was able to pull herself up, supporting herself with one elbow, and turned her gaze to Sam. Her eyes were back to their sparkling beauty, but lost, pleading, and filled with sorrow. Inside Sam's head, she heard Elle say in a dead voice, *Sam . . . Run!*

Sam took two steps toward her sister and was reaching for her when the floor that stood between them shook and fell away. Elle had used the last bit of her strength when she took the witch's sword—she had none left to fly with and no spirit left to save herself, and Sam could do nothing to help. So Sam turned away from her sister and ran.

The last thing Sam saw as she and Akasha and Thorn fled down the stairs was her sister disappearing along with the rubble, as the tower room disintegrated in stone sheets of searing red-and-white flames. As they ran, Sam found that she was clutching her sword with both hands, and that her arm was wet with her own blood from the wound to her shoulder. Her body was still on fire with the bluish-white flame, and the image of her sister falling to her death beat at her until she lost control and had to scream. Then her scream, the sharp snaps and the crunching, grinding sound of the falling stones all rose together into one deafening, thunderous roar, as the walls of the witch's black tower gave way, crashing and rolling like a giant stone tsunami, crushing everything in its path.

"Your hands!" Sam yelled over the booming wave of falling blocks of stone, her breath racing in and out of her chest as fast as a bird beats its wings. "Give me your hands!" She reached out to Akasha and Thorn, and with great effort, more effort than she could've imagined possible, she grabbed their hands, unfurled her wings, and flew along the staircase, corkscrewing down and down and zigzagging around the heavy fragments of black stone and wood debris that shadowed them. Thorn yelled, closed his eyes, and in the next second, they shot out of the entrance and were rolling on the ground far enough away from the crumbling tower to keep from being crushed.

In the next instant, there was nothing but silence.

The great roar of destruction had vanished, and a large cloud of dust fell upon them, turning their skin, clothes, and fur a pale grayish color, making them look like ghosts on Hallow's Eve. Slowly, they sat up and looked back at the rubble. Sam gingerly felt the places she had fallen on and looked severely at Akasha, amazed they were both alive, as Akasha coughed and spat grit-filled saliva on the ground. "I've had bruises enough before," Sam choked out, spitting and coughing along with Akasha, "but this really hurts." She looked over at Thorn and watched him roll over onto his back, exhaling a gray, powdery, dust cloud of ash, followed by a deep, harsh, painful moan. The corners of Sam's mouth lifted slightly; she was relieved to see that he too had survived their narrow escape, but she winced when she moved her legs to sit up.

The next thing she knew, she was rewarded by Jo's ear-shattering whinny as he appeared behind them. The horse tossed his head happily and shook his back, sending a cloud of grimy, chalky dust into the air. He trotted up and nosed her eagerly and pushed at her, getting more ash and grit on his face. Sam stood, grabbed Jo's head with both hands, put her cheek to his jaw, and without meaning to, rubbed even more ash on the horse. "Good to see you too," she said.

Then she leaned into the solid reality of Jo's shoulder and pressed her cheek against his body to soak in his warmth, took in a deep breath, and coughed again.

Twenty-One

Sunlight was breaking through the dust cloud left behind from the falling tower. The morning air was chilly and filled with the same foul scent of evil as before. Shafts of hazy light fought through the thick, smoky ash and fell gently on the rubble. In the soft glow of the dawn, Sam could see the fallen tower clearly and still held close to herself the adrenaline from the battle with the witch.

Her heart was racing and her breath hurried.

Sam, Akasha, and Thorn stood looking at the destruction, brushing the dust and ash off their bodies, shaking it out of their hair. Sam was amazed that it was early morning, as time seemed to have been suspended from when they started climbing the witch's tower until now, standing next to, and surveying all the fallen stones.

She poured water from her canteen onto her crown to clean the ash from the grassy shoots. They shivered and shuddered in delight, pleased to wash away some of the grit and grime, when suddenly her abused body—especially her legs—turned abruptly to jelly. She sat down and put her head between her knees, clutching her wounded shoulder. "My sister," she said quietly, her eyes pooling.

"I'm so sorry," Akasha said, sitting down beside her.

"When we meet the witch in battle again," Thorn said, "you will have your revenge."

"Revenge won't bring back my sister," Sam replied harshly, looking at Thorn through watery eyes.

Thorn blinked owlishly in the dusty light. He murmured and apologized, "I meant no offense, milady."

Sam nodded, stood up, reset Jo's saddle, and tightened the flank cinch. "Apology accepted," Sam replied after a moment, her voice resigned. "Let us move forward and do what must be done." Then she looked back at all the fallen stones and stared at the ground, wondering how long it had been since they had eaten. *Food might help*, she thought. But to stay any longer in this contemptible place was unthinkable, and the idea of eating simply rolled across her mind and vanished. She could think of nothing else but her sister, and like a lightning bolt, Elle flashed into her mind and it brought memories of her family flooding vividly back to her. An overwhelming longing hit her so hard her legs gave way. She slid down Jo's leg and sat in the dirt. She hugged her legs as her eyes welled up again. She clenched them shut, and hot tears rolled down her cheeks. Then she thought of the Wicked Witch and she ground her teeth together and wiped angrily at her tear-smudged face.

As if reading Sam's thoughts and trying to keep her friend focused in the right direction, Akasha said, "The witch's army is already laying siege to your mother's castle as we sit here gathering our wits and dusting ourselves off." Akasha took in a deep breath and continued. "Where's your bow?"

"Lost in the rubble," Sam said softly, staring at the trembling, tear-soaked palms of her hands. She still felt shaky, and when she rocked forward onto her heels and clambered back to her feet—using her shield as a prop—her ankles cracked, her knees shook, and her legs ached. But the pain of losing her sister seemed impossible to face, and it superseded all the other aches and pains she was feeling. A sudden burning sensation stung the wound on her shoulder. Sam clutched the cut, feeling the hot wetness of it, and watched as Thorn swiftly scampered up on the flat top of a small mountain of rubble.

Off to his right at his foot, Thorn looked down at Akasha shaking ash off her body and Sam gazing vacantly up at him. All around him was the destroyed black tower, nothing but waste and rough fragments of stone and brick. He could not believe they'd been able to survive such destruction and believed—and was certain the others felt the same as he did—that Sam's sister had fallen to her doom, that she had perished.

The sunlight fell like dusty beacons across the debris, and the sizeable, rubble-covered clearing left by the destroyed tower seemed as tall as a mountain. Thorn looked around at the wreckage that had knocked down most of the outer walls of the entire castle, with huge stones spilling into the moat. Fortunately for them, it had not touched the drawbridge. "So, what now?" Thorn asked loudly, looking down at Sam and Akasha.

"We ride till we can't ride any longer. To my mother's castle," Sam said, looking up at Thorn with exhaustion showing on her face.

"And eat?" Thorn asked.

"And eat," Sam replied, trying to smile but only slightly, since it was difficult to find anything to smile about with all that had just happened and all that lay ahead of them. But it was so much like Thorn to think about food at that moment that she couldn't help but let her lips lift into a grin. She nodded her head, acknowledging Thorn's question but in truth, was dismissing it. This was not the time to worry about ones stomach. She pulled out a small satchel from Jo's saddlebag that held her fire ointment. She rubbed the healing balm on the open wound on her shoulder. She winced and felt the sting of the red sword all over again, took off her empty quiver, and tied it to her saddle.

She then walked over to Thorn and gently rubbed some of her healing balm on his gash as well, and did the same for Akasha's ear. Then she made a proper bandage for herself, soaking it in the medicinal salve, and with Akasha's help, firmly attached it to her shoulder. Again she winced, but the ointment was cool and soothing, and she could tell it was already numbing the pain.

They mounted their horses.

"At your command, milady," Thorn voiced with steadfast determination.

Sam kicked Jo in his in ribs with a firm purpose, as did Akasha and Thorn, clicking their tongues and calling out, "*Hah! Hah!*" The horses reacted instantly. The brave but exhausted souls leaned forward in their saddles, galloping toward Glinda's castle—Sam's home—kicking up clouds of ash and dust behind them. When they pounded across the drawbridge, the wood slats made a thunderous, romping sound that echoed across the plain where everything was dead or dying. *It will take decades for this land to reclaim itself,* Sam thought as they rode east to fight by her mother's side. She was sure if they did not stop the Wicked Witch, the entire landscape of Oz would become like this valley where nothing grew, lifeless for decades to come.

As they rode away, Sam looked back, but only once, at the fallen, black tower. The thought of her sister slapped her hard again, as she replayed that moment when she ran away from Elle. Her eyes instantly filled with salty tears, and she let them spill out and roll down and drip off her jaw. Her crown reached out and gently stroked her face, but it could not stop the flood of sorrow rushing through her, nor could it stop the emptiness filling her heart. She knew she had to accept the choices she had made, but the consequences sat on her shoulders like a lead weight. Then she gazed at her friends. *They are waiting for something great from me,* Sam thought tiredly. *By the grace of the Great Head they shall have it.*

They rode until the sun could be seen crawling behind the trees, and the sounds of the awakening insects and creatures of the night echoed all through the dense forest.

They had left all the signs of the hard-fought battle with the Wicked Witch far behind them; most of the fight, though, still reeled in their minds. But Sam began to breathe a little easier. She was weary enough for hunger, but too weary for everything else she knew she must do. She needed to close her eyes, if only for a few hours, to recharge and regain her strength.

She looked at the fading pink in the sky. Twilight would soon be upon them. She pulled back on Jo and he responded immediately, coming to a quick halt. Following her lead, the others did the same, and then she sat very still and listened. Off to her right hidden somewhere in a grove of trees, she heard gurgling, the sound of running water. She pulled Jo around and softly kicked his ribs, and as Jo trotted toward a small island of trees, Sam opened her wings and flew ahead of him. The horse instantly picked up his pace and followed her. "We'll camp here," she said to the others as she flew. She quickly came upon a small river and followed it until it narrowed and became clean and slow, gently splashing and swirling against large boulders over a rocky bank.

Not far from where Akasha and Thorn were setting up camp, she found an inlet where the water had made a wading pool and where the current was sympathetic and kind. Dirt and ash still clung to her hair and body, and she could smell her own sweat when she moved. She flew back to Jo and escorted him to the hidden inlet, unbuckled his saddle, and placed it on the ground with all the other gear he carried, then took him by his jaw and walked him to the water's edge. She squeezed his ears and said kindly, "I'll brush and wash you later." Jo leaned his head down and sniffed the water first before slurping up large mouthfuls. Sam took off her boots and dropped them on the ground by the water's edge. Then she took off her tunic and leggings and soaked them, ringing them out and hanging them on a nearby branch as she watched Jo drink. It had been a long day, and the horse looked worn out, exhausted, the same as she felt.

She crouched on the bank and put her hands in the gently moving stream and did the same as Jo, slurping up handfuls of the cold, refreshing liquid. She splashed her face, glad to wash away the residue from the falling tower, and then set her crown on the sandy bank of the inlet next to her towel so it too could drink and clean itself.

Without hurrying, she waded out to the middle of the small, narrow river up to her knees, then sat down in the water, stretched herself out arms above her head, and let the water wipe the grime from her body and the pain that pricked at her heart. She could feel the grit and ash trickle away like a smoky cloud as the river carried it downstream. It made her feel better, but it could not cleanse her of the dread or the dark mood and rage lingering in her chest. She clenched her eyes shut and lay as still as she could to relax and ease her mind, but still her thoughts returned to the ruin of the black tower and the voice of her sister ringing inside her head.

Sam . . . Run!

She could not bear to be without Elle, but she knew she had no choice but to accept it. And still, she could not. *Perhaps one day the Scarecrow will explain all this to me,* she thought, *if he is willing.* Sam pressed hard on her temples with the palms of her hands, trying to tamp down her frustration, but her anxiety doubled. Then another terrible thought came to her. Her mother. *If I lose her . . .* Sam opened her eyes, blinking back tears, and stared at the night sky. There was no moon, but the stars shone fiercely down on her, and there was no room amongst the stars to hold her fear or shed any more tears. The sky was enormous and made her feel small, alone, defeated.

Then all at once, she realized that the witch's determination to control the land of Oz and make slaves of all its people and animals had never been quite so real to her as it was at that very moment. Her terror, to be sure, had been real enough when she was clashing swords with the old hag. Sam clearly saw the demented and purposeful look of pure, undeniable evil on the face of the Wicked Witch, who was determined to destroy everything and everyone Sam loved. But the thing that had held her, the truth that drew her on, was not to save her sister—although that was part of it—it was that she believed, just as Elle had believed, that the light would tear open the dark. It had nothing to do with her birthright or proving to her mother she was a worthy warrior and could stand alongside the very best the queen's army had to offer. It had everything to do with the battle of good over evil. That was something worth giving one's life fighting for: freedom and the right to choose your own destiny and *not* have a collar around your neck.

She closed her eyes again. The air was so still, so incredibly tranquil, she could hear Jo shuffle his feet and the crackling of a fire. Then the scent of hot meat stew wafted across her nose and settled on her tongue. She got up and walked out of the stream, picked up her tunic, and dried herself off with her towel. Something was cooking, for she could see smoke drifting lazily through the trees in the direction of the campsite and could smell roasting meat.

❧ ◆ ☙

S am inhaled deeply as she spooned the steaming meat stew into her bowl. But the mood was somber, and eating only satisfied the group's hunger but did not feed their low spirits.

"You look clean and refreshed," Thorn said softly. "And the food has brought the color back to your cheeks."

Sam nearly smiled and was about to respond, but the impulse dried up quickly as she stared into the fire as though hypnotized. The warm fire felt good against her skin, but she was still shivering from her cold bath in the stream, first her chest and then spreading to the rest of her body. She placed her tunic on three sticks that she had tied together to form a tripod, close enough to the fire to dry it out by morning, then pulled her towel close to her, sat on her bedroll, and wrapped her blanket over her shoulders. As she watched the flames of the campfire leap and dance, her mind was still finding it difficult to settle.

"We need to sleep," Akasha said, circling her own blanket until it was shaped as she wanted it. "There is always hope for tomorrow." Then she laid down, curling her tail around her body, swishing its tip back and forth as if brushing dirt away.

Sam knew Akasha was right, and hearing the Tin Woodman's words was comforting. Without hesitation, she obeyed her dear friend, put her bowl down, and stretched out. But her mind kept turning, and she had to force the whirling, angry thoughts back to the depth of her subconscious—back into dark shadows. She swallowed hard, tasting something sour in the back of her throat. It was difficult for

Sam to nod off when her brain was crammed with questions that had no answers. Sleep didn't come for a very long time, but finally her heavy eyelids stayed shut, and she slept the numbed, restless sleep of one who has failed to beat her foe in battle or save her sister. Shortly after sleep consumed her, she woke, startled, and thought she heard rumblings like massive boulders crashing along a hillside far away. Perhaps she was dreaming, and when she sat up she knew it was another vision to place worry upon, and she could feel it vibrating all around her. At first, as she gazed into the pitch-black, all she heard were the sounds she'd become accustomed to at night: Akasha's gentle, soothing purring and Thorn's heavy breathing, and sometimes his loud snorting and snoring. *For an assassin*, Sam chuckled to herself, *he's not all that stealthy when he sleeps.*

She had hoped for a more profound, rejuvenating slumber, but she'd had less of a peaceful time of it and had quickly learned that when a vision decided to show itself, she had no power to stop it. Then the cold, horrifying cries of battle rolled over her, making her skin prickle and the hair on the back of her neck stand at attention. Her shoulders shivered.

In this vision she heard Saran's voice, weary and hopeless. And in the distance, she heard the spine-chilling, hellish wail of the red dragon. Saran cried out, *"We are outnumbered on the ground and from the sky!"*

"Yes, we are outnumbered," another voice shot through the air, higher-pitched—it was Lillith. *"Nothing we haven't faced before."*

And then, to her surprise, Sam heard her mother's voice. *"Be not afraid,"* the queen said in a voice without fear. *"We have the light on our side, and our wits still with us. Let us rally and defeat this Wicked Witch!"*

Now she was awake. Wide awake. Nerves on edge. No longer a prisoner to her vision. Her crown cupped her ears and tugged firmly, warning her. Then she heard it, a rustling in the shadows, behind the trees. Sam quietly pulled her sword from its scabbard. "Tell me who you are," she said forcefully into the darkness. Akasha and Thorn woke instantly and stood up holding their swords with a firm grip.

Sam looked at them both, put her finger to her lips, and warned them. "*Shhh*, listen."

They did not move. More rustling. Their eyes were slowly becoming accustomed to the darkness, and the shadows that could be seen were the blinks of gold, green, and tawny eyes staring back at them. Sam looked over to Akasha and saw her smiling, which Sam thought was strange. Then Akasha growled, low and deep, but not in a way that sounded like she was ready to engage an enemy, more like a greeting, as if it were a signal. The shadowy creatures came from behind the trees. At first Sam saw two, then ten, a dozen, fifteen, twenty—no, more than fifty black cats. Some were the size of Akasha, some larger and others smaller. Jo laid his ears back flat to his skull and rolled his eyes until the whites showed. "No," Sam warned him and rubbed his nose to hush him. "They are not our enemy."

The great cats roved evenly through the undergrowth, low and flat as they approached, keeping a steady eye on Sam and Thorn, for like cats of all sizes, they pretended that they could not be seen or heard, always on the prowl. The thought came to Sam that they must be the mountain cats, like Akasha (her kru, perhaps), all of them dressed in their battle armor.

As the silence between the throng of cats and the three warriors became painful, the largest of the beasts stood up on two legs, a fierce monster of a cat, larger than all the others, and shook his body, looking straight into Akasha's eyes. He was the biggest cat Sam had ever seen, as tall as the Cowardly Lion and with paws as thick as tree stumps. She was confident this great cat must be their leader, for he wore a sash made of gold and onyx with a waistband that held a scabbard made of the same stones. And what stood out the most to Sam was that the handgrip of this great cat's sword had one black stone embedded in it, where the guard met the hilt; it had a glimmer that caught the eye.

Thorn kept very still as one of the furry creatures twined itself around his legs, releasing soft mewing sounds, then licking his trousers and rubbing its thick-furred head affectionately against Thorn's left cheek. He reluctantly but carefully patted its head.

The great cats were conversing together in low tones, gesticulating and cocking their heads and shifting their beady, almond-shaped eyes with suspicious intent toward Sam and Thorn. Thorn slowly placed his hand on the hilt of the long, curved knife that he had sheathed at his waist, hidden under his tunic. But by some telepathic force that must have warned Sam, without looking at Thorn she gently put her hand on his wrist to stop him. These giant cats' impenetrable eyes and inscrutable countenances would have been intensely calculating and skeptical if it weren't for the fact that Akasha was standing with them, purring deep down in her throat with no great alarm, facing the sizeable cat standing whisker to whisker and lowering her head.

If it had been otherwise, the cats would have looked upon them with much ferocity; but as Sam learned later, the thing that weighed most in her favor was the fact that she was a princess and the daughter of Queen Goodwitch, and the great beasts were actually regarding her as an ally to protect rather than as an enemy to annihilate.

Sam and Thorn stepped back two paces and watched as the largest cat, wearing what Sam thought was a royal sash, walked up to Akasha and opened his arms, growling in the same low tone Akasha was humming.

"Father," Akasha said, and bowed her head further, letting him embrace her. She buried her arms in his thick black fur and held him tightly. She looked up at him and he rubbed her head, pushing back her ears until they lay flat. Akasha sat back on her heels, sniffed, and then said in a soft and broken voice, "It's good to see you."

"I knew you were safe," he replied in a gentle, caring tone, and placed his own bristles-and-velvet face on top of hers. He looked over at Sam with tender, loving eyes, and said to his daughter, "The Scarecrow told us where to find you, and told us of your great battle with three dragons and how you saved the life of one of the Goodwitch princesses." He blinked and gently pushed his daughter from him to look at her face and then rubbed both of her cheeks with his paws and smiled. The other mountain cats sat before them in a semicircle, watching with green-and-gold eyes. Some sat neatly, tails curled around four paws, while others were sprawled out like kittens, lashing their tails back and forth in anticipation. They were of all ages, from the young who were trying to prove their worth to those who were gray-muzzled with age like seasoned warriors.

As Sam watched in awe, Thorn leaned closer to her and said in a whisper, "Looks like we have another princess riding with us, Princess."

"Looks like it," Sam said through the corner of her mouth, grinning. She looked at Akasha's father, the cat king, and then around, noticing how the other cats were watching her intently through slitted eyes. Sam looked at Jo, whose ears were still flat to his skull.

The cat king unclasped a small, gold-encrusted metal pin in the shape of a dragon and held it in his paw toward Sam. Then he slowly blinked and gently nodded, as though waiting for a reply. Stretching her hand toward the chieftain, Sam advanced forward and took the pin from his open paw, cupping it into a fist and putting her hand over her heart, bowing low, and taking a step back to stand next to Thorn's side. The cat king's wide grin spread into an answering smile.

Sam raised her head, looking at Akasha and back to the cat king, then smiled and said, "Your Majesty." His actions spoke of nothing but peace and a kind of friendship that at that moment was most dear to Sam's heart.

Satisfied with the display of royal respect and unity, the other cats repositioned themselves around the fire to take advantage of its warmth. Some of them formed heaps, and some of them stretched out alone in individual curls, licking their paws and grooming themselves with their thick, coarse tongues.

The cat king dropped his paws to his side and took a step forward toward Sam, lowered his head in respect, and then looked at the princess more intently. He put his paw on her shoulder and said kindly, "It is an honor to meet you, Princess Goodwitch." Then he handed her a large leather pouch, stepped back, and put his arm around his daughter. "The Scarecrow said you might need this." Sam knew instantly that it was her pouch, the one she'd given to the Scarecrow, and she opened it. When she saw the angry, sharp yellow shards from the three teeth she had yanked from the heads of the three dragons that she and Akasha had slain, she felt a twitch in her thigh, a small prick of pain, a memory left by the claws of the red beast.

Then the cat king looked at Sam calculatingly and said, "Your mother's army is being overwhelmed. As we speak, the Great Head himself is leading his Emerald City militia to engage the Wicked Witch from the north, and the Munchkins have joined him. But I fear it will not be enough."

Sam tied the pouch to her waistband. "Then we have no time to waste. We must leave immediately."

☜ ◆ ☞

As Sam was tightening Jo's saddle, she looked over the seat at Akasha doing the same to her horse. "So, Princess," Sam said to Akasha, smiling, "are you ready to fight that crusty old tart of a witch again?"

Akasha turned and smiled back, and said, "Yes, Princess, I am."

"Good," Thorn voiced loudly to both of them, pulling back on the reins of his pint-sized horse to keep her steady. "Then let's quit mucking around and get to it." He didn't wait for Sam and Akasha to mount their horses. He kicked Billy in the ribs and trotted off, bouncing in the saddle as he rode away. Jo reared and snorted, turning a shimmering coal black, and then Sam and Akasha took off with hoots and hollers, the growls and snarls of warrior cats following close behind them.

Sam looked over her shoulder and saw the horde of brave furry warriors strung out behind her and flanking her sides, leaping and running with incredible speed and agility. She hoped they could make a difference and that they could turn the tide in this battle. It did give her great comfort to have them by her side—but then, in a flash, her sister jumped back into her thoughts.

She dug her heels deeper into Jo's ribs to spur him on, and she felt the muscles in his neck tighten. His great frame stretched out like an arrow racing with the wind. Her body became rigid, and her eyes became slits. She crouched against Jo's neck and took the pressure off his reins. Her crown gripped her ears as the gusty current pushed her hair back, and she stared straight ahead, ready to ride once again into the fray to see where destiny would take her. They were tearing through the forest now, so fast that Sam could no longer distinguish the warrior cats from the trees, only a continuous blur of green. She found herself laughing, wild out-of-control laughter that was instantly cut to shreds by the wind.

In the next instant, Sam had the conviction that Elle was dead. And she couldn't rid the thought from her brain, despite the exhilaration of riding Jo at full gallop and having a small army by her side. It was a distressing kind of desolation. A feeling of profound emptiness and terrible loss. The same tortured feeling she had when her father was stolen from her when she was so young. She knew this pain would come at unexpected times, with no warning. And as before, the horrible ache made her eyes sting and her breath catch. She tried to keep it from happening, but when the wave hit her she couldn't stop it.

So Elle was gone, and Sam had to face the reality of it, but it was so hard, almost impossible. She knew everything about her sister. Her likes, her dislikes. What she liked to wear, and what she'd never try on. What she liked to eat, and food she'd never place on her tongue. Sam could not keep thinking about it. But by no fault of her own, Elle had opened up areas in Sam's head that Sam did not want to think about: *What will happen next? What will my life be like without my sister? How will I live without her, knowing she'll never be there to keep me levelheaded?* It made Sam wonder at the unfairness of feeling annoyance and anger toward Elle for subjecting her to wave after wave of sour realization.

As Sam was thinking about all these things, the painful wave crested again—a forceful, foamy, and curling surge of guilt—and it hit her hard, straight on, stinging her chest. "Elle is dead." Jo's ears twitched as if he understood. It was perhaps an accident, or an experiment, to say it out loud for the first time. Tears ran out the corners of her eyes, blurring the trail in front of her. She wiped her eyes, and her crown soothed her ears, rubbing them gently, and she let the rocking of Jo's steps bring her back, away from her grief.

The air was fresh but the sky was hazy, and the sun's shadows had soft edges, so it could barely push through the overcast sky. But Sam could see things more transparently now, the trail more defined. Her mind was returning to the truth of what lay ahead, and she knew what she had to do. She knew that she *would* do it, without question, without hesitation, even if it meant giving up her life to do so. And then she heard in the back of her mind the faint, ghostlike whisper of the Sisters of the Lake: *"There will come a time when everyone you love is all that matters."*

Then she said to herself, *Everything comes with a price. Some things just cost more than others.*

Twenty-Two

hey rode in a daze and were making good time, tired as they were. Sam, like her companions, was anxious to reach the edge of the hillside overlooking her mother's castle. They had ridden their horses hard, but the horses never seemed to mind, and the cats had run nonstop, not once needing to take a break. But all were clearly exhausted, and Sam thought it was foolish of them not to rest before they laid their eyes on the battlefield. She might have gone on until she dropped in her tracks, were she on foot like her furry entourage or flying on her own, but she was not. They had been following a creek upstream for most of the day, stopping occasionally to let their group and horses drink along its banks. The sun had finally been swallowed up by thick, dense layers of clouds, and the day had grown warm and humid, the air filling with moisture and the promise of rain.

"Hey," Thorn huffed, wiping sweat from his brow. His face was bright red. "Any chance of a break or making camp?" A few cats eyed him with suspicion. Sam and the rest kept plodding onward, her eye relentlessly searching for any of the witch's spies that might be lurking behind trees, rocks, or bushes.

"Y'know," Akasha said after a moment, "a break might not be such a bad idea. I could use some rest. You too, Sam."

Sam gently pulled back on Jo's reins and stopped, as did her companions including all the cats; then she carefully scanned the surrounding timberline. The cats slowly closed in around Sam and waited as Akasha's father circled back. He walked in a careful, furtive manner, taking in Sam's slouched posture and tired face. "We can stop for the night if you like, Princess. We have made good time."

With some effort, Sam released the reins, rubbing the ache out of her fingers. Her voice, when it came out, was hoarse and unsteady. "I trust your judgment, Your Majesty. We'll go as far as you think necessary."

The cat king stared at her for a moment and then looked around the small clearing next to the running brook. "This will do, milady," the cat king said. "We should rise early anyway, and we've been long on the drive forward thus far. But I think you and I should scout ahead. We don't want the enemy surprising us in the middle of the night."

Thorn and Akasha also dismounted. Sam, stiff and exhausted emotionally, made a clumsy hop to the ground, nearly fell, then stumbled around until she regained her footing, instantly appreciating the cat king's wisdom to stop and make camp. She bent to the ground, relishing the cracking in her spine. Thorn and Akasha led their horses to the creek's edge to drink and nibble on the fresh green watergrass. Thorn stroked his mare's silken neck gently, but Billy tossed her head, shaking away his touch and whinnying, unwilling to be petted, and Thorn backed off. "Fine, girl. I get it." He smiled. "A drink is more important than I am." Thorn dropped his reins and left Billy to tend to her own needs, and he collapsed atop a large flat stone on the bank and watched Akasha's father and Sam walk away.

Then he heard the cat king growl and huff and growl again before disappearing into the woods. Immediately, some of the cats set out to gather wood for a fire and hunt for food, while others continued to drink from the brook and dunk their heads. Thorn let out a tired sigh, wiggling to the edge of the rock and joined the rest, dousing his own head and getting a long drink. The sweetness of the water and its coolness was just what he needed.

"I can't believe evil has taken so much so quickly," Akasha said to Thorn as she spread herself out next to him on the large flat stone, shaking the water off her head and licking her paw. "Never would have thought it possible. Not again, wickedness consuming everything." She reached over and picked a withered flower growing from a crevice in the rock. "Have you noticed the trees, even the flowers? They look dull, tired, bent over, some withered and colorless. Evil is choking the life out of everything." She threw the lifeless flower into the creek and watched it slowly flow downstream.

"I feel it cutting into my skin," Thorn said as he lay back on the rock, looking up at the trees. "Everything is dying."

"I do wonder if we have the strength to defeat the witch," Akasha said. "Without Sam, I fear it would not be impossible."

"That is something we agree on, Cat," Thorn said. "But we're a kru now, a clan of our own. I would rather die trying to fend off evil than to live with it."

"Like you, I will do anything to bring back the light."

Thorn could hear the truth in Akasha's words and see it in her eyes. He could tell how strong she was, like Sam, a true warrior. He saw it in them both when he watched them fight the dragons and when they fought the Wicked Witch. For the first time in his life, he didn't feel alone. He liked the idea of working as a team instead of lurking alone behind shadows. It was a new and unfamiliar feeling for him, and then this newfound emotion of actually being part of a family completely swelled and took him by surprise as a tear rolled down his cheek. "Together," he said, "we'll bring peace back to this land."

Akasha's father and Sam returned after finding no sign of any of the witch's scouts. The other cats, Akasha, and Thorn had built a fire and were roasting rabbit. The smell of food was abundant and robust and made Sam's stomach gurgle, but there was an unnatural essence hanging loosely around everyone. A sinister presence Sam knew was taking hold of everything she loved.

But after she stripped Jo of his saddle and gear and brushed him, she let him wander. The gently running water of the stream as it trickled over rocks and the occasional bird calls made it seem that good was at least trying its best to beat back the odious power of the red-skinned witch. Before she let Jo roam, Sam rubbed him down with a dry cloth and then massaged him with what was left of the fire ointment, not to repel dragonfire, but for its soothing healing powers to ease the dull ache that comes from a long ride; she kneaded it deeply into his muscles and joints. She had to scrape the remaining bits of goo from the bottom of the satchel to use for her own wound, which was almost completely healed. Now only a faint scar was left to remind her of the task ahead and what was at stake.

As she looked around the small meadow at the cats, she felt weariness overtaking her. Some of the cats had found a large boulder to sprawl out upon, while others had smoothed down beds in the tall grass to find a private place to purr. Rest would do them all good. So Sam and her friends, and her army of great cats, took a much-needed moment to find a little bit of peace before moving on. Sam laid out her bedroll and used Jo's saddle as her pillow. Jo moved close to Sam and nibbled on the fresh, tasty grass, snorting softly in delight and shaking his head. Akasha was napping next to her father, and Thorn had found a warm spot between two furry beasts.

୬ ♦ ୬

H aving Jo close to her always gave Sam comfort, relaxed her, made her feel safe. She wanted to sing when thinking how she loved to catch the first breath of the early morning breeze from the kindly trees that surrounded her home and drink from its clear, fresh streams. But she knew the song she had in her heart for her home would be a long time coming before she could sing without worry.

It broke her heart that the only scent wafting through the air was the smell of smoke and death. Her worries surrounded her. She remembered what the Scarecrow had told her when she last saw him, just before they parted ways, about not letting herself worry so much.

And it was good advice, but she couldn't help but feel the depth of her concern for the ones she loved and the life she'd always thought could not be shaken. She knew she had to rest, that she needed to keep her body and mind alert and subdue the rumblings racing in her mind.

All things narrowed toward tomorrow.

Riding toward death, whether it was to be her destiny or not.

Sleep, restless as it was, did find her but for only a short while. She dreamed of endless poppy fields, the fields surrounding her home, torched and on fire, black smoke rising to the clouds. She woke startled, keyed up, sweating, forehead gleaming wet, her fists clenched and her nerves jumping. A black furry head was resting in the hollow of her lap, and another stretched out and pressed firmly against her back. As she stirred, the cats began to purr. She sat up and pushed the giant head away, but the cat rolled over and put her heavy paws over Sam's legs to keep her from moving. Sam pushed the paws off her legs and shoved the cat away, then sprang up and paced back and forth. She was dizzy with exhaustion and filled with anxiety; she was riding her quiet army into a battle that could very well be their last. She remembered each and every vision she had been given, the flashes of the red dragon, the Wicked Witch, and her sister, all of which invaded her daily thoughts and now were her nightmares when she slept.

The dream she had just witnessed during her short, restless slumber was bone chilling, filled with more than burning poppies. It was also filled full of battle and shouting and groans of the injured and dying, and the horrid, ghastly sound of the screams from the flying monkeys. Then she thought of the Scarecrow, the Tin Woodman, and the Cowardly Lion, and tears ran down her face.

Standing before Jo, she bowed her face in her hands and wept. "This will not do," she said to the horse, choking on her words. She put her face into Jo's neck and took in a deep breath of his earthy smell, rubbing her face in his mane to wipe away her tears. Staring at the ground under her feet, the dirt felt dead, dry, and brittle, slowly decomposing and crumbling into dust. She turned back to Jo and whispered, "I need to stop feeling sorry for myself," and then softly patted his neck three times. She picked up his brush and started grooming him, even though she'd already done so earlier. "Isn't that right, Jo? I need to stop feeling sorry for myself." Talking to him and doing something that was familiar to her, something she loved to do, would hopefully help quell the continuous, awful whir beating inside her head.

"Can't sleep?" Akasha asked, sneaking up alongside her.

Sam jolted and turned her head. "Jeez, you are as quiet as a cat."

"I am a cat," Akasha said with a sly grin, like a big, hungry cat looking at a plump canary. "Answer my question, Princess. Can't sleep?"

"No, I can't sleep," Sam replied, brushing down Jo's hindquarters, tilting her body with the brush stroke. "I never know what I'll see these days when I shut my eyes at night or during the day. And you? Can't sleep, either?"

"I can't. Are you worried?" Akasha asked.

"I am," Sam said, wrinkling her brow and looking at her friend. "But the Crow said to me once that if we worried about everything, then we'd be too exhausted to do anything about it."

Akasha smiled again, hoping to ease the tension. "That sounds like the Crow."

Sam sighed and stopped brushing Jo, putting her face against his ribs. The horse shivered as she patted him lovingly while saying, "But how can we stop the wind from blowing or smash a mountain or bury the ocean . . . or change the past? It is impossible."

"Together," Akasha replied, not at all surprised by Sam's pessimism. She gently draped her paw over Sam's shoulder. Sam's crown reached out and rubbed the cat's paw and stroked Sam's cheek. "We do it together."

Thorn walked up on the other side of Sam with his little pony, ducking his head under Jo's neck. "What's to worry about? We're riding into battle to fight flying monkeys, a giant fire-breathing monster, and a powerful, depraved wicked old witch . . . Oh, not to mention her evil army of groveling, deranged minions." He smiled and repeated, "What's to worry about?"

Sam laughed, a cracked sound, half a choke. "Thank you, Thorn. You make a bleak situation look even bleaker."

"At your service, Princess." Then he looked at Akasha and smiled. "You too, Princess."

Sam could hear many of the other cats talking in low voices. And she could feel how anxious Jo had become. She knew he sensed he was close to home, and she also knew he could sense the urgency she was feeling. Maybe it was the way she'd groomed him, but she was certain he could feel the heightened tension. "Soon," she said to him, and he cocked his ear at her and grunted only a little when she tightened his girth. "My mother—and all of Oz—need us, and we shall help her soon. What's to worry about?"

꙳ ✦ ꙳

After a while, Sam and her troops moved on. She began to feel a bit more relaxed when they were moving forward. It helped lighten her mood, and she realized it was also the security of having a small militia of her own watching her back that made her feel better. She snuck several sidelong, covert glances at the cats while they marched together through the forest, stopping every now and again to listen to the stillness of the woods, that perfect silence so at odds now where the abundance of life was no longer anywhere to be seen.

There was something mystifying about these warrior cats, Sam thought, something regal, something formidable. Perhaps it was the wildness she saw in their eyes that she found so exhilarating. Or perhaps it was their raw strength that captivated her. From their gentle purring gestures to their cunning, stealthy way when they prowled, so light on their paws, so sure and aware, and so confident of themselves— bold as brass they were, as though daring any beast, human or not, to challenge their right to be there. Nothing escaped their attention, not a fluttering moth, cooing pigeon, or falling leaf. And they were ever glancing up at the stars, making sure they were headed in the right direction. Sam was pleased to have them as allies and cringed at the thought of it being otherwise.

Dawn was quickly creeping above the trees, but it was barely a lessening of shadows, and the clouds hung so low, gray, and mixed with black smoke that it took effort to stand and not bow her head beneath the weight, heavy and saturated as it was with despair. Even through the complete absence of hope, spring had found a somber and muted voice, with only a few flowering trees in full bloom.

Sam reached up and picked a flower from a tree and held it carefully in her hand. She looked at it as if it were something completely foreign to her, something that had been lost to the world, and she thought to herself, *Such beauty amongst such hopelessness.*

When she mounted Jo, he stepped out as if all his joints ached, and Sam was willing enough to go slowly, mainly to work out his pains, but also because they were close, very close to their home, and there was no telling where the enemy might be hiding as Sam and her company approached the battlefield.

Sam paid careful attention to Jo's stiffness, but she knew that he'd work it out swiftly. As they cautiously rode through the forest, they came to a small pocket clearing and Sam could see, off in the distance, the fell that was the pass to the valley before her mother's castle. Her heart jumped in her throat, and Jo shook his head as if he knew exactly what she was thinking. The breeze sang to her, but floating with it were strange sounds, and she smelled peculiar odors. It was her crown's restlessness and constant tugging of the points of her ears and Jo's heavy breathing that told her what was happening, for these were the smells and muffled sounds of battle.

The air had grown thick and heavier with moisture, the scent of rain adding weight to the deluge and butchery of war. Off to the east, the direction they were heading, thunderclouds were building, sun-white on top, ominous blue-black underneath. They cut off all the sunlight that was trying to break free. At times a gust of wind turned the leaves over on the trees and spun up dust on the ground. Sam did not want to climb the ridge. She knew she would come in sight of the castle and was fearful of what she would find, fearful that she had come too late, fearful that even now, with her newfound strength and her newfound powers and the small army by her side, it would not be enough.

Their edginess increased with each step they made, and the cat army that accompanied her was moving through the brush much more carefully now, stopping every few seconds to listen and sniff the air. It was a sea of furry backs, some black and gray, some a brownish or ruddy color with streaks of black and white, all wearing their battle armor and swords. Their ears were pointed in the direction they were going, and their tails were low and rigid, swishing only slightly when they stopped to sniff and listen.

She let go of Jo's reins, stretching her arms outward, palms up, then she closed her eyes and tilted her head up to the black washboard cloud-covered sky to let the first light droplets of rain sprinkle down and dance on her face. She could feel the wetness running into her eyes, her mouth, her hair, and then the mist-like drops grew in size and slapped the leaves, tapping against her crown and shoulders. The hard rain had begun. As they continued their march, it started coming down in huge, heavy pelts, and all Sam could think about was wishing she could bathe the day away, scrub off all the bad she was about to face. She let the wetness saturate each and every pore. Rivulets ran like veins down her neck.

A chill ran down her spine and skimmed the length of her arms, moved along her waist, and swirled around her legs. She wiped at her face as if brushing away the tears she hoped were not ahead of her and opened her eyes. She blinked into the pouring rain, and her crown's grassy shoots shivered and shook off the rainwater as she pulled her hood over her head and crown and pulled herself out from the depths of worry.

Once again, she remembered what the Scarecrow had said to

her and it echoed inside her head with a powerful voice she couldn't ignore: *If we worried about everything, Princess, then we'd be too exhausted to do anything about it, now wouldn't we?* She was worn out, her body sore, and dread was wearing on her nerves but she was alert, ready. The forest path turned ashen and soggy underfoot, then muddy, grabbing at the horses' hooves and the cats' paws. The fog thickened, clinging to the ground. Then the trail narrowed, weaving its way through dense underbrush, towering trees, and giant boulders. The trees pressed in around them and seemed to shrink, to wither, bending from the weight of war, their jagged limbs clawing the sky like a crowd of drowning people praying for salvation.

Everyone had fallen deathly quiet, all of them creeping, weapons out, keeping a tight watch on the trees and bushes. *It is one thing to prepare to fight the monsters*, Sam thought, *quite another to engage them and know they are not only real but will kill you without remorse.* Sam's heart sped up and she had to force herself to slow her breathing. Her eyes darted everywhere, trying to peer through the ground fog; every bush, thorn thicket, and boulder looked like a monster. Sam patted Jo's neck to ease his doubts and whispered, "We're here. Everything will be fine."

Thorn nudged Billy with the heels of his boots, and his horse pushed up to Akasha. He spoke low, so as not to be overheard. "At least this fog isn't trying to kill us." One look at the wry grin on Akasha's face told him she agreed.

They wound their way upward along the smooth, broad, muddy path at the bottom of a steep ravine that led to the top of the ridgeline. Silently, Sam and her comrades pushed through a mesh of undergrowth at the edge of the steep slope and had to gallop up the rest. Jo snorted and shied away, and Sam clung to the saddle and pulled him around, facing front. Akasha and Thorn sidled up next to her, along with the great Shadow Mountain cats standing behind them, making three rows of soldiers, fifty in each row, with Sam leading them all. Akasha was on her right flank, and Thorn was sitting on his horse as tall as he could to Sam's left.

They all stood silent, horses shifting their hooves in the mud, anxious, not believing the glimpse they now had of the scene below them. The time-honored, magnificent trees Sam had spent her youth climbing were gone, burned as black as night, and smoldering. It even seemed that the gentle hills had been flattened, and where there had been fields of corn and barley, and flower gardens of tulips and poppies that should have been in full bloom, there was now nothing more than a lifeless field of smoldering, scorched ground.

Jo tried to sidle sideways, eager and wanting to bolt headlong into the melee, but Sam kneed him and pulled back firmly on the reins to make him stand still; he obeyed her but stomped his feet in protest. He had already turned a fiery red, and she could feel his muscles curling as tight as a spring, ready to charge.

Between the rolling waves of low-lying clouds, and the grisly sounds of the heaving and thrusting cries of battle, Sam scanned the burned and ravaged land—her home. The Wicked Witch's army of Winkies was between them and the castle, and the flying monkeys blackened the late-afternoon sky where it was almost impossible to filter out the vile creatures from the dark clouds. Sam and her army could see small bands of her mother's command, the largest near the castle gates, fighting desperately, but they were outnumbered. Sam could tell, though, that they were fighting with ferocious aggressiveness, and fighting defensively, mainly because of their honor and duty to their queen, but also because of the fear of being captured alive by the witch's army and turned into slaves of evil.

The smoke and dark cloud cover had consumed the sun, turning the day into a nightmarish dream. Sam stared numbly at the ragged, scarred landscape that had once been lush and green and full of hope. She listened to the terrible cries of the monkeys and the horrible *whoosh* of their wings as they flew, as well as the heavy sound of clanging sword blows. The smoke from the fires choked her and made her eyes water. Her crown held her face, wiped her eyes dry, and tugged at her ears at each wail of the wounded. It was as though the forest she had seen each morning since she was a child from the turret roof above her bedroom had never been, never existed at all. It was as if she were some other princess, thrown into some other time, on another planet on a distant shore of disheartenment and hopelessness, where there was no light, only darkness.

She watched in horror as the death-dealing machines, the trebuchets, shot balls of fire at the castle, breaking its back, destroying outer walls, setting them on fire. In what looked like a hundred places, the enemy horde and the red dragon had applied their torches, and columns of dense smoke were rising above the city as though to blot out from the eye of heaven the horrid sights of ferocious hostility on the battlefield. *Better to die in battle,* Sam thought, *than fall into the hands of the witch.*

෨ ◆ ෬

S am could tell Jo had settled down and stood tall and committed, ears forward, tense, waiting for her orders. Sam glanced heavenward. *Somewhere above the low-lying clouds, the sun lights up the sky,* she thought. *Let it light our courage.* She scanned the gray mud and burned husks of the ancient, mighty trees and wondered if the sun's face would ever grace this tortured landscape again. "It is time to end this," she whispered to herself. "One way or another, it *must* end."

The furry cat soldiers who surrounded her were all standing up on two legs in their fighting stance, elbows level, swords drawn and pointing forward, ready and waiting for her signal to set the charge and jump into the fray.

Sam looked quickly at Akasha and Thorn. Their faces were grim as they took in the battle scene that was raging before them. *Comforting to see such severity on their faces,* Sam thought. What Sam saw in their eyes looked wild, committed, confident—*deadly*.

Her face hardened and adrenaline took over, pushing any fear from her mind. She untied the large leather pouch from her waistband, opened it, and scooped out a small handful of the dragon teeth fragments, then held the yellow, crusty pieces in the palm of her hand. They felt warm and rough. She opened her wings and lifted a short distance away from Jo, and as hard as she could, she threw in the air what she had in her hand. Without hesitating, she took another handful from the pouch and threw it. Then another and another, until the pouch was empty.

The dragon teeth fragments landed on the ground about thirty feet in front of the small army, each landing with a loud, low thud. In the next instant—before Sam had time to return to Jo—a shock wave moved through the warriors, jolting them, pushing at their faces, and making them close their eyes until it blew by. The horses snorted, showing the whites of their wide-opened eyes, and they let out a series of high-pitched neighs.

The ground shuddered and shook, pushing itself out and up, and each dragon seed grew into a cloud of dirt. The dirt swirled and twisted like a dust devil on a desert bed of dry, barren land, transforming into flying dragons on two legs wearing full armor, sword in one hand and shield in the other—ready to fight, one thousand savage, bloodthirsty creatures in all. They were taller than Jo, with wingspans twice their own height. Their deep, yellow, reptilian eyes all stared back at Sam, their mouths foaming, waiting for her orders.

"Dragon warriors!" Sam shouted as she hovered in the air, the calmness of her own voice frightening her. "You will do as I command!" Her tattoos glowed blue, and the hot, bluish-white flame from within her shot up her arm. It rippled up over the hilt and grip of her sword, then rolled along the sharp edges of her blade to the tip, sparking and spitting white-hot, bubbling droplets of fire that fell sizzling to the dirt. "Fight for me! Fight for our queen!" Then she pointed her blazing sword toward the sky and, once again, with a stout and steady voice, shouted, "Fly! Fly! Fly!"

The dragon warriors instantly obeyed, snarling and foaming and gnashing their pointed teeth. They slashed their swords, flapped their wings, and lifted off the ground to engage the flying monkeys, leaving nothing but clouds of dust in their wake.

☞ ◆ ☜

There was a strange, subtle tingle from the bluish-white flame covering her body and her crown, not unpleasant but rather invigorating, calming her nerves. She watched as the dragon-teeth warriors engaged in battle, then turned to face her companions. "My friends . . ." She paused. "I ask for your service to fight for our right to exist." Then she pointed her flaming sword in the direction of the battlefield and it shimmered brighter, and Akasha's and Thorn's eyes glinted against it as they looked at Sam. Then Sam shouted louder, "To fight for our freedom!"

The air was punctuated with loud shouts and the sharp clanging of metal against metal. When Sam gazed across the battlefield, in the midst of the carnage she saw the Tin Woodman, the Lion, Saran, and Lillith holding off the enemy's advance at the castle's gate and the Great Head himself fighting by their side.

To Sam's great surprise, in among them all, wielding two swords was her guardian, her Augie, slashing and cutting, defending the castle and the queen. The venomous anger Augie cast with each blow as besieger after besieger fell before her prostrate to the ground showed Sam that her protector was as mighty a warrior as any twice her size. She could see that Augie was more than she had appeared to be when Sam was growing up, and watching her now fighting alongside her friends bolstered Sam's resolve to the next level.

Across the eerie, blackened ground, she also saw her father slashing and spinning his pike, and the Scarecrow deflecting each powerful blow. And next to them were her mother and the Wicked Witch, going blow to blow with their swords, her mother with her glowing white sword and the witch with her blazing, long, straight, needlelike, red sword. But the Wicked Witch's red sword was now a grisly extension of her arm, growing out from the stump where Elle had lopped off her hand.

And there, hovering above them both, flapping its gigantic wings was the red dragon, lifting itself high into the sky, whipping its long, nasty neck around and spewing its scorching inferno. Her mother slammed the tip of her sword into the ground, dropped to one knee, waved her free arm back and forth, and then a white translucent bubble encased her, pushing the witch back and deflecting the dragonfire before Glinda could be baked by the hot lava flame.

"Listen to me now!" Sam called out at the top of her voice, and all the pairs of bright eyes in her small band of furry warriors turned to her. She swallowed and took in a deep breath, continuing, "Let our blades quell the dark. Let us fight with an unwavering hand." She paused and looked to those on her left and then to those on her right. "Let us fight for our tomorrow!" Her voice echoed as if the bluish-white flame surrounding her enhanced her words, and the look of unwavering determination on Akasha's and Thorn's faces and the faces of the great cats held her together and gave her a sense of relief, almost a sort of triumph.

Silence hung in the air over the cries of war, as Sam quickly flew back onto Jo's back and took hold of his reins. The troop held its collective breath. Sam raised her sword above her head, as did everyone else in the company, yelling out their war cries. "For Oz!" Sam shouted with all her might, and Jo rose up on his hind legs, kicking his front legs and leaping forward. Akasha, Thorn, and the great warrior cats followed behind them, snarling and gnashing their sharp teeth.

⧉ ✦ ⧉

And thus, amid the wild conflict filled with the chaos of war, with death and destruction reaping their terrible harvest like a hammering wedge, the stouthearted warriors galloped into the battle,

Sam leading the charge, cleaving a split one hundred feet wide.

Sam's senses were alive, rushing down upon the enemy soldiers with their weapons high, making a sound like thunder as their horses hammered across the ground while their adversaries all beat their swords and spears against their shields.

The first of the witch's soldiers to feel the sharp teeth of Sam's army fell beneath Jo's lashing hooves and was trampled to death. The second was skewered by Akasha, and the third pulled down by the great cat king. Behind Akasha, Thorn yelled out a curse each time he thrust his sword into the enemy. And above them, the dragon warriors fought the flying monkeys with uncontrolled savagery.

The air came alive with the enemy's screams and cries of pain and terror, as Sam's valiant soldiers hacked their way across the battlefield.

Sam looked up at the sky and saw the evil flying creatures falling to the ground; many monkeys limping away with broken wings.

For an instant, she thought they might have a chance to win this conflict and bring the wicked old witch to her knees. Push wickedness back into the dirt from whence it came and bring peace back to Oz.

And in that instant, it all became clear to her. She understood. From the moment she was born, until that very second, this was her destiny; to fight for the ones she loved or die trying.

Twenty-Three

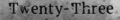

 he witch's army had no scouts looking back over their shoulders, for they had no reason to consider a watch necessary, since they thought they had the only airborne army in Oz. Along with that, on the ground their fiercest troops had their enemy bottled up at the castle gate, on the edge of defeat. There was no need to send out scouting parties to look for stragglers. Only a few folks who were scattered in small villages across Quadling townships and Munchkin Country were brave enough to fight and stand by Glinda's side in battle. The red dragon had terrified all the others so thoroughly they stayed in their hovels, shivering with uncontrollable fear. Everything seemed to be in favor of the witch's army. Victory, they thought, was theirs. Plus, the witch would have sensed any adversary approaching from any direction before they arrived.

Or so they thought. But the Wicked Witch was too distracted by Glinda and the Scarecrow. Her evil army had no forewarning of Sam's approach. If it had been given the foreknowledge, scouts could have been sent out on their riding beasts, some of them nearly like horses but most of them nothing recognizable at all, more like brindled gnus with sharp killing tusks on either side of their skulls. They could have tracked Sam and her army down and cut them to pieces, and they could have won the day. But not this day. All they could do was flee from Sam's cat army and her battle-seasoned friends, Akasha and Thorn, for fear of losing their heads.

Sam looked to her left and saw the cat king disappear into the melee, slicing and snarling. Sam raised her sword above her head and then brought it slowly down before her, pointing it toward the trebuchets. Seven blasts of white-hot, energy-charged lightning spheres sizzled and crackled. And the sword spit them out one by one, destroying each and every one of the wooden machines. Sam could tell that the bluish-white flame engulfing her frightened most of the witch's soldiers. It stung their eyes when it came too near and felt like teeth at their throats, so they scrambled to be free of it. Sam's flaming sword spurred the great cats on, as they spread out in clumps with their growls and their snarls, skillfully fighting the enemy with their swords and sharp claws and using their powerful jaws to break the necks of those who opposed them.

Out of the corner of her eye, Sam saw Akasha leap off her horse and join her father and the other great cats. She watched Thorn do the same, kicking his leg up and over his horse's neck and cutting his own path through the throng of invaders. As Sam pushed on, carving her own incision through the enemy army and splitting it apart, she'd see a cat or one of the beefy shapes of the dragon warriors fling itself onto the back of one of the rival soldiers, taking them down to the dirt and ripping them apart. She did not think about how many she killed or maimed herself. She thought of them only as obstacles that must be overcome so she could join her mother and fight the good fight with her. There was no question that Sam was appalled by war and the great dismay and death it brought. But she would do absolutely anything—anything at all—to save her family and the land she loved, no matter how appalling her actions might seem to be. And so her sword rose and fell, again, and again, slashing and cutting through the enemy horde.

The heaviest fighting was at the castle gates. Saran and a small attachment of her elite castle guards, along with Lillith, Augie, the Tin Woodman, and the Cowardly Lion, were desperately holding back the witch's elite guards. Saran gave a muffled exclamation when she saw Sam and the others. "To me! Quickly!" she yelled with what little spirit was left in her. "It's Sam, and she's brought reinforcements." She urged her companions and the rest forward, and her excitement gave her new strength. They regrouped, and those who were able mounted their warhorses and charged head-on into the throng of besiegers.

The Tin Woodman and the Lion looked up when they heard Saran's cry to arms, and when they saw the bluish-white, flaming rider and the sea of great cats, they smiled at each other. Then the two furrowed their brows and galloped forward with mighty war cries, swinging their swords with all the strength left in their weary bones and tin joints.

They gave all they had and more.

Sam's arm was tired, but it did not matter. Her sword found the necks and vitals of the enemy well enough on its own volition. The enemy could feel the heat and flame from Sam's sword consume the air around them, biting at their throats. Only a few brave souls would approach and fight Sam, but now most had capitulated to the sting of her flaming sword.

With the path in front of her open, Sam then turned her attention and focused solely on the witch and her mother. She turned Jo hard and he was quick to respond, lowering his head and rushing toward the queen with all his magnificent warhorse toughness.

She saw the red dragon circling above her mother and thought it was about to make another run and spew deadly fire, but instead it flew into the smoky sky, vanishing into the black. In the next instant, it swooped out from the dark clouds, as silent as dust settling on your shoulder, leaving misty streaks of gray cloud behind it. It tilted its wings just enough to slow its speed and brought its head up, curling its barbed tail underneath. Sam screamed, "Mother, behind you!"

Sam could feel cold sweat start from every pore in her body. She kicked Jo as hard as she could with her heels but there were still a few enemy soldiers who stood to oppose her. As they tried to step out of Jo's way, they still showed the glint of metal, aiming to disembowel Jo if they could, or hurl a spear and strike Sam from behind. Sam had to use precious time to stop them, but again the blue flame engulfing her and the blazing-white sparks spitting out from her sword, along with the powerful red chest of the warhorse she was riding on, made them eventually flee, and only her sword's quickness stayed their flight. She slew them as they sought to escape.

"Mother, look out!" Sam yelled again. But the queen did not hear her daughter's cry. Sam felt it as surely as if she were standing where her mother was, looking through her mother's eyes. She felt the crushing pain at her mother's back; she felt the wind knocked out of her. And then, with wide eyes, Sam saw the dragon's barb protruding from her mother's chest.

Jo neighed with war fury, and Sam heard the great cats cry their harsh hunting cries. Jo galloped across the evil sea of fighters that separated them from her mother, and Sam watched in horror as the dragon slowly pulled its tail free. Her mother sucked in air as her lungs gurgled from the long, deep gash. She dropped her sword, fell to her knees, and placed her hands, one over the other, on the open wound. Sam whispered to herself, "Mother . . ."

And there, at that very moment, the queen heard her daughter call her name, turned to look upon Sam's face one last time, and smiled. Sam cocked her head slightly, hot tears momentarily blurring her vision, and her heart stopped in her breast.

The Wicked Witch ran forward, sliding a few feet in front of Glinda before she stopped, just inches away, throwing up dirt and dust and small pebbles that scattered around the queen's knees. They looked at each other. The witch grinned, and without hesitation she plunged her red sword between Glinda's cupped hands, forcing it through her heart. The Good Witch of the South closed her eyes, and Sam thought she heard her mother say, "*Samantha . . .*" But she was too numb to know if it was real or if it was her imagination.

Sam's face was on fire, but not from the flame surrounding her. It was the burning anger that was choking her as she watched the witch pull her red sword free.

As if time stood still, Sam watched her mother's body become limp and fall to the side.

The Wicked Witch stood over Glinda in jubilation, an evil smirk of victory etched upon her face. Sam dropped her shield and let go of Jo's reins, leaped off him with fantastic speed, spread her wings hard and fast catching the wind, and screamed through the air. She held her sword with both hands, arms stretched out in front of her, unyielding, rigid, like an arrow shot from a bow. She gave a strong push down on her wings and then up, feeling her shoulder muscles burn as they moved her faster and faster through the air, then she banked sharply, flying straight toward the red dragon. Her speed was so great the sky around her burst into blue flames and an earsplitting, thunderous shock wave of white light exploded from her wake, spreading out in all directions.

Akasha, Thorn, the Scarecrow, the Tin Woodman, the Lion, and all the soldiers—from both armies—stopped their fighting and looked up toward the sound, as an intense burst of hot air blasted downward, hitting them hard and fast in the face and chest, knocking some off balance and pushing back the fur of the great cats and other animals who were fighting for freedom. Jo and all the horses laid their ears back, eyes full and white, and snorted and whinnied, shaking and stomping the ground.

ᕤ ◆ ᕥ

Without stopping, Sam pierced the belly of the red dragon, flying straight into its body and coming out through its spine. She hovered above the monster, and hesitating for only a second, turned back and punched straight through its body again. The second she came out again, covered in dragon guts and flesh, she flew up and over the colossal monster and looked him directly in his one good eye. The dragon was falling, and the enormous creature was twisting and turning and gushing out vast amounts of dragonfire from its wounds and mouth, growling from pain as the flames fell back to earth.

Sam saw fear at the edges of its glowing yellow eye and then death when it started to fade. She flapped her wings and shot up above the dragon's head, and with one mighty swing of her sword, sliced right through the great beast's neck. She hovered and watched its body tumble and twist, falling along with its severed head. The dragon crashed into the dirt with a tremendous explosion, making a dust cloud that shot fifty feet upwards and shook the ground so violently the Wicked Witch fell to her knees.

Sam watched the witch regain her balance, and not hesitating for an instant, she flew toward her evil adversary, her mother's killer. The witch stepped back away from the fallen queen, and planted her feet firmly, setting her stance to fight the princess. But instead of exchanging blows with the Wicked Witch, Sam landed softly by her mother's side. She stood for a second, looking helplessly down at her mother. Sam's bluish-white flame faded as she watched the light leave her mother's beautiful, ice-blue eyes and fade to gray. She fell to her knees, placing her sword on the ground next to her queen, and cradled her mother's head in her arms. Sam gently put her hand on the queen's cheek, carefully brushed the dirt off, and whispered, "Mother." She had no tears, only sorrow. She pushed her mother's hair behind her ear. Sam's body and her mind went numb. Sounds of the battle became pale, insignificant. She did not care about living or fighting. Nothing mattered to her anymore, because what was most precious to her was now gone. No magic spell or even the powerful Wizard of Oz could bring her mother back to her.

The only sounds Sam did hear were the witch muttering and the sparks and sputtering of one of her red fireballs. Without looking at the Wicked Witch, Sam waved her hand and the blue flame ignited and covered her and her mother in a white, blazing, pellucid bubble, protecting them. When the witch's ball of fire hit the white, frothy, effervescent barrier, it burst apart and fizzled out. The witch tried again, throwing another red ball, and another, and another, and then she bent forward, slashing her sword left and right to no avail, and screamed, "You insolent child!" but she could not penetrate the flaming white shield.

Off in the distance, somewhere touching the edges of her mind Sam thought she heard someone calling her name and she shook her head, thinking she had imagined it, but then she heard it again.

Sam.

The witch continued hitting Sam's protective bubble with her red sword, over and over, each blow taking its toll and draining Sam of her strength as she fought to ignore a dizziness that rose and fell like the tide.

Then she heard the voice again, closer now.

Sam.

The voice echoed loudly in her head, and it occurred to her that it sounded like her mother's voice, like she was calling her name from beyond, from heaven. Sam shook her head again, knowing that was impossible. She turned her head slowly, feeling as if she were caught in a dream, and watched in slow motion as the Scarecrow and her father continued their hard fight, pike against sword. The crash of their weapons rang out above the sounds of battle, stinging her ears. She blinked her eyes and wiped the sweat away with the back of her hand. Her father flew up and over the Scarecrow, knocking him off his feet, and aimed his pike at Sam, throwing it hard and straight.

Sam closed her eyes, thinking this was the end because she could not hold the protective spell any longer and she was not going to leave her mother's side. The white bubble vanished, and out from the shadows, Jo jumped in front of her. The spike hit him in the shoulder, and he fell with a scream and a snort, shuffling his legs, and then was silent. Sam opened her eyes and wanted to run to Jo, but she couldn't leave her mother alone. Her crown tugged hard at her ears. She smelled it first in the wind that rushed past her, pushing her hair and the grassy shoots of her crown forward.

Cinnamon.

The wonderful sweet scent of cinnamon.

Then the voice spoke to her again.

Your sword!

She didn't try to think, didn't try to analyze. She kept her eyes on her mother's pale face and without looking, threw her sword into the air. Whispering inside her head and moving her lips like a silent prayer, she said, *Believe*.

Out of the corner of Sam's eye, she saw a blurry streak of green and then heard the cracking of bone. Sam shivered, not out of fear or exhaustion, but from absolution. It was Elle, and her sister was alive.

The bluish-white glow of Sam's flaming sword sputtered and flickered, transforming from its fiery bluish-white glow into a blazing, sizzling green, igniting the fire inside Elle and covering her entire body the instant Elle's fingers wrapped around its hilt.

Elle exhaled, letting out a surge of hot breath and a shuddering scream as an electrified pulse shot down her spine. Her hand held true as she struck the witch squarely, cutting through and through, piercing the witch's chest with a harsh, ugly sound, shattering the witch's sternum and puncturing the old crone's evil, wicked heart. As Elle pulled the sword out, she quickly reached into the gaping wound and grabbed the witch's heart. With one swift motion, Elle tore it free and held the ugly black mass in the palm of her hand, still beating and pumping the witch's green blood.

Elle poured water on it from the canteen she had attached to her waistband, and the heart sizzled and spit. A small plume of steam erupted and the black heart liquefied into a viscous, bubbling, black goo, dripping off of Elle's hand, sputtering and spilling onto the dirt at her feet, and finally disappearing into the ground. Elle let the buildup of adrenaline escape with her next breath as she wiped her hand on her tunic.

For only a moment, the witch stood in horror and watched wide-eyed as her heart melted away. In the next instant, small cracks and tiny, burning orange fissures appeared on the tips of the witch's fingers (on her one good hand) and turned to ash. They hissed and spread out like wildfire to each knuckle, then her wrist, working their way around the elbow, over her shoulder, and finally up her neck to the side of her face, as bits and pieces of the witch's body broke apart, piece by little piece. With her eyes wide open, gaping in horror at Elle, the witch tried to speak but she couldn't, her mouth opening and closing like a feeding guppy. And then in the next second, the Wicked Witch turned completely to ash and blew away into the wind like thousands of tiny, nasty, black fruit flies searching for rotting garbage.

Elle looked over at Sam and dropped Sam's sword. The green flame that covered Elle's body ceased to burn. It started from her feet slowly working its way up her body until the last bit of fire danced for a moment across her shoulders, arms, face and head, and then, it drifted off vanishing into the stale rippled air of battle.

At that very moment the fighting ended; the only lingering sounds were those of the dying. The dragon warriors had instantly turned to dust, and their ash was scattered to the wind. And the very second the witch drifted away, her entire enslaved Winkie army and the flying monkeys dropped their weapons and fell to their knees, overcome with shame for what they had done. But Sam knew it was through no fault of their own, as they had been controlled by the Wicked Witch to do her dirty work.

But shame, Sam thought, would stay with them until the end of their days, for it was something she believed they would never forgive themselves for, nor would they ever forget. She knew that feeling well. She felt it now, and it hammered at her—and would follow her for the rest of her life too. This she was sure of. She believed she'd never truly forget the horrifying choice that she'd made to mercilessly cut down the good Winkie people who had been so hypnotized by such terrible and powerful dark magic. Everyone who had fought would carry with them battle scars hidden deep under their skin for the rest of their lives.

The moral implications alone of what she had done would be written about and debated by Ozarian scholars for years to come. And rightly so. In the darkest corners of her soul Sam was certain, at least for her, that shame would remain constant, concealed behind every sunrise and sunset from this moment forward. It was a heavy burden for anyone to bear. Her eyes pooled every time the thought forced its way into her mind. She felt profoundly sorry for all who fought and died that day—and for those still standing—as she would hold the indignity of war and the contrition that comes from the aftermath of battle deep within her, forever, until the light in her eyes vanished and celandines and poppies were growing above her head. For this, she thought, would be the only way to release the ache that was now branded on the hearts of everyone.

The air was heavy, filled with pain and much suffering. All the Winkies looked around in horror and had no idea how they could have been so duped, and worst of all, they remembered each and every horrible thing they had done.

Sam watched her father as his eyes went from orange to his beautiful aquamarine blue. She could actually see a wispy cloud of smoke seep from his eyes and escape his shoulders, and then disappear into the air. He shook his head to rid himself of the vile image of the loathsome devil-woman who had bewitched him. Closing his eyes, he pressed his palms hard in the sockets to squeeze out all his shame. When he opened them he stood there, looking across the battlefield at all the dead and hearing the moans of those soon to die, and then he remembered. He remembered everything. It flooded in like a raging storm, drowning him—falling in love with Glinda and asking her to be his wife, the birth of his daughters, being taken away, tortured to do the witch's bidding. It all came back to him, the beautiful and the hideous, all at once.

He reached down and extended his hand to the Scarecrow. The Scarecrow took it, and Lucius helped him stand. The Scarecrow put his hand on the man's shoulder and said, "Lucius, it is no fault of your own. Your daughters need you."

Shaking his head, trying to rid himself of the memories, Lucius walked up to Elle and opened his arms, and they held each other and then knelt down next to Sam. He put his hand on Sam's shoulder, and she cupped her hand over his. His hand was warm and loving, and she held it with all the strength she had left. Her eyes pooled, and she wept.

The Tin Woodman, his tin body dented and splattered with blood, and the Lion, his mane also matted and caked with blood, walked up and stood next to the Scarecrow. Then Akasha and her father, along with Lillith, joined them. Both armies had formed a circle around the queen, kneeling and bowing their heads. Without warning, the Wizard, the Great Head, appeared out of thin air, standing as if he'd always been there next to Sam, and put his hand on her shoulder. Sam's crown gently rubbed the Great Head's bloodstained hand. The air was stale and smelled of death, and he, like all the others, removed his helmet, kneeled, and bowed to the Good Witch of the South.

Suddenly, the rain stopped and one honey-colored beam of sunlight found an opening through a small rent in the dark gray clouds covering the battlefield, casting an eerie, mournful glow on Glinda, but lasting only seconds as if highlighting the event they all had just witnessed. The light faded as a raw, bitter wind stirred Sam's crown and brushed across her skin, driving the anvil-black clouds over, pushing back the sun, leaving only a dark veil of lamentation covering the hearts of all who looked upon their fallen queen.

Twenty-Four

After the war was over, after the unforgettable spectacle of death and destruction had ended, the day didn't belong to anyone. As Sam scanned the landscape, she felt as though she were in a dream; the whimpering and groaning of the wounded and dying echoed along with the sad song of senselessness. She blinked back what tears she had left to shed and let the stiff, smoke-filled breeze play with her hair. Her crown rubbed the sides of her face, and she closed her eyes, saying a silent prayer for herself and for those who had lost their lives, and for all those who had not yet surrendered to death's cold and unforgiving embrace. *So much loss*, she thought, her heart so heavy she felt she might suffocate. "Why?" she asked out loud.

Sam set her jaw and pushed the despair behind her. She tried to concentrate solely on putting one foot in front of the other, as though she could truly filter out all the suffering. But it was a hopeless effort. She could no more let go of the heartache than she could stop the rain from falling from the sky. "Mother," she whispered to herself. "I'm so sorry."

She heard the hard, labored breathing and deep moan of a dying soldier, and the tears bit at her eyes, though she thought she had nothing left to give. She slumped against Jo, felt his warmth and listened to his beating heart, relieved he was alive. The tears for her mother, and for everyone who lost loved ones that day, poured freely, and they gushed out and kept coming until a harsh sob shook her frame.

Eventually, the brisk wind blew again and pushed the clouds away, letting the somber, late-day sunlight cascade across the devastation. Sam inhaled deeply and shivered from the cool air filling her lungs. But there was something more—a trace of spring. Her skin prickled. The night suddenly felt as if it had just opened its eyes, as though the trees, birds, and animals were coming back to life, watching her, giving her a sign. *Hope*, she thought. *Yes. There is still hope. There is still hope for tomorrow.*

She closed her eyes; more hot tears leaked from the corners. She heard a whispering behind her, a soft, tender, loving voice calling to her and telling her not to be sad. It was her mother. And with the palms of her hands, Sam wiped away the tears rolling down her cheeks. Then she recalled the night of her sixteenth birthday, when her mother came to her bedchamber and gave her the sword, honoring her, choosing her to stand by her side as an equal and not as a child. Understanding suddenly dawned on Sam, and she began to smile. She opened her eyes. Her mother had left her another gift, a great gift to remember her by, and not only the beautiful sword.

She had passed on her spirit too.

It had been a fight of light against dark, a battle against one misguided and deeply disturbed wicked witch. A demon who'd used good people by controlling their every thought for her own wicked and malevolent desire to rule over Oz and all its citizens. But it was nonetheless a long and bitter day for those who were left to pick up the pieces and regain their dignity and self-worth. There had been many losses on both sides of the camp—many were not seasoned soldiers, but were merely simple folk who had never held a weapon in their lives before, only a pitchfork to bale hay and a hoe to till the ground or a hammer to build a home. In this war, there were no captives to be taken, only the living left to help the wounded and dying.

It was not until the night grew deep and heavy that the Scarecrow,

Sam, Elle, and their father, along with the Tin Woodman and the Cowardly Lion, were able to carry Glinda's body up to the royal bedchamber so the queen could be prepared for burial. And when they carried her lifeless form across the battlefield, those left standing and those helping the wounded kneeled and bowed their heads in sorrow for the fallen queen.

❧ ◆ ☙

Later when they gathered before the castle gate—or what was left of it—they sat down to think about the rest. Akasha, as well as the great cat king and his army, had gathered at the castle gates to rest and decide what needed to be done next, lucky to be some of the few standing upright on their paws and feet and not prostrate face-first in the mud.

When Augie came to sit, Sam held her in her arms, and Augie wiped soot and blood from Sam's cheeks and reached over to hold Elle's hand, squeezing with what strength she had left to give.

The loving old Munchkin turned a blurry gaze toward Sam and wiped tears from her blood-stained cheeks. "I am so sorry for your loss."

There was no rejoicing, no celebration that the Wicked Witch was dead, for all were weary, bone-weary. They'd had so little hope at the beginning of the day that now, in the evening, as the sun was dipping below the horizon and turning everything to long, sorrowful shadows, they had not really begun to realize that the war was over and that good had once again triumphed over evil, that light had once again torn through the darkness and saved the day. For now, there were the wounded to attend to, and the few souls who were left on their legs who could help had to muster up the energy to do what they must.

Many of the survivors were children, for those who were old enough to carry weapons had taken up a sword or knife or sickle and gone into battle, and in the end, had met their Maker. But the children at least now could help carry bandages, collect wood for fires to burn the dead, and carry pails of water, as there was not a child among the lot who had not lost a father, mother, sister, or brother. The work was, in a way, the only comfort they could offer themselves, for it would be years before they would ever find peace and be able to follow the colorful brick roads now tainted and overflowing with Ozarian blood.

The battle took many to the grave on that day, and Saran was one of the brave souls who had fought to the very end, fought for her queen and country. Saran had died on the battlefield fighting, leading her company of warriors through the last endless days. Her soldiers had followed her loyally, with respect if not with love, for they trusted her courage in battle. And even when Saran had become worn and haggard as the siege from the Wicked Witch's cutthroat army continued day after day, her cries to carry on cut a sharp edge in their ears to fight the good fight. She was unscathed until the end, and her horse came back without her after darkness had fallen, the saddle still on its back, stained with her blood.

Lillith was kneeling with a waterskin for one of the fallen soldiers when Saran's horse, the horse of the First Consola, returned to the battlefield and someone whispered the news of Saran's death to her with a cracked and frightened voice. Lillith looked up at the messenger, a small child she knew from her village and simply said, "Thank you for telling me, child," and then lowered her eyes to carefully tilt the waterskin to the lips of the soldier and quietly wept.

The fallen soldier looked upon Lillith anxiously. She was a beautiful young woman and Lillith's cousin, whom Lillith had known since a child and assisted in her birth, and she looked upon Lillith anxiously. Even though the soldier was weary beyond life's breath, she reached out and held Lillith's cheek saying, "I am so sorry for your loss, Cousin." This had become the phrase of the evening, echoing to each of those who had lost a family member or dear friend: *I am sorry for your loss.*

Her name was Truly, and she was young. The fallen soldier had just celebrated her nineteenth birthday four days before the Wicked Witch attacked the castle. Her face held none of the scars and wear that were tunneled into the faces of the more seasoned castle guards. She was lovely, with smooth dark skin, dark hair, a soft, angelic face, and a gentle, kindhearted spirit, which made it all the more difficult for Lillith to watch her cousin slip away.

S am and Elle had consoled Lillith, held her firmly—which Sam tried to do for all those left to deal with the wounded, the dead, or the dying—for the princesses shared Lillith's ache for the loss of such a close and dear comrade. And when Lillith returned to her task of helping the wounded, she was conscious that her helmet was missing, that her armor was bloody, that there was a gash on her leg, and aware too that her hands would be trembling were it not for the weight of the waterskin she held. Sam was particularly aware that an innocent child had just told Lillith that Saran was dead and that Saran's horse had returned with a blood-stained saddle. So each time Lillith gave a drink to one of her fallen comrades, she cried a little more for the loss of her friend and captain, but did what she knew she had to do: help those who could not help themselves and do what she could to heal the terrible blemish left from the ravages of war.

But the First Consola was not the worst of their losses. Everyone knew the queen had fallen in battle, and it was hard for anyone to believe that such a tragedy could happen. It lay heavily on everyone's minds, making the task of healing and repairing all the more difficult.

Some of the great cats had fallen too, and everyone, including Sam and Akasha, had lost sight of a comrade. Thorn was missing. He had not been seen since Sam saw him leap off of Billy and sprint into the mix at her flank when they first rode into battle. Sam and Akasha looked for him anxiously, and it was Akasha who found him, limping with one good leg, grinning from ear to ear, his swords still in both hands. He had a long, grim gash along the length of his thigh so that he could not move around much, only hobble forward a few feet at a time then rest against his swords and hobble some more.

When Akasha found Thorn in a such a state, she instantly imagined him battling enemy soldiers with his swords rising and falling, slicing through the air like little machines that never tired or felt pain from their wounds.

"Where's your horse?" Akasha asked. "Where's Billy?"

"She was taken down and slaughtered by a pack of gnu," he explained, and let it go at that.

"Step up and get on my back," Akasha said. "I will carry you to the gates. The others are there waiting." But Thorn shook his head. "Get on," Akasha said with a slight growl.

"I can't," Thorn said in a huff, growling back. "I cannot throw myself up onto your furry back with only one good leg." Akasha lowered herself to stand on all four paws and with horrible slowness, Thorn eased himself onto her back, grabbing tufts of fur to steady himself and using her elbow as a step up. Once he was on the cat's back, he let out a thankful sigh. He leaned forward resting his head along Akasha's neck, nestling his cheek deep into her soft warm fur. He closed his eyes and teased his friend. "That's a good cat. Forward."

"Be thankful I like you," Akasha teased back with the first smile of the night, "or you'd be my breakfast in the morning." It was difficult to find humor amidst all the suffering, but what little humor there was to be had, helped to ease some of the tension that floated around each and every one of them.

⤙ ◆ ⤚

Lillith told them later that night that the castle had been besieged barely a week after the queen had returned from the meeting with Rumpart. "I killed the horrid sod, Rumpart, on the second week of the battle, and before all hell broke loose from the surprise invasion of the witch's army. We had planned a covert raid on Rumpart's castle to rescue Elle. But we felt defeated before we even began, since their numbers were so great on the ground and in the air." Lillith explained further, "We would advance a little, only to be pushed back to the keep. We were weary and discouraged, and we never rode out with the hope we'd be victorious." She paused a minute and stared at the fire where they were boiling water for the wounded. "We would gain a little ground, always riding out a little less each time, and each time always bringing a few more survivors from more burnt-out villages and towns back to the castle for shelter . . ." She paused again and sighed deeply, looking from Sam to Elle and then vacantly at her feet.

Akasha and Thorn had been keenly listening and were eager to hear the rest. "Please, continue," Akasha prodded.

Looking up from the ground, Lillith eyed Sam and continued with her account. "It began shortly after you left on your camping trip, Princess. When you didn't return as you said you would. We sent a search party out for you, but they never returned. I am sure they were killed by the witch's scouts. We all thought you to be dead, milady."

It was difficult to learn how disheartened Lillith and Saran had become. "When the search party didn't return, we had lost all hope. From then on, everything unraveled. Battling evil day after day tears a person's soul wide open from the inside out."

Sam shivered and later spoke in snatches with Lillith as they tended their horses and tended the wounded.

S am and Elle were numb with shock and sorrow, and tried not to think of their mother, so they went from one painful cry of a fallen soldier to another around the castle—what was left of it—giving water and tying bandages. But somehow, they managed to stay near each other, and the presence of the other was to each a much wanted and needed comfort.

When there was a moment, Elle explained to Sam and her friends how she escaped the burning rubble of the witch's tower. Sam was not surprised in the least concerning Elle's tenacity and her cunning ability to crawl out alive from underneath the massive pile of scattered stone debris. And she admonished herself for not taking the time to search for her sister among the mounds of broken and burning stones. But at the time, the chance of Elle surviving had seemed so small, and the threat of war from the Wicked Witch was pounding at them with stronger cries to forge ahead and cut the head off the snake. It was a choice Sam now regretted dearly.

But Elle would have nothing of it, and did not allow Sam to wallow in self-pity, as she told her in no uncertain terms. They held each other and cried, grateful to be reunited, both aching from the death of their mother.

Sam crouched for a moment by the campfire, which cast long shadows on the walls of the castle, and she thought of the words spoken by another person that had made her life more than ordinary: *If we worried about everything, Princess, then we'd be too exhausted to do anything about it.* Abruptly, she turned to Akasha and asked, "Where is the Crow?"

"I am here, Princess," the Scarecrow said, appearing out of the shadows, holding the reins of his horse. "I've been tending to your mother." Sam reeled to her feet and held the Scarecrow, crunching his straw body, bits of it poking out at her, but she didn't mind and held him even tighter. After some time, she quietly said, "You're leaving, aren't you?"

"I am," he said, rubbing her back. Then he released his hold to look directly at Sam, and he gently rubbed her cheek with his hand. His rough burlap glove gave Sam comfort, and she closed her eyes. "I've heard of rumblings in the north—just rumors, but I think it best I take a look."

Sam opened her mouth to argue, thought better of doing so, and shut it. The Scarecrow did almost nothing spontaneously; everything he did was deliberate, so the chances of changing his mind with words would be wasted words. Plus, she was much too tired to argue or weep any more. She sighed, and perhaps the Scarecrow heard something in that sigh, for when he put his arms around her again, he held her a little tighter.

"One day, explain all this to me," she hesitated, "that we did what needed to be done, and that it was good."

"Good?" the Scarecrow questioned, looking across the battlefield at all the destruction and death. "What does that really mean, *good*? One day the stars will no longer shine in the night sky, and there's not going to be anything or anybody left. Nobody is going to remember anything that happened here, cruel or kind." Then he paused, let out a labored sigh, looked down at Sam, and gently rubbed her shoulders. "In the grand scheme of things, my dear princess, none of this matters."

"It matters to me," Sam said kindly. "You matter to me." Then she smiled back at the Scarecrow and let out a soft, breathy chuckle. "You think too much, Crow."

"Life was a lot less complicated for me when I was hanging on a wooden post in the middle of a cornfield, wishing I had a brain."

"Will I see you again?"

"Why wouldn't you?"

Sam smiled again, as much of a smile as her weariness allowed. "Because you are so mysterious."

"Not as mysterious as you think, Princess," he said, grinning back. "I will always know where to find you, no matter where you are."

Sam pulled away from the Scarecrow and looked at his painted face so she would not forget how beautiful he was, and what he meant to her. "I miss you already." He put his hand on her cheek, and she felt the comfort of its roughness on her skin. Then she gently placed her hand over his.

"The Tin Woodman and the Lion are staying to support you and will help rebuild your mother's castle," he said. "Watch for me in your dreams, milady." Then he mounted his horse and rode off, not looking back. "You never know when I will need you next."

She watched for a moment as he evaporated into the dark of the night while the spitting and sputtering and crackling of the fire caught her ear. The fire reminded her of times spent eating and laughing with the Scarecrow and her friends by the fireplace at his Silver Lake retreat. It seemed ages ago, but it was a good memory and gave her some solace, a place to go in her mind, something good to help ease the woe and gloom that lay heavily upon her.

Then the moans of the wounded abruptly brought her back to reality and, once again, she tended to the injured.

The castle's keep was deserted, except for those who were putting out the fires. Tomorrow, many of the sick and wounded would be taken there for healing, but for now, this night, they would stay by the fire at the foot of the castle's gate, for no one had any strength left to do more.

Sam felt a loving, familiar hand touch her own and held it firmly.

"You need to sleep, Your Highness," Augie said. "In your own bed."

"Now?" Sam replied, exhaustedly, looking around. "I can't. I must tend to the wounded. They—they need reassurance. They need hope."

"Let the healers give them hope. You've done all you can."

Sam noticed blood on Augie's shoulder. "You're injured!"

"It's nothing," Augie said with a distant and vacant voice. "More of the enemy's blood than my own."

Sam could tell that Augie, like herself, was much too tired to explain and would attend to her own injuries when she could. Augie put an arm around Sam, holding a torch in the other hand, and they walked up to the castle together, leaning on each other.

The castle was eerie in its silence and solemn in its darkness. Sam's exhaustion made the shadows from the torch dance like evil sprites at the corners of her sight. She had spent her entire life in these halls, but now they seemed unfamiliar and dangerous, and after so much time of being away, she could not remember how to navigate through them.

As she walked up the spiral staircase to her turret room, she remembered the never-ending staircase in the witch's black tower, very much like the stairs she was now climbing—her own stairs—and she shivered violently as her breath whistled through her teeth. She stopped and put both arms around Augie, and Augie held her firmer until the shaking stopped, until they could continue, step by agonizing step.

Augie let go of Sam so she could open the door to her bedchamber. Sam put out her hand and leaned against the doorframe. When they entered the large vaulted room, the torchlight danced on the ceiling, and it reminded Sam of when her mother had given her the sword for her birthday and the hundreds of candles she'd lit with her magic that night.

When they reached the bed, Sam fell into it with a gasp and shudder, and started shaking violently again. "I'm so cold," she said through chattering teeth. A blast of grief hit her, from her mother's death to Saran's end and Lillith's anguish, and all those she knew and didn't know who had fallen in battle. She opened her mouth to speak of all that had been lost, but despair rushed in, bitter and crushing, and she mumbled, "Why, Augie? Why?"

"Shush," Augie said with a kind, consoling voice, as she pulled the covers over the princess to help ease the chill of the night. Augie pulled a chair up next to the bed and stayed by Sam's side till Sam fell asleep, saying a silent prayer for the princess.

Before Augie knew it, slumber had taken her as well.

Twenty-Five

S am crouched like a spider clinging to its web, waiting patiently for an unsuspecting insect to fall into her trap. Her right hand grasped the gilded flagpole, while the other gently moved across the scabbard that held her sword. The triangular flag above her head—frayed at its tip—whipped and snapped as Sam waited and watched the faintest glow of dawn touch the low-lying clouds rolling over the mountaintops, highlighting them underneath with a pink and golden flare.

Her stomach churned.

Bubbled.

The *rush*.

The rush still felt the same, a tickle that she loved, and the thrumming of her heart, albeit rapid, was under control. But her days were different now—*she* was different now—and a feeling of sorrow followed her at each sunrise and sunset. Her grief was something she knew she would accept in time, but it was also something she knew would travel with her. It still came in waves, and when it curled and crashed hard against her mind, she needed private time for herself to settle her swirling thoughts.

Her father and Elle, Augie, Lillith, and everyone who lived in and around the castle and all the small towns and villages throughout Quadling Country were leaving today for Munchkin City for her mother's celebration of life. It was a two-day ride she didn't feel like being a part of, mainly because there was always so much fuss and brouhaha when the royal caravan left the castle keep, but more because the tear in her heart was still fresh and painful. *Then again,* she thought, *it would be fun to ride Jo and go on a little adventure.* She was sure Akasha and Akasha's father, along with many of the Shadow Mountain cats, would be at the funeral proceedings, as well as Thorn, the Tin Woodman, and the Cowardly Lion. She didn't believe the Scarecrow would make an appearance, based on what he had said to her when he rode off into the shadows that night after her mother had been killed. But even though she had little hope of seeing him again, she missed him terribly.

Despite her lack of desire to make the trek to Munchkin City, it would be wonderful to see her dear friends again. She missed Akasha deeply too, and the others as well, though Akasha most of all. Sam had become partial to the mountain cat's peaceful purring when she curled up to take a nap, or when she rubbed her side against a rough and gnarled old tree to ease an itch. The last time she'd looked into the sparkling-yellow almond eyes of Akasha and talked with the others was right after they had buried her mother on the shoulder of a peaceful knoll overlooking the castle, surrounded by magnificent flowering trees. It was a place where her mother had loved to have picnics with her and Elle when they were children.

When they buried her mother, it was a small private ceremony. Only the castle guards and a few close friends were allowed to attend and show their respect. The Cowardly Lion tried to be brave, but his tears spilled out nonstop, and the Tin Woodman gushed so much that he had to use his oil can to keep his eyes from rusting shut. But the Munchkins who so dearly loved their queen asked to have an official state funeral, one befitting a great ruler, so all of Oz could mourn.

Everyone still felt gray, and perhaps in the aftermath of the Wicked Witch's treachery, the Munchkins were right—a final farewell to Glinda Goodwitch, the Good Witch of the South, was what all the citizens of Oz needed. For Sam, it was much more complicated than just saying a final farewell and then moving on. She desperately tried to push to the back of her mind the image of her mother looking back at her and smiling just before she was killed. But it was always there, like a misty glade waiting for her to return to that terrible moment. And each time that image pressed hard against her skull, she would shed a tear that made a small space around her heart to prevent it from beating out of anger. Still, there were times when the image of her mother being impaled by the red dragon and run through by the Wicked Witch was heavy and loud and pounded her ears with such force that her rage crashed in on her like thunder, and her vision was stained red.

But it was her family and friends who were her salvation, an arm around her waist that helped her stand and stagger forward to walk across a peaceful bridge of reclamation.

ॐ ✦ ॐ

Before Sam had flown to the roof of her bedchamber, she woke that morning in her own bed, under her own covers, in her mother's castle—her castle now—as she had been doing for the past month. Her muscles were still sore and stiff, but not so painful as her sorrow.

It was a rustle from somewhere just beyond her sleepy eyesight and the dim haze before dawn that woke her. And as it had happened each morning, she couldn't at first imagine where she was, and she groped vaguely for the hilt of her sword. But then she would recognize the raspy, gruff voice of her caretaker.

"Sam," Augie grunted. "Time to wake. Get up, Princess."

"Augie?"

"Aye, milady, and *yes*, it's me. Every morning it's the same. I wake you, and you're not sure I'm real." Augie pulled the bed curtains apart, letting the morning light flood in. Sam winced and shielded her eyes. "I'm real. And it's time to get up and put yourself together. We have a long two days ahead of us."

"What day is it?" Sam asked.

"The day after yesterday," Augie quipped. "Every day it's the same with you, the same questions. Now, eat." She placed a tray of food on the bed next to Sam and handed her a cup of orange juice. "And before you ask, yes, Jo is doing wonderfully. He is still limping a bit, but your fireproof ointment is a miracle, a health-giving tonic. We have made enough for everyone to use, and the people are so grateful."

"Yes, right," Sam said sleepily as she drank the juice. "Right," she repeated quietly to herself. The aroma of bacon filled the air, and she bit into it; the bacon tasted like it was the first time she'd ever tried it before, a strong, woody flavor that made her tongue swell for more.

Augie opened her eyes wide in the same way she had done to terrorize the very young Samantha when she was caught in some childish misbehavior. "You'll need more than just one piece of bacon before you go off flying. The sun is almost about to show itself, but," she said in a tone of suppressed frustration, "I need to tell you again that I do not approve of your animal friends, meaning some of your mountain cat friends that stayed behind. Mute or talking, it makes no difference to me, but they feel they can sleep wherever it pleases them to lay themselves, and that simply won't do, milady. We need to find them their own pillows and blankets and their own rooms."

"We will," Sam said, and snickered in a way that made Augie join her. But Augie turned down the corners of her mouth to suppress the smile, and tears pooled in her eyes. She turned away from Sam and leaned back onto the bed, staring out over the balcony into the grayness of the early morning. Sam could feel Augie's grief and understood her sorrow. Sam deeply regretted that the very last time she spoke with her mother, she had a little girl's tantrum and had argued with her mother about wanting to go to Rumpart's castle with her.

Her childish behavior then was a memory that would be impossible to forget, but one that she gained insight from, about how gracious and loving her mother was to always forgive her for her shortcomings. And just thinking of that made her feel better.

"I'm so very sorry, Princess, but I miss her so," Augie said, wiping away her tears.

"Me too," Sam said softly. As she dragged herself out of bed, she felt that each and every part of her body would never move quickly again, and she stretched her wings slowly to work out the ache that had been a constant reminder of the hard-fought battle with the Wicked Witch. When she touched her feet to the floor, she let out a short, quick yelp from the cold stone. Sam leaned back onto her bed, stood beside Augie, and put her arm around her. Being that much shorter, Augie put her head in the crook of Sam's arm, and they leaned against each other for a long time. Augie's eyes pooled, and tears gently rolled down her puffy, wrinkled red cheeks.

The princess saw the long bandage wrapped around Augie's forearm under her sleeve. "How's your wound healing?" Sam asked, changing the subject.

"Thanks to your ointment, it is mending quickly. Soon I will have no scar to remind me of that terrible war, only that which is left on my broken heart."

Sam held Augie closer, hugging her as tightly as she could, and said softly in her ear, "I love you, Augie. I will always love you."

Off in the distance, Sam heard Jo whinny, snort, and stomp, and she grinned and giggled to herself.

"I put some apples in your satchel," Augie said, wiping away more tears with the back of her hand as she gently pushed Sam away from her. She put the palms of her hands on Sam's cheeks and smiled. "Go. Jo's waiting for you."

After Sam put on her clothes, she grabbed the satchel of apples and her sword belt. Because of all she'd been through, now she never left the castle without her sword. But before she leaped out and over the balcony, she stood on top of the railing, turned toward Augie with outstretched arms, and gave her a sly wink. Then she tilted her head back and let herself go. She fell backward over the edge and let out an excited howl. Augie ran to the railing and yelled after her, watching her drift down toward the ground. "You be back here in time to get ready, do you hear me?"

Sam waited as long as she dared before she unfurled her wings, and at the very last second, before the ground swallowed her whole, she quickly spread them to the wind, twisted and looped, and shot up to the clouds leaving a trail of snowflakes in her wake. Another tickle caught in her throat and she grinned, thinking to herself, *Good old gruff and bossy Augie, always looking after me.* Then there was nothing but the sky and the wind, and the rush.

And now, as Sam waited on top of her bedchamber roof, the moon was silently setting in the west as she looked across the landscape. The vast land around the castle remained scarred from the battle with the Wicked Witch. But already, a hint of new grass and poppies were poking out of the ground and scattered among the blackened trees and scorched underbrush. Still, the scene was a sad reminder of the anguish and suffering which lingered in the air. The early morning light was fading quickly. The moon seemed only a delicate, translucent orb resting against a hazy waking blue sky, waiting to be swallowed up by the sun. The fiery edge of the sun was just showing itself over the rise, and a fine mist covered the low dips along the rolling hills and upper valleys.

Most mornings the wind was cold, but Sam's body was always warm when flying down to the horse barn to give Jo his breakfast treat of fresh apples. He would nicker and thrust his nose into the satchel and sniff it to greet her, then nudge her to hurry along and give him his morning treat. And when she teased him and didn't take the delicious apple out right away, he'd impatiently blow air on her face and turn a dazzling scarlet to show his irritation. Then, with a petulant stomp of his back foot, he'd shake his mane and snort and shake it again. It was a game they played with each other every morning, and when Sam finally pulled the delicious fruit from her satchel and Jo was finally allowed to munch down on his prize, his hide would slowly change to a serene pale blue, and then to his calming coat of cream, and Sam would gently rub the fire balm onto his wound and groom him until he sparkled.

Thinking about Jo made her smile. Now the most simple things made her happy: arguing with Augie, eating breakfast in bed, long walks, and long naps. The mornings she loved the most, as they brought a new breath of hope to her, which she needed a lot of now. Her mind drifted, and she wondered what it would be like to stand on the creamy surface of the moon and gaze down upon her own world.

And then she thought about how many other worlds like hers might exist in the universe, worlds that had magic, talking trees, a wizard ruling them, good witches and bad witches, and war.

ॐ ◆ ॐ

The pinkish golden glow of the sunrise was becoming more intense, filtering up and scattering against the clouds and floating around the mountain peaks—soft hues of color danced underneath the clouds and brilliant white skirted the tops.

The slate shingles were cold under Sam's feet, and she wiggled her toes to warm them. She could see the wind stir the treetops, and the surface of the forest next to the castle seemed to ripple beneath the steel blue sky; the breeze, when it touched her, smelled of leaves. Sam grinned. Off in the distance she could almost hear the apple trees boasting with self-satisfaction about how their new crop of delicious red apples were the best they'd ever made.

She turned her attention to Jo and looked out over the meadow, and spied him munching on sweetgrass with Vail. Sam's grin grew and stretched from ear to ear into a full smile knowing that he was happy and content.

The castle guards were bringing saddled horses out from the main stables and walking them to the keep for their trip to Munchkin City. But she ignored their scuttling and turned her eyes toward the early morning light. This had always been her favorite time, in the morning before the sun peeked its head out to share its warmth with the living; to sit and wait for the rush. And these days, it had become an even more critical part of her morning routine than ever before, as it gave her a much-needed feeling of normalcy. There was no place like home to repair a wounded heart.

As the sun moved higher, she watched the plume of a newly forming cloud shift and sway and rise above the others. It was as if this billowing vapor was a living, breathing, thinking creature—swirling, shifting, growing, changing. A sudden flash from the sun made her squint, and she turned her eyes from the light. She looked over to Jo's barn, where the horse was shaking his head and stomping the ground. He looked healthy and robust, and the ointment was healing his wound at a fast pace. She giggled to herself, knowing he was waiting impatiently for his treat.

Sam thought he was strong enough to make the trip to Munchkin City, and she had decided to ride him. Even Roman and Augie were in favor of the journey, and Roman thought Jo's wound had almost healed entirely and believed the little jog would raise his spirits tremendously. "If Jo becomes a bit sluggish," Roman had told her, "just sit and rest. Take all the time he needs and enjoy the day together. It will do you a great deal of good as well, milady." This, Sam thought, was an excellent idea—and the reason she decided to heed Roman and Augie's suggestion. They would take their good old time about it and would not worry about when they arrived. She was in no hurry—the Munchkins could wait.

Each time she sat on top of the turret roof, she'd wait until the second she saw the sun's searing yellow edge. Then she would close her eyes and whisper, "Crow, are you there?" But like every morning since the war, he did not respond. This concerned her a little, but she knew him well enough to know he could take care of himself. She still worried after him, though, despite the fact that she knew he did not like her doing so.

The sun was higher, and the wind had settled to a gentle breeze, and with it came the smell of cinnamon. The corners of her mouth stretched into a gigantic smile, and her crown wiggled her ears and tugged at her lobes. She opened her eyes and said, "It's about time you got here. Oversleep?"

Elle had gotten the same wake-up call from Augie as Sam, but must have flown out of the castle before Augie had a chance to fuss and spout her feelings. "No," Elle said as she hovered in front of Sam. "The grumpy old Munchkin was just being emotional—"

"And wonderfully bossy," interrupted Sam.

"Yes, and wonderfully bossy," Elle agreed, and then she mimicked Augie with her best impersonation of Augie scolding them. *"And make sure you're back in time to get ready."*

They were both giggling when suddenly Sam's crown violently tugged at her ear, warning her. A bluish-green flash zipped by them. In its wake, the wind tickled their eyelids and played with the grassy shoots on Sam's crown. It was their father, and they both smiled and flew off to catch him. It had become a morning ritual, something they shared with each other that was theirs and theirs alone. And as they did each morning, they ended their aerobatic chase at the queen's grave, where they would sit and talk and tell their father all that had happened after he was taken from them, just to have the private time to get to know each other all over again.

As they were sitting by their mother's grave and watching the late-morning clouds shift from one color to another, their father stood up and walked over to Glinda's gravestone, pensive in his stride. He kneeled down next to it and rubbed his hand across the top edge of the coarse granite. "I—" Lucius broke off and rubbed his finger along the writing on the stone, then stood up, paced around her grave, and stood behind it. He turned to face Sam and Elle like a nervous man trying to explain the facts of life to his daughters, and reverently said, "I am to be made king when we return from Munchkin City, and there will be a ceremony . . ." His voice trailed off once more.

"Yes, we know," Elle said.

"Of course, you're the king," Sam chimed in, almost stepping on Elle's words. "It's what Mother would have wanted. We both know that and—."

Elle jumped in, "It's what the Quadlings want as well."

Lucius stared at Sam fiercely. "You should be queen. It is your birthright."

Sam shook her head. "Elle would be a better queen than I would. My birth has nothing to do with it. You will be a great king, Father."

Lucius shook his head. "May the Great Head give me patience. The people will never forgive me for what I did. I tried to kill your mother—my wife, our queen! And I tried to kill *you*, Sam. If it weren't for Jo, my pike would have run you through."

"But it didn't, Father. The people know you were under the spell of the witch and the golden cap. And they also know—as do all the citizens of Oz—that anyone who possesses the golden cap will have three wishes. And when the people saw you throw the cap into the fire that night after the war was over so it could never be used for evil again, you were forgiven. The war, mother's death . . . none of it was your fault. I think you are just using all that as an excuse to not be king."

Elle smiled and put her arms around her father. "It's true, Father," she said. "Sam's right. It wasn't your fault, and you should be king. So be a great king . . . for us, and for Mother, if not for yourself."

Lucius swallowed hard. "Yes, of course," he said. He knew it was his duty to carry on the goodness Glinda, his wife, his queen, had given to the Quadlings and to all of Oz.

When he lost Glinda, he had begun to feel he belonged to no one, and no one belonged to him. But his daughters' love and respect made him feel once again that he was part of something important, something special he needed to protect, and he vowed he would never let them down.

EPILOGUE

❧ ━━━━━◆━━━━━ ❧

VALEDICTION
FOR
QUEEN
GOODWITCH

Gone . . . But Never Forgotten

They came in droves. There were so many people and animals that one could not see the Yellow, Red, Blue, or Green Brick Roads that circled out from the center of Munchkin City, only shoes and paws. Thousands of Ozarians, people and animals, all wanted to say their final farewell to their most beloved Good Witch of the South and help ease their heartache and grief.

It took three days for everyone to lay a white rose next to the life-sized painting of the fallen queen. The roses spread out from Glinda's portrait like a vast white ocean of sorrow. Sam was shaken by the kindhearted gesture from the citizens of Oz. It was extraordinarily beautiful, yet at the same time a little unnerving to experience so much love and so much admiration for her mother. Sam wasn't yet beyond having to blink back tears when she thought of her mother. And when she was feeling smaller and more worn at the edge than most days, she still found herself brooding about that day, and brooding sometimes brought on a tight headachy feeling around her temples—like now—a feeling of tears scratching at the back of her eyes and the haunting question: *What could I have done differently?*

The gathering crowd was making Sam anxious, just as she had been before falling into the waters of Silver Lake. It was the same feeling when she and her friends entered the deadly fog surrounding Rumpart's castle, or when they did the long climb to the top of the witch's dark tower and confronted the witch for the first time. She tried to push the uneasiness aside in the vain hope that it might pass as suddenly as it had fallen upon her, but she couldn't. It kept pounding on her, making her neck shiver and her shoulders tighten.

Several times during the morning, and for days after her mother's death, Sam thought she heard faint sounds behind her as if someone, or some kind of thing, was moving in and out of the dark shadows, following her. Even her crown had sensed it and had been tugging firmly on Sam's earlobes, demanding a response. Sam had pushed aside her crown's exhortations but even now, surrounded by so many loving and caring people, that feeling of being followed had increased and was growing, and her crown continued to pull or prick her ears and pinch her cheeks, trying to warn her.

The great and powerful Oz stood high up on an oversized rostrum, looking out across the throng of citizens who'd come to pay their respects. The murmur and rustle of the enormous rabble slowly diminished when he raised his arms in the air, the change palpable. When a child cried, the large densely packed crowd of people and animals was so silent that its whimpering could be heard by everyone. It was an awe-inspiring sight to see so many, from all over Oz, who wanted so much to show their love for the Good Witch of the South and all she had sacrificed.

Sam and Elle and their father were standing with Akasha and her father on the large stage next to the Great Head's podium, overlooking the enormous crowd. The Tin Woodman and the Lion were there as well, inches from Sam's shoulder, listening to what the Wiz had to say about the fallen queen and gazing across the thousands of heads, almost all of them holding handkerchiefs and dabbing their eyes.

When the Wiz finished his grand speech, the crowd milled around to talk to friends and to those who had traveled from the far reaches of the world. Sam's father was shaking hands with the Wiz, and Elle seemed to be enjoying her conversation with the Tin Woodman and the Cowardly Lion. Sam turned to Akasha and reached out with a gentle and loving smile as they embraced. After a moment, Sam pulled back and said, "It's good to see you again, Akasha."

"You are looking well, Princess," Akasha said.

"As are you, Princess," Sam replied, her smile growing as they embraced again.

They heard a deep-throated rumble roll across the sky and noticed a massive, dark thundercloud slowly approaching. As Sam gazed at the distant tempest, her suspicion of being followed by some shadowy foe returned, making her shoulders tighten again.

"What's wrong?" Akasha asked. "What is it?"

"Nothing," Sam replied. "It's been a long morning—a little tired, that's all."

The stillness of the damp air was incredibly misleading, but anyone who was listening carefully, truly listening, would have heard all the signs. Sam's crown was listening, had been aware from the start, and was now tugging even harder at Sam's ears and poking her face to make her listen to the strong presage coming from the sky. Sam shooed her crown's grassy shoots with the brush of her hand, ignoring her crown and trying to focus on the ceremony for her mother and visiting with her friends. But there was a little something about each poke that nagged at Sam, something she couldn't put her finger on, something wicked, something—*dangerous*.

❧ ◆ ☙

Thorn was standing with them as well, looking dapper in a bright orange-and-green tartan twilled shirt with florescent-green overalls.

"It's good to see you, Thorn. You, you . . . ," Sam said but hesitated, thinking about whether to comment on his outrageous outfit and the brightness of his clothes. But when she started to tell him what she really thought, she stopped and her eyes widened. "You look taller?"

"New shoes," he said with a puffed-up grin.

Sam grinned back, biting back the chuckle growing at the back of her throat. She turned to the Tin Woodman and the Cowardly Lion and asked, "Have you seen or heard from the Crow?"

The ashen clouds continued to growl, and the hot winds were getting stronger. Sam's crown seemed even more agitated and started pinching Sam's eyebrows. Sam once again shooed the grass shoots away. They tried again, and she slapped them to stop.

"Have you heard any news from the Scarecrow?" she repeated, ignoring the growing storm, and her crown's warnings.

"No, we haven't," replied the Tin Woodman, speaking over the thunder.

"He likes being mysterious. I wouldn't put much thought into it," the Lion added loudly, as the winds became more robust, frantically swirling and twisting at his fur. "I think we should take cover?"

An awful moan broke upon Sam's ears, and there came again from the black shadows the sound of a moving thing and the loud rustling of dead leaves, and she felt the air thicken. That feeling she'd been having, that a creature or some kind of evil was following her, suddenly came to life. Like a great wave of locusts swarming a field of wheat, there came a howling roar—not from man or beast, but from the wind itself. The ominous, dark, angry clouds quickly covered the entire sky above the crowd, rolling and billowing into each other and surrounding the great horde. Then something gave—lightning— white-hot and gnarled. It's fiery fingers lit up the sky; sharp cracks like the snapping of a thousand leather whips. Then more lightning and thunder so loud people had to cover their ears.

The wind was screaming, blowing hats off people's heads and knocking many to their knees as they darted for shelter. Everyone and everything all at once felt the gale's blustering fury. Trees bowed to its booming demand, and the rain came, hard and fast, and poured down in sheets, straight-lined sheets, stinging sheets. Then the hail came. People scrambled everywhere—children screamed, and mothers held them close to their bodies to protect them as they ran.

Sam and Elle, their father, Akasha, everyone raced with the

frightened crowd, everyone trying to outpace the storm. The blinding bolts of electricity crackled and sparked, making Akasha's fur stand at attention. Sam looked over her shoulder and saw giant, tubular formations that lowered themselves out from the raging, fuming clouds, reaching and whirling and stretching out to the ground like massive fingers grabbing handfuls of earth. In the next second they melted into each other, one large fist slamming into the dirt with a crash that shook the ground. The funnel whipped, twisted, and shifted from side to side, moving forward as if with a mind of its own, as if it knew exactly what it was doing . . . as if it were purposely chasing Sam and Elle and their friends.

The Munchkins' homes and buildings began to creak and fall apart under the pressure of the attack. The trees that lined the sidewalks exploded like a string of massive firecrackers. The Tin Woodman and Cowardly Lion were picking up small children, dodging debris as they ran from the ferocious wind. But when they looked over their shoulders while they ran, they watched Thorn being thrown against a small tree. Thorn hugged the tree with all his strength and closed his eyes. The wild, driving squall ripped the tree out of the ground, roots and all, flinging it in the air like a giant toothpick and taking Thorn with it, a whipping beacon of brilliant orange and green sucked up by the violent storm.

Akasha was thrown into much larger trees. She used her claws to cut deep gashes into the bark to keep from being taken by the tempest. But the gusty blasts were determined, and like they did to Thorn, they grabbed Akasha, violently pulling her in, flinging her around as though she were nothing but a sack of straw.

When Sam looked to her left, she saw a house being picked up and swallowed up by the massive storm, undamaged by the whirling mass, and people and animals thrown hundreds of feet into the air. She remembered her mother telling her about a mighty wind she'd called a cyclone, and how it could destroy anything it came in contact with. Sam yelled over the roar of the wind as she and Elle ran for safety, "It's a cyclone!"

"A what?" Elle yelled back, her voice swallowed up by the storm.

Suddenly, Elle was lifted off the ground and was pulled into the funnel. Elle opened her wings to fly out of danger but couldn't, and in that same moment, Sam unfurled her own wings and grabbed her sister's hand. They flapped their wings as hard as they could, but the wind was too fierce, and it continued to suck them up and into the swirling mass. Sam saw a flash of black fur zip past and realized it was Akasha being wildly thrown around inside the cyclone.

Then with great effort, Lucius flew in to try and save them. He reached for Elle's ankle, but held onto it for only a mere second as he too—as strong as he was with his mighty wings—was unable to fight against the intense pressure of the air and the wailing wind. As if by design, the powerful windstorm spit him out, throwing him away from his daughters as if he were nothing more than a child's toy.

The next thing Sam and Elle knew they were rolling on hard pavement, and Sam heard the yells and screams of Akasha and Thorn before they hit the ground with two big thuds, one right after the other. The wind swirled and shifted for a quick moment, losing its strength; then in a flash it was gone, leaving only scattered debris and white roses falling from the sky.

Then nothing but silence—absolute silence.

The shock of hitting the ground was so sudden and severe, Sam was surprised she didn't hear the crack of bones as she rolled to a stop. She moaned and groaned, moving her arms and legs, and hands and feet to make sure everything was working. The transition had been swift and so unexpected that it left Sam for a moment forgetful, and her first thoughts were, *Is this death? Have I passed over forever into another life?* But her heart was thudding hard against her ribs, and the ache in her bones told her she was very much alive and not dead. Her breath was coming in quick short gasps, and cold sweat leaked from every pore of her body.

She suddenly heard another shadowy moan coming from the depths of her mind, and she opened her eyes with a start to find that her cheek was resting on a hot, hard surface that looked like a long black road with a painted yellow line running down the middle of it. The grayish blue sky above was dotted with small puffs of bright white clouds. It was now midday. The sun was shining full upon her, and its heat was intense. It was quiet and serene, like the catastrophic whirlwind had never whisked them away. Only the sound of a few clicks and chirps of insects could be heard, mixed with the lazy springing sound of cicadas flexing their muscles. Sam sat up on her elbows, and when she inhaled, her ribs screamed. When she lifted her head, the cornrowed strands of her hair lay in a tangled mess across her eyes. She peered through the hair at her surroundings, a lost soul in a foreign land. Colors were muted, dull, as if they were rusting away, nothing like the vibrant colors of Oz.

On either side of the road were row upon row of corn plants standing ten feet tall and a small, faded green sign mounted on a rusty metal stake that tilted slightly at an angle. She read the sign out loud to herself, like a whisper, wiping the sweat off her brow from the heat of the sun. "Welcome to Kansas." She knew this place. Her mother had told her about it and she had read about it in books. She and Elle even saw a play about it. A land where there was an ocean of corn, and chickens, an Aunt Em, a dog named Toto, a cyclone, and a farmhouse falling from the sky. Such were their bedtime stories. Sam stood up, then helped Elle to her feet, brushed the dirt off her arms and legs, and looked around.

Akasha was shaking dirt from her fur, and Thorn was still lying on his back, moaning. "What in the Great Head's name just happened?" Thorn said with a tremulous groan, as he rolled over and stood up, stomping his feet and shaking his body to rid himself of dirt and debris. "And where are my knives and swords?"

Sam looked at Thorn, scrunched her brow, and was about to say something, but decided to wait. She opened her wings and slowly lifted a few feet into the air, leaving a small dust cloud behind, and gently flapped them to stay above the corn, which glistened in the sunlight. A brisk wind raced over the stalks, making them shift and sway, rattling their broad, sun-baked, faded green leaves. A little to her left, perhaps thirty feet away, stood a ratty scarecrow mounted on a thick wooden stake, its hand-painted face vacantly staring back at her. A large black crow was sitting on its shoulder, stealing a piece of straw with its beak. It flew away when it saw Sam, cawing as it scooted across the sky. Watching the crow take flight, she instantly felt a sting in her chest. She missed the Scarecrow's counsel and his crooked painted smile. Sam wondered how he was, and wished he were with her. She wanted all her friends with her, especially her father.

The black road stretched out for miles and miles in both directions, disappearing into a muggy gray haze. As she gazed upon it, she felt a spell of overpowering fascination. It seemed to call to her, to lure her to it, to draw her as a hummingbird is attracted to a flower. Sam laced her fingers together and placed her hands on top of her head, then took in a deep breath of the thick, loamy air. It was filled with moisture, hot and sticky, hard to swallow, and it sat heavily on her lungs.

Then she remembered . . . the whirlwind had snatched her crown from her, and she'd watched it hit her father square in the face as he was trying to grab onto Elle's ankle. Vivid was the image of that last moment, but stronger still was the memory of spending quiet time together, telling him in low tones of how she missed the loving embrace of her mother and how bittersweet it was to lose one parent while the other was returned to her. She rubbed her head, wishing she had her crown. She felt lost without it, naked, vulnerable. Then she reached for her sword, and it too had been taken by the wind. *Great*, she thought. *No crown and no weapons.*

For some inexplicable reason, as Sam hovered above the corn she felt as if she were on the verge of some great new truth, but it turned to nothing when she tried to put it into words, and she just let it out with a soft sigh and a quiet chuckle, saying to herself, "I have a feeling we're not in Oz anymore."

Elle was brushing the dusty grit off her body. She combed her hair with her fingers and shook out more earthy grunge. When she spat out dust and dirt and wiped the sweat from her forehead, she noticed the road sign. She looked up at Sam, shading her eyes from the glaring sun with her sweaty hand. "Sam, is this some kind of cruel joke? Kansas? We're in Kansas?"

"It's Kansas, Elle," Sam said, putting her hands on her hips and floating back down to the ground. "You know, somewhere over the rainbow and all that stuff—"

"Yeah, yeah. I know, I know," Elle interrupted. "All the stuff Mother and Father used to tell us when we were children." Elle took in a deep breath of the hot, humid air and let it out with a *humph*. "This is nuts, Sam."

"What now?" Akasha asked, standing next to Thorn.

Thorn was trying to speak while rubbing corn silk out of his hair, creating a cloud of silky threads around himself that shifted and swirled and sparkled from the bright sunlight. "How do we get back to Oz?" He coughed and sneezed, waving his hands in front of his pudgy Munchkin face to push the silk cloud away. Akasha did the same and let out a low growl to show her disapproval, her eyebrows drawing together. When she shot him a sharp look, Thorn just shrugged his shoulders, smiled, and coughed again.

"Follow the painted yellow line in the middle of the road," Sam replied.

"Okay . . ." Elle said, frustrated, as she shook her shoulders and unfolded her wings to shake loose the last of the dirt. "Then what?"

"We find Dorothy Gale."

Δεν Υπάρχει Μέρος Σαν Το Σπίτι

(Greek to English: *There's No Place Like Home*)

CPSIA information can be obtained
at www.ICGtesting.com
Printed in the USA
LVHW030315251120
672446LV00032B/758/J